STEALING

FIRE

SUSAN SLOATE

Covfefe Press

STEALING FIRE
By Susan Sloate

Published by
Covfefe Press
USA

Author Photograph by Chris Halm

Cover by danny_media through Fiverr

Formatting by dream_books through Fiverr

ISBN-13: 978-0692116937

ISBN-10: 0692116931

To EB and
To Robbie

"To love one who loves you,
To admire one who admires you,
In a word, to be the idol of one's idol,
Is exceeding the limit of human joy;
It is stealing fire from heaven."

— **Delphine de Girardin**
(1804-1855)

PART ONE

PROLOGUE

Autumn 1963

Her mother liked to sing show tunes to her, putting old records on her battered record player and singing along with the tinny recorded sounds of Broadway orchestras. She'd wanted to be a singer on the musical stage, her mother, but settled for marriage and children the first time it was offered and spent the rest of her life droning unhappily to her daughters about the opportunities she'd missed.

Still, in between complaints there was a lot of good music. Her mother's voice was sweet and almost always on key, and she sang the words clearly, so even little Amanda understood what the song was about. By the time she was five, she knew all of Rodgers & Hammerstein, not just the mammoth hits but also the more modest ones, like *Flower Drum Song*, right down to the flops no one remembered: *Pipe Dream, Me & Juliet, Allegro*. Even her mother was astounded at how accurately she could pipe the songs along with the records.

"I haven't heard this in awhile. I used to love it," her mother murmured, almost to herself, one rainy fall afternoon, as she took a long-playing black vinyl record from its cover and put it on the turntable.

Six-year-old Amanda wandered over to the table and picked up the album cover. The name of the show, *The Life and Times*, was printed in bold letters across the top, with a pencil sketch of a black top hat and neatly folded white gloves in the middle. A splashy yellow sun, its rays streaming diagonally, filled the rest of the cover. At the bottom were other names. Her mother had explained carefully that those were the people who made up the tunes and the words and the stories of the shows. Amanda glanced at these now but could not quite sound them out; she was just spelling her way through the Dick & Jane books, and while she could read the title, these names were longer and harder. She forgot about them altogether, though, as the record began to play.

She loved it instantly.

"Again, Mommy, again!" she said excitedly when the first song ended. Her mother shook her head. "Listen to the rest first."

Amanda sat down on her favorite soft footstool near the big brown rocker and listened. She loved it all.

There was one song especially that she liked. It was about blowing bubbles:

"A prick in time, a pin to pop—

The bubbles burst, the glories stop.

So fragile is the joy of night—

Like bubbles bursting into flight."

She didn't understand the verse, but she sang along with the chorus: "

… Bubbles bursting, bursting bubbles.

Breaking dreams with every blow.

I'll remember each dream burst

Till the final bubbles go."

She didn't really understand the song, but it seemed sad to her. She had bubble set, like most little girls, and sometimes, something hurt deep inside her when she watched a brightly-colored bubble pop, just out of the reach of her eager fingers. She thought she knew what the words meant.

As with most show scores, Amanda asked to hear the record again and again, till she'd memorized all the music, lyrics and orchestrations. As her reading skills improved, she also studied the names on the album cover. A few months later her older sister Josie, tossing a ball carelessly around the room, smashed the record as it was coming out of its cover, on its way to the turntable. Amanda cried and asked her mother to please buy it again, *please*. Her mother explained regretfully that she had gotten it as a gift. The show had been a flop years before, and no record store nearby had any copies to sell. No one was interested in buying it anymore.

Amanda cried harder and said *she* wanted to buy it; please couldn't they take the money in her piggy bank and find a store that would sell it? Her mother said no, decisively now. There were no copies around, and Josie hadn't meant to smash it; it was an accident. "Stop crying now, Amanda," she said sharply. She listened to her mother and stopped crying. And as the years went by, she learned many more show tunes—by Rodgers & Hart, Cole Porter, George Gershwin, Jule Styne, Frank Loesser and others.

But she never forgot the record album with the streaming sunrays and the top hat, or the song about bursting bubbles.

CHAPTER 1

Beau

Los Angeles
September, 1982

Sixty would be a milestone, he thought. The age of uncertainties would be past. No more worry about where he stood. No more decisions about the future. He was looking forward to it, had sworn to himself that he would approach old age gracefully. No attempts to downplay the years. No excuses about his lack of achievement. And as he mentally framed that resolve again, he accelerated.

The little MG shot forward. He worked the clutch expertly, leaned into the canyon bend coming up. His favorite curve in the whole canyon, and he knew just how to approach it to get the maximum thrill—hard into the right side, then a quick left. If you took it right the car bounced off the pavement; wrong, you went over the side. He'd never been wrong yet. And he'd never driven it any other way, at any slower speed.

One of the joys of working with Jules was commuting to work sessions at Jules' house deep in the canyon above Sunset. The drives up and back more than compensated for a lousy day, and accented the pleasures of a day that went right.

Today had been a pretty lousy day. He and Jules rarely quarreled, but when they did, it depressed them both.

The quarrels always followed a period of creative drought, when Beau felt frustrated and empty, but this drought felt more exhausting than usual. He couldn't remember such a long period without a single useful idea. He pushed away the thought of old age creeping up. It was just one bad day. He'd had them all through his career. But this one didn't feel like the others.

The arena had changed. No use trying to ignore the inescapable truth.

"Musical theatre as we know it died years ago," he'd said flatly, after they'd tossed ideas around fruitlessly for an hour. "Face it, we're fossils. Our old shows wouldn't get a dollar's worth of backing in today's market." Jules had been the boy wonder composer in his twenties when Beau was hitting his stride; now Jules was over fifty but still trim, fit, radiating health.

By comparison, he himself looked ready for a major overhaul. He brushed that thought aside as he went on. "We're not Andrew Lloyd Webber—not that I'd ever want to be. But that's all that sells today. They don't want what we used to do."

"Well, then," Jules said reasonably, "let's do something else." He sat at the piano, waiting, as usual, for Beau's suggestions. Whenever there was a problem, Beau often thought resentfully, it was always the librettist's job to come up with a solution.

He remembered now the silence that had fallen between them. The memory triggered more discomfort, and he pushed the MG up to seventy. He'd learned from experience that it was the maximum speed at which he could hold the car on the narrow bending roads.

He caught the flash of light that signaled another car coming from the opposite direction and veered over slightly. Good eyes, still, after all these years.

Jules had noodled with a melody, something he often did while thinking. "Well," he said at last, "what would you like to do?"

I want to be a hit again! he'd repressed the urge to scream. Control, remember. Think clearly. He looked down at his expensive Italian loafers—a concession to Jean's taste—and noted the first threads fraying at the toes. Goddamned imported junk. Ten times as pricey and never lasted half as long as the American stuff.

"We need something new," he said carefully. "A new twist, a new idea. Something."

Jules nodded patiently. "Audiences won't sit still for the old stuff. Not at forty bucks a ticket. But do you want to try for a *Cats*?"

"I thought we were clear on that. That shit doesn't even hold up as a revue, let alone theater. It's nothing but expensive production. Christ, can we afford to write a show that costs four million dollars to mount?

No. Not with our track record."

"Hey, hold on. We've had hits."

"*Had* hits is right. Not one since '70, and we were damned lucky with that. Even then the trend was changing, with *Hair* and that other godawful garbage. It was the last of the old guard showing up for us."

The silence thickened, and Beau glanced up. Jules wasn't looking at him. His eyes flickered, for an instant, to the wall behind Beau, jammed end to end with gold records and certificates. All for hit songs: Television theme songs, some impressive movie themes, written with other lyricists, young guys, a few women. All in the last few years.

Thinking about it, Beau pressed down harder on the accelerator. The needle began to edge toward seventy-five. He could feel the MG's wheels lightening on the pavement, but that rage burning in him had to be appeased somehow. He saw the stoplight which signaled the end of the canyon and touched the brake, downshifting reluctantly. Sunset would be bumper to bumper all the way past the Strip; he'd have to stay below thirty. The MG halted smoothly, if a trifle abruptly, at the edge of the crosswalk.

"I don't like to think of myself as obsolete," Jules had said quietly, when he saw that Beau had noticed. "I can change. I'm not that old."

"Are you saying I am?"

Jules sighed. "Neither of us is. You're way too sensitive."

The light changed, and Beau had the MG spinning around the corner in a split second. He was looking forward to the stretch beyond the Sunset Strip, where there were few lights, pretty scenery, and, he reminded himself, lots of very alert cops. At Jules' house, he had stalked off his frustration around the spacious living room. Jean often told him tartly he looked like a gazelle in full flight, and physical grace, he would concede, was not one of his strong points. Still, he got a lot of good thinking done, frequently fixed a lyric to his satisfaction while pacing, and kept his legs in good shape. It sure beat the tennis his contemporaries were taking up to ward off their boredom.

Jules watched him for awhile. Then, tentatively, he ventured, "Maybe we could option a book. Like *I'm Okay, You're Okay.*"

"And do a musical about pop psychology?" His mood was bleak, and it was unlikely that he'd be able to shake himself out of it. Sometimes they lasted for days.

"They're doing heavier stuff in musicals these days," Jules suggested. "Someday they may even try something like *Equus* as a musical."

Beau shuddered. The eye-piercing scene alone made him fervently hope that he'd be long dead before it opened.

He had quickened his pace, shoving his hands into the pockets of his windbreaker. Jules waited, respecting his silence, knowing it was likely to be germinating something good. He never spoke until Beau addressed him; at such times, he'd learned, it could be treacherous to break into an unformed thought.

"Okay." Beau spoke finally. "What do we know, anyway? How does the world work? It's a young people's world, right?"

"That's what the demographics say."

Demographics! Shit, that's just what he meant. How to live creatively in a world that was increasingly addicted to classifying and analyzing everything? Beau took a deep breath and tried to stem his irritation. "Okay. And we're not so young, right? We're the people who've been shoved aside and left behind by the young people, who are marching off with the world on their shoulders. We're misfits who once had the world on our shoulders, and—"

He'd have continued, building up to his point, but for the blazing eyes of Jules' third wife, Marie, who stood in the doorway. If it was a mistake for soft-spoken Jules to try to best Beau, Beau also knew from the look on Marie's face that now he'd better back down.

She glared at him, pushing back her short blonde hair, her dark blue eyes glowing not with warmth but with anger. She couldn't be more than twenty-eight, Beau had figured, meeting her for the first time, and right now every fiber of that youth was energized by her rage.

"No more of that," she said icily. "Not another word."

"It's just an idea—" he'd started, but she cut him off.

"Forget it. That *idea* is dead. Jules will never do a show about misfits and old fogeys. He's still young."

He'd felt himself getting worked up. "You don't even know what I'm going to say!"

"And I don't want to hear it, ever." She looked at him squarely. "Maybe you'd better call it a day now."

"Honey—" Jules had risen from the piano and come to embrace her, but though she rubbed against him affectionately, her eyes hardened and held on Beau, while she spoke to her husband.

"I'm tired of it, Jules. You're too young to be thinking about crap like this. Let him do a big song and dance show about geriatrics, if that's what he wants. He knows more about getting old than you do."

The words burned acid into his brain. Even thinking back on them upset him. He'd said a subdued goodbye to them both and tried not to look at the antique clock over the fireplace as he left, but he knew they'd cut short their work session by a good hour. It wasn't quite four.

Up ahead, a woman in a well-crunched red Datsun was making up her mind about moving into the turn lane. Beau leveled his horn at her and tore ahead, missing her fender by only a few inches. Damn, how do these people keep their licenses? It was enough to make you crazy.

He thought again of Marie's long-legged figure and bouncy manner, the smile and warmth with which she'd greeted him at the door earlier, and felt his breath tightening. He remembered joking, months before, with Jean, when he'd read the announcement in the trade papers about Jules' marriage to a much younger woman, but watching them together, it seemed less preposterous. He had caught from the first the feeling of fun and playful lust between them, in their frequent small touches and whispered asides. Thinking about it now caused a tightening in his chest that he refused to think of as resentment.

He roared down Sunset, into Beverly Hills. The street was wider here, with lush foliage on both sides to hide the expensive houses just a few yards away. He shifted up again, remembering when he and Jean had that kind of relationship. It had been so many years ago.

Now, if he tried to joke with her, he knew how she'd react: a shrug, a sigh, and on to another subject. While some women turned into hysterics during the menopausal years, Jean had simply turned dry. Quiet. Less in touch with him, as though she no longer needed to communicate her thoughts with him. He, feeling the rebuff, had responded in kind.

They seldom had conversations these days, unless spurred by an outside source: a television talk show, a newspaper column, a phone conversation with someone else. She had taken to writing short polite penciled notes and leaving them in his study, asking him to lower the heat before he went to bed, pick up a carton of milk, pay the phone bill. Always with "please" and "thank you" attached, widening the distance between them.

The speedometer's needle hovered at seventy as the car curved up the hill that signaled the end of Beverly Hills. He was anticipating the bend coming up, when he saw the red lights flashing behind him. Reluctantly, he pulled over.

"Good afternoon, sir." The police officer looked a little startled as he squinted at Beau. Well, he probably didn't look like the typical teenage speed freak—or like the owner of an MG. Beau handed him his driver's license and registration without being asked.

He hated the picture on his license, but who didn't? Since it had been taken, his thick, unruly hair had turned from salt-and-pepper to all silver, and he'd let it grow out to a rakish length. The photograph emphasized the high cheekbones, the wide mouth, the deep liquid brown eyes with their dark lashes. Not a handsome face—okay—but distinctive. Unique. Out of the range of the photographer's lens, his long, lanky frame belied a better-than-average appetite.

The young officer studied his license for a moment and turned a searching gaze on him. "Don't I know you?"

For a moment his heart rate sped up. It would be something if his name actually meant something to this kid—he had to be under thirty. Then he remembered that in Beverly Hills, policemen assumed most of their traffic stops were people whose names they should know. It was probably part of their training.

The officer was still waiting for an answer, looking from the license to his face. He tried to sound unconcerned. "Uh, no. Probably not."

"Director? Producer?"

Beau wondered if he would be spared the ticket if he said yes. Then he realized the cop might want to audition for him. Didn't everyone want to be in the movies?

He decided to go with the truth. "Song lyricist."

"Oh?" The officer still looked polite and interested. "Anything I might know?"

His automatic response seemed to sum up the whole lousy afternoon. "I doubt it. I was probably before your time."

"Too bad." The policeman became briskly professional again. Obviously, there was no point in fawning over a civilian. "Are you aware of the speed limit on Sunset?"

"No, Officer."

"Well, it's fifty, Mr. Kellogg, and I clocked you at seventy-three."

Beau nodded politely and watched as the cop took his time writing up the ticket. Another incident not to be mentioned to Jean.

The officer tore the ticket off his pad and handed it to Beau with the usual instructions about traffic school. He signed off with "Have a nice day, sir"—the standard southern-California-ism—and watched carefully as Beau started west again.

He passed the Bel-Air gates and skimmed past UCLA. Grudgingly, keeping an eye on the patrol car framed in his rear-view mirror, he kept a steady slow pace, cursing himself again for letting himself be talked into buying a blood-red MG, which he'd found to his sorrow was ticketed more than the quiet black he'd actually wanted. It was always open season on drivers who liked to drive.

As a cluster of smaller houses peeked through the shrubbery, Beau turned off Sunset and climbed up the hill, past one street, then two. A quick right onto his own street and then into the driveway of a pleasant low-slung red brick ranch. It had more of an eastern influence than the Spanish origins of southern California, but it was comfortable. And paid for, thank God.

He smelled Jean before he saw her, and caught a whiff of expensive perfume, whatever was this year's favorite. Unlike some women, who wore the same scent for twenty years, Jean liked to switch perfume, lipstick—he'd had a tough time persuading her to keep her hair the same color. She had a real enthusiasm for change, at least the little things.

Yet he couldn't articulate what he somehow knew to be true—that losing a well-loved scent he associated with her weakened their relationship and robbed it of continuity. He rather doubted at this point that she would care. He cautiously ignored the thought that popped, unbidden, into his mind: at this point, he didn't, either.

"Hi." She smiled at him, interrupting his musing. She was at the kitchen sink, surrounded by fresh flowers she was sorting into vases, one of her weekly rituals.

It seemed as though her hands moved more slowly these days, though her movements had always been measured. Not like him, he thought ruefully, who was always told to slow down, wait for her. He'd heard it even on their first dates.

Her auburn hair bobbed to her shoulders, almost exactly as it had the night they met, and though the depth and hue of the blue oval eyes hadn't changed, it seemed to him that the recent years had added a tinge of—was it discontent? Bitterness? Only he seemed to notice it, though; other men still turned to look at her on the street. The long, slim, almost boyish lines of her body had given way to an appealing softness, and the few fine lines in her skin could not obscure the beautiful bone structure. She was a stunning woman and could still pass for ten years younger than her age, whereas he looked like hell, and he knew it. When they stood together in front of the bedroom mirror, their twin reflections made him a little sick.

When he thought of Jean, he thought of beauty and grace. It was her contribution to their marriage. She didn't have to say a word or do anything special. Just standing at the threshold of a room, offering a tentative smile to a gathering of strangers, she gave him reason to stand taller. *What any woman should be able to offer any man*, he thought sometimes. He had friends for companionship, produced his own income, thank you, and could easily have turned for physical relief to any number of women. Jean gave him class.

He continued through the kitchen to his study and sat down at his desk. She'd stacked the mail there, as usual. He was thumbing through it when her voice at his shoulder startled him. "Jim called again."

He didn't realize she'd followed him. The study, by tacit agreement, was his. She'd paneled it in dark wood, stacked solid floor-to-ceiling bookcases for his massive library, added a sofa with cushions he could sink into, a sizeable desk for his typewriter and a sturdy file cabinet, then quietly backed away. It was unusual for her even to approach the door.

"What'd he want?" Must be important, for her to be standing there tentatively.

"The same thing, I gather. I thought you were going to tell him no decisively, and let that be it."

"Ah—he won't take no for an answer."

"Or you aren't saying it decisively." She smiled. It wouldn't be the first time he'd fudged an answer to his agent.

"He keeps saying it's a lot of money, and we can use it, Jean."

She shrugged. "If you think it's important."

"You're the one who keeps talking about retirement. How can I if I don't have something put away? This would help a lot. It might even raise my price permanently."

"He told me part of the deal was that you spend time in New York."

"So?"

"You know you hate to travel. At your age, is it really necessary?"

The crack about his age stung. His answer was to pile the bills into a stack on the desk. She hesitated, knowing that he'd won that round. Then—"Your birthday party's at seven o'clock. It would be nice if we could be on time, since we're hosting it."

He didn't turn around, but he heard her scurry out, closing the door softly behind her.

(HAPTER 2

Amanda

New York City

It was a sign.

It had to be.

Stephanie and Fleur were late again—as usual—and she, prompt to the minute, was as usual waiting for them, killing time in the tiny Village record shop near Houston Street, thumbing through a stack of old records and searching, as she had for years, for one particular album.

And there, stuck high on the wall, was the unframed theater poster. It caught her eye when she looked up from the rack and tilted her head back, stretching her sore neck. The paper edges were faintly curled, and the sheen of a shiny original had long since worn off, but it was the logo she remembered from the album her mother had discarded so many years before: a top hat, a pair of neatly folded gloves, and the streaming rays of the yellow sun.

She stared at it, and the corners of her wide mouth began to lift. Her heartbeat doubled.

She hadn't seen that picture for almost twenty years, but it was unmistakable, familiar as her own face in the mirror, a beloved talisman of the deepest part of her childhood.

It had to mean something. She could feel it. She could even smell it—the cool drift of air through the open shop door quickened her senses and lifted her spirit.

These sunny autumn afternoons, with puffy white clouds drifting lazily across high blue skies and a hint of smoke and mystery in the light breeze, always evoked something deep inside her... something she couldn't quite name, something that made her pulse double, as though the next corner she turned would be the one that led to... whatever it was she felt she had been waiting for all her life.

She wished she knew what it was.

But she was certain that it did lead to *something*... something that would change her life.

She looked at her watch, then at the black and white theater-mask clock on the wall. Both timepieces agreed: Stephanie and Fleur *were* unforgivably late, and she had to be at work by six o'clock, less than an hour from now. You showed up promptly at the Lorelei or you didn't stay long. She'd never been late.

Yet she knew that today she'd wait until they arrived; their news was too important. It would be nice if they could manage to be somewhere on time, just once. Her eyes went back to the theater poster taped on the wall. Just looking at it made her want to smile.

"Looking for something?"

The store clerk looked down at the section she was browsing in, and the faintest curl of contempt crossed his young face. Amanda saw the look and winced inwardly, though she was used to it. Unless it was Andrew Lloyd Webber, who was racking up millions these days with his high-glitz, high-production shows, most Broadway show music met with similar reactions.

She *hated* Andrew Lloyd Webber.

"Help you?" The clerk was still waiting.

"*The Life and Times*. An old show from the '50s—do you have the cast album?" She asked the question with hope. After all, they had the show poster... that was more than she'd seen anywhere else.

The clerk, wiping the back of his hand across his pudgy nose, frowned. "I've never heard of that one... hey, Alan!" He yelled it so suddenly and loudly that Amanda flinched. "Do we have something called—uh—"

"*The Life and Times*," Amanda said again, this time to the taller, older man who turned from the cash register with a polite questioning look.

The man's bushy eyebrows rose in surprise. "Good grief!" he said. "I haven't been asked for that one in—well, I forget how many years. I saw it when it first opened... not very good, but a wonderful score. Too bad more people don't know it." He nodded at the fading poster on the wall. "That's from my own collection. I'm not sure you could find another one."

"Probably not," Amanda agreed, her heart sinking. "What about the album?"

"Oh, dear, no. Let's see, we've been open here since 1967, and I don't remember ever having it. It was a flop, you see. They never re-issued the album after the original run."

"I know."

"Do you?" The man looked at her more attentively. He saw, Amanda supposed, what everyone saw: A slender girl in her mid-twenties, a few inches over five feet tall, light brown hair held back by barrettes and curling softly under, not quite to her thin shoulders, wearing a simple, unmemorable gray skirt and crisp white blouse. Nor was she especially pretty, something Amanda had been reminded of all her life. What she didn't realize was that discerning people looked past the quiet clothes to her arresting gray eyes, edged with thick dark lashes, which could be merry, thoughtful or stern, but always alert, always responsive. Those eyes gave most people pause and led many of them to give her a second, curious look.

Amanda knew what the man was thinking as he considered her. He confirmed it by saying, "You don't look old enough to know that show."

Amanda flushed. It was yet another reminder that she was out of step with her own generation. She'd heard that, in one form or another, all her life. And it was true; she was. On the other hand, she knew the score of just about every musical that had ever had a Broadway run, from the turn of the century to *Hair* to Lloyd Webber and his garbage.

That and a dollar would get her a cup of coffee. It was probably all that the knowledge was worth.

When she made no further comment, the man moved away to wait on a new customer, and the theater clock on the wall chimed. She looked at her own watch for confirmation. Both timepieces agreed. She was due at the Lorelei in forty-five minutes. What was keeping them?

She looked around the store once more and spotted a potential gold mine: A small section in back devoted to sheet music. Judging by the faded and yellowing pages some patrons were leafing through, it was old stuff, and maybe... just maybe... some show music.

If she could find something in that stack to sing for her coach, it would be well worth her time to browse.

As she started toward the back wall, the shop door burst open, the little bell swinging from the doorknob jangling discordantly. "Amanda!"

It was Stephanie, dark, slender and swift, moving quickly and calling loudly enough to turn every head in the place. Behind her, as always moving more slowly—a bit like a lumbering elephant—was Fleur.

Stephanie grabbed Amanda's arm, almost bruising it in her excitement. "Oh, God, the rumors were true! A real revue at the Hot Grill, for *real* producers and show organizations. Auditions in a few weeks. Finally, we have a chance!"

Amanda didn't say anything, but Stephanie didn't wait for an answer, and Fleur, as usual, felt no need for words. She communicated mostly through her music.

"Amanda, will you listen? What are you looking at that's so important?"

Amanda was looking regretfully at the curling, tattered theater poster on the wall behind her. She knew she should be excited about singing in front of the influential theater people who would turn out for the revue, and tomorrow she probably would be.

But tonight her mind was reeling backward to the remembered sound that had once issued from her mother's phonograph. And instead of thinking of the new song that she, Stephanie and Fleur could put together, she was wondering if she'd ever find that piece of her childhood again.

***

"Happy birthday, buddy!" Beau winced, both at the greeting and the ringing tones—Christ, Jim could be loud. "How's sixty?"

"So far, so good. But it's only been a few hours; give me time to work up some symptoms." Beau lit a fresh cigarette and scanned the page he'd left in the typewriter, scrawling notes for changes on a scratch pad while he listened to Jim's pitch. He'd long since decided that pumping up his clients was Jim's primary function in life. And true to form, he'd made Beau his last call of the day—the little clock next to the typewriter said ten after six.

"Beau, you gotta at least talk to these guys. It's a lot of money, and they're serious about you."

"Why me? Nobody in New York advertising knows me."

"Why look a gift horse in the mouth? It's twenty grand for one month's work! Don't tell me you can't use it."

"I can use it." Beau drew on the cigarette and crossed out a typo, wondering why Jean couldn't remember to keep sharpened pencils on his desk. She knew he hated using pens—too easy to mess up a lyric sheet crossing out in ink. He always used stiletto-sharp pencils and asked her to keep a supply close at hand. Yet his pencil cup was empty. Again.

He shook himself out of his irritation at her and tried to pick up the thread of the conversation. "Why me? How'd they even get my name?"

"Ben, naturally. He said you were 'the best lyricist since Gilbert'—he really said that—and he may even have exaggerated your price a little. You should thank him."

"Hm. Sounds like stuff *you* should be saying."

Jim ignored the jibe. "So what can it hurt? Go to New York for a few days, meet with these guys, think it over. They'll pay expenses, of course. Even if you insist on that little hole in the wall you usually stay at—"

"The Lorelei. It's not a hole in the wall. It's a lovely small hotel with a lot of charm."

"It's not the Waldorf, which they're willing to pay for."

"No, thanks. I like the Lorelei. An old army buddy of mine runs it. He'd be hurt if I didn't stay with him."

"So you'll meet with them?"

"Do I have to give you an answer now?"

"Hell, no. Think about it. Take your time. Just so I know by, say, tomorrow. Oh, and many happy returns."

Beau chuckled as he hung up. Just like Jim to demand an answer to a question that could probably wait. He shrugged. That's what agents were good for, though. Hell, they had to be good for something.

He was still thinking about it when Jean called him to dress for dinner. She gave him a swift appraising glance when he joined her, after a quick shower, in front of the bedroom mirror, where she was dabbing on makeup. "Are you really going out like that?"

"Like what?" Though he knew he sometimes picked bizarre combinations, she couldn't fault his choice tonight. He thought he looked pretty sharp: Gray slacks, tweed sports coat, white shirt. "What's wrong?"

She nodded at the ink stains on his fingers, and scowling, he went off to wash his hands again. When he came back to the mirror and picked up his comb, she was almost finished.

It was remarkable. Just brushing down her hair and patting on light makeup, she could still command all the male attention in the room. The years had been good to her. By anyone's standards, she was a stunning woman.

And yet, how long had it been since he'd felt any real desire for her? Many months—no, more than a year now. And how long since he'd done something about it? A lot longer than that. He knew the reason, of course, but sometimes he wondered whether his equipment would still work, if he wanted it to. As the years had gone by with their sex life stalled, Jean had begun to indicate wordlessly that she didn't mind. Her whirlwind of activities and social events left her too limp to be very responsive anyway.

Beau comforted himself with his usual thoughts. Of course he still loved her—was truly in love with her. Nobody pants and misses heartbeats—not after being married thirty-two years. They certainly understood each other. She knew all his jokes and how he liked his eggs scrambled and what he thought of the present administration. He remembered to compliment her on her new outfits and listened when she described the latest chapter meeting of any of her myriad charities. Really, he could count himself lucky that she'd put up with him. In his moods and rages, he was no lamb.

It was his fault, in a way, that their sex life was non-existent. But he couldn't help it, any more than he could help liking blue instead of red.

And sex wasn't everything, he told himself, not at their age.

"Did Jim get you to say yes?" she asked.

"Jim doesn't 'get' me to do anything." He patted his pockets for his car keys. "He wants me to think it over. So I will think it over—and tell him no tomorrow. Ready?"

She pivoted away from the mirror, smiling over her shoulder for his approval. He nodded and smiled back—she did look lovely—but God damn it, she still made the same gesture inviting his flattery that she had all these years, and he hated it every time. "We'd better hurry," he said quickly, forestalling any more personal comment. "It's past 7:30 now."

"Don't you want cologne?" She held up a bottle of some stuff she'd picked out as an advance birthday present. He didn't like cologne particularly; smelling clean was about all he cared about. But it was this year's designer fragrance, and when something was 'in', Jean couldn't resist it. He rubbed on a little hurriedly. She sniffed approvingly. "Now you smell like a prince."

"Now," he retorted, "I smell like every other damn fool husband whose wife likes designer labels."

They were the last ones to arrive at their own party. Jean slipped among the couples, greeting and chatting, laughing with the wives, charming the husbands. Beau tried to follow her example, but he never felt comfortable trying to make others comfortable. He detested cocktail-party talk, and he was never sure his handshake was firm enough, or dry enough.

Yet he'd known everyone there for at least fifteen years, some closer to thirty. With every face he could connect a dozen anecdotes, a hundred little intimacies. It was a group that hadn't varied much over the years—a few deaths, a few divorces. A sprinkling of new faces that soon settled into the lines of the old crowd. Beau should have felt soothed and comfortable among them. Instead, tonight, he felt a creeping alarm.

He shook hands mechanically, smiling, pecking the proffered cheeks of the women, sitting down finally at the head of the long table. At the foot, Jean chattered easily, glowing under the candlelight. God, he envied her polish and grace. How she could pull things off!

"Beau, you certainly don't look sixty," remarked Nancy Callahan. She was a smooth pampered blonde married to his close friend Dave, whose ad agency had been the first to hire Beau five years before, to do a coffee jingle.

Dave cast a disgusted look at him as they dug into shrimp cocktails. "Don't be ridiculous, Nancy, he looks eighty. And if that crazy metabolism of his didn't burn up everything in sight, he'd be at a fat farm right now, trying to sweat it all off. The SOB doesn't even exercise! I've never seen a guy who could eat so much." Dave glared at Beau's long-limbed body and pushed away his plate. "God, I hate you. The gray hair only makes you look *distinguished* or something. You know you're the oldest one here?" He gestured down the length of the table.

"Don't mind him," Nancy cut in. "He's been jealous of you all afternoon—Dr. Stern cut him down to a thousand calories again. He hates it."

"I'm not jealous—" Dave started.

"Never mind," Beau said wearily. "It's not all it's cracked up to be."

"What is?" Dave asked practically.

Chronologically, Beau thought, he probably *was* the oldest one in the bunch. He had never noticed; he didn't feel any age in particular. But looking down the length of the table, he saw Shelley Christendon furtively slipping a pill into her mouth; across the way her new (much older) husband leaned close to Jean, the better to hear what she was shouting in his good ear. Dave's hair had remained dark blond, but there were rolls of fat around his waist and neck, his concession to his fifties.

Beau strained to enter the stream of conversation flowing around him. Phyllis Horowitz was bubbling over in her excitement to share the prices she'd just wangled for a family plot at Forest Lawn. "Can you imagine," she was saying delightedly, "four people all together—and you can take up to three years to pay for it!"

"'Climb every mountain'," Dave confided to Beth Mastin on his left. "Great recognition factor. First thing you think of is the movie, right? Man, that slogan's gonna sell a lot of baby diapers... and it was Nancy's idea, wasn't it, hon?" He patted his wife's hand affectionately.

Beau closed his eyes against the sudden wave of nausea that rolled over him. Though drops of sweat ringed his face, his body was chilled. He gripped the edge of the table with one hand and with the other clutched his water glass as a lifeline.

Too late. The water acted as a catalyst for the undigested shrimp revolting in his stomach. Phyllis was still trying to interest him in a family plot on a hill when he bolted for the men's room.

***

The ride home was considerably slower: Jean was driving. Beau slumped in the passenger seat, still pale, but the Coca-Cola she had forced into him had quieted his stomach enough to finish out the evening.

Though he couldn't touch the birthday cake she'd ordered, he had listened, wincing, to the multi-key rendition of *"Happy Birthday"*, made the obligatory wish (he'd wished to be spared any more birthdays like this one), and blown out the candles.

"Feeling better?" Jean asked. He nodded, turning his head to gulp in the California night air. She slowed down for a dip in the road and said without looking at him, "Sometimes it just hits you out of nowhere." She knew his habits. Even at opening nights on Broadway, he'd never had a nervous stomach.

"I'm going to talk to those guys in New York," Beau said suddenly. "I'll call Jim tomorrow."

Jean frowned without taking her eyes off the road. "Why now, Beau? Why not fifteen years ago when you could have done it without so much strain?"

"What strain? I've been meeting deadlines all my life. I could write songs at the studio all day and work on a new musical at home at night. Besides, fifteen years ago I didn't need the job. Now I do."

"You wouldn't have taken this job fifteen years ago."

"I didn't have a birthday like tonight fifteen years ago!"

She paled. "You didn't like it?"

"Did you hear what those people were saying? Our best friends for over twenty years—diaper ads and cemetery plots! That's what they think about, when they're not thinking about retirement! I'm not ready for it, Jean!"

He wanted to say more—try to explain that sense of soaring anticipation that had colored his life until—was it only ten or twelve years ago? When he began to realize these were the only colors life would permit him. And the only choice he had left was to change the shadings every so often. But he couldn't explain, because he suddenly felt sick again, and he had to beg her to pull the car over in time.

***

Sunday was always Visiting Day. Beau knew it amused Jean to see him, who disliked attending the bedside of a flu victim, dressing carefully for the drive to Pacific Palisades. "Give him my love," she said as Beau stuffed his wallet into his jacket.

Beau grunted. Jean had never cared for Ben when he was healthy. Come to think of it, he himself had never felt completely comfortable around his boisterous, leprechaun-like friend. *But he's my friend,* he told himself. *That's why I'm going.*

It gave him a momentary pang to see the gray-rimmed body as Ben stepped slowly into the living room to shake hands. God, the guy used to be a dynamo. He could live for days at a clip on Dexedrine and cigarettes, stay up rewriting later than anyone Beau had ever known. Yet look at him now—a diagnosis of lung cancer, and suddenly he'd become a gray old man.

Beau tried to repress his shudder. *Could I ever look like that?* he wondered. Desperate to hide his thoughts and act normally, he wrung Ben's hand so hard it made him wince. Too late, Beau remembered the guy was still weak. *Easy,* he told himself. *Try to take it easy.*

"So, what's the news?" Ben seated himself gingerly in the plumpest part of his favorite sofa. "Did the agency people talk to you?"

Beau nodded. He hadn't expected the subject to come up so soon. Usually there was a ten- or fifteen-minute period of chitchat, a superficial inquiry after Jean's health (Beau suspected Ben felt the same way about Jean that Jean felt about him), gossip about mutual friends.

Perhaps Ben was deliberately leaving out the gossip period because there were fewer people to gossip about: more and more of their mutual friends were dying.

"You gonna take it?"

Jesus, the guy got right to the point. "I don't know," Beau said carefully. "They gave me a few days to think it over."

Ben grunted. At first Beau thought he was in pain, but no, he was just signaling his nurse to bring him a glass of water. "Better grab it," he advised. He coughed, gulped the water, coughed again. "If you don't, somebody else'll get a plum deal. And probably all the work that comes after it, too."

"Well, it helps that you recommended me."

Ben waved him away. "Don't kid yourself. They're up to their asses in lyricists. And what the good ones can't do, believe me... for the right price they'll get a lousy one. You think they know the difference?"

Beau shrugged. "You're not telling me anything I don't know."

"Then do something about it!" Ben leaned forward, his pale blue eyes bulging. "Christ A'mighty! I'm *handing* it to you on a platter. It would've been me if this thing hadn't happened!" He gestured at his little gray body folded into the couch.

He knows, Beau marveled. *He knows how helpless he is.* God, isn't that worse—knowing how much you've lost? Awkwardly, he plucked at the first words on his tongue. "But you'll be back in shape any time now. And once—"

"Ha!" The older man snorted, bringing up a mass of phlegm and a subsequent coughing fit. Beau thought longingly of the pack of cigarettes in his pocket. He didn't dare light up here—but he could feel his entire being shaking for the soothing influence. *As soon as I get in the car,* he promised himself. *The very* second.

Ben seemed to sense his thoughts. When the coughing subsided, he said bitterly, "I've done three rounds of chemotherapy, and every day of it I wanted to die. But I did it because I wanted a little more time. That's the worst thing about all this. Damn doctors expect you to change your whole life. They know they've got you. You're so damn scared you'll do whatever they say, if they can only keep you breathing a little longer!"

He gestured irritably to Beau, and they rose for the torture of the weekly walk. Beau, with his long strides, could easily motor half a mile ahead of Ben even before the cancer. Now he forced himself to slow to the leisurely gait of a convalescent. As he reached out an arm to steady his friend, he saw the blue eyes flash at the pack of cigarettes stuck carelessly in his inside pocket.

"Never gave them up, did you?"

Beau shrugged. "No willpower."

"Not a good enough reason, you mean!" Ben rasped. "A doctor shows you x-rays of your own lungs, and you see what rotten shape you're in— it's funny how quick you give up smoking. Look at me—I was three packs a day for forty years. Quit cold turkey a week after the diagnosis."

There seemed to be nothing to say after that. They strolled without speaking through the back lanes. This was the kind of house Beau had always coveted, with both land and privacy. He also envied Ben's solvency, fostered by hit shows that peppered Broadway regularly for twenty years. As they passed a plump lilac bush that he had always particularly loved (though it was not currently in season), it slipped out. "The bush that *Battle-Ax* bought, hm?"

Ben snorted. The snort turned into a prolonged cough. "*Battle-Ax* didn't buy a blade of grass on this whole damned lawn. It barely paid the rent on my New York apartment."

"But it ran for two years!"

Ben flicked a hand at him, like brushing away a fly. "Grow up, Kellogg, will ya? I was the guy they brought in to fix the show. I got paid by the week, and I spent it like it was water. Until five years ago, this place was mortgaged to the hilt." He saw the stricken look on Beau's face and amended himself. "C'mon, it's what I wanted. I got to do the job. And the songs turned out okay—"

"Oh, Christ, Ben." Beau increased his pace, annoyed, unmindful that his friend now lagged behind him. He didn't want to hear this, not from Ben. The commercial shit was choking Broadway. Either you held out for your worth or you groveled—just for the chance to get the songs heard by a real breathing audience.

It disgusted Beau to see the number of talented people who had succumbed to the lure of the bright lights and lost their dignity in the bargain.

Ben nodded solemnly as he caught up to Beau. "Don't kid yourself. We both know the money isn't in Broadway. Nobody gets rich on it... yes, yes, I know, Rodgers & Hammerstein and Lloyd Webber. Okay. But probably in the producing, not the songwriting."

He'd been rambling on, spitting the words at a graceful poplar in the distance, but at a sound of protest from Beau, he turned. The powdery blue eyes softened. "Give it up, Beau. Take the damn agency job. That's where the money is, *and* the security. The blasted things'll pay the mortgage for a helluva long time. Write your own stuff for yourself, and don't expect to see it on Broadway again. We're too old for dreams. The world has passed us by."

Beau had listened without a word, his eyes sparking. Now, glaring at Ben, he snapped the pack of cigarettes from his pocket, flipped one into his mouth and lit up defiantly. As a cloud of smoke whirled over his tufted head, Ben spun away, coughing harder. Beau, steely eyes fixed implacably on the distant poplar, marched ahead, puffing like a steam engine.

***

It was a terrible night. He tried to shut out Ben's admonitions, first with half a bottle of red wine, then smoking one cigarette after another, lighting a second while the first was still fresh in his mouth. He filled up the ashtray beside his bed, until the sight of the crushed butts and streams of ash disgusted him. He padded into the kitchen to empty them into the garbage, only to find a note from Jean propped up against the little enameled clock he'd always hated. "If you're working with Jules tomorrow, please pick up 75-watt bulbs on your way home. We're all out. Thank you."

Was this what passion came down to? A request for 75-watt bulbs? Where were the bulbs that had once flashed between them? He emptied the ashtray, tapping it furiously against the porcelain in the sink, swearing as he saw a piece chip away. Damn! His favorite ashtray, a hotel-room souvenir from *The Life and Times*. His face turned grim as he stared at the chip.

Nothing ever stayed the same, damn it, not when it was perfect to begin with. Except he hadn't known it was perfect... hadn't appreciated what he had when he had it. Always, he'd been sure that tomorrow would be better. Now look what his tomorrows were going to be filled with: diet soda.

At 2:00, Beau made his way quietly to the little upright piano at the far corner of the den. If he played softly, he wouldn't disturb Jean. It meant hardly tapping the keys, and keeping his foot off the pedal, but if she'd taken a sleeping pill she'd be dead to the world, and he could count on spending a couple of hours with the old songs. It sometimes relaxed him enough to sleep.

He rolled smoothly into the score from *Glory, Glory*, grinning as he played. His first show, at the age of twenty-three. What a wildly eager young theater man he'd been! First one present at every rehearsal, the last one leaving the stage door at night. Scribbling new lyrics on the backs of napkins (some cloth), on leftover call sheets, on scraps of old handkerchiefs.

Of course, on that show he was little more than an apprentice to the great Annie Dean. Annie was really the heartbeat of the show. She still ranked as one of his favorite lyricists. He'd been damn lucky that the schoolboy charm of his college letter to her had caught her attention. It was his first opportunity in the theater, and it led to everything else.

He'd blossomed under her tutelage, and learned something from Annie's gentle attitude toward him, and from Trevor Runeman's.

Trevor was everything Annie wasn't—loud, rude, without a discernible trace of humor and inflexible about timetables and schedules. He was the type of producer who peered over writers' shoulders and clucked when he saw their pencils slowing down.

"Something New". His fingers unerringly found the right keys on the piano for his first professional song, first solo lyric credit. He'd written it painstakingly, so proud to be trusted with a patter song, as they were called in those days. Four complete verses, a snappy chorus, and a dozen topical references, in effortless rhyme. Though it seemed as distant now as his boyhood, he still felt something warm inside playing the first notes.

The piano went abruptly silent as he thought back to Trevor, and the three shows they'd done together. *Glory, Glory* had been a nice-sized hit that ran for eight respectable months, and Trevor seemed satisfied with his return. *He damn well ought to be*, Beau thought smugly. Ticket sales, plus album sales, plus all those road companies... he got his money's worth out of both that show and their second, *A Trace of Morning*, which ran nine months and featured two hit songs, one by Beau.

Spinning Disks was probably fated to be a disaster even if he and Trevor hadn't faced off. He just wasn't on the same wavelength as composer Denny Hubert. Hubert came from the tradition of Gilbert & Sullivan and Victor Herbert—operettas with grand melodies and full-blown, overly dramatic lyrics. Beau had always tried for the simplest expressions, feeling they were the best, truest, clearest to put across, easiest to sing. And he had enough experience at that point to feel that his opinions should carry weight.

Trevor didn't think so. As usual, Denny had whipped up a frothy, high-toned melody. Only it was supposed to be a comic piece—Beau needed something simple on which to build the frame of his lyric, which would serve as the real attention-getter for the audience. Keep the range small, he pleaded. Easy to sing. Please.

All Denny knew was writing big melodies scored with lots of strings and horns. The funny, almost a-melodic patter songs that evoked big laughs were beyond his ken.

Beau didn't blame him for his creative limitations. He did blame him for his politicking. Denny knew just when to run to Trevor with a creative problem, so that a discussion between composer and lyricist inevitably became a showdown mediated by a crazy producer. It wasn't the way to handle things. Still, Beau put up with it... until that final patter song.

It was the best he'd ever done. God, he was proud when he finished it. Light, witty, each phrase delicious in all its shades of meaning. He'd even gotten in a couple of wicked puns. The male star, Cam Berman, was going to love it.

Cam did. Unfortunately, Denny couldn't match it with an appropriate melody. All he came up with was a series of brassy, soaring waterfalls of notes. Over and over, Beau explained—patiently, kindly, diplomatically— that they were beautiful, but inappropriate. Put them in the trunk and try again. Please.

Finally, Denny wouldn't try again. Instead, he went to Trevor. Trevor screamed that he'd yank the number rather than let his composer and lyricist poison the company with their personal feud.

Beau couldn't believe it. Yank that beautiful lyric? A sure showstopper? A sure hit record—possibly even a signature song—for Cam Berman? Was he out of his mind?

When he understood that Trevor was very serious, that power was the issue here, not the creative peak he'd finally achieved after years of sweat, something snapped inside him. He'd never played the game very well, relying on his lyrics to speak for him. This time, it was a mistake.

The only words he could come up with when he understood the full extent of Trevor's—and Denny's—betrayal, were unprintable, and shouted at the top of his lungs, in front of every single person connected with the show— lawyers, backers, record executives. It was a colossal mistake.

That was when the slide began. The lyric, of course, never found its mate in Denny's music, and as Trevor had promised, managed to get lost in the shuffle. Beau felt physically ill when he saw the final printed show program minus that beautiful song. But that was only the first disappointment.

Of course he never worked for Trevor again. That meant never working with some of Broadway's creative cream, and losing a shot at writing some of the finest librettos of the '50s, shows that embedded themselves into the American psyche. He sometimes felt a little sick when he thought of the shows he might have written.

Still, he tried to stay optimistic. All wasn't lost. He picked up lesser Broadway jobs, and went looking for work in movies as well. But movie musicals were becoming overly expensive in a studio system that was running itself rapidly into the ground. Movie jobs dried up. He was reduced to the occasional theme song. It kept him eating, since he was prudently stashing his money away in stocks, planning carefully for a graceful retirement around age sixty. Then the market plummeted.

All the years of studying investments, reading books and seeking professional advice, all the careful choices wiped out in a seesaw of blinding speed, and none of it his fault. He didn't have enough, suddenly, to retire. The unthinkable had suddenly become the inevitable. He had to continue working—but doing what?

His other lyricist friends, not so proud, had for years been writing commercial jingles, and they urged him into it. Good money, they said, and fast, easy work: no more spending six months on a score. If you own a rhyming dictionary, you can live like a king.

They were right, too: Beau's Broadway credits shone like a lighthouse beacon through the sludge of minor lyricists clawing and kicking for the chance to write coffee ads, deodorant jingles, odes to the immortal douche. L.A. ad agencies knew his name. Some of the older executives—thirty-five, forty— could even occasionally remember some of his lyrics. Inevitably they bungled them, of course, and just as inevitably, they were so proud of their creaky memories they sometimes insisted on singing them when he met with them. He swallowed his winces and gave them tight smiles and brief handshakes. They gave him lucrative contracts.

So here he was—hiring himself out like a conscientious whore to the highest bidder, looking for long-range campaigns that would give his work a shot at national exposure, where the real money was.

He swung into the score from *The Life and Times*, beginning with his favorite lyric, *"Bursting Bubbles"*, his fingers rippling gently over the keys, keeping the music soft.

Remembering that reminded him of what he didn't want to be reminded of. All this musing over his career was just a distraction, he knew, from what really bothered him, though after all these years he wondered why. It wasn't as though he wasn't used to it.

Jean.

The stunning woman he'd been so proud to win, after frenzied years of dating New York girls, many of them professional beauties, actresses, singers and dancers. She'd been the most beautiful of all, a luscious bloom from southern California that men had rushed to court. Yet she had chosen him. He often wondered how that had happened.

Had he caught her at the right moment, the moment when she realized she wouldn't be a movie star, and so had decided to escape her disappointment in marriage? He was one of at least a dozen, he knew. Had he been exotic to her, a New York-based guy working in the theater, unlike the others, native Californians in banking or business or entertainment? He'd been doing a short stint writing forgettable songs for a hybrid musical at Universal when he met her through friends at the Brown Derby, of all places.

God, he'd never recover from that first look—creamy soft skin, tip-tilted sapphire eyes, the cat-like smile he'd seen on Vivien Leigh in *Gone with the Wind*, and the prettiest auburn hair, just brushing her shoulders. A girl with poise and taste, a girl who didn't need to run after anyone.

He'd done all the running, he remembered, and he was still surprised that after a six-month courtship, she had said yes.

The first few years had been so happy. She'd agreed reluctantly to live in New York, though he understood that she really wanted to return to Los Angeles, where she could feel comfortable, not breathless. ("New York is so *fast!*" she'd said in wonder on her first visit.)

In those days, returning from exile on the West Coast, he got Broadway jobs easily, one after another—doctoring shows in trouble, contributing storylines or lyrics to others, building up credits, eventually being the sole name as librettist-lyricist. Despite the setback with Trevor, he could envision a glorious future. A good life stretched in front of them, full of hope and promise.

Until Charlie.

He hadn't cared much about becoming a father, but after awhile, Jean began to talk about having a baby, at first mentioning it wistfully once or twice, then more often, finally incessantly and insistently.

All right. He didn't mind having a child. He knew it would make her happy. And when she became pregnant while he was doing a paste-up job fixing *The Wishing Well*, where he first worked with Jules, he was happy—happy for her and for himself.

All seemed to go well during the pregnancy, with Jean having little or no morning sickness, few symptoms, glowing with health. But something went very wrong at delivery. He still didn't know how it happened.

The child they'd named Charles Beauregard Kellogg had been born dead.

He never wanted to go through anything like it again.

Jean was distraught, and inconsolable. Inevitably, she blamed herself. Something she'd done had caused it. Something she hadn't done could have prevented it. Again and again she went over it, while he tried to comfort her, to shift the blame off her shoulders, to ease her pain.

He himself never had a chance to mourn the child, or even feel a connection with him. He'd never even held the baby; the doctor had come into the waiting room where he had stood for hours, smoking ceaselessly, and briefly told him the bad news. "She's going to be fine," he said quickly, "but— there could be repercussions, emotionally."

Repercussions. Oh, God.

Beau had stared at the little closed casket, as though that would somehow make him feel fatherly, make him understand why he was at this strange funeral where he and Jean were the principals. She was, as always, faultlessly groomed, beautifully dressed, softly spoken. Even at this most tragic of moments, she had an aura that drew all men's eyes.

That was the problem.

It had started two months after the funeral. He had gone back to work on the advice of the doctor, who advised a return to routine as soon as possible—therapeutic for both of them.

A dance rehearsal had ended unexpectedly early one day when a pipe broke backstage, flooding the place. The producers shut things down and called for plumbers and maintenance people.

He thought he'd take Jean to an early dinner, then maybe dancing, if she felt up to it. Getting dressed up and going out often cheered her up.

This time it didn't, though she agreed to go and spent the usual amount of time dressing, perfuming and making up. He told her how beautiful she looked before they left, and again when they were seated in Twenty-One. She smiled faintly and said nothing in response, but he noticed her eyes roving idly over the other diners, something she ordinarily never did: He'd always prided himself on keeping her attention when they were out together.

She chose something from the menu and ate most of what was on her plate. Afterward she agreed docilely when he suggested dancing at El Morocco. They shuffled around the dance floor for an hour or so, her eyes still roving restlessly.

Then her gaze stopped on someone across the room—a young man in an elegant suit and tie, with a feral smile. "Who's that?" Beau asked her irritably.

She seemed surprised. "I don't know. Why do you ask?"

"You've been looking at him for the last five minutes. Do you know him—or are you attracted to him?"

"Don't be silly." She tightened her arm around his neck. "Oh, good, they're playing 'Night and Day'."

He'd allowed himself to be distracted, and held her closer. There was nothing to be concerned about. She was just... restless. Grieving.

Doing her best to go on with her life.

Three days later a second pipe had burst backstage.

When Beau walked into the apartment, two hours earlier than usual, he'd heard a soft whisper, a sigh, like something borne on the wind, except that what he was hearing wasn't a phantom sound.

He didn't call out to Jean, as he usually did. Just walked quietly into the bedroom.

And saw her in their bed, naked, astride the guy with the feral smile from El Morocco.

They were too caught up in the final moments before climax to notice him, and he was too staggered to make a sound, or turn away. Horrified, he watched them finish, the climax remarkably loud for Jean, as though she were shedding all her inhibitions at once. She was sobbing, her hips moving frantically, her glorious auburn hair sticking to her perspiring face in clumps.

Beau still couldn't think of anything to say when their breathing finally slowed, and turning her head slightly, Jean saw him. Her body stiffened.

"Get out," he said. It was the first coherent sentence he could summon. "Both of you. Now."

With speech, his emotions began to thaw from the frozen lump they'd coalesced into when he first walked into the bedroom. Rage and pain were beginning to war inside him, licking his heart with stripes of burning red. He couldn't believe anything could hurt so much. His hand curled for support around the edge of their dresser.

Jean rushed into the bathroom, scraping up her skirt, blouse and underclothes from the floor on the way. The guy kept his eyes on Beau as he picked up his pants and shirt (custom-tailored, Beau noted sourly), then edged backward in the same direction Jean had taken. "Bastard," Beau muttered. "Prick. Asshole."

The guy said nothing, but his eyes measured distances, gauging the chances of either a quick escape or shadowboxing past Beau to the front door. Both, at the moment, were dim: The doorway where Beau stood was the only egress from the bedroom. His first rage was cooling from molten incoherent thought to the smoking heat of pre-meditated murder. He felt more than justified.

The guy disappeared into the dressing area near the bathroom, emerging two minutes later more or less dressed, his shirt inside out, shoelaces knotted untidily. Jean came out of the bathroom at the same time, looking more hastily put together than he'd ever seen her. Her hair was flipping around her shoulders, her lipstick smeared, her blouse creased and buttoned wrong.

The guy, to his credit, stood in front of her as they moved toward Beau. As they came closer, Beau's eyes stabbed at them; he hadn't moved.

They stopped four feet from him.

Impasse.

Beau never knew who swung first, but in a minute he and Feral were rolling around, half in, half out of the bedroom, punching and kicking at each other. Fists landed. Then came groans and fountains of blood.

Fifteen minutes later, Feral staggered out of the apartment, his eye blown up to half again its normal size, his nose cracked, his mouth trickling blood.

Beau's hand had swelled; his knuckles were skinned. His cheeks felt sore; his teeth hurt. Blood had stained his favorite shirt, and he wasn't sure whose it was.

His heart ached unbearably.

How could she do it?

He wondered this aloud to his friend Frank, who patiently bought him drinks for three hours that night at the Algonquin Bar (he loved its famous literary associations). Jean had left and not come back. He had no idea where she was, though she had gone at his express order. He had no idea whether he wanted her back. He had no idea where his life was headed.

"It's not about this guy," Frank said for the twelfth time, watching Beau down his sixth scotch. "Come on, you know it's not about him."

"Then what?" Beau mumbled. He was becoming sleepy as well as drunk. In a few minutes, he knew, he'd probably pass out.

"It's about the—" Frank hesitated. "Beau, it's about the baby."

Beau tried to focus on him. "What?"

"She's grieving. This is her way."

Beau felt adrenaline flooding his veins in spite of the drinks, felt his rage coming back. "She was fucking a total stranger in our bed, right in front of me! That's grief?"

"A stranger she first saw when you took her out dancing. Maybe she was mad at you for being able to have fun so soon afterward. Maybe it was a way of pouring out her anger at you for seeming not to care." Frank shrugged. "I'm no shrink. But it could have been that way, couldn't it?"

Apparently it was.

She came back the next day around noon, hesitating just inside the door. He had gotten up to wait for her, trying to shake off his towering hangover, and called in sick to rehearsal, for one of the few times in his life. Neither of them knew what to say.

She tried to explain. He tried to listen, tried to say he understood. He choked on the words. He didn't understand. He'd never understand.

Yet they stayed together.

And it happened again and again. A month would go by, sometimes two, and Jean would announce she was taking classes at a local college, or joining a book club that met in the evenings. She'd be out at certain times.

He learned to dread it.

He knew what she was doing, what she never seemed to stop doing.

At first he confronted her—hired private detectives who cost him a fortune, assembled irrefutable, unanswerable proof. Told her in scornful, well-turned phrases what he thought of her.

She would cry and admit it. She'd beg for forgiveness. She'd say she didn't know what had come over her, that she couldn't live without him, that she'd never do it again.

At first, he believed her. He *wanted* to believe so badly that this was the last time, that it was over and behind her, and they could live their lives as before. He knew he was more than justified in seeking a divorce, but he couldn't bring himself to do it.

He'd seen the look on his mother's face, all those years ago when his father left... haunted and shocked and helpless. At the age of fourteen, he'd been the one to shoulder the burden for the family until she could pull herself together, get a job, begin her life again.

It had never been much of a life afterward, and she'd died before his first show even opened. Beau knew he couldn't do that to Jean. He knew she couldn't manage on her own. She relied on him for everything.

He was a better man than his father. Better this half-life of doing what he knew was right, rather than the pain of feeling he'd destroyed her by walking out.

And if he couldn't leave, he could try to improve their life together. He agreed to move back to Los Angeles, where she had family and memories and had always claimed to be happy, even though it put him further from the center of the action professionally. He thought being back on familiar soil would give her stability, might finally end her torment.

Instead, it continued, constantly, blatantly. He'd never caught her again with a man in their bedroom, but he had once found Polaroids in the drawer of the night table. Seeing her, naked and abandoned, with some guy whose face was turned away from the camera, made him sick at heart.

It wasn't just the humiliation. It was the heartache, and the jealousy, the wondering how he had failed her, whether it was somehow his fault.

That question had finally driven him, reluctantly, to a psychiatrist, a good one recommended by an actor friend. The psychiatrist had told him unemotionally after half a dozen sessions that the cheating ('nymphomania', he termed it) did relate back to the loss of their baby. This was a grief reaction, and to some extent, it was to punish him, as well, perhaps for seeming to recover from the baby's death more easily than she did.

After he heard this, he never went back. What was the point? Frank had told him the same damn thing that very first night, and paid for his drinks, too. No point in spending more money for more of the same.

Grief ends, but her cheating went on and on. It stopped being about grief; it became about the emptiness of her life, the pointlessness of her days, but anything could set it off. He dreaded it, even as he braced himself to deal with it.

But eventually, something had to give.

What finally gave way, though he wouldn't admit it, were his feelings for her.

He told himself he'd never stop loving her. He'd loved her when they married, and that would never end. Her behavior was something hurtful she couldn't stop doing, like taking drugs or drinking too much. Taking care of her was part of his wedding vows, like taking care of a healthy woman who after marriage had become blind or deaf, or lost a limb. This was part of her, and part of his responsibility. To abandon her when she couldn't help herself was heartless and impossible. It became the prime focus of his responsibility as a husband.

Still, the mark it left on him was deep and lasting. The jazzy romantic lyrics he was known for gave way to crisp, bitter poetry in perfect syntax and rhyme, which singers at first gingerly and then bluntly told him they didn't like to sing—they were just too depressing. The soaring sense of beauty and possibility that had been a trademark of his early work was gone. And with it went a lot of his marketability.

This is life, he told himself. *This is what they mean by playing the hand you're dealt. She's the love of my life. Neither of us can help what's happened.* Even if he was little more than a caretaker now, he felt it was a role he could never abandon.

But there was one thing he couldn't get past.

His friends in college had always laughed about his fastidiousness in matters of the heart, or further down. He tried to laugh, too, but there were things that just couldn't be helped. He'd always been a man who conducted one relationship at a time, not looking for others, concentrating on the woman he was with, automatic fidelity even without a vow. It was just his way.

And the thought of having sex with Jean again, after the many men she'd been with, made him shudder in revulsion. It put her on the same level as a whore.

He couldn't stop thinking of the men who'd had her, how they'd kissed and stroked and screwed her, when she belonged to him. His imagination was too vivid.

From the moment he'd walked in on her and the nameless guy she'd picked up and brought home, he'd never been able to touch her again.

Sometimes he thought, when she lied cheerfully to him about her latest art class or get-together with her girlfriends, that he'd driven her to it, by his refusal to make love to her. He told himself that she was almost— almost!— justified in looking for it elsewhere. But he couldn't help it; the thought of making love to her now was sickening, a final, loathsome humiliation.

As the years went by, he occasionally wondered if he would eventually become impotent, and if *Use it or lose it* also applied to his dick. He knew his sexual feelings were, for the most part, completely submerged, in a fog of pain he couldn't bear to probe. It sometimes surprised him that he felt so little. But sex meant Jean, only Jean, and the thought of Jean in bed with him repulsed him. At first, whenever she cheated, she'd want to make up with him in bed. She learned soon enough that her coaxing would set him off all over again.

The king-sized bed of their early married life gave way to two double beds, then to separate rooms, which turned into a blessing when middle age led to snoring and nighttime perspiration. He was restless much of the time, getting up in the middle of the night to play the piano, drinking more than he should. On rare occasions, driven by an impulse he had to satisfy, he paid a hooker. He wasn't proud of it, but he told himself as long as he closed his eyes and pretended she was Jean, the young Jean he had courted and loved long ago, he wasn't really betraying his marriage. And being with a hooker let him know he could at least still function, if only mechanically.

Then came the fiasco of Nancy.

He wouldn't do that again.

He loved Jean, he told himself repeatedly. She was his one great love. She was all he ever needed. It was no one's fault, really, that their romantic life had ended so long ago.

Love was shared experience and companionship, nothing more, and he had more shared experiences with her than with anyone. They laughed at the same jokes, liked the same books and movies, shared the same friends and holiday memories. A few years ago, on a whim, she'd taken a job at a friend's upscale boutique on Melrose Avenue. To his surprise, she enjoyed it. What had been a lark eventually became a full-time, sometimes six-day-a-week job, and she had risen to the position of assistant manager. It made their lives a little easier together, now that she had responsibilities she seemed to thrive on.

It was more than enough. Sex was overrated, anyway. And at sixty, for God's sake, he should be winding down. There were compensations that came with age, he told himself. This was undoubtedly one of them.

Romantic dreams were for teenagers. He'd lived his romance. It was behind him now. He refused to see his restlessness as anything but the last vestiges of youth before the onrush of old age.

He hadn't given up all his dreams, though. *One more show*, he thought, *one more shot at immortality*. As his restlessness mounted through the spring and summer, he clung to that lovely dream as to a life raft.

He renewed his friendship with Jules, the hotshot boy wonder who, it was rumored, could write a movie score in a week and orchestrate it as well. He had a real ear for melody, too, and a passion for working in the musical theater that had not been sated by his own three Broadway shows, two hits, one flop. He wanted it too, so badly he could taste it. So there they were, two old dinosaurs hoping to hear the sound of cheers one more time.

Meanwhile, he'd agreed to discuss a campaign for a new diet soda so he could keep eating long enough to become immortal.

CHAPTER 3

October

Anticipation was the enemy.

Amanda considered this as she walked south on the quiet tree-lined street in the mid-seventies, just off Central Park West. Behind her, three blocks away, was the Museum of Natural History. To her left was the park. Ahead of her lay an ordinary work night... yet something inside her, something she couldn't name or understand, was making her heart beat faster and high color surge into her face. It was as though her heart knew something, something her mind didn't yet know, that was making her feet want to dance on the pavement and her soul soar with excitement.

It was happening again, like it had the day she'd met Stephanie and Fleur at that record store in the Village. She could feel it: something marvelous was just around the corner.

She had had this feeling so many times before, on so many nights just like this one. But this soaring, glowing, 'something-wonderful-is-coming' feeling had never led to anything that justified this surge in her heart. Yet no matter her disappointment, no matter that she couldn't name just what she wanted from nights like these, she remained hopeful that someday it— whatever *it* was—would arrive.

What she had now—the hotel job, her voice lessons, the upcoming showcase they were working on—would be more than enough, she often thought, if she hadn't always felt there was *something else* waiting out there. She didn't know what, or where to look for it or how to call it to her. But there had to be something else, something to fill that space in her heart reserved for the most important moments of life, something that prompted her to think, "This is *living!*"

Lately, it had come more and more insistently, as though she could meet it around any corner, at any moment. And still she didn't know what *it* was.

Just because the early October night was unseasonably mild and clear, with a full moon rimmed by soft, pillow-like clouds and winking diamond-like stars overhead... just because looking into that beautiful sky and breathing the cool, crisp air lifted her heart and quickened her step, didn't really mean anything.

She had no logical reason to feel so buoyant. Steven had finally and irrevocably gone. Not that she wanted him back; his parting shot, that she would never get anywhere as a singer, still rankled. She was trying to forget it, trying to convince herself he had spoken out of rancor and she would prove him wrong. Still, a faint doubt niggled at the back of her mind. She told herself she wouldn't succumb to it.

So why, in spite of that, did she lift her face to the evening sky feeling so suddenly joyous? Why did she have the persistent feeling that around the corner lay a grand adventure?

Actually, around the corner lay only the Lorelei, the small elegant hotel where she worked four days a week.

Stupid, she chided herself. *You've read too many fairy tales. It's just another work night. Who cares what the air feels like?*

Still, she slowed her usually brisk pace as she came closer to the hotel and took deep, luxurious breaths. It was too pretty a night to work. It was a night for adventure, for laughter, for romance.

She sighed. Unfortunately, her idea of romance didn't coincide with her contemporaries'. Theirs tended to start in crowded, noisy, smoky bars, lead to alcohol-fueled laughter and end in fumbling acrobatics in the bedroom.

Where was the Fred Astaire and Ginger Rogers in that? Where was the Audrey Hepburn? Where were the delicious conversations, the quiet romantic dinners in tiny bistros, the breathless meetings in elegant bars, the knowing smiles, the companionship and sparkling dialogue? Where was the across-a-crowded-room explosion of feeling when you looked at the one person whose presence in your life turned the world to Technicolor?

Her friends told her gently that movie romance was not real, that she should strive for companionship and understanding, which was the basis of real love. Her mother told her bitterly to look around at the mess that love could become, and beware. Her older sister Josie, flitting carelessly from one affair to another, told her that hormones were reality and romance was a fantasy. Oh, and her skirt was wrinkled. Perhaps this breathless anticipation was for that dream, the one she'd secretly, guiltily hugged to herself all her life, the '50s-type romance she had always intended to star in herself someday. But a glamorous '50s romance was not likely in the unromantic '80s. And if that was the object of her anticipation, then she knew, turning into the revolving doors of the Lorelei, that she might as well give it up, if she didn't want her own life to become as bitter and unfulfilled as her mother's.

Meanwhile, she was on duty, and romance was not on the agenda tonight. "Evening, Madelyn," she said to the woman behind the desk, her voice calm and businesslike.

"Evening, Amanda."

Madelyn eyed her, seeing the same presence the record-store clerk had seen. And Madelyn, whose hotel uniform was never less than starched and fresh, whose makeup stayed artificially moist and glowing hour after hour, was unimpressed with Amanda's less than remarkable looks. Even she had to admit, though, that half of Amanda's success with hotel guests came from her smiling gray eyes.

She also had something else Madelyn had never quite figured out. It had something to do with the energy she emitted, even while standing still. It made even the simple navy skirt and blouse she wore seem interesting. *How does she do it?* Madelyn wondered. *How can she work longer than any of us and never seem to wilt? How can she stay calm and controlled in the middle of a dozen crises?*

The energy and those expressive eyes weren't her only assets. The other half of Amanda's success with guests came from her silvery speaking voice, which was at once calm, warm and comforting. Guests with problems listened to her and forgot why they were offended. That lovely clear voice, remarkable in a girl that young, was her secret weapon, along with the ability to cut to the root of a problem.

She was the best assistant Jerry had ever had.

Amanda let herself in behind the desk and looked at the stack of mail in her box. She had only been away for eight hours, but it was bulging. Memo from Jerry... check on the faucet leak in 801... postcard from Mrs. Glenda Beaty signed "Love & kisses"... Memo from Jerry... get a list of registered guests on his desk by 10 a.m.—he always asked, though she did it every day... note from the front desk... three complaints tonight from the guest in 214 about the room next door, which happened to be vacant... Memo from Jerry... get a terrific double room ready for an old friend of his arriving from the Coast...

The sudden blare of loud music startled her. She spun around and marched into the little office behind the mailboxes. Sure enough, there was Cherry, tapping her feet to the hard-rock music pouring out of the radio and fiddling with the reservations list.

"Cherry!" Her voice came out a squeak against the music. She snapped off the radio and actually felt the sudden stillness in the room. Cherry took her time looking up.

"Hi, 'Manda." Cherry could never be bothered saying all three syllables. It probably took all her energy to put on her elaborate makeup. Where she wasn't colored and highlighted, she looked tired and sullen. Her neatly pressed navy uniform was the only part of her that looked professional.

"Why are you working tonight? Madelyn didn't tell me you were here."

"Well, she told me all right, loud and clear. I had to cancel a big night just so's I could come in." Cherry looked mortally offended.

"Well, good." Amanda smiled at her. "Because I need your help with the guy in 214."

Cherry snorted, "That creep. He's hearing things, and calling us every five minutes about it. He's been bitching all night about the noise from 216."

"I know. I want you to—"

"216 is *empty*."

"Cherry, I know. I want you to go into 216, close the door, and start banging things around. Stamp on the floor, turn on the TV, whatever you can do to make a lot of noise. Turn on the faucets—or better yet, the shower—"

" 'Manda, he's already screaming about noises he can't even hear. If he hears *that*—"

"Go on." None too gently, Amanda propelled Cherry out of the chair. "I'll call you in a few minutes. Pick up when it rings."

She watched Cherry disappear into the elevator, told the switchboard operator to put through any complaints to her and watched the clock at her desk tick off five minutes.

For once, Cherry did an impressive job. Of course, Amanda mused, no one else was so well suited for it. Eight minutes later the phone buzzed in the office. Amanda, grinning, picked it up. A stream of high-pitched abuse poured from the receiver, punctuated by sharp intakes of breath. She listened mischievously to the threats spewing out, and finally broke into the next breath, in her sternest voice.

"Thank you for letting us know. I am *so sorry* you've been disturbed. I'll go up there right now and clear out that room. We don't put up with that kind of behavior here. Anyone who disturbs our guests can just get out right now!" Amanda was working herself up into a credible imitation of outrage. "I will not pamper those people who think this is some kind of circus! Our guests *deserve* a good night's rest!" She was charging on, but the voice at the other end of the line had altered pitch, to her amusement.

Thanks for your help. Sorry to have to mention it. When might things— er—quiet down?

"I'll have them out right away. If you'll just please be patient for just a few minutes... oh, thank *you*, sir. So sorry you were disturbed. Good night." She dialed room 216. Cherry answered on the first ring. Amanda could hear the blare of the TV and the sound of the shower behind her. "Great job, Cherry. Close up and come on down. And be sure you turn off the faucets and lights."

Cherry reappeared looking puzzled. "What gives? I made enough noise up there to wake the dead. Aren't we gonna hear from our friend in 214?"

Amanda was already going over the reservations sheet. "I expect not," she answered placidly.

Grumbling, Cherry went back to her magazine and radio. Typical— Amanda comes on and the problems never materialize. It never occurred to her to wonder why.

***

By ten o'clock, Amanda had handled Jerry's memos, typed the next day's registration list, and taken a seven a.m. wake-up call for Mrs. Patricia Ellis. She was Mrs. Ellis's longtime favorite and the real reason the garrulous and very wealthy old lady returned again and again to the Lorelei on her visits to New York. While desk clerks, telephone operators, and maids fled at the prospect of a conversation with her, Amanda had found her fascinating from the first.

She had only been on the switchboard a month when Mrs. Ellis phoned for room service at one a.m. Amanda had told her pleasantly that there was no room service until seven o'clock. Mrs. Ellis's distress had been as genuinely touching as it was funny.

"Oh, but I'm out of my crackers, and I have to have them! I get so jumpy without my crackers. Couldn't you just open up the kitchen for a minute and find them? Everyone has Ritz crackers, don't they? And I really don't sleep well without them. Why, one time when I was visiting my son, it was *terrible*. I had told Hallie—that's my daughter-in-law—at least four times before I came that I eat six Ritz crackers at bedtime. And of course I thought of bringing along my own box, but that really would have been silly, wouldn't it? I'm sure they would have broken in my suitcase. So I got all the way there—they live in Vermont—and there wasn't a Ritz cracker in sight and the nearest store was ten miles away and it was already 11:00, and—"

Amanda stifled a giggle but took note nonetheless. The next night Mrs. Ellis found a gift-wrapped package of Ritz crackers on her night table. She called to thank Amanda, and ended up telling all about her son's unhappy, stifling marriage to the thoughtless, heartless Hallie. "If he'd just *listened* to me," she said repeatedly, and Amanda, grinning, felt she had a friend for life.

At 10:06, the night stretched ahead of her without problems.

At exactly 10:07, trouble started. With a bell, as usual.

"Amanda?" It was Carole, the night-shift operator. "We got a screaming lunatic yelling for Jerry."

"Jerry left at six."

"I know. He says he won't talk to anyone else. But when I try to take a message, he just starts screaming again."

"Did he say what it's about?"

"No." Carole sounded desperate. "When I ask him, he just swears."

"All right. Put him through. I'll talk to him." Carole heaved a sigh, and Amanda heard a click and girded herself for battle. "Hello, this is Amanda. May I help you?"

"Jesus Christ! Where's Jerry? I asked to talk to Jerry."

"I'm his assistant. Is there something I can do for you?"

"No, Miss, there is *nothing* you can do for me. I asked to talk to Jerry, and that stupid operator's tried to fob me off on every dumbbell in the hotel. Now why don't you tell Jerry I'm waiting at the airport for the limo he promised. This call is costing me money."

"I'm sorry, he's gone for the day. I can page him, but he probably won't respond for at least an hour." Amanda's tone was chilling rapidly. She reached for a pad and pen. "What's your name?"

"Tell him it's Beau Kellogg, and that I'm goddamned sorry I saved his ass in France and that I'm getting the hell out of this screaming inferno *without* his goddamned limo, and coming over to that dump of his to personally finish the job now. You got that?"

"I got it," she said evenly, restraining a great urge to slam down the phone. "Are you sure you trust me to give him the message?"

"Not really. But I've taken every precaution." The rich voice turned steely. "If you don't change a thing, he may get it the way I intended it." The phone went dead in her hand.

Amanda slammed the receiver down hard. The rude, inconsiderate son of a bitch. Waiting for a *limo* at the airport. Who does he think he is?

She was still trembling ten minutes later, when she heard a familiar voice in the lobby.

"Evening, Amanda." A man in a bulky suit with a scrawny mustache had come in quietly, a natty tweed hat in his hand.

She turned with a start. "Jerry! You're supposed to be at the Plaza dinner! What's up?"

He grimaced, but the blue eyes under shaggy eyebrows were dancing. "Forgot the events list for next month. I wanted to go over it at home." He balanced the hat reflectively in his palm, poised himself for an instant, then hurled the hat at the nail above her head on the wall. As usual, the hat went wide by at least two feet and landed on the floor behind her.

Usually Amanda laughed; Jerry only wore the hat for the pleasure of tossing it at the nail, though he missed ninety-six times out of a hundred. This time, though, she gritted her teeth. Her hands were still shaking as she handed it back to him. "Come on, I was pretty close that time. Amanda? What happened? The kitchen pipes didn't buckle again?"

"Your friend," she hissed. "Your nasty, inconsiderate friend from the Coast, who—"

"Hey, he's here! Terrific! Where'd you put him?"

"He's not here. He was waiting at the airport for a limo to pick him up. Says you were supposed to order one for him?"

"Oh." Jerry thought this over for a minute but as usual, didn't admit to any wrongdoing. "He was upset, huh?" Amanda just glared at him. "Well, he's like that," he said placatingly. "High-strung. Fusses over little things. One of those creative types. Really, he's a terrific guy."

"I'll bet," Amanda muttered. She handed him the reservations list. "He's on his way now, by cab, I guess."

Jerry glanced over it. "Well, where are we putting him? Let's give him the best we've got."

"How about a broom closet?" she said tartly, and related the gist of the message. To her surprise, Jerry laughed heartily.

"Yeah, that's Beau," he said fondly. "Amanda, you can't get so steamed at him. It's not like you. And he cools off fast."

"*After* he upsets everyone else," she retorted. Then she relented. Jerry looked crestfallen—which was Jerry at his most appealing. "Okay, the best double room in the house. How about 704? Overlooking the park. He can watch the muggers outside when he can't sleep."

Jerry laughed. "When he gets here, I'll treat him to dinner. That should cool him down."

Amanda thought privately that it would take a lot more than that.

***

Beau was exhausted: too tired to move, almost too tired to speak. He had hardly slept since the night of his dismal birthday party the week before, and the transcontinental flight had taken a further toll. He had waited almost an hour for his luggage to come off the carousel and then had to fight for his own bag with a screaming shrew who claimed it was hers and had dragged an airport security officer into the fray.

On top of all that, Jerry had promised him ebulliently on the phone to have a limo waiting for him. "Nothing but the best for you, buddy! Don't you worry!" That was a laugh. Beau had scanned all the terminal traffic in vain, had questioned skycaps and airport personnel, even had himself paged in the hope that a driver would hear his name and seek him out. Another of Jerry's fancy promises unfulfilled.

Why do I always fall for it? he thought wearily, as he watched a husky cab driver sling his bag none too gently into the trunk of the cab. *Why don't I remember the way people fail me? Why didn't I remember Jerry, in particular, with his gift of outrageous hyperbole and his habit of always falling short?*

He figured his rage at the hotel personnel would be his last burst of energy on the entire trip. He watched the well-lit Manhattan skyline come into view and wondered how it would look if he fell asleep during his meeting the next day. "Gentlemen, really, I'm very interested," between snores. He shook his head, stirred despite his fatigue by the unmistakable New York upbeat under the cars, the buildings, and especially the people. No one strolled on the sidewalks of midtown Manhattan; everything was brisk, blunt, snappy movement. Even late at night, New York was undeniably alive and moving.

"Traffic jam." The cab driver pointed to the street ahead, one block from the hotel, which was blocked by three cars, a police car with a revolving blue light and a swarm of shouting people. He leaned back, stoically prepared to wait it out. Meter ticking, of course.

"At 11:00 at night? Jesus Christ!" Beau hissed between clenched teeth. His stomach was rocking, his vision blurring. "What the hell's holding everything up?"

He peered through the windshield but could see little beyond gesticulating policemen and screaming drivers. The meter climbed for five minutes while they sat immobile in traffic. He had no energy left to walk two blocks, but unless he wanted to wait a half hour for traffic to start moving, that was his only option. At least soon he could drop into what he remembered was a soft, inviting bed.

Steaming, Beau paid off the cab driver and took his bag from the trunk, his rage giving him a second wind. He hoped it would get him through the hotel lobby.

***

The events list was nowhere to be found. Amanda was sure Jerry had taken it with him but lost it, so she would have to type a new one. She wasn't surprised; he couldn't be trusted to hold onto a piece of paper for more than five minutes.

She was just sitting down at her tiny desk in his office behind the reception area when she heard a bellow from the lobby. "Jerry! Get your cowardly ass out here!"

"Hey, Beau's here," Jerry said, pleased. Amanda stifled a snort, and he gave her a reproving look. "He's really a great guy."

"I think I'll sit this one out." She rolled a fresh sheet of paper into the typewriter, and Jerry, shaking his head, went out to greet his friend.

"Hey, Beau! Long time, huh?" Jerry shook hands enthusiastically. "You still look great. You just never get older!"

"I look like hell," Beau corrected him, smiling in spite of himself. Jerry's placid good humor was hard to shake.

"He's my old army buddy," Jerry told all the staff within earshot. "He even saved my life once."

"And you've all been paying for it ever since," Beau said, and brought down a wave of appreciative laughter.

Jerry slapped him on the back. "We gave you the best double in the house. View of the park and everything. Come on, we'll send your bags upstairs and I'll take you to dinner."

Beau turned pale at the thought. His stomach, whose rumblings had dimmed beside the headache and jet lag, suddenly made its presence known again, violently. He was trembling as he scrawled his name on the hotel register.

Jerry was going on, heedless of his discomfort. "Just think—a thick steak, garlic mashed potatoes, and—"

Beau knew he couldn't listen to any more without vomiting. "Jesus, will you stop it!" The chatter at the front desk ceased. Without looking around, Beau headed for the elevator. Jerry and a bellman, toting his suitcase, trotted in his wake.

Jerry's good humor remained unabated on the elevator ride up, with Beau still shaky and hard put to listen and look around him, though at this point, his stomach quieting down, he felt fully as embarrassed as Jerry's courtesy could make him. Screaming as he had suddenly seemed inexcusable. "Jerry," he said weakly.

"Right this way, Beau... isn't this nice?" It really was. Amanda had sent up the full VIP treatment: Fruit basket and a bottle of champagne chilling in a fresh ice bucket. With undiminished bonhomie, Jerry took Beau's bag from the bellman and set it on a luggage rack. Beau shrugged and tipped the bellman his usual dollar. The bellman thanked him and discreetly disappeared.

Jerry pointed to the park below. "There! Isn't that a pretty view?" He beamed as though Beau could really see it through the darkness.

"Lovely," Beau commented. "Should I tip you, too?" He sank down on the bed, the soft carpeting rocking wildly beneath his feet.

CHAPTER 4

Jerry stayed only until Beau was settled in the room, since Beau was quick to assure him he couldn't eat such a late dinner and really *needed* to go to sleep.

Amanda worked all night, as usual. After she dealt with the items in her mailbox, she took over from Carole as night operator at the switchboard.

By 7 a.m., she was more tired than usual. Either it was because of her shorter-than-usual afternoon rest, or because the creep Jerry called his friend had upset her so much when he phoned from the airport.

She didn't know why—God knows she was used to demanding guests—but this guy had gotten under her skin. He'd treated her like she was both brainless and incompetent, which she loathed.

What she resented most of all was the difference between the promise that had hummed all around her last night and the reality.

Forget it! she told herself irritably. She would nap when she got home and when she got up, do extra practice. She was singing a new song for her coach tomorrow, and at $75 an hour, she wanted to get the most out of his time.

Wearily, she made her way to the formerly gracious brownstone northeast of the hotel where she lived, picked up yesterday's mail and rode up to her apartment on the eighth floor. Inside, she dropped her handbag on the rickety three-legged table, already crammed with unopened mail and hotel schedules.

She liked the job, she told herself. True, she'd only joined the staff eight months before, but already she'd settled into the fabric of the hotel's life. The everyday situations intrigued her and taxed her for creative solutions. She'd already learned from Jerry, a past master at the art, to avoid a down-and-dirty fight with a guest at all costs, no matter how well deserved.

"We're in the business of creating comfort," he'd told her in her first week. "Our guests have to feel that while they're under our roof, they're at home. Whatever makes them happy, no matter how outrageous it might be, is what we have to give them. And arguing with them—even when you're right—destroys that illusion."

Amanda smiled, peeling off her sweater. If he'd only known how perfectly she fit that mold.

She went out of her way never to confront anyone: her mother, her older sister, her voice teachers. She had earned a reputation for efficiency and serenity in every situation. The hotel staff respected her. Jerry adored her. Nothing ever seemed to rock her.

She flicked on the kitchen light. Despite the golden autumn sun outside, the light in her apartment was always dim. The window over her bed, in the corner alcove, was set so high that she had to pull herself up on tiptoe to peer out before deciding what to wear each day. But it was a steal: a large living room, small kitchen alcove with breakfast nook, cramped little bathroom and tube of a dressing room—with two closets!—at only a little over half of her monthly salary.

She'd been lucky to get it, she had thought with satisfaction. It beat living at home under the oppressive eyes of her mother. True, the comfortable cul-de-sac in Long Island was roomier and safer than Manhattan; it seemed to have been passed over by the periodic tidal waves of crime and progress, and most of the residents were faces Amanda remembered from her childhood. But happy? *Not on your life*, she thought with a grin.

The flip side of living in glamorous Manhattan was high prices, cramped quarters, cold impersonal contact with hundreds every day. But she accepted it cheerfully. No place was perfect. If constant vigilance was part of the price you paid—well, that kept you conscious, didn't it? And being conscious stimulated adrenaline. And adrenaline, she told herself, was the body's way of letting you know it was terrific to be alive.

While she ate buttered toast and drank hot tea for breakfast, she shuffled through the stack of mail. Con Ed, a renewal notice on her renter's insurance (a necessity if you lived in Manhattan), syrupy-sweet enticements to join record clubs and book clubs. The literature she'd requested from Julliard.

She stacked the bills on the three-legged table, the other stuff on her dresser. The club offers went into the wastebasket. She'd go over her checkbook after practicing, write checks for whatever she could. It gave her a thrill of satisfaction now to remember the piles of bills overflowing the three-legged table only a few months ago, with demands for payment and overdue notices, all because she'd spent so much engaging a voice coach. Now, only today's bills sat on the table. She'd come a long, long way. She slept for two hours, and woke feeling much refreshed, surprised that it was only ten-thirty. *Time for practice*, she thought. She showered and took her time drying her soft brown hair and pinning it back off her face, a few strands, as usual, slipping through the barrettes. The battered upright piano in the corner of the room waited patiently, but for some reason she didn't want to leap into her work, as she usually did. She kept finding ways to put off starting her vocal warm-ups, and she wasn't sure why.

Her mother had tried to become a singer on Broadway in her own youth. That she gave up that dream as soon as she found a man to marry and harass was unimportant to Amanda, who determined at a young age to live her mother's dream while telling herself it was her own. She could sing entire scores by Rodgers & Hammerstein, Rodgers & Hart and Cole Porter before she could read.

By the age of ten she also knew Gershwin, Frank Loesser, Lerner & Loewe, Jule Styne, Harold Rome and Meredith Willson. She knew the work of Adler & Ross, who wrote *Pajama Game* and *Damn Yankees*, and most of the less-heralded shows that played on Broadway from the 1930s on. While other girls her age sang songs by the Beatles and the Rolling Stones, and boys tried to imitate Jimi Hendrix's guitar licks, Amanda absent-mindedly hummed *"How Do You Speak to an Angel?"* from *Hazel Flagg*.

It didn't make her wildly popular with her contemporaries.

However, it did catch the eye of older people, especially her teachers. She sought out musicals on television, spent her meager allowance on hard-to-find albums (her mother owned many and she listened to them frequently), and saved up assiduously for tickets to local productions. By age twelve she was beginning to pursue a singing career, quietly and seriously, blocking off practice times, soliciting extra help from her music teacher, choosing chorus and drama over afterschool and summer sports.

Her teachers and coaches seemed to think she had it all: A clear, sweet singing voice, personality, an uncompromising work ethic, and persistence. Her one weakness made them frown and cost her innumerable nights of worry: a tendency toward stage fright that could overwhelm her even after arduous preparation.

She would literally sweat buckets as she waited backstage to make an entrance in her high-school musicals, despite the fact that her director told her she was the most talented person in the cast. Nothing she heard from others mattered; she felt sick to her stomach most of the time while performing and looked forward only to coming offstage afterward, not reveling in the performance itself.

"You'll get over it," she was told over and over again. "It just takes time and practice."

She had to believe it. What choice did she have? What other career interested her? She *must* be meant to be a singer, she told herself. Musical theater was all that interested her. No other field appealed to her, unlike her sister Josie, who drifted in and out of various jobs in various industries, equally indifferent to all of them.

Once she moved to Manhattan and chose her coach, she focused on his goal: finding a few songs she could work up into audition pieces, the more obscure the better. "Everyone sings Rodgers & Hammerstein," he told her disdainfully. "What can you possibly do with '*My Favorite Things*' that these guys haven't already heard? If you're going to stand out, you have to sound like your material was written for *you*. And that means digging for stuff all these musical-comedy mavens don't know."

She understood the logic, and together they dug, and uncovered a gem.

"*The Siren Song*" from *Leave It to Jane* was first performed in 1917. Amanda thought privately that it was the best song Jerome Kern had ever written, and she worked stubbornly at it. "Think about what you're singing, Amanda," her coach told her over and over. "Think about the words. Who are you in this song, and who are you singing to?"

She knew what was being asked of her; the trouble was she didn't have the faintest idea how to deliver it. The overriding quality of the lyric was sexually alluring. How to convey that with soft confidence, when she'd never felt confident of her own sex appeal?

She told herself that barring her own meager romantic experience (and six months and one week with Steven was pretty much the extent of it), repetition would help her find the right tone. At least, she thought it would. She didn't know what else to do. The song was so beautiful and so perfect for her range; she was determined to get it right.

She still didn't know how to handle the sickness in her stomach when she faced an audience. It seemed as though, far from abating with experience, at times it was worse. It seemed like the most indomitable obstacle to the career she'd dreamed of for fifteen years. How could you look forward eagerly to performing when it was the one thing you most dreaded?

Luckily, Stephanie and Fleur, the songwriting team (and romantic couple) who lived in the Village, believed in her and what she could do for their songs. They had met her at an open night for singers, taken a liking to her and asked if she'd sing their songs in Open Mike nights at a local nightspot, the Hot Grill. So now, besides her twice-weekly voice lessons and coaching, she met with them regularly to learn and rehearse new songs. The upcoming revue at the Hot Grill could be a huge breakthrough, and they'd decided she would sing a comic song, not a romantic one. No pay, of course, but if producers and show organizations *did* come, it could be the beginning.

She closed the piano and stretched out on the bed, suddenly tired again, her thoughts swirling around the song's interpretation. It was a promise held just out of reach, like the promises made to her as a child. "Amanda, wait till Christmas. Maybe Santa Claus'll bring you that sled you want." "Amanda, stop complaining! I told you if you got all A's that you could wear my dress at the commencement party, and you got one B." "Amanda, no one said you could go away to college; you know we can't afford it."

Promises that were never kept. That's what I understand, better than the sirens. Promises from my mother, from my sister, from the sky and the wind last night!

I never make promises I can't keep. I know how much it hurts when a promise is broken.

Maybe I'm at the wrong end of this song. What I need is a song full of yearning for something I may never find. Nobody would find fault with my interpretation of that.

CHAPTER 5

All day long he'd been exhausted, but as darkness wrapped the city, he was awake and restless, his brain humming with bits of words and disconnected thoughts. He glanced at his watch: 11:30. Nowhere to go, no one to see. Damn it! He felt charged up, ready to start a full day of meetings or work. He could imagine the look on Hattie's face if he called her now. She was a 9-to-5 girl. She closed the piano at 5:01, and that was it for the day: creativity on the assembly line. He thumbed through his notes from the day's meetings, unwilling to get down to serious thinking about a jingle for the new soft drink. It was just too pretty a night for those kinds of thoughts.

He sighed. He'd brought nothing interesting with him to read. He'd sat in the hotel bar for an hour, killing time, listening to the blur of conversations around him, nursing a scotch, and finally left without talking to anyone. It was too late to phone any of his New York friends; he'd call them tomorrow after his meetings.

Right now, though, he wanted to do *something*. He checked the time again and placed a call to Jean.

"How's it going?" she asked.

"Oh, you know. Busy. Hectic, at first. Then it quiets down."

"How's the job look?"

"Fair. They *say* they know what they want; that's different. Usually I have to hang around waiting for a consensus. Now all they have to do is figure out how they're going to get it."

"Well." Jean sounded brisk, as though she were checking off items on her list of questions to ask. "Any jet lag?" He knew that would come up.

He kicked his shoes off. "No big deal."

"I packed your pills, in case you need them for a night or two. They can help you sleep better."

"I told you, I'm fine. Fact is, I don't feel sleepy at all."

She hesitated for a moment, as though wondering how far to push.

Then she said, "Well, that's good."

"How're you?"

"Oh, everything's fine. We got that shipment at the store, finally."

"Hey, that's great!" He had no idea which shipment she meant. But he figured enthusiasm couldn't hurt. "You've been waiting for that."

"Right." She hesitated again. "Well, as long as you're okay—I was going to bed early. We have inventory early tomorrow."

"Oh, sure. I forgot."

"No. I didn't mention it to you."

He felt himself flush, tried to recover. "Didn't you? I thought you had."

"If you're okay—" she repeated. "I'm really beat."

Christ, it was only 8:30 in L.A. They'd been on the phone two minutes. But he was carefully polite. "Okay. Call you in a couple of days, all right? I'll probably be busy tomorrow."

"Fine. Don't work too hard."

She had hung up before he even said goodbye. *Thanks for nothing*, he thought. Then he had a second of remorse. Maybe the work was harder than he knew. It wasn't as though he'd ever even visited the store with her, seen her in action. For all he knew, she was a dynamo behind the counter, though it sure didn't seem like what she'd want to spend her time doing.

He ran a bath, hot, and whistled bits of the old songs he'd heard in the bar downstairs. Funny how that pianist had played songs he knew, which were old, and not very popular, many from shows that had once been hits but were hardly remembered today. He'd recognized the main love song from *Hazel Flagg* and the title song from *Wish You Were Here*—not your average show repertoire. When he had some real time on his hands, he'd spend a couple of hours with that pianist, slip him a few bucks. It would be worth it to hear a song *he'd* written, for once.

He thought back to his favorite failure as he stepped into the steaming tub. The libretto had been too gentle, too soft to compete with hard-plot shows like *My Fair Lady*. It could have held its own against an *Oklahoma!* maybe. Maybe. But the score was lovely. What a waste. He'd written the best lyrics of his life for Malcolm's music. They'd liked each other, respected each other's abilities... and the show closed in six days, after a year of backbreaking work.

He unwrapped a bar of his own soap, brought from home, and dipped it in the water, then scrubbed his skin with it. *The Life and Times* was the title. And they'd loved it, all of them, which was unusual. No matter that he hated Vernon Delaney, the director, or looked down on the pansy choreographer, what's-his-name, and no matter that the art director and the lighting director fought like cats and dogs, or that the sound guy was screwing the costume designer while he blackmailed her husband, who stage-managed the show. The point was, individually and together, they all loved the show, but they'd tried to do too much. It lacked focus, depth, clarity. The audience couldn't understand it, because the story points were fuzzy and diffuse. Excited backers had compared it to *Allegro* by Rodgers & Hammerstein. He should have remembered that *Allegro* was a flop.

For years he'd railed at everyone except the creative hands responsible. But now, he was beginning to realize it had been their fault.

We tried something and weren't old enough or wise enough to pull it off. Or maybe to realize no one could pull it off. We were all in love with different pieces of the show and fought like madmen to keep the pieces we wanted. And the end result made no sense at all.

And the score—like all show scores, it depended on ticket sales for radio airplay, and on radio airplay for record sales. And with ticket sales dropping to nil in the first two days, after brutal reviews, it wasn't likely they'd get air time for any of the songs, no matter how pretty. By the end of the run, people stopped buying copies of the cast album. A month after the show closed, Jean got one as a favor at a charity luncheon.

Beau stepped out of the tub and toweled dry standing on the bath mat, humming what he could remember of the title song, then swung full blast into the love ballad. He'd never forgotten a word or a note of it. It was the first song he and Malcolm had written together, the first of the score, and the simplest song possible, in his opinion. He loved it but hated the memories it brought back.

Nancy.

The soubrette who should never have been a soubrette. She couldn't act, couldn't sing, had no sense of comic timing. But she was so beautiful. That, everyone agreed on. It was Beau who had pushed her for the soubrette role, the best role in the show, and the pivotal one on which the plot hinged.

"Is this the stage door?" she'd asked innocently, peering at the sign. "I can't see a thing without my glasses." She'd twisted her gold hair under a wool hat, turned her collar up against the cold rain, huddled down in the warmth of her coat. Beau melted, watching her.

He argued for her against the producers and the director. "She has it. What we all talked about. Vulnerability, beauty, innocence. Wasn't that what we all agreed?"

"Just because you have the hots for her doesn't mean she has to carry the damned show," Vernon observed dryly. "We could stick her in the chorus, if you want to get laid."

Beau had him out of his seat, by the collar, before he'd finished the sentence. And after Vernon got a crack over his forehead that Beau figured was probably still there, unless he'd had plastic surgery, the others separated them, and Nancy got the part.

She was grateful to him. Five weeks' worth of grateful, in hotel rooms and country places he barely remembered now. As rotten in bed as she was on the stage, and he was so enamored it didn't even matter until the last few days, in that last little inn, which for some reason he remembered vividly:

Nancy snuggled up to him, naked, a glass of champagne in her hand. He patted her soft skin, searching his memory for the nagging thought she'd interrupted earlier with a provocative kiss in an unlikely spot. She snuggled closer, cooing to him, and when he tried to shush her, she exclaimed petulantly, "There you go again! You're always doing that!"

"What?"

"Trying to get me to be quiet. Don't you like hearing me talk, honey?"

Actually, not in the least. The less she spoke, the better. When she did, it was invariably to complain about the other actors in the show, all of whom blindfolded and with laryngitis could sing better than she, or to coax him into getting her more attention from the costume designer. "Wouldn't I look just peachy in that new shade instead of this old blue?" He grew to dread it, and at last dealt with it simply by ignoring all but the most blatant requests.

It was beginning to come now—he was beginning to remember—he could feel the mists of distraction clearing out around the thought he was anxious to recapture—when she tucked a long slender finger under his chin and stroked. He pushed it away, his eyes darting about to imprison the thought visually. She leaned closer, tried again, and this time he made a noise of real frustration. And as he swung his legs over the side of the bed, it came back—a lyric he could fix now, before the opening. The right phrase, the right rhyme--all there, like clockwork.

"Pencil. Damn it, find me a pencil! Hurry up!" She was startled, but sat up slowly and opened the drawers of the night table next to her. "Here's a pen. And some note paper." She held them out obediently, but he pushed her hand away.

"Didn't you hear me? A pencil! I don't want a pen. Get me a pencil to write with! Christ, aren't you useful for anything?"

There was just a moment, when her eyes looked bewildered, before she dissolved in tears. He swore through her sobbing, still rummaging for the pencil—he always wrote a lyric in pencil, to forestall problems in the inevitable rewrite. It was such an ingrained habit that he could no longer write without one. Damn, and he always carried them, too—he had more pencils than extra toothbrushes.

Terrified the words would get away from him before he could set them down properly, he rushed into the other room (they had a tiny suite in the inn) and threw open his suitcase. When he realized he'd left his precious store of pencils in New York, he dumped out the contents of Nancy's handbag. Lipstick, worn emery board, makeup-smeared handkerchief, change purse— the girl never carried more than two dollars in cash, claiming she was afraid of being mugged in the big city. What that also meant was that someone else always picked up her tabs.

He didn't realize she was watching him. She had come quietly into the room, just far enough to see him pawing through her personal things. He thought he'd heard every tone of voice she was capable of, within her limited range, but he was wrong. He wished she'd brought that kind of richness to her songs. "You miserable prick—what do you think you're doing?"

The fight that ensued exhausted both of them. He called her a whore, a no-talent, an opportunistic chorus girl, a hick... she got in more than a few good shots herself. After she elaborated on his advanced age (he was just over thirty) and speculated on his few remaining good years and the horrors of prostate trouble and finding false teeth that fit, he found the first threads of gray in his hair.

He never spoke to her again. On opening night, he distributed flowers and congratulations to every dressing room except hers, managed to hug and squeeze everyone involved at the cast party except her. Funny, too, that after all these years he remembered her so well. Her face was the last thing he saw clearly before he stumbled into bed and slept.

***

He woke humming the love song. It was quiet and dark in the room, though he'd fallen asleep with the heavy inner curtains still drawn open.

He rubbed a hand over his eyes to blot out the distant lights shimmering beyond the window, but it was too late. He was wide awake and suddenly hungry as hell.

He groped for the light switch and reached for the telephone.

Squinting at the lighted dial, he pushed the buttons for room service. "Good evening. May I help you?"

"Yeah, this is room 704. I'd like a milk shake, chocolate and thick as hell, and a toasted bagel and cream cheese. How fast can you do that?"

***

Oh, God, it was him, the bastard who had upset the switchboard operators and bellowed through the lobby loudly enough to alert all five boroughs. At three o'clock in the morning, asking for room service. Unbelievable.

Amanda leaned back in her chair. Her stomach was tightening inexplicably. "I'm sorry," she said finally, when she could control her voice. "Room service closes at midnight."

There was a pause. "Oh. What time is it now?"

She looked at her watch. "Ten after three."

Another pause. He seemed to be thinking that over. Well, let him. The small desk lamp at her elbow cast only a faint yellow light, and the switchboard was quiet. She hadn't spoken to anyone in almost two hours.

"Then whom am I speaking to?"

"I'm the night operator. This is the main switchboard."

"Well, main switchboard, you must all sound alike down there. I could swear I've talked to you before."

Shouted was more like it. Odd that he'd remember, though. "You've got a good ear, 704. I was on duty last evening."

"Good Lord. How long are the shifts around here?"

"Eight hours for everybody else. I'm working a double today." A red light was flicking on somewhere else. "Can you hold a moment?"

"I'm not going anywhere."

"Okay." She dealt with the other call, an elderly man asking for directions to a building in Greenwich Village. It took a long while, not only to explain, but to repeat at the top of her lungs and spell out the names of several streets. She was surprised to see the light still flashing when she finished. She thought the creep might have hung up.

She pushed the button for 704. "Sorry. You were saying?"

"No, main switchboard, *you* were saying. About working sixteen hours in a row. Why? You own stock in the place?"

"Maybe." She sensed encouragement in the silence and decided to plunge on. "Maybe I just love it here."

"I guess you must. But I hope you're well compensated."

Trust a man to think of money first. "That's not my major concern."

"Glad to hear it."

Okay, enough's enough. It's been a long day, made even longer by him. No reason to shoot the breeze with this guy. "Excuse me, I have other callers. Sorry I couldn't help you."

She thought she heard an odd, disjointed chuckle at the other end, but dismissed it as impossible. Spoiled babies don't laugh; they have gas attacks. That's what she was probably hearing.

"Well, better luck with them." The sarcasm was unmistakable.

She heard it and bristled. "Look, if you'd called earlier—"

"Absolutely. My fault entirely, for falling asleep after a cross-country flight, a time change, and a screw-up in hotel administration, not to mention business meetings all day. Forget I even mentioned it." The phone clicked off in her ear.

She sat for some moments before she noticed she was trembling. This was the second time he'd undermined her—and it bothered her.

She jotted a note on her steno pad: "Order chocolate shake and toasted bagel with cream cheese for breakfast, 704."

***

The wake-up call was late. He'd half-expected it would be the girl on the main switchboard, and was surprised when he glanced at the travel clock on the night table and saw that it was already ten past seven. Damned idiot. You couldn't trust anybody to do anything right. "Yes!" he almost shouted into the phone.

"Good morning, sir. This is your 7:00 wake-up call." It was definitely *not* the girl on the main switchboard; this was a much older woman, and her voice was huskier. And damn it, she was late!

"It's now *ten past* 7:00, Operator. Can't you tell time?" And he slammed down the phone. He had an 8:15 breakfast scheduled with Hattie and wasn't sure he'd make it; early-morning New York traffic was murder. But he could still try.

He gulped down vitamins, a concession to Jean, and brushed his teeth while hastily unbuttoning his pajamas for the fastest shower of his life. He could make it. He still could make it, with the slightest luck, as he splashed water on his face, shaved. Yeah, twenty minutes to go. If he called downstairs for a cab—The unexpected knock on the door startled him. For a moment, he couldn't think of anything to say. "Who is it?" he finally croaked.

"Room service, sir. Breakfast."

Beau pulled a towel around himself, combed his hair back swiftly and opened the door a crack. "I didn't order—," but the waiter was bustling in like he owned the place, setting down a tray on the table in the corner overlooking the park. Beau pulled the towel closer.

The waiter wasn't even looking at him. He surveyed the placement of the tray—and following his gaze, Beau saw a toasted bagel with a small cup of cream cheese and a tall glass overflowing with foamy chocolate soda, with a long spoon and a straw set neatly beside it. "Have a nice breakfast, sir." The young man started toward the door with a pleasant nod and a smile.

Beau simply stood there. As the man brushed past him, he remembered and fumbled. "Just a minute—"

"All taken care of, sir. Have a nice day."

He admired the breakfast tray for a full precious minute. Then he tore off the towel, slid into a shirt, and pulled up his pants. Maybe there *was* some efficiency left in this world, after all.

***

He met Hattie with a minute to spare, but his thoughts were on a much more important meeting two hours later, and he was pinning all his hopes on the outcome. He cut Hattie short after an hour and a half and reached his destination five minutes early.

It was all for naught, of course; a half hour later, he shifted impatiently in the soft leather chair in the lobby of the Fieldston Brothers Theatre Organization. There was no indication that he'd be ushered into the inner sanctum any time soon. The receptionist sitting behind a pane of glass took and directed calls in a quiet murmur; she hadn't looked at him since he gave her his name.

He'd long since finished reading the trade papers and flicked an eye over the glossy magazines on the polished low table in front of him. Now he felt like moving around.

He struggled out of the chair—those deep cushions held you in like flypaper—and strolled over to the framed posters and show photos crowding the wall. Hits, one after another. Big, expensive, well-financed hits, all the Fieldstons' most recent triumphs. Gorgeous sets, striking costumes, smoke machines, sound effects, light effects. No stories to speak of, few memorable songs. He felt slightly nauseated. This was what Fieldston was producing these days?

Why not? he answered himself silently. It made money. That was what they were about, after all. He had seen almost all of them, and they made him yearn for his own days on Broadway. They also made him wonder if he still had anything to offer.

He was studying the photos one after another, trying to find some redeeming quality in these new shows, when the receptionist called to him through the sliding glass window in front of her desk. "Mr. Kellogg? Mr. Fieldston will see you now." She pushed a buzzer located discreetly at her elbow.

Through the heavy security door was a thickly carpeted aisle. On either side were cubicles with functional-looking desks and chairs, all occupied by important-looking, well-dressed people he guessed couldn't be over twenty-five. None of them glanced at him.

He started down the aisle, only to be intercepted by a young man in a navy pinstriped suit, hand outstretched. "Mr.—er—Kellogg? I'm Jason Fieldston. Pleasure to meet you. This way, please."

He shook hands mechanically and followed Jason to an office at the end of the hall. It wasn't a corner office, and the furniture was a hodgepodge of various periods and styles. The woods clashed; the file cabinets didn't match; and the walls held more than a dozen framed photos of Jason with this or that current Broadway luminary.

Jason closed the door behind him, nodded him to yet another leather chair—which didn't match its mate—and seated himself behind a beautiful polished mahogany desk, which looked too large for him.

"A pleasure to meet you," he repeated. "I've heard great things about your shows."

Beau looked around, trying not to feel the humiliation seeping into him. "Excuse me. I had an appointment with Mr. Fieldston."

"Yes." Jason had the grace to look self-deprecating. "That's me."

"I thought—" Beau began, and then stopped. Clearly he was being fobbed off on the least important member of the family, someone so young he wouldn't remember anything Beau had done.

His first instinct was to be enraged. His second, coolly superseding the first, was to tell himself to calm down; it had been a long time since his last hit. He'd gotten the appointment, anyway, and Jason seemed disposed to listen.

The young man smiled at him. "I'm learning the business. My father and uncles felt I should be part of the organization on the bottom levels before they'd trust me to run anything with their names on the door. So... I've done some stage managing, some minor producing, sat in on creative meetings, done some negotiations with the unions. Now I'm in the office for awhile."

He seemed to be waiting for Beau's reaction. Beau managed a civilized smile. "An all-around apprenticeship."

"Yes," Jason agreed. "I'm sorry I've been so busy I haven't had a chance to hear your work... but my father and Uncle Perry both spoke highly of you." He tapped a pencil on the desk, smiling brightly.

Then why am I not meeting with them? Beau asked himself. *Why am I meeting with this little snot-nose who has no idea who I am?*

He refused to let himself dwell on the first thought in his mind, which was that it was much easier for a little snot-nose with no idea of his background to turn him down. He still had a chance. A ghost of a chance, maybe, but he was taking it.

"Jules Hamner and I are collaborating on a new show." It made him feel a little sick to realize that at one time, that would have been all he needed to say. There would have been immediate demands to hear the score, the libretto, questions about when and where they wanted to mount the show, and the checkbooks would open.

And now? Oh, God. For a fleeting instant, he really did want to cry.

Jason's brow furrowed for a moment. Then a bright smile of recognition burst forth on his round, vapid face. "Oh, yes. Jules Hamner. He wrote that song for the Carpenter movie—what was it called?"

Beau struggled to remain calm. "He's also," he said carefully, "a renowned Broadway composer."

From there, it only got worse.

Jason admitted he had glanced at Beau's credits in some reference book—though he also admitted a little sheepishly that he couldn't whistle a single tune to which Beau had ever set a lyric. And of course he knew none of the lyrics or librettos. Beau had hoped that the pairing of him and Jules would be enough to get an offer of backing, but with Jason here so ignorant he probably hadn't heard of *West Side Story*, that dream went up in smoke in just a few minutes.

Jason said in a deepening voice, as they approached his specialty, that Broadway money was getting tighter—productions getting more expensive all the time—and the shows of years past just wouldn't cut it on the current Broadway scene. People wanted spectacle, clever sets, lots of flash to compensate for the rising ticket prices. Now, Andrew Lloyd Webber had figured it out; his stuff sold like hotcakes. Had Beau seen *Cats*? Wasn't that a breakthrough?

Beau managed to nod, and hoped the nod did not convey the truth, which was that *Cats* represented not a breakthrough but a breakdown of the musical theater as he knew it: it made him want to vomit. The rising ticket prices Jason spoke of so knowledgeably were tied partially but directly to all that flash, which could not disguise the fact that those shows—he used the term loosely—were empty spectacles without story or meaning.

But he let that slide and went patiently to his subject. He and Jules were choosing now between several exciting scenarios. The score would be their best in years. And he'd always had a warm spot in his heart for the Fieldstons, etc., etc. Jason listened, nodding, his face serious. "Well, look, Beau—you don't mind if I call you Beau?" He didn't wait for Beau's weak nod, but shot his cuff expertly and consulted a thin gold watch on his wrist. "I'm really on the run this week; they've booked me back to back in a dozen places, like I can bypass city traffic and just use my cape." He smiled in a comradely way. "Sorry I can't stay for more, but look. You and the Fieldston Organization apparently have a long relationship. And I know you don't do the Lloyd Webber kind of shows. But, well... I can't promise you anything—my father and Uncle Perry would disown me—but I know they'd want to see whatever you come up with, as long as they're at the head of the line. As old friends, can we ask that? A first look?"

A first look. That was all. He once could have demanded thousands of dollars for a first look at his work, and a commitment up front. Now they considered it bestowing a favor on him to see his stuff without the slightest obligation on their part.

How the mighty hath fallen, he said to himself. It would almost be funny, if he didn't suddenly feel as though his heart had fallen into his shoes.

Jason was already rising, not looking at him, expecting him to do the same. His big meeting was over, in less than fifteen minutes.

He got heavily to his feet. "A first look?" he repeated. "Well, sure. That's what I was hoping you'd say."

Jason, showing what a regular guy he was, insisted on walking him to the elevator. "Say, I hear you live in L.A.," he said out of the blue after he'd pushed the call button.

"That's right."

"Great town. I'd rather live there than here. You here on other business?"

Beau resolved hastily not to mention the commercial. He hadn't fallen quite that low yet. "Yes." Jason had stopped listening; he was humming one of the songs from *Cats*. Fortunately, the elevator came jangling up a few seconds later.

Hastily Beau shook Jason's hand. "Thanks. Say hello to Harlan and Perry for me." At least he could let Snot-Nose know he did know these people on a first-name basis.

Jason nodded, but his eyes looked distracted. "Great score, *Cats*, don't you think?"

"One of my favorites," Beau lied.

He wondered if he could go to hell for saying it—or if this *was* hell, and he just hadn't realized it yet.

***

By evening he'd decided that the only thing he could do was forget the whole disappointing mess. He remembered that he hadn't thanked his benefactor of the morning, and remembered, too, the silvery tones of her voice the night before.

Well, it was better than re-living that ghastly meeting in his mind. He decided to find her and offer profuse and sincere thanks. It wasn't her fault the day had turned to such shit. She'd at least tried to make it start right.

Without a name or an inkling of a title, he didn't stand much chance of finding her among the sixty-odd staff at the hotel. His best shot was to wait until the early-morning hours. Perhaps she'd be on duty at the switchboard again. If not, her relief probably knew who she was. Either way, he could get a message to her somehow. It was the only part of his day that had gone well.

He flopped onto the bed, aware that without thinking of it he was suddenly very aroused. By what or whom, he wasn't sure. And it wasn't supposed to happen—not this strongly—at his age, was it? God, he hadn't felt such a rush in years. It pleased him, even though he was aware that he had no real use for it now. Jean wasn't here, and even if she were, that part of their life together had been over since the first time he caught her.

He threw off that thought and tried to concentrate on the presentation they'd shown him at the agency the day before.

"It's a new taste!" the young man in the tailored suit had insisted, holding up a bottle of what looked to Beau like iodine. "Delicious. Snappy. We want a jingle that tells how snappy it is. How exciting. How it'll enhance everyone's life who drinks it!"

He and Hattie had exchanged amused glances. Trust account execs to blow their own horns loudly enough to be heard in the next county. And to remind everyone else what their jobs were. Most of them had been doing them for longer than the little punk had been alive. This morning was the first time he'd ever wondered whether that was an asset or a liability. Before, experience had always counted as a plus. But these days, who knew?

The presentation had gone on for over an hour, the questions and arguments about the jingle for longer than that. What was their *angle?* the punk kept asking abrasively. What were they trying to *accomplish* here?

Beau forgot the angle, his arousal, and even the humiliation of the morning, in the sudden overwhelming urge to sleep that overcame him.

CHAPTER 6

When he woke, he realized he'd fallen asleep in his clothes, shoes on, everything. It was very dark. He held his wrist up but couldn't read the digits on his watch. *It must be pretty late. I should undress and get under the covers.* But he knew it was useless. He was awake for the day.

Maybe food would be a good idea. And thinking of food reminded him of his plan to phone the main switchboard, looking for his phantom benefactor. It's possible she wasn't working tonight. Sixteen-hour shifts day after day would kill anybody, no matter how young and strong and willing. But when he thought back, she'd sounded calm. And capable. It was possible. He owed her at least a thank-you.

He reached over for the phone and punched the keys. A voice answered— young, female—and immediately put him on hold. He couldn't tell from that quick greeting. But he would wait.

***

The phones were ringing off the hook, and it was after three. And Amanda was tired, though she'd tried not to admit it to herself. She'd been burning the midnight oil at both ends, and she was ready to wilt.

She disposed of all the calls, even the ones she knew personally; she didn't think she could be bright and bubbly tonight. As she started to put down her headset, she realized she'd left one call on hold; the red light winked tantalizingly at her. She pushed the button, and was startled to hear a light, clear whistle delicately sounding one of her favorite old songs.

For a moment, she just listened, holding her breath rather than risk losing the notes floating across the wire. Then she started to hum along, filling in the words where she could remember them, leaning on the melody when she could not.

The whistling stopped, and the voice she'd come to recognize and dread pushed out at her. "So you know it."

"It's one of my favorites." She hummed a few more bars, hesitatingly. "I've known it for years."

"Remember the title?" It was a challenge.

"*Bursting Bubbles*." That was easy. Pieces of the lyric were coming back to her as she remembered the scratchy old record that Josie had broken years ago. Even now she felt a small pang at losing it. "From a show called *The Life and Times*."

"Well, well. I'm impressed. Two points for you."

"And for you, 704. Are you into trivia games?"

He chuckled. "So you know who I am. That makes you one up on me. I don't know who you are."

"Why do you want to know? Gonna complain to the boss?"

"I wanted to thank you. I don't often have a chocolate shake for breakfast, but it really hit the spot this morning. It was very thoughtful. And unusual. I never get service like this, not even at the Lorelei."

There was a pause, and a softening of her voice when she answered. "Well, you're very welcome, 704. Glad I could help."

"But you still won't tell me your name?"

"Won't you snap my head off if I do?"

"I suppose I deserved that. But I was pretty sick when you first talked to me, and waiting an hour at the airport for Jerry's non-existent limo didn't exactly make me feel better."

"Oh." She thought this over for a minute. "I'm sorry."

"But not sorry enough to tell me your name, right?"

She laughed. Perversely, she was enjoying his persistence. Silly, too, because she told hotel guests her name as a matter of course. Yet she was reluctant to satisfy his curiosity, because she suspected that he might then hang up and leave her to the suddenly unappealing solitude of the switchboard and the night. Why that should bother her, she didn't quite know.

"All right, the name is off limits. Tell me about yourself. Why does a young woman who is obviously intelligent and interesting lock herself behind a switchboard night after night? How does she know songs that only old fogeys like me know—"

"Stop it! I love that song. I always have. It's a terrific song. In fact, it's a terrific score."

"You think so?" He sounded pleased.

"I certainly do."

"Well, thank you again, then."

"Why thank you again?"

"I wrote it." He amended that hastily. "Well, half of it. I did the lyrics for the score."

"You did?" She sat back and hastily scanned the guest list. *Beau Kellogg. Of course.* Perhaps subliminally she'd realized it, but it had been years since she'd read the names on the album cover. And when he'd yelled his name at her that first night, she'd been so angry she hadn't thought about

it. "You worked with that composer, then—Malcolm—"

"Malcolm Gooden." She could hear the smile in his voice. "He was something."

All traces of frost disappeared from her voice; now she fairly bubbled into the phone. The serene control was gone. "I loved that score! Always, from the time I first heard it, when I was a child."

"Well, that certainly dates me, doesn't it? And I really thought I could manage to stay young forever."

"You sound young." Actually, he didn't sound any age in particular at all; he just sounded—well, vibrant. Bursting with energy, even now, in the middle of the sleepy night, when she could barely keep her head up. Even as that thought occurred to her, she realized she felt much more alert now. It was probably just having someone to talk to.

"A night full of compliments glowing in the dark. I don't deserve that— but please don't take it back. It's made my whole trip worthwhile."

"I can't believe I'm talking to a celebrity in the middle of the night. It's so fantastic, somehow." Somehow he knew she meant the literal sense of the word, not the exaggerated lingo of the youngsters today. This was no Valley girl. The thought made her—even unseen and unknown— much more appealing.

"Oh, please. I'm not a celebrity. But I've known some over the years, and they never seemed happier to me than other people. In fact, most of them were pretty miserable. I wouldn't want to be famous that way, would you?"

She paused for a moment. "I'd like to be special."

The answer was swift and sincere. "But you are special, main switchboard. You have to be, to remember a score that old as though you just heard it yesterday. I can almost feel now like I might not die alone and forgotten."

***

They'd been talking for half an hour, but Beau hadn't noticed. It surprised him that he felt suddenly re-charged; he realized he was enjoying the unexpected conversation. But he didn't want to impose on her. "Do you have something else to do when the phones aren't ringing? Or do you just read to pass the time?"

There was a pause. Usually she tried to practice, quietly, when the phones weren't ringing. Or scribble some of her silly verses, when they occurred to her. "I don't have time to read much," she said finally.

Hastily he revised his opinion of her. "Oh. Well. Then you must keep busy with other hobbies."

Again the peculiar silence. "Don't you? Or does working late at night preclude doing anything else?"

"No... "

"But you don't want to talk about it."

She fidgeted in her chair, wondering how much she should say. He seemed genuinely interested in her, and being a Broadway librettist and lyricist, her ambition would be right up his alley, but she was wary of revealing too much. For one thing, he might think she was angling for his help, and one experience with his dark side was more than enough for her. And men could be funny, if they heard something that didn't match their picture of you. Then they'd blame you for it, and you'd never hear from them again. And abandonment was something she dreaded. She'd never learned to handle it well.

She had been that route before—with Steven. God, what fun they had together, until she told him he had been mistaken about her: She wasn't going into business. She was going to sing in clubs and on stage and records. He hadn't really believed her.

When he finally realized she was serious, the relationship ended. He didn't want to encourage what he said was her 'fantasy of a career', and didn't want to waste his own time on people who pursued fantasies. He was too busy preparing for a career at his uncle's merchant bank.

It had hurt for months. Even now, she felt a twinge of pain thinking about him. She'd really liked Steven, liked the silky brown hair and the serious expression in his hazel eyes, liked the neat, conservative shirts and ties he wore and the way his cheeks flushed when he got excited in conversation. Or any other time, she admitted to herself with a blush.

The voice from 704 broke into her reverie. "I'm listening. So what *do* you do in your time off? Or don't you have any?"

"Of course I have time off," she said impatiently. Then she said quickly, "Sorry. I was thinking about something else. I didn't mean to snap at you."

"You didn't. Don't be so sensitive. Okay, if you won't tell me, I'll guess. You're—um, an athlete. A demon swimmer or tennis player. Right?"

"Uh—no. Haven't played tennis since I was ten and seldom get the chance to swim."

"But I'm on the right track, right? How about jogging? Or aerobics? You do seven killer workouts every week, right? Jane Fonda tapes and all? My wife swears by those."

She hesitated. This was the first she'd heard of a wife. "Sorry. Wrong again."

"Come on, then. Give me a hint."

She thought hard. "Well—it's physically very hard work, but you can't really lose weight or tone up your muscles doing it. It just makes you—feel good."

There, she thought. *That should end the conversation, if he really wanted to.* She stared at the red light on the switchboard and wondered if he really wanted to.

***

It didn't occur to him to end the conversation. He was too busy trying to figure out the answer to the riddle. What kind of exercise could you do that didn't give you those kinds of benefits? God knows, Jean was only interested in those most likely to increase your circulation, stimulate weight loss and give your skin some kind of much-vaunted 'healthy glow'. That seemed to be her major criterion for taking up an activity—that, and who else was doing it. If expensive accessories went with it, that was a plus, too.

He was silent for a long moment, thinking about it, and then... he heard her laugh.

The sound was oddly fresh and stimulating, and once more he found himself becoming aroused. He could feel the blood rushing through his veins, and every one of his senses was filling up... he could open his mouth and drink in the air he was breathing; he could inhale all the sounds of the night and hear all the special fragrances. It wasn't possible, was it... just hearing a voice at the other end of the phone?

When he could control his voice, he said, "Sounds to me like you're being deliberately evasive."

The pause at the other end stretched for a long moment. Then he heard her clear her throat.

"Can you hold for a moment? My other line's buzzing."

"Sure." He wasn't even sure what they were talking about; he just knew he felt a singing in his veins he hadn't felt for some time. He remembered, with odd clarity, how aroused he had become for a brief moment, the summer before, strolling through the Renaissance Faire.

Hundreds of people, on a wilting-hot day, wore heavy velvet tunics and ridiculous hoops that swayed with the slightest movement. He remembered the young girl—no more than sixteen, he'd judged— dropping him a careful curtsy as he entered the fairgrounds. There was something about the fair skin set off by that ornate lace that started his blood pounding. When he turned to give her a second glance, she was giggling over something her friend was saying, and his sudden fever abated as swiftly as it had descended. Still, he'd been grateful for the momentary rush of his senses. *I'm not dead yet*, he'd thought, vaguely comforted.

He remembered Jean in enticing lingerie on their honeymoon, delighting in their isolation... was his memory accurate or wishful? The question haunted him. In his darkest moments it seemed as though she'd been play-acting about her sexual passions in every moment they'd spent together. *Maybe we never had what I thought we did*, he thought bleakly. Why not? One can shut out almost any unpleasant reality with enough willpower. Or anesthetic.

That skin-prickling moment at the Renaissance Faire—could it have lasted fifteen seconds?—was the last time, until now, that he'd experienced what he'd always taken for granted. Sometimes it seemed as though the mechanism had shut down in him forever. But maybe... it hadn't. Not quite yet.

Meanwhile, that silvery voice was evoking feelings he'd thought were gone forever. He wouldn't hang up until she eased him off the phone.

***

Amanda pushed the hold button and leaned back, watching the red light winking in the semi-darkness. She didn't have another call, but she wanted a moment to think.

Jerry was right; he was a character. She didn't remember ever meeting anyone like him before. She could swear he almost knew what she was going to say before the words came out. There was no reason in the world to continue talking to him; it could lead to personal involvement, which would reflect badly on the hotel. She'd seen it happen with the Tyler girl and the wealthy Canadian businessman: she didn't last, and he never came back to the Lorelei. *A word to the wise*, she reminded herself grimly.

Ridiculous. The man is old enough to be my father. There's no romance here. He's just interesting to talk to. It's just talk, she thought defiantly. *What's the harm?*

Staring at the winking light became a form of hypnosis, and she felt light-headed, almost woozy, when she snapped the button down. "You getting sleepy?"

"I was just thinking I'd never felt more wide awake. What time is it?"

She glanced at the overhead clock. "Five to four."

"Hm. I guess it would be silly to get up now."

"I think it's crazy—unless you're in the flower market, or something."

"That's a lot more dignified than what I'm doing in New York."

She wanted to ask him what that was, but while the unexpected rush of feeling was lifting him toward throbbing wakefulness, Amanda was realizing suddenly she was very, very tired. She'd worked the night shift—plus classes and extra practicing for her audition—for three nights straight. She tried to stifle it, but she was sure he heard her yawn through the phone.

He did. In every nerve from his scalp to his fingertips.

***

They'd been talking for more than two hours when Amanda gasped.

Beau was talking about the volume of song lyrics he'd published years before. It was one of his proudest professional moments, and though he knew it was bragging, he wanted her to know how few lyrics were ever published apart from their music. It was an honor he felt to this day.

He was talking about the days just after the book's publication and how silly he'd acted (he admitted to taking midnight walks down Fifth Avenue so he could peer into bookstore windows and see it, something he thought he'd never tell anyone).

Still, her gasp cut off his stream of talk. "What?"

"It's almost 5:30. Did you know that?"

He hadn't glanced at the clock since starting to talk to her. The conversation was so pleasant he'd simply turned over on his side, pulled the telephone close to him, and propped himself on a pillow. It felt as though they'd been chatting only a few minutes, though he'd found himself telling her stories about his life that he hadn't thought of in years.

He rolled over, keeping the phone close to his ear, feeling remarkably at peace. "Do you have to go?"

She paused. "Not yet. But aren't you tired?"

"Is that a crack about my age?"

"Lord, no! But I had a nap this afternoon. You've been going all day long, and now you've been awake all night. Aren't you even a little sleepy?"

He took a deep breath and realized he felt a hum in every cell of his body. "I'm really not. I might fall asleep in my meetings today, but that would probably be all to the good."

She laughed. "You don't mean it."

"I do. Otherwise I'm liable to tell these idiots what I really think of their product, and that could be fatal."

"For you or for them?" she asked.

He burst out laughing. It was 5:30 in the morning, and he felt as fresh as though he'd slept for ten hours. And somehow he knew, in every fiber of his being, that it was going to be a wonderful day.

Reluctantly he said, "I suppose I'd better let you go. You're off soon, aren't you? At six?"

"Seven." She sounded reluctant to go, too. "Hope you have a good day. I really enjoyed the talk, Mr. Kellogg."

He smiled. "I enjoyed it too, main switchboard. More than any conversation I've had since I got here. And for the record, my name is Beau."

There was a pause, and he could hear the smile in her voice when she answered. "*My* name is Amanda."

And she hung up.

He smiled again before kicking off the covers.

***

Jerry had arranged to have breakfast with Beau before he went to his desk. Beau was waiting for him at the entrance to the hotel dining room at 7:30. He looked unusually fresh and clear-eyed and was as usual tapping his foot impatiently.

Jerry raised an eyebrow when he saw him. "Slept well, I take it?"

Beau smiled. "Hardly at all, but right now I'm starving. Let's eat."

Jerry led the way to his favorite booth in the corner of the walnut-paneled room and barely lifted a finger before a waitress materialized in front of him with her pad. "Good morning, Jerry." She nodded professionally at Beau.

"What's good today, Fran?"

"The French toast," she said promptly. "And the strawberries are beautiful."

"Berries in October?" Beau asked.

'From South America, sir. They're delicious."

"I'm impressed," Beau said to Jerry. "You really go the extra mile." To Fran, he said, "French toast and strawberries sounds fine." Jerry asked for the same, and Fran disappeared with a smile to get coffee.

"Now, what's this about not sleeping? I don't like hearing that from my guests."

"No, I feel fine, honestly. It's good to be back."

Jerry toyed with his napkin before settling it in his lap, carefully avoiding Beau's eyes. "I always thought you loved it here. Never did understand why you moved to L.A."

"Jean prefers it. It's her hometown, you know. And I've had plenty of work there. I don't mind."

Jerry started to say something, but stopped. Instead, he glanced around the coffee shop, at the quick movements of his wait staff and the smiles of the patrons.

"Stop worrying, Jerry. You still run the best hotel in New York."

"I hope so."

"With staff like Amanda, you should triple your business. Where did you find her?"

Jerry looked up, surprised. "You met Amanda?"

"Just on the phone. I called looking for room service after midnight, and she answered. The next morning she sent up exactly what I asked for. So I had a chocolate milkshake and bagel for breakfast."

Jerry chuckled. "She does aim to please."

"She seems awfully efficient for just a telephone operator," Beau probed. He didn't know why he was suddenly so interested in pursuing the topic.

Now Jerry really laughed. "Telephone operator? Amanda's the assistant manager. I don't know what I'd do without her."

Several pieces fell into the puzzle in Beau's mind. "Well, that makes sense. But why is she answering phones so late at night, then?"

Fran brought them a pot of steaming coffee and poured cups for each of them. Beau sniffed the rich aroma appreciatively. As usual, it was perfect. Jerry really did know his business.

Jerry added cream to his, stirred in sugar, and drank deeply. He seemed lost in thought for a moment, so Beau persisted. "About Amanda?"

Jerry started. "Oh, yes. She's been here eight or nine months, walked in off the street and asked for a job, and now I think she could run the place single-handed. Of course, she's not management-trained, but it's not really her thing anyway. I can only imagine how good she is in her chosen field, if this is just her day job."

Beau carefully added sugar he didn't want to his coffee, to avoid looking directly at Jerry, and tried to sound casual in his questioning.

"What's her chosen field?"

"Music. She wants to sing on Broadway."

"Oh?" Many more pieces fell into place: Amanda's saying what she did was 'physically very hard work that made you feel good'. Singing, he knew, *was* very hard work. But if that silvery speaking voice he'd listened to for most of the night was any indication—and usually it was—he'd bet she was probably a pretty good singer.

And no wonder she knew *his* work. Singers did comb through old scores looking for good material. He felt a sudden sinking of his happy mood; was that the only reason she knew his stuff? She'd said she'd known it 'for years', though; and she'd also said she loved it. He hoped she wasn't trying to flatter him, but then, she'd said it before she knew who he was.

"Hey, Beau!" Jerry put a hand over the sugar bowl. "Easy." Beau looked at him blankly. "You put in six sugars."

Beau looked down at his coffee and tasted it cautiously. God! It was horrible. He looked apologetically at Jerry. Jerry signaled for another cup, which came quickly. This time Beau deliberately added just one sugar and then looked up. "You still haven't told me why Amanda works the night shift."

"Oh, that's where she started. She has lessons or something during the day, so she sleeps in the morning, has her lessons and practice in the afternoon and comes in around six."

"But that's—" Beau tried to figure it out. "She's putting in more than a twelve-hour day."

Jerry shrugged. "She's only here four days a week."

"Still—doesn't the union put the kibosh on that?"

"No union for management, friend. And she's listed on the books as management. Anyway, she seems happy. The job pays for her voice lessons, and the guests just love her." He grinned rakishly. "You too, huh?"

"Me? No," Beau lied. "But I do appreciate efficiency."

"That she is," Jerry agreed. "Unusual in somebody so young."

"How young?" Beau tried to sound nonchalant. He'd really wondered about this.

"Ah, the food!" Jerry gave Fran a big smile as she set down plates of well-browned French toast and small bowls of—she was right—delicious-looking fresh strawberries. She poured water into their empty glasses, asked if they needed anything more, and with a smile, vanished. "Dig in," Jerry told Beau. "Breakfasts were my main concern here for a long while, but I think we've really gotten better."

Breakfast was not his main concern right now. He cut the French toast into bite-sized pieces and dipped it in the grape jelly on the side of his plate to give himself something to do, but he really wanted an answer to his question and couldn't figure out how to get it now that Jerry had been sidetracked, as he so frequently was.

How old *was* she? She sounded like a girl in her twenties, but her conversation was that of a woman in her thirties or possibly even forties— or was that just wishful thinking on his part, hoping to narrow the gap between them? And why was that important, anyway?

Jerry tasted the French toast appreciatively. "Perfect. That new chef is a jewel. Now if I could just figure out how to bring more business to the lounge at night."

"What's wrong with the lounge?" Beau asked automatically, not caring about the answer. He looked around the bustling, noisy room and wondered how to bring the subject back to Amanda. Subtly, of course.

Jerry grimaced. "The guests sleep here and often eat here, but they're not drinking here. And we make a good profit on booze. It's a nice place, too—good atmosphere, great bartender."

Beau tried to forget Amanda and consider Jerry's problem. "Well, it's New York. Plenty of famous bars have a lot more atmosphere, and your guests are out-of-towners. They want a little nightlife while they're here.

What about adding some entertainment?"

"We have the pianist... he's good, but not a real draw."

"Bring in a singer," Beau said absently, fiddling with his French toast and wondering how to bring the conversation back to Amanda's age.

"Can't afford one... Beau, you're not eating." Jerry looked genuinely disappointed. Since his major idea of hospitality was feeding people, every dish refused seemed a rebuff to him.

"I am," Beau said hastily, spooning up some berries. "I guess—you must have hired lots of young college kids."

"When I can. They do work cheap. They don't stay, of course. And their minds are on their majors or their significant others, most of the time."

"What's the average age?" Beau tried to be casual about it.

"Oh—twenty, twenty-one."

Beau put down his spoon. He felt a little sick. Was Amanda really only twenty or twenty-one? He didn't think he could bear it.

"Not everyone," Jerry assured him hastily. "There are plenty of old geezers like me around, too. Berries are good, aren't they?"

"Perfect," Beau said, his appetite by now completely gone. He forced himself to take another spoonful. He couldn't think of a way to bring the subject back to Amanda indirectly, and he dared not ask about her again directly. Even Jerry, obtuse as he could be, might think it was strange.

He smiled and made small talk for another half hour, until he could excuse himself to meet with Hattie again. And for the rest of that awkward breakfast, they never said a word about Amanda.

***

She couldn't understand why she felt wonderful, but she did. And the whole day went beautifully, too. Even her voice coach was effusive, and he was never effusive. "You see?" he bellowed when she'd finally sung "*The Siren Song*" to his satisfaction, for once sounding languid and seductive. "You see what you can do when you put your *heart* into something, Amanda? You see what is possible?"

She didn't have time to answer; she was running to join Stephanie and Fleur at the Hot Grill, and she was already late.

The girls greeted her with fond cries and hugs and thrust a roll of sheet music into her hand. "Hurry," Stephanie ordered, her dark curly hair damp with perspiration, slender form aquiver with electricity and worry. "Warm up. Auditions have started."

"Shh!" Fleur warned, as a few people at the tables in front turned to glare at them. Her cascading red hair corkscrewed around her head, and her outfit, as usual, looked as though she'd painted a wall while wearing it. Hard to believe she wrote such beautiful melodies to Stephanie's edgy lyrics, Amanda thought, but there it was: Fleur was the slow-moving, always-calm eye of the storm, Stephanie the jittery fireworks at the outer edges. Their romantic relationship was as on-again, off-again as Stephanie's self-esteem, but the songs they produced together were always tuneful and clever.

Amanda's job was to sing the new song so well that they'd secure a place in the upcoming revue. She could feel her stomach turning in knots as she contemplated it. Below them, on the postage-stamp-sized stage, a couple of young men were trying to harmonize, but they sounded like nails scratching on a chalkboard. "Ugh," Fleur said, covering her ears. "No matter what you do, you'll sound better than that."

"That's not enough," Stephanie said, her dark face tense, her fingers drumming on the metal edge of her seat. "There are twenty spots and at least sixty groups trying out for them."

"Amanda'll put it over," Fleur said confidently.

Amanda gave her a grateful look and hoped that she would. That she *could*. But before she could say anything, Stephanie grabbed her. "Listen, I wrote a new last verse. It's a lot better, but it means you have to memorize it right now."

Amanda nodded and took the sheet music with her to a remote corner. Even if she never caught the eye of a Broadway producer—though she intended to!—singing at the Hot Grill was terrific experience. She was surrounded by people like Steph and Fleur, who she was sure were the next generation of Broadway composers and lyricists, she was getting to know them, and she was singing, really singing, great new songs.

She read over the new lyric. Stephanie had followed her. "What's wrong?" she said suspiciously, looking at the slight frown on Amanda's face. "I don't like that look in your eye."

"Steph, anyone ever tell you you're paranoid?" Amanda said, trying to parry Stephanie's accurate reading of her face.

"Yes, and they're right. So don't be diplomatic. What's the problem?"

Amanda hated to hurt her feelings; she hated to hurt anyone's feelings. But the words on the page were not going to work, and she didn't know how she could sing them to make them sound any better. She pointed at the lyric. "That doesn't sound exactly… right."

Steph read over her shoulder and then frowned. "All right, you have thirty seconds to fix it. Go ahead."

Amanda was taken aback. She was the singer, not the lyricist. But Steph was challenging her. Amanda took a deep breath and looked straight at her. "Okay. 'The dark' doesn't scan right. Why not change it to 'scarlet'?"

"Yeah, why not?" Fleur had followed and was looking thoughtfully over her shoulder. She peered at Steph. "With 'scarlet', the accent is on the first syllable; 'the dark' is on the second. It scans perfectly. Amanda's right."

"'Dark' rhymes with 'park', which is the last word in the previous line," Steph objected.

"And the rhyme isn't necessary," Fleur said calmly. "It's nice, but it still sounds better with 'scarlet', even if it doesn't rhyme. Try it that way."

Steph, outnumbered, said grudgingly, "Well, let's see if it works."

Amanda sang the line softly to the girls as they bent forward to hear her above the scratchy sound of the tenors onstage. "That is better," Fleur approved. "Do it just that way."

Steph snorted, dug a pencil out of her purse and carefully notated the change on the sheet music. "Okay, so this time she's right. Ever think about writing your own lyrics, chicky?"

Before Amanda could answer, they realized the tenors had finally stopped singing and a disembodied voice from the sound booth was floating toward them. "Amanda Harary and 'The Girl With the Basket'."

"Here," Steph called out. She pushed Amanda toward the front of the house.

Amanda went to the man sitting at the piano near the tiny stage and handed him the sheet music. He looked it over and played a few notes. "Key?"

"B flat, please." He gave her a couple of notes again and she hummed them and nodded. "That's fine."

She should have been nervous, but the informal atmosphere was calming. She had nothing to lose, and few people were actually focusing on her. From their corner, Fleur and Steph watched her with fixed, tense smiles.

The pianist waited till she'd climbed onto the stage and positioned herself by the microphone, then played the lively introduction. Amanda came in on cue, singing the clever ditty Steph had fashioned to Fleur's bouncy music, of the girl who dressed up as Red Riding Hood for customers of certain refined tastes in a French brothel—until the day she met a guy who was a real wolf.

There was some laughter in the audience, and when she bowed her head at the end, even a few of the groups waiting to go on gave her some light claps. Amanda smiled and nodded. The tenors, still dawdling hopefully on the left, gave her a sour look.

"Thank you," called the disembodied voice. "Just a minute."

That was always a good sign. Amanda waited, standing squarely on both feet, a slight smile on her lips, even though her legs were now trembling in reaction. She hadn't had time to think about herself while she sang, but now her throat was closing up. She glanced out at the tables. Fleur and Steph could hardly contain their glee; they knew it had gone over well.

There was a crackle of paper from the front tables. "Here, please," called the voice, now distinguishable as a man sitting at the front table leaning into a microphone. Amanda came offstage and went to stand in front of him; Steph and Fleur moved quickly forward as well.

He leaned away from the microphone to address them privately. "Cute song. You girls wrote it?" He squinted at Steph and Fleur, who nodded mutely. "Great. I'll give it a nice slot. 9:30 Sunday night, two weeks from now. You get six minutes. Costumes not necessary, but desirable—your responsibility. We'll have four pieces here—piano, drums, trumpet, bass. You got charts on this?" Charts were the arrangements of a song for various pieces in a band or orchestra.

"I'll have them," Fleur said with authority.

"Good. Bring them." He turned a grin on Amanda. "Nice job. You really put it over."

"Thank you," Amanda said, hoping she wasn't stammering with delight.

He nodded again. "Do it just that way on show night, okay?"

"I'll—do my best."

He nodded again, dismissing them, and leaned into the microphone to call the next act.

Fleur, Steph and Amanda walked outside without speaking, in a daze of delight.

On the sidewalk, they gave way to their joy, jumping up and down, hugging and shrieking. "You," Fleur pronounced, "are singing all my songs from now on."

"Even the ones written for men?" Amanda asked, laughing with such happiness she felt as though her face might split open.

"Even the ones written for *baboons*. That was perfect, perfect! Did you hear him? 9:30 Sunday? That's prime time! Talk about a showcase!"

"Celebration!" Steph announced. "*Big* celebration. Where we going?"

Sardi's might have been traditional, and Mamma Leone's or the Stage Deli were full of hot and ample comfort foods, but this celebration started, at Steph's insistence, with expensive cocktails at the Plaza's Oak Room. Because they were also young and giddy, and because Amanda herself felt a need to return to her roots for this special day, the celebration ended at Rumpelmayer's, over the biggest, most lavish banana splits that establishment offered.

***

It was past four when Amanda finally left Steph and Fleur, who were going to Fleur's loft off Houston Street to work on more verses for the song, if they were needed. They wanted Amanda along to sing the results as they wrote, but she begged off, claiming she had an early dinner date.

Instead, she caught a bus to the public library.

Inside, she asked diffidently for a copy of Beau Kellogg's collected lyrics. He hadn't mentioned the title to her, but the librarian, after clucking and checking the card catalog, came up with it: *Words for All Occasions*, published originally in 1959 (not long after I was born, Amanda thought wryly). She checked it out.

Apparently it hadn't been popular among the habitués of the library. The library card was crisp and untouched, the dust jacket unchipped, covered in protective mylar, as pristine as a bookstore display. Amanda promised herself she'd take very good care of it.

She went home on the bus with the book cradled in her arms, and read the entire volume, cover to cover, before she went to sleep. To her delight, it contained not only the lyrics for his eleven Broadway shows (and his best-known movie themes), but detailed synopses and notes about each production—all written by him. The bits she liked best were the unintentionally personal notes he managed to inject, which she read over and over. When she finished, she set the book carefully on her night table, so it would be the first thing she saw when she woke in the morning.

CHAPTER 7

Promptly at 1:30, Beau phoned the switchboard. A sleepy female voice answered.

Unbelievingly, he asked, "Amanda?"

"Amanda's not on tonight. Can I help you?"

"Not on tonight," he said stupidly. "I thought—I thought she was on the switchboard every night."

"Not on weekends, sir. Is there something I can do for you?"

He was silent, as disappointment flooded his mind. Why? She was entitled to her weekends off, wasn't she?

He realized then that the operator was asking him something else. "Excuse me?"

"I said, would you like to leave a message for her? She'll get it tonight."

A message? What would he say? 'I'd like to continue that great conversation'—she probably couldn't care less. Being nice to guests was part of her job. Obviously, she has a life outside the hotel. What would she need with some old geezer?

"No," he said abruptly. "No message." He hung up.

Amanda relieved Tiffany on the switchboard unexpectedly at six o'clock. Tiffany, an elegant-looking blonde, was surprised to see her. "I thought you were off the whole night."

"Couldn't sleep. Might as well get on with things." Amanda took the list of wakeup calls and shooed her out. "Go on. I'll clock you out at seven."

Tiffany was almost out the door when she remembered. "Oh, you had a call earlier. He didn't want to leave a message, though."

"Oh?" Amanda's heart started to beat faster. "Did he leave his name?"

"No. But it was the guy in 704. Does that help?"

"It helps a lot," Amanda said, her heart hammering harder. "Thanks."

She settled in at the switchboard as the sound of Tiffany's footsteps faded and debated whether to phone him now. If he was still having trouble sleeping and had just fallen asleep—well, that would be unconscionably rude. There was no excuse for it. He might even complain to Jerry.

She sighed and decided not to call. Then she looked at the list of wake-ups. Good; he was on it for 6:30.

She phoned everyone else with a 6:30 wake-up call at 6:25, so she could reach him on the dot. "Good morning!" she said cheerfully. "Rise and shine. I hear you called for me last night?"

***

He'd been awake most of the night, smoking and pacing the room, more irritated than he wanted to admit at not being able to talk to her. The sound of her voice, promptly at 6:30, lifted his spirits, and he crushed out his cigarette and settled on top of his bed. "Well, good morning. You know, you didn't give me many clues to your secret identity."

He was picking up their conversation almost exactly where they'd left off, and she sounded like she was smiling. It felt so familiar and so pleasant. "Oh? So you think you know what I do?"

"Better than that—I asked some questions and got some answers. You're a singer."

She paused, then guessed. "Jerry told you."

"I should have realized. I can hear it in your voice. You're probably a very good singer."

"Well, I'm not working this hard to be a very bad one."

He chuckled, and tried to keep his tone light, to maintain her trust.

"Of course, there are still two things I don't know about you."

"Oh? Just two?"

He could tell she was curious, so he pressed, just a little. "I don't know your last name. What will it say on the marquee when you star in your first Broadway show?"

She hesitated only an instant. "Amanda Harary." Without waiting for him to ask, she spelled it for him, as she had spelled it for other people hundreds of times.

"Harary is unusual." He'd never heard it before.

"Hungarian, I think."

"Your father's Hungarian?"

She hesitated. "I'm not sure. My mother doesn't talk much about him. He left when I was four."

"Oh." But he wouldn't dwell on it; the silence that was so companionable now could become uncomfortable.

Before he could think of something soothing to say, she added, "What else don't you know about me?"

So the channel was still open, after all.

How to ask the big question, the one that had been bothering him for the entire day? Suddenly, he knew the perfect way to ease into it.

"Actually, you've been confusing me."

"Oh?" He could tell that had caught her interest.

"You're a contradiction," he went on. "You have all the knowledge of a woman in her 40s, but the outlook of a woman in her 30s. Yet you sound like you're in your 20s. How could that be?"

She laughed. "I don't know, but thanks for the explanation. Maybe that's why I felt like such a misfit in high school. Too much interest in things my peers didn't find interesting."

"That will do it." He wished he could get her to answer the question. How else was he going to find out?

But before he could think of how to pursue this line of thought, she gave him the answer. "I'm twenty-five. Thirty just around the corner, and fifty lurking right down the block."

"You're a baby," he retorted, but he was relieved. Twenty-five was young, but not beyond the pale. These days, there were twenty-five-year-olds running film studios and Wall Street firms. Jason the snot nose was probably around that age himself.

"Well? Have I satisfied all your curiosity? Is there nothing left to talk about?" Her tone sounded bright, but there was a curious wistfulness underneath.

Relieved, Beau blurted out, "I thought you'd be at the switchboard last night, but I was disappointed."

"Were you?" Now she sounded pleased. "Well, they do let me off occasionally. And last night I was glad to be off; I was reading something extra good. In fact, I couldn't put it down."

"Oh?" She was reading and enjoying herself, while he was thinking of her and sleepless. At least she hadn't been out with some young stud. Somehow that made him feel better, so he tried to sound interested. "What were you reading? Shakespeare? Eighteenth-century English fiction? Or one of those trashy paperback novels they turn into expensive mini-series?" He hoped it wasn't the latter but very much feared it was.

Her answer was the very last thing he expected. "*Words for All Occasions.*"

He snapped to attention. "You got my book?"

"Well, not for keeps. The library had it." She paused. "I thought it was—really wonderful."

His mood suddenly soared. "I'm so glad."

"And I liked what you wrote about the shows—how they were conceived, what you needed to change and fix, all the backstage stuff. I love stuff like that."

"That was my favorite part of putting the book together. It's fun remembering those shows, even the flops. In fact, I think now that was the very best part of my life, even if I didn't realize it at the time."

***

He didn't sound sad, but the words did. She felt a pang inside. He felt he'd passed the best time of his life already, when her best time hadn't yet come? As cheerfully as possible, she said, "Well, the book certainly holds up. I read it straight through, and I enjoyed it so much, I'll probably read it again tonight."

She hoped he'd tell her they could talk the night away, but instead he said, "Well, that's good. By tonight I'll be on a plane headed home."

"Oh?" She hoped she didn't sound too disappointed. After all, they'd only had a couple of conversations; what made her think he would want to talk to her again, after such a long conversation last night?

"Yep. And a good thing, too. You don't need any old geezers wasting your time."

"You're not old."

"I just turned sixty. Never thought it would happen, but you know the old joke: 'If I'd known I'd live this long, I'd have taken better care of myself.'"

She laughed. "I've never heard that."

"That's because you're so young." He felt better about her age, but still, there was a world of difference between twenty-five and sixty, even if it didn't seem to matter in their conversations.

He wondered if she felt the connection between them, or if she thought they *were* worlds apart. And would she comment on it?

She didn't. Instead, she said, "But you're not going away for good, are you?"

"Not possible. At some point, these jerks will decide they understand songwriting and summon me back to hear more of their wisdom and rewrite accordingly." He paused and said, "I'll be back pretty soon."

"Are you sure?"

She sounded pleased, and it made him smile. "Positive. And if I stayed anywhere but the Lorelei, Jerry would have my head. So you'll hear from me again in the middle of the night, I'm sure."

The silvery voice brightened. "Till then, I guess I have to content myself with our resident lovers and the ghost on the seventh floor."

"*What?*"

"It's true. We have a husband and wife who each come here on Tuesday nights—which would be fine, except they both come with their lovers, and they both insist on sixth-floor rooms facing the park. Jerry about has fits trying to make sure they don't run into each other."

Beau laughed. "I don't believe it. You're making it up."

"Nope. Truth is stranger than fiction. Honestly, the whole staff knows about this couple, but nobody's blabbed yet. We keep their business, they keep their rendezvous, and I guess somehow their marriage limps on."

"And a ghost? On this floor?"

"Yes, and she can be pretty crabby."

"Who was she? Supposedly?"

"Rumor has it she was a middle-aged duchess who fell in love with a young butler who worked for the American family that owned this place a hundred years ago. She was English and lonely, and he was English, too, so maybe she felt a bond between them. The duchess invited the family to dinner at her mansion often, so they would be forced to invite her back, and she could see the butler. One day she finally found a way to be alone with him. She summoned up her courage and told him she loved him and wanted them to have a life together. He bowed to her politely, left the room and immediately told his employers, so he could avoid even the appearance of wrongdoing. They threw her out. She held her head up, accepted the slight and left them with an elegant bow. Then she went home, closed the windows, turned on all the gas jets, lay down on her bed and... breathed in."

Beau chuckled. "Love killed her, hmm?"

"Well, in a way. She—" She broke off as she noticed the time. Two minutes after seven. "I'm sorry. I'm late with my 7:00 wake-up calls. I have to go."

He felt a curious reluctance to end the conversation, but tried to be genial. "Well, thanks for waking me."

"Actually, you sounded wide awake when I called."

He wasn't going to tell her he'd paced half the night, just thinking about her. "No. Well—I might have woken up a little before you called."

"Have a good flight back."

"Thanks. You have a good day now." He hung up, looking thoughtfully at the phone. It was stupid to feel reluctance at leaving a disembodied voice. Just—stupid. He should be relieved to be going home.

So why wasn't he?

***

Jerry found himself humming as he strode into the lobby to start the day. He didn't know why. True, he was delighted with the new chef at the Bistro. The guy was doing beautiful breakfasts, and the number of guests eating there now had risen dramatically, in just a few weeks. Even better, the number of guests ordering full breakfasts instead of just fruit and pastries had skyrocketed. Mrs. Sarandon would be pleased, when they sat down over the quarterly reports.

Breakfasts at the Bistro had been a problem since he first started there twelve years ago. He'd persuaded Mrs. Sarandon to see it as a possible profit center and therefore to shell out the money to hire someone top-notch to do breads, pastries, omelets and pancakes. Now not only were guests stopping by for breakfast, local businessmen were coming in twice a week.

That problem had clearly been solved. But why else was he humming?

Because, he realized, there was another problem he hadn't been focusing on to which he'd just found a solution, thanks to his old friend Beau.

It was one of Amanda's rare early days. About once a month she came in at eight in the morning and worked till six. She was going over the list of expected checkouts when Jerry came in cheerfully and tossed his hat across the room. Surprisingly, it fell neatly onto the hat rack and stayed there.

Amanda looked up in surprise. "Bulls-eye! Hey, Jerry, what's going on?"

Jerry was so pleased, both with his idea and the fact that he'd actually managed to hit the hat rack for once, that instead of sitting down at his desk he found himself strolling around Amanda, who was sitting at the smaller desk in the corner. "I just had a flash of genius."

She put the list down and looked at him.

"We need a lounge singer," Jerry announced.

"A lounge singer." This was the first she'd heard of it.

"Really. Somebody who could liven up the place would probably increase profits big time. *But...* Mrs. Sarandon probably won't authorize it for the budget."

"There goes the lounge singer."

"No." Jerry stopped and shook a finger in her face. "How'd *you* like to sing in our lounge—say, once or twice a week?"

***

She had no idea what to say. Delight, dizziness, excitement warred in her. "You want *me* to sing here?"

"Extra work," he warned her. "With no extra pay, I'm afraid. And you're already working a lot of hours. But... you can sing whatever you want. Work it out with Martin. Think about it and let me know."

She was thrilled. "I don't need to think it over. I'll do it, Jerry. Thank you." *And stage fright be damned!*

He cocked his head at her, a half-smile on his face. "You may not thank me after doing it for a few weeks. What time does Martin come in?"

"Six," she said promptly.

"Okay. When you get off tonight, go see him and work something up. You can start whenever you want."

At Amanda's grin, Jerry grinned too, and started humming again.

She felt like humming too. In fact, she felt like singing right there in the office. But at the same time, there was a sinking in her stomach. She wondered why. Here she'd just been handed a huge opportunity—the biggest one yet, even if it didn't pay—the exposure and experience would more than make up for it.

Then she realized why she felt so disappointed: Beau Kellogg was returning to L.A., and he wouldn't be hearing her sing.

CHAPTER 8

L .A. meant more sleepless nights. Beau lay staring at the ceiling, bits of words tearing through his mind in the darkness. Knots in the rough stucco above him shimmered in the half-light, seeming to scurry across the ceiling like bugs. Beau had a horror of bugs and insisted on having the house exterminated every six months, though Jean told him repeatedly she hadn't seen any kind of bug there except summer spiders since they moved in. He thought of this as he watched the holes snaking across the ceiling and finally decided to trust her: it was too late at night to climb on a chair and check.

It was too late for many things, actually. Like work. Yet the bits of words continued to nag at him: find us a place, Beau, set us in place. He was almost finished with his second draft of the jingle, but Jules was still waiting patiently for a libretto—even an idea for a libretto. Beau tossed in bed, feeling the sheets around his body softening with sweat. He lit a cigarette in the darkness and lay back, pushing aside his solemn promise to Jean not to smoke in bed.

Here was a dilemma, all right: the leisure to write a great piece, anything he wanted, and absolutely no ideas. What could he devise that would be worth a four-million-dollar investment?

Let your mind wander, he told himself. Just... go off and think of other things. He thought of other things... and the pictures in his mind focused and puddled on the Lorelei. Amanda's voice at the switchboard... the beautiful wax-glossed banisters leading up from the lobby... the soft carpets... the doors leading in and out and up and down... the valets and backstairs servants and butlers of a hundred years before... the story she'd told him of the absurd little duchess and her tragic love...

Ah, he wasn't going to sleep anyway. He kicked back the sheet and stood up, sucking at the cigarette as though his life depended on it. Play more show tunes? He was sick of them. Nothing on television, and there wasn't a book or magazine in the house that he hadn't read twenty times. Shit.

He looked at the dial on his watch. 1:30. Unbidden, the thought floated into his mind: 4:30 in New York. Amanda might be on duty at the switchboard.

Without thinking, he picked up the phone. And just as suddenly slammed it down. Jesus, was he crazy? He glared at the silent placid instrument as though daring it to nudge him into action. Run up a huge phone bill, just for some pointless, unnecessary conversation?

He began to pace the room, to work off some restlessness, but only found himself more frustrated. He remembered Jules saying that the gym he'd installed at home worked wonders for his late-night insomnia. Beau had scoffed inwardly. How like Jules to follow the crowd, jump on the fitness bandwagon, because it's the hip thing to do. He'd have built in a marble microwave if the designers told him everyone else was doing it. Besides, if regular workouts with Marie weren't helping Jules to sleep, it didn't seem as though anything else was worth trying.

There wasn't anything in his house to work out with, unless you counted sprinting over the coffee table or chinning up in the doorway between kitchen and dining room. And frankly, he wasn't in the best of shape to tackle either. Just like him to break a bone or something and end up *really* wasting time lying in a hospital bed.

He glanced at the watch again. Two minutes had passed, in which he'd circled the room aimlessly, feeling the harsh brush of the carpet under his bare feet. Hell, it couldn't hurt just to dial the place, could it? If she wasn't on duty, big deal. It was just a one-minute call. If she *was* on duty—well, he'd worry about that later.

He pecked at the buttons on the phone, not realizing until the line was connected that he hadn't needed to consult his address book. When had he memorized the Lorelei's telephone number?

"Good evening. The Lorelei." It was her.

"Still awake, are you?"

She knew his voice right away, and he could feel her professional manner ease into friendliness. "Well, hello. I didn't know you were in New York. How come you're not staying with us?"

He hesitated for a split second. "I'm not in New York. I'm home. In L.A."

"I see." He thought he could hear a slight chill in her voice. Or was it simply a shade of understanding? "You can't sleep at home, either?"

"Don't get snide with me." But he couldn't work up any real animosity. It felt so damned good to talk to her.

"Sorry." But she didn't sound sorry; she sounded saucy and teasing, and he loved it. "What are you doing awake at 1:30 in the morning, then? Want to be the first to tee off tomorrow?"

"Brat," he growled. "If you want to know, I was thinking about your stories."

"Which stories?"

"About the old days at the hotel. Tell you the truth, I wanted to hear more."

"Long distance at 1:30 in the morning? Maybe I should give up singing and take up writing."

"Well, for damn sure you won't get anywhere unless your manners improve," he hissed at her, secretly enjoying every word. "Now are you going to tell me some more or are we going to fight?"

"I thought we *were* fighting." Amanda's voice had taken on a lighthearted lilt, which made him smile as he searched for a pack of cigarettes and settled himself comfortably in his favorite leather chair. "Or is this what they call banter?"

He couldn't hold back a snort of laughter, and she joined in. It was hopeless even trying to sound indignant at her. "All right, all right. What're you singing these days? Anything I would know?"

She began to tell him about the revue at the Hot Grill, now only four days away, where she would sing *"The Girl with the Basket"*. He listened, puffing contentedly on the cigarette, and realizing that he suddenly felt at peace. She also told him about Jerry's offer to sing in the lounge in her free time. She had met with Martin, the lounge pianist, and they were working out a repertoire. She would be starting there on Friday, two days before she sang in the revue.

Beau exclaimed over her good fortune, even as he remembered his conversation with Jerry over breakfast and wondered whether his casual comment, "Bring in a singer", had helped spark Jerry's idea. He hoped so, if it meant Amanda would get a break. He had actually been thinking of her when he made the comment, and trying to bring the conversation back to her. Funny if it turned out to benefit her.

Amanda went on eagerly, telling him it had been Martin's idea to intersperse standards like *"That Old Black Magic"* with little-known but melodic show songs written by well-known Broadway composers. "I might even try *'Bursting Bubbles'*, if I can find the sheet music."

His heart lifted at the thought. "I'm sure you'd do it justice."

"You haven't heard me sing. Maybe I'd sound horrible."

"Impossible." The silvery tones of her speaking voice sent a delightful shiver down his spine. He'd heard the same silvery tones in the speaking voices of other singers whose work he loved, and he was sure she would be every bit as good. And if she actually did sing the song, he would have to find time to hear her on his next trip to New York.

She was still talking. "... And my finale choices are either *Something Tells Me*' or *'I Wish You a Waltz'*."

"What's that last one?" He shook himself out of his own lazy reverie. "I've never heard of it."

"From *Ballroom*—a couple of years ago."

"Must've missed it."

"You? The man who knows every show ever written?" Her voice was teasing now, as wide awake as he was suddenly feeling limp and drowsy. "I can't believe it. Wait, let me get out my tape recorder and you can say it again."

"Brat." He tapped out the cigarette and glanced at his watch. Jesus, they'd been yakking for over fifty minutes. "Hey, what're you doing to me? How can you keep a tired man on the phone so late at night? Haven't you got any manners at all?"

"Hey, now wait a minute. Seems to me you called me, Mister, asking about old stories I haven't even gotten to yet—"

"And which I now can't afford to hear," he interrupted. "Next time, when I ask a question, don't get off the subject, okay? You're costing me a fortune."

He felt her smile through the phone. "Well, since you put it that way—"

"Yeah, yeah. I'll wait on those stories till next time. Have a good day, honey. Don't work too hard." He hung up.

In New York, Amanda pressed down the button releasing the call, staring thoughtfully at the silent switchboard. *He called me honey. Funny how nice it sounded.*

In Los Angeles, Beau made his way to bed, almost toppling with a sudden, welcome fatigue, and slid effortlessly into a wonderfully refreshing, dreamless sleep.

***

She should have been bouncing off the walls with jitters and restless energy. That was how her stage fright usually started. But as Friday night approached, Amanda felt calm and confident, as though this first performance was her hundredth. She couldn't understand why she felt so relaxed.

Martin had helped enormously. She'd known him since her first week at the hotel and spent many evenings at the piano, singing along with his more obscure selections; he liked to see if he could stump her, make her stumble on an old lyric. So far, he never had.

For her 'debut', as he jokingly put it, he'd chosen eight songs that showcased her voice and personality, and worked out simple but effective arrangements. She'd been disappointed that hard as she'd searched (and she'd searched very thoroughly), she couldn't find sheet music for *"Bursting Bubbles"*, and Martin had edged away from trying to fake it, claiming he didn't want to mess her up if he got it wrong. But she was happy with the others; they were all wonderful, and she knew she'd enjoy singing them.

Steph and Fleur had promised to come and clap like mad, part of their strategy to keep her feeling good: with Amanda singing at the Hot Grill only two days later, "We want you high and happy," Fleur told her. "Besides, watching you is a lot more fun than watching Steph agonize at home."

Steph didn't smile. "You're just as nervous."

Fleur shrugged.

Martin had decided it was better not to introduce her formally, but just to let the patrons become aware of her gradually as they were talking and drinking, though she would have a microphone in her hand, so she would seem like a professional entertainer and not a half-soused patron.

At 8:00 she sat down casually on a bar stool next to the piano, her navy silk dress demure and inconspicuous. She felt surprisingly relaxed; somehow the familiarity of the Lorelei was lending her support and banishing her usual terrors.

She wriggled around on the stool until she was comfortable, and nodded to Martin, who played the introduction. Four bars later, she quietly began to sing *"That Old Black Magic"*. The first few notes were unsteady, but after the first eight bars, she was feeling better. By the time she got to "Those icy fingers up and down my spine", she was breezing.

No one seemed to notice until she was halfway through the song. She smiled at the patrons (mostly men) glancing her way, and sang a few bars softly to each of them. But with each line, she deliberately increased the volume, so by the end, she was singing full out, at performance level, her eyes and voice reaching everyone in the room.

And surprisingly, virtually all eyes were on her as Martin ended the song with a flourish.

At the last note, the patrons broke into genuine applause.

Stephanie and Fleur were clapping hard, as they'd promised, and so, Amanda noticed, giving a quick glance around, was almost everyone in the bar, the soft lights reflecting sparkles off the men's watches, the women's jewelry, as they nodded to the music and swung their hands together. She dipped her head appreciatively and gave a little smile before going into her next song, *"Something Tells Me"*, from the forgotten musical *High Spirits*. It was a melodic waltz, and she loved it.

So did the audience.

An hour later, she had sung her entire repertoire twice and accepted the personal congratulations of the patrons who spoke to her or shook her hand on the way out. (A hefty number stuck bills in the tip jar on the piano, and a couple of half-crocked businessmen had tried to grab her backside, but she figured this was par for the course with lounge singing.)

Under his breath, as the patrons nodded and smiled at her, Martin said, "Way to go, baby. A first-round knockout." (Martin was gay, and Amanda had long since decided his sports metaphors were his way of sounding butch.)

"That," Fleur said with approval, "is almost as good as you're going to sound on Sunday." Steph's olive skin was flushed even darker than usual, a good sign.

So she didn't quite understand why she didn't want to celebrate with them. Or why instead of feeling thrilled and on top of the world, she felt just... pleased. Well, not quite pleased. Actually, sort of... relieved.

Well, not even relieved.

More like... well... let down. After singing to an appreciative audience and not feeling even a flutter of fear, she also didn't feel much of... anything.

Something was not quite right.

CHAPTER 9

She told herself everything had happened too fast on Friday. That was why she hadn't felt as thrilled and fulfilled as she should have. She was sure Sunday would be different.

It was.

The Hot Grill, always crowded, was jammed when she, Steph and Fleur arrived. A haze of smoke—both from the namesake grill in the middle of the room and the customers' cigarette and cigar smoke in front—floated softly overhead, where the murmur of conversation and clinking of china and cutlery blended with the tuning-up sounds of the band.

Amanda felt a flutter at her throat, and a tightening in her stomach, the familiar beginning of her stage fright. It seemed as though everyone who had auditioned for the revue was here, along with half again the usual number of customers. It was noisier than she'd ever seen it and suddenly seemed completely overwhelming. How had she ever stood and sung on that huge empty stage, even at the audition?

She clutched Steph's arm. "I can't do this!" she whispered.

"The hell you can't," Fleur retorted. Ignoring Steph, whose face had gone several shades paler, she took Amanda's other arm. "Come on, let's get to the dressing room."

The women's dressing room on the second floor, ninety percent smaller than the main room, was even more packed, and filled with the smells of perfume, cosmetics, smoke and sweating girls. Amanda felt nauseous.

She couldn't bring herself to walk in. Though she was carrying the plastic garment case holding her costume, and Fleur held her makeup case, she had to lean against the outside wall and take deep breaths. Her face had gone paper white.

"Stop worrying," Steph told her. Her own eyes had dilated enormously in her thin face. "This is just like singing at the Lorelei."

Amanda shook her head and gulped in more air. The small friendly lounge at the Lorelei was a far cry from this chaos. This was overreaching. She really couldn't do it. Why had she ever thought she could?

Fleur, the calmest of the three, saw the panic in her face. Deliberately she set down Amanda's case and said, "Do you want to forget about it?"

"Are you crazy?" Steph demanded. "She *can't* not sing tonight!"

They had never seen her so frightened; she always tried hard to project confidence and capability. Singing along with Fleur's piano was so much more relaxed, so much less demanding, than what was waiting out there tonight.

Her coaches had told her for the last year that she'd work through it. Her mother had told her she was being silly. She also said she was too busy helping Josie get ready for two weeks' vacation in Europe to make the long trip into the city to see Amanda sing and brusquely wished her luck.

Amanda thought if she had to walk out under those white lights, which were even now increasing in brightness as the club readied the stage, her trembling legs wouldn't hold her, and she knew she'd tumble into a heap on the stage... assuming she didn't faint or throw up first.

Under all the fear came a cold voice saying quietly, *These aren't nerves. This isn't fun. This* isn't *what you want to do with your life.*

It was the voice she had tried not to hear through all the years of training and coaching. On her darkest days, she wondered if that voice wasn't the one she should be listening to.

But there was no time for it now. Steph's face was freezing into a furious mask, and even Fleur, always phlegmatic, was beginning to look concerned.

There was a sudden blast from below, as though someone had blown into a microphone, and the band began to play an up-tempo, urgent medley. "They're starting," Fleur said, her usually calm voice vibrating. "Get changed and do your makeup. You still have about an hour, so we'll stay up here with you. We can listen to the others before you go." She put her hand on Amanda's arm again. It was ice-cold.

Fleur's own hand began to tremble.

From there, it got much worse.

Amanda managed to get control of herself, at least outwardly, and marched into the dressing room.

There were plenty of frazzled nerves in there too, and a variety of methods to soothe them, from nervous chattering and smoking to a surreptitious bottle of scotch to a handful of pills or a line of white powder. Amanda grimly ignored it all, found a mirror far down the row where she could see two inches of herself, and kept her eyes on her own reflection while she made up her face with shaking fingers.

Her throat was tightening again, and she was having trouble breathing. When she finished her foundation and powder, she had to stretch upward to try to draw oxygen into her lungs. Usually this calmed her down, but tonight it hardly made a dent.

She still could hardly inhale when she went out to warm up with Fleur, and her voice sounded like Minnie Mouse on helium. Steph listened for a few moments, bit her lip and walked away, while the straight line of Fleur's mouth grew tighter and tighter.

"We got you some hot tea," Steph told her when she finished. She pushed a mug of tepid liquid in front of Amanda, spilling a quarter of it.

"Maybe that'll help."

Usually it did. Tonight it didn't.

They sat at a back table shoved into a corner. One after another, like wooden soldiers, the other acts were being introduced, coming on to perform, then taking bows.

"No one's making a great impression," Fleur said hopefully after listening to the first eight. She was right. The applause, except from pockets of friends and supporters, was polite, rather than enthusiastic.

Amanda nodded, but the fluttering in her stomach made even casual speech impossible. At 9:15 she got up to go backstage, still unable to say anything. The girls looked worriedly after her.

She threaded her way through the house, noticing the VIPS who had been invited: those sitting at ringside tables, in silk blouses and Armani jackets, were the people the Hot Grill had set out to impress. All the work came down to their opinion. A few more lukewarm responses from them, and there would be no second Talent Revue Night at the Hot Grill.

She felt faint.

The stage manager, wearing a headset and managing to be in six places at once without raising her voice or losing her unruffled calm, saw her stark white face and pushed her into a chair. Amanda knew she should check her hair and makeup once more—God forbid there should be lipstick on her teeth!—but she couldn't bring herself to move. She just sat, staring at nothing, hearing the sounds of the group ahead of her. Lucky guys. At least they had each other out there. Despite Steph and Fleur's heartfelt emotional support, she would be alone.

"Two minutes," the stage manager told her. She nodded and tried to breathe. When the announcer began her introduction, the stage manager had to physically help her up. "You'll be fine after the first note," she said to Amanda, who had gone even paler.

Amanda nodded her thanks and hoped it was true.

But this was not the Lorelei. When the band finished the eight-bar introduction and she did her rehearsed sashay onto the stage, even the audience's warm laughter at her Red Riding Hood outfit didn't help. She knew she had only six minutes to win them over.

About four minutes into the routine, she gave up the effort.

***

"It wasn't *awful*," Steph said an hour later. She'd been saying the same thing for almost that long, as long as it had taken Amanda, on trembling legs, to get offstage, then upstairs to change, and emerge from the dressing room. "You were on key the whole way, your diction was fine, and you finished."

"But no zing," Amanda said bleakly. They all knew it, and no one could say it didn't matter.

All the sparkle and sauciness she had brought to the audition—which had gotten them the coveted 9:30 spot in the first place—had vanished in her terror. The applause had been scattered and perfunctory, when it could have been wildly enthusiastic. That it hadn't been was all her fault.

She'd blown a huge opportunity, for herself and for the others. She felt all the weight of it, though neither of the others said a word.

"Lots of people get stage fright," Fleur said stoutly. "*Barbra Streisand*, for God's sake! You'll get over it."

They were sitting at a table in a bar on the Upper West Side, near the Lorelei. It was one of Fleur's favorite places; she swore Cole Porter used to come in all the time. Amanda used to tease her that Porter was so rich he wouldn't be caught dead on the West Side, but tonight she wasn't in a mood to joke.

She knew she'd let them down.

From their silence, they obviously thought so, too. They might never want her to sing another song for them again.

All her confidence on Friday night had evaporated.

The thought of ever singing in front of an audience again, no matter how small, made her feel sick to her stomach. She didn't know if she could even sing with Martin again, though she was scheduled to, next weekend.

She'd been so excited about this revue; she was sure that this time, after the extra coaching and the work with Steph and Fleur, *this time* she wouldn't be paralyzed by stage fright.

She knew the song cold, knew all the gestures and little dance steps they'd worked out to punch it up, could do them all in her sleep. What would her coach say? She knew he'd been there, though she hadn't spotted him. She feared what Steph and Fleur might say next week, when they all got together for another work session.

But far above that was the thought that upset her more than anything else. *What would Beau think?*

***

"Shake it off," Beau advised her. It was the following night, and he had phoned the switchboard, eager to hear how she'd done. Somehow she'd known he would, and she forced herself to tell him how bad it had been. "You didn't write the song, and if it was as good as you say, someone will have noticed it. This audience was full of professionals. If you were on key and enunciated the words clearly, someone will pick up on it. If they don't, it's not your fault."

"But I was awful!" Amanda could hardly get the words out, and yet it was so true.

"Doesn't sound like it to me. You were scared. Big deal." His voice softened. "Stop beating yourself up, honey."

They'd already been on the phone for an hour, and most of that time had been her recounting of Friday and Sunday nights. He had listened patiently, wondering why she could tell a long story and he was riveted by every word, when if someone else took longer than a minute, his mind began to wander. He wanted to tell her that, to build up her confidence, but thought it would sound too much like a pass.

He let the chance go by.

He was beginning to think there might be other chances to tell her.

He wondered if he would take them.

CHAPTER 10

After the fiasco at the Hot Grill, Amanda temporarily suspended her voice lessons and coaching. She wasn't sure what to do about her stage fright, and she didn't want to keep shelling out her hard-earned funds until she knew. She spent her free time in the evenings scribbling more of the verses that had crowded into her head since she was a child. She told everyone the hiatus was temporary, but she took on more hours at the Lorelei, which Jerry admitted was a relief: he relied on her more than he'd realized. She continued to sing twice a week in the lounge, and continued somehow feeling relaxed and at home with the small friendly crowds and close atmosphere, but more and more, she found herself thinking hotel-related thoughts.

She also kept renewing the slim volume of show lyrics at the library, each time for two more weeks. Each time she had to bring it back for renewal, she felt a little stab of anxiety; what if this time, they wouldn't let her take it out again? It made her feel odd to think someone else could check out the book and then lose it on the subway or in a deli. Silly as it seemed, she felt an odd sense of well being when she had the book in her hands.

She combed used bookstores, thrift stores, even a few flea markets, looking for a copy she could buy. No luck. She left her name and number with bookstore owners, librarians, and salespeople. No one called. She knew she couldn't just copy the book into a stack of photocopied pages. The spirit of the thing had to do with the fact that this book had existed during this wondrous time she still dreamed about. It had once been for sale in the bookstores on Fifth Avenue, and people of that vanished era, who she felt had to be brimming with joy and a thirst for living, could choose, or not choose, to buy it. The volume that remained stubbornly in her hands, week after week, was a remnant of the time she still hungered for and knew she could not be a part of. It was a link to a world she could never enter. And so she refused to let it go.

Jerry recognized it when he saw her thumbing through it in a free moment at the hotel. He was surprised. "Where did you find that? Must be long out of print."

"You know it?"

"Sure. Beau's biggest thrill. He bragged about the damn thing so much, we were all sick of it by the time it was finally published."

She couldn't think of a thing to say, but she wanted to know more. She nodded encouragingly.

Jerry picked up the cue. "He and his wife threw a big party here in the city when it was published."

She tried to sound casual as she asked something she really wanted to know. "What's his wife like?"

"Jean? Oh, stunning. Tall, great figure, auburn hair... a real knockout. I think she even used to do some modeling in L.A., where she grew up. It's funny, because Beau isn't exactly a leading-man type. They're quite a contrast."

She was silent. It was hard for her to picture the man she was getting to know—and thinking about often—with a knockout beauty. Men who married gorgeous women tended to have insecurities they thought the woman's looks would mask. He hadn't seemed like that, somehow; in fact, his confidence about himself was something she liked about him.

She sighed. It seemed as though a woman's looks always trumped her other qualities, though, in the end. Isn't that what her mother had always said? She certainly could never compete there.

But Jerry was going on about the party, and she forced away those thoughts to listen to him. "People kept coming in and out all night, dozens of them. Beau had taken over some posh restaurant on the East Side, I forget which one. There was a piano in the middle of the room. Anyone who could play did. And the guests—God! Steve McQueen and Mary Martin and Pat Boone and Tony Curtis, and Jack Lemmon noodling on the keyboard—we had a great time."

Amanda nodded again. Her eyes were very bright.

"And around 1:00," Jerry went on, "Beau was so drunk he volunteered to write a lyric to anybody's music, right then and there. And David Susskind, who couldn't carry a tune in a wheelbarrow, volunteered to sing it, and I think it was David Merrick who offered to play. That was something, let me tell you. We all almost split our sides laughing."

"Were any of his lyrics any good?"

"You know, they weren't bad." Jerry thought back for a moment. "In fact, I could swear that he made something up—they were going around the room, picking out titles for songs, and Beau would make up something on the spot, and David would play some little thing to accompany it—and then somebody said 'mirage', and by God, he came up with the neatest little ballad in just a minute. I think he used it in a movie theme a few months later. It was terrific."

He broke out of his musing and turned to her, struck as always by the frail hand with its long, slender fingers lying on the desk. He eyed her with some bemusement. "He's a real character. But it might be best for you not to take him too seriously."

She tried to laugh, but all that emerged was a dry bark. "Jerry! He's a guest. It's just interesting, that's all. He seems to have had a fascinating life."

"He can certainly make you think so." He paused, trying to think how to caution her diplomatically, without seeming to butt in. Somehow he didn't think her fascination with Beau was in her best interest.

But she's a grown woman, he reminded himself regretfully, *with a good head on her shoulders. She knows how to deal with all kinds of people.*

He shrugged. There was no way he could think of to phrase a warning that wouldn't seem as though he were a middle-aged man crying wolf. He wondered if he was misreading the heightened glow about her these days. God knows it was a ridiculous thought. And there was no basis for it, for God's sake—she said they'd talked on the phone, that's all. And Beau had said he admired her efficiency.

Forget it! he told himself. *You're asking for trouble.*
And if there was one thing Jerry never inquired into very deeply, it was something that might cause trouble.

***

Somehow, she knew, her yearning to own Beau's book was tied up with her own past—no, with her parents' past, the fabled past her mother had painted in vivid words for her when she was a young child. Her mother had communicated relatively little, except to scold or nag, and Amanda was an affectionate child who wanted to feel connected to her. So when her mother, homesick for the Chicago suburbs where she'd been raised, reminisced about her girlhood, Amanda listened and asked questions. And her mother told her stories about a time that seemed much more exciting than the one she was living through now.

As she grew up, she dreamed about it—a world of summer picnics and autumn hayrides and winter sleigh rides, where romance was just behind a handsome young man's Pepsodent smile and charming manners, and every girl was lovely and popular. By the time she realized her mother had colored the stories too brightly out of unhappiness with her current situation, it was too late: Those vividly-hued descriptions *were* the past to Amanda, no matter how inaccurate they were, anchored as they were in her earliest memories.

In some dim recess of her mind, she believed—hoped—she might still, somehow, bridge the present and the past. All she had to do was turn the right corner, touch the right person, follow the right path... and she could be part of it, too.

The problem was that she already *felt* herself to be part of it, more than she'd ever felt part of the imperfect present. The customs and practices of her mother's generation seemed natural and familiar to her. The language and customs of her peers were bewildering.

When Cherry talked about motorcycle races on the weekends and dates in video arcades and late-night showings of *The Rocky Horror Picture Show*, Amanda looked at her through the eyes of an alien. It was as though she didn't even understand the language Cherry was speaking, their frames of reference were so different.

In Beau's stories she glimpsed more of the world she'd been introduced to as a child, the world she thought she'd join herself when she grew up. But the '60s had changed everything, social traditions had been thrown aside, and now the hectic, hard-driving world of the '80s felt foreign to her. So she drew closer to him; he symbolized the beloved familiar in a way none of her contemporaries could.

And his book of lyrics, a memento of that vivid past, was like a message from lost but dearly-loved friends. She wouldn't return it permanently to the library until she had no choice.

***

He swore, looking at the phone bill.

It was the long distance that was the killer. God, the calls to New York alone—he ran down the list hurriedly, hoping that he could palm off most of them as business. But he knew the numbers, and while there were two legitimate (short) calls to the ad agency and two more to Hattie, all the others were to the hotel, and he winced, looking at them: 56 minutes. 59 minutes. 114 minutes. God, how had he managed that? He hated talking on the phone.

But it didn't stop him from picking up the phone that very night, when the sounds from Jean's room had quieted down, and he judged she was safely asleep.

***

She knew immediately when the board lit up who was calling. She was so sure, in fact, that she abandoned the official hotel greeting. "Hi, there."

She could hear the smile at the other end, in his voice. "How did you know it was me?"

She glanced at the clock and laughed. "Can't imagine. So *many* people call me at 3:00 in the morning."

"I'm having trouble sleeping these days."

"Want me to order up a chocolate soda?"

That was all he needed to relax. Forgotten were Jean and his unending worry about her; forgotten was the unfinished jingle under the pool of light on his desk. She had a way of making whatever came out of his mouth sound so clever, so special. "Why is that?" He blurted out the question before he realized that she didn't know what he was talking about.

But somehow it didn't matter. "Oh, I don't know. Seems logical, doesn't it?"

He laughed delightedly. "You don't even know what I'm talking about."

"No, but it's comforting when someone agrees with you, isn't it?"

She didn't tell him she was keeping a death grip on his book, renewing it faithfully every two weeks at the library, just to keep it safe on her bedside table. She didn't mention her doubts about her singing career. He didn't tell her about his domestic situation, his ongoing concerns about Jean and his worries that he would need another job after this one, if he were to build up a decent retirement account.

Neither told the other that these funny, far-ranging, unimportant conversations were becoming important to both of them, in different ways, for different reasons.

It didn't matter. When they talked, nothing else mattered.

It was only when he looked up at the clock over his desk that he realized that they'd been chatting aimlessly for almost two hours.

"For Christ's sake!" He said it loudly enough to make her jump at the other end of the phone. "How do you do this to me? Don't you realize how long we've been talking?"

"Okay. I'll bite. How long?"

"It's almost 2:00 my time. Jesus, I should have been in bed long ago."

Her answer was arrow-swift and unexpected. "That's interesting to contemplate."

It stopped him cold, in fact. "Why would you want to?" he asked gruffly, to hide the equally startling lift of his heart. She couldn't have meant what he thought she meant... could she?

The only reply he got was a giggle, but even that was tantalizing.

"I don't even know why the hell I'm bothering," he grumbled, and hung up before she could hold him back with one more tantalizing giggle.

CHAPTER 11

November

Jim sounded doubtful when he called the following week, not sure whether he was imparting bad news. "The agency people want you back in New York. Something about the new jingle not working. I think they want to supervise you directly for now. Is that a problem?"

Beau's first thought was: *Now I can meet Amanda.* He fought to keep his voice from sounding too eager. "No. I had a feeling they would. They've been hinting about it since I started. How long do they want me for?"

"Oh, a few days. All expenses, of course. First-class flight. And they're okay with your staying at the Lorelei."

"Good."

"So, can you fly in early Friday? Meet with them that afternoon?"

"I'll be there."

***

Autumn in New York was his favorite time in the city, and his favorite memory: it was when *The Life and Times* had been in rehearsal. They'd opened on November 5, and his memory dimmed after that, not surprisingly. But that last month, when they were all so high and sure of themselves—working like slaves to correct minor problems, all with precious spot blindness to the glaring major error, the one that would do the show in—they'd been united in their appreciation of the sights and smells of the city in autumn. More often than not, instead of giving notes on the stage after each day's rehearsal, Vernon would invite the cast into the alley outside to breathe in the crisp fall air as he went over each day's work. This was where Beau would introduce a new lyric, where the choreographer tried out a new dance routine. He'd never forgotten the late-afternoon light and how it seemed to bathe them all in a strange and wondrous halo.

He got flight reservations and dialed the hotel, glad that for once he had a business reason for calling. His fingers went unerringly to the right digits.

Amanda picked up the phone in Jerry's office and smiled at the familiar voice. "How are you, Beau?"

"In need of a favor. And don't start talking to me, because I just got my phone bill and I never want to speak to you again. You're costing me a fortune. Damn near a thousand bucks over the last couple of months."

"Probably the best thousand you've ever spent." Little smart-ass.

"Is this how you get all that repeat business? Insulting Jerry's guests?"

"I'll have you know most of them love me."

"Well, none more than me."

She dimpled at the gruff-tender tone. By now, the lift in her blood pressure when she heard his voice was very pleasant. She had been concerned that her offhand comment in their last conversation would be... misconstrued. Or would it? She felt so comfortable with their long-running conversations that she'd gotten careless; often spoke without considering the consequences. She hadn't even thought before tossing off that remark.

What *was* she thinking, exactly?

And what was *he* thinking, with *his* last remark? Was he flirting back with her?

She didn't have time to worry about it now. He was already asking about a reservation. He'd liked 704 when he stayed there before; could he have it again? She wondered if it had associations for him now, associations with her and their conversations in the middle of the night. Somehow it seemed important that he have it this time, too—as though their relationship would continue to grow if he did.

She tried to figure this out rationally, while the rest of her thrilled to the idea that he was coming back. Perhaps this time they could actually meet. "We have guests in that room now, but they'll be checking out that morning. I'm not sure if it'll be completely cleaned if you arrive at 1:00, though. I'll leave a note for the cleaning crew, but I can't promise. Is that all right?"

"Yes, it's fine. I trust your judgment." There was a smile in his voice. "And I'll expect you to meet me for a drink while I'm there. Might as well meet the face behind the voice."

She tried to sound calm, though her heart was hammering against her ribs. "I'll do my best to break free."

"Good. I'll talk to you when I get in Friday." And unceremoniously, he hung up.

***

He didn't mind the flight delay this time, or the traffic coming into the city. New York *felt* like fall now, in a way Los Angeles never did, and he'd missed it. The wonderful smoky tang in the air reminded him fleetingly of other autumns, when he was growing up in Chicago, and he savored it.

He'd rented a shiny new white Buick this time, and enjoyed the drive from the airport to midtown. The hell with it; the agency was paying for it, anyway, and he always preferred driving himself. It was around 2:15, and he figured she'd be at the desk when he came into the lobby.

He wondered what she looked like. He'd never thought to ask. He was almost sure she wasn't very dark or a redhead. But blonde? She didn't seem the bleached, flashy type. When he thought of her, he thought of colors, but not the colors of her skin and eyes. Mostly he thought of bolts of burgundy silk, flashes of silver, beams of golden morning mist. All his favorite colors, actually. Her voice sounded like those colors, he thought, trying to pin it down. Rolling up into laughter, sliding down into serenity, edged sometimes in ice, sometimes in the softest of flower petals. His heart began to beat faster as he thought that in a matter of minutes, he would be meeting her.

He found a garage a block away and parked the Buick on the ground floor, another bonus. And then, impatient to meet her, he lifted out his suitcase and hurried down the block and through the revolving doors into the hotel lobby.

He stopped in the lobby and surveyed the girls at the desk. Several were about the right age: a nice-looking brunette, a redhead wildly chewing gum, a tall, exotic-looking blonde. He eyed the last one a little longingly, but at last decided, no. Not the type at all. The brunette was a likely candidate, though. Her uniform was neatly pressed, her manicured nails coated with a clear polish, her hair tied back.

He approached her, wondering, and the brunette gave him a professional smile. "Welcome to the Lorelei, sir."

"Thank you." He searched her face for a sign that she recognized him, but saw nothing. He gave his name. Still nothing. She found the reservation and offered him a pen to sign the register.

When she nodded to a bellman behind her, he asked, "Is Amanda here?"

"Let me check." And turning, she called into the office behind her, "Is Amanda in?" He cocked his head, trying to hear the answer, but she had it before he did. "No, sir, she's apparently out running an errand. She should be back any time. Shall I leave a message?"

He was hideously disappointed, but he tried to sound composed. "No, thanks. I'll catch her later."

By the time she had returned from buying the cleaning supplies and a box of Ritz crackers for Mrs. Ellis (who was checking in that night and already anxious about her nighttime snack), it was 2:45, and room 704 was empty. Beau had rushed off to meet with Hattie (opting for a cab so he could keep his excellent parking space), hoping he could persuade her to see things his way and stave off a long dinner afterwards.

"I like it," Hattie said frankly, as he hummed the jingle. "It's what they asked for."

"Let's hope they remember that tomorrow morning." He scratched notes on his pad. "'Need' or 'want'—what do you think?"

"Give 'em their choice and let them decide." Hattie glanced at the antique clock over her mantelpiece and turned away from the piano. I think that's it. Let it ride till the monsters hear it."

They both chuckled. The image of the sober young man lecturing them on corporate responsibility and vision—about a diet cola!—was too absurd to take seriously. Beau got up, leaving a half-filled coffee cup on the long, low marble-topped table. "Thanks, Hattie. We'll see how it flies tomorrow. But thank God, one way or the other, I'm leaving tomorrow night."

"Why do you suppose they called a corporate meeting on a Saturday morning? Don't these people know that's what the Hamptons are for?" she asked.

He laughed. "They'll be the death of us, Hattie. God help us—we were never that pompous when we were young."

From that moment on the day sailed, his phrase for those rare miraculous days that unfolded just right. He caught a cab immediately on his way out, and the driver was young, pleasant, and articulate. (A hopeful writer, he found out on the ride across town. Only this one seemed sure enough and smart enough that he might even turn out to be talented.) He recommended an excellent restaurant near Rockefeller Center, a less expensive one (which Beau knew to be mediocre) near Times Square, apparently under the impression that Beau was new to the city. They discussed sports amicably, and Beau found himself impressed enough to ask to see a sample of his work. Unlike the usual wannabes, however, this one did not stammer or back away from the opportunity to display his work to a professional. He only asked, politely, whether it would be convenient for him to drop off some chapters at the hotel. Beau agreed, feeling pleasantly philanthropic, and resolving that if the stuff was even decent, he would recommend the man wherever he could. He liked his style.

He decided not to walk up to the front desk for his phone messages. It was doubtless enough time for Amanda to have returned, and curiously, he found himself wanting to keep the telephone contact, if only for one more conversation. He returned to his room, opening the windows wide. Thank God Jerry was one of those old-fashioned innkeepers who believed in the value of fresh air. A good gust of wind from the south carried with it all the smells and vigor that California lacked. He drew several good deep breaths, feeling energized, and at the same time a little sleepy.

A disinterested voice on the switchboard gave him his messages crisply. Jean wanted him to check in. The agency confirmed its meeting tomorrow, for brunch at a restaurant he didn't know near their offices. Probably new and trendy, he figured. And pricey. Dumbbells. Afterward they would listen to the new work at their office studio. A memo from the hotel that his room had been cleaned, per his request, but a few supplies were still missing. Please inquire through the front desk. *You bet*, he thought.

"You did it!" His voice rang enthusiastically through the wire. "I wasn't sure you could have it all clean before I checked in."

"We aim to please," she answered lightly.

"I'll say. What supplies am I missing here? Did you send someone out for them?"

"I went for them myself."

"I'm impressed."

"So am I. That's why I like it here. It's not just a job, it's an adventure." She told him about having to stop in three pharmacies before she found the right kind of soap and shampoo, and then almost being run over by an old lady pushing a shopping cart, prompting a hearty chuckle from him.

"Well, now. This deserves a reward. What time are you free for drinks?"

She hesitated. In a curious way she too wanted to keep this contact at arm's distance, as badly as she wanted to know the man behind the voice. It had been so lovely the last two months that she was reluctant to spoil it. Perhaps he couldn't live up to her inflated expectations. *But who could?* she thought wryly.

Into the silence came his reproach. "Now come on, Amanda, I'm not here for long. And I'm not as dreadful as you think. Only maybe half as dreadful. One drink. In the bar. I'll be there at 6:30." The line went dead.

CHAPTER 12

She wished she'd had time to change clothes and use hot rollers. But for that she'd have had to hurry home. It was a choice of looking only slightly better, or being on time.

She made do. She took the last precious fifteen minutes of the day to duck into the lobby restroom to re-comb her hair, clamp the barrettes more securely into the soft brown locks, and renew her makeup. She started to re-apply blush to her cheekbones and halted when she saw the high color surging into her face. Clearly, more blush would be redundant. She applied a fresh layer of powder and lipstick and then put her makeup kit away.

She had never given much thought to what he looked like, and now, as she crossed the lobby and headed for the bar, she wondered about this. Somehow the voice had seemed complete in itself, with no need to attach a face and body. Jerry had said once that he was restless, always moving, and used his hands to punctuate his conversation, but never given particulars of his height, weight or hair color. *Wouldn't it be funny if we both wandered around the bar for an hour and couldn't find each other?* she thought in a moment of near-hysteria. Tiny invisible fingers seemed to stroke her vocal cords, causing an unbearable tickle. She willed her feet to move faster, but every step felt like pushing through a wall of molasses.

At 6:30, the hotel bar was filled, but not overflowing. Amanda stood peering hesitantly inside. The dim flattering light cast shadows into the faces she was trying to read, and she knew she would have to stroll in and look closer, especially as she had no idea what she was looking for. Still, just from his voice, she thought she knew what *not* to expect from him.

She ruled out any men sitting with other men or women, and those wearing flashy jewelry; she suspected Beau would have better taste than to sport a pinky ring larger than his knuckle. The one or two who flashed obvious hairpieces were the next ones out. Somehow, she felt, even if he turned out to be bald, he wouldn't apologize for it, not with a cheap toupee.

She went over the faces scattered around the bar. Too young, too old, wrong race... over and over. She looked at her watch: 6:41. He was here, by now. She looked again, and noticed two men lounging by the bar, each nursing what looked like a double scotch. Either could be him... possibly. They were alone, they were clearly waiting... one was pudgy and playing with the dish of olives in front of him; the other was cracking jokes that were too far away for her to hear but that clearly weren't amusing Alex, the bartender. Between jokes, the second drinker was picking his ear. She hoped neither would turn out to be him.

She was faintly aware that music had begun. Martin had started his nightly set. Within a few bars she recognized the title song from *Do I Hear a Waltz?* She loved the score, played it often, knew almost every word and note of it. She turned around to look at the piano.

There he was.

There could be no doubt about it.

He sat next to Martin on the piano bench, one finger lifted in a conducting motion, silver mane dancing energetically with the sweep of his head. The flash of recognition that shook her was decisive. She knew she was looking at the man behind the voice that had haunted her late nights at the switchboard, and didn't know how she knew.

He hadn't seen her. He was concentrating wholly on the pianist, eyes fixed on the piano keys.

She approached quietly, staying away from the lights above the piano. He had begun to hum the song, dropping in pieces of the lyric when the spirit moved him. The bits she heard confirmed it: this was the voice she knew.

She'd made no sound, but he looked up, as though he sensed her presence. Looked her over, noting her features, her presence, her clothes. And smiled dead into her eyes. "Amanda," he said. And held a quick finger to lips, indicating the pianist. She understood.

They listened to the final bars, glancing furtively at one another every now and then—she at the silver locks, the high cheekbones, the deep-set brown eyes so strangely familiar; he at the soft hair, the upturned nose, the flush on her pale skin. Martin ended the song with a flourish, and struck up another at once. Beau rose, dropped a five-dollar bill in his glass, nodded his thanks. Amanda gave Martin a wink; his answering grin was impish.

Beau held out his hand to her, not to shake but to lead her—and docilely she followed him, her hand arrested in his, to a tiny secluded booth at the very back of the lounge, near the fireplace, which was blazing in response to the crisp November day.

She didn't remember ordering a drink, but she must have, or he had extraordinary ESP, because her favorite whiskey sour was set in front of her, and he was talking animatedly, telling her stories, never dwelling on the same topic for long, a word or thought spurring him into another subject as naturally as a car rounds a corner. He seemed completely at ease with her, as he had on the phone. She followed what she could, still feeling dazed at the reality of his physical presence, the paper-white skin, the short, dark eyelashes, the warmth of his fingers, the even curve of his nails. There was a faint, clean hint of cologne about him.

She could not comprehend the conflict in the messages transmitted by her senses.

He's old, she thought, bewildered.

"And then the driver said to me, 'Are we really goin' for it, Bud, or do we stop here?' And I said, 'Look, if they're not slowing down, we're not slowing down ...'"

Yet his vitality was overwhelming. He burst with movement, with gesture, with a tumbling flow of words. He seemed to have more energy than she did. "After rehearsals, we used to walk down Broadway and play a game with the passersby. If they could out-walk us—beat us to the corner—"

His eyes, darting about to pinpoint his thought in specific phrases, seldom stopped at hers, yet she couldn't take her eyes off him. Dressed, no doubt, for a meeting with his partner, he had unbuttoned a crisp white shirt at his neck, belted narrow black leather over gray slacks, topped it all with a tweed sport jacket. He wore no jewelry, just a watch (a bit frayed around the edges of the brown leather strap) emphasizing the slender bones of his wrist. The varying impressions fluttered past in split seconds, caught her consciousness briefly, then vanished, replaced by new ones. She wished she could grasp it all clearly, not in such disconnected jigsaw pieces. What was the matter with her?

More disconcerting than anything was the over-arching sense of familiar warmth. *I know him*, she thought. *I've met him before.* But she hadn't. She knew she hadn't. Yet her overriding sense was that she was meeting him *again*. She didn't understand it.

He stopped the cascade of words suddenly, broke into a smile—eyes and mouth signaling his pleasure—and drank down half his scotch and water at a gulp. "I haven't let you get a word in edgewise," he said. "I'm acting more conceited than usual today." He patted her hand briefly, the merest feather touch. Amanda managed a natural-looking smile of her own, even as her heart lurched, and tilted the whiskey sour to her lips. Half of it vanished. He stared at her. "Well! I didn't know you were a drinker. Another one?" He lifted his hand to signal Alex, but she reached out a quick hand to stop him. Their fingers bumped, accidentally, and she felt a sudden surging warmth flowing from his hand to hers. His eyes were on her, warm, ironic—and perhaps something else? She couldn't tell.

"No, thanks," she said, as easily as her hammering heart would permit. "One's more than enough. I still have some work to do tonight."

***

He chuckled, shook his head and finished his drink. She was a wonder. If she turned sideways he was sure she'd be transparent, she was so thin. Even her bones seemed fragile. The soft hair and translucent skin belied her luscious voice and the sparkle of those many phone conversations, as though all her color radiated from inside her physical being, through those extraordinary eyes, which followed his easily, picked up his changes of thought as fast and easily as he did. He hardly glanced at her, yet saw her, as he talked, in his peripheral vision. Her chin dropped lightly on one thin hand, but the gray eyes framed in surprisingly inky black lashes wandered with him.

Why do I feel as though I know her? It was true that she could have been any of a dozen girls he remembered from his years on Broadway. He wondered why he associated her with that earlier time, and not with the girls he knew now. *Because,* he answered himself silently, *she could have stepped right out of the New York I knew in the '50s. She could have been a girl I dated in those years. She's so familiar…*

He turned to her swiftly and stopped in mid-sentence, abruptly changing the subject. "What did you really think of me?" he asked. "The first time we talked. Remember?"

She rolled her eyes, laughed and reached for her glass. He stopped her. "Come on, no evasions. You hated my guts, right?"

"You weren't very polite, as I remember."

"I'd been standing in the airport for an hour, fighting for my bag with some witch, and waiting for Jerry's fictitious limo to show up! That's what I remember."

He started to say more, to justify himself, until his attention was arrested by the sight of her long slender fingers curled lightly around her empty glass. She was listening to him, liquid gray eyes fixed on him, a faint smile on her wide curving mouth, fingers fluttering gently, unconsciously, on the cold surface of the glass.

The flash of desire that went through him like summer lightning made his knees weak.

Hastily, he raised his eyes to her face. He had to stop watching her stroking that glass, or he didn't know what he would do. Quickly he took charge of the conversation again.

"All right, let's forget that. When did you decide you didn't hate me, after all?"

Amanda smiled again, trying to still the hammering of her heart. She wondered if she looked as nervous as she was feeling, poised on a knifeedge of trembling anticipation, certain she was about to tumble into some delicious, unknown abyss and eager for it to happen. She realized she was fingering the empty glass and that he was looking at her curiously. He probably thought she was an idiot.

She shook off that thought and answered mischievously, with the first hint of the sparkle he'd heard in her voice through dozens late-night conversations. "What makes you think I ever really did?"

He smiled back. The glow in her face was reflected in his eyes. "Well. It's worth coming all the way to New York just to hear that. Even if I'm only here for one night."

She was suddenly pierced with disappointment. She hadn't thought he'd leave so soon.

He was looking at her with a half-smile. She struggled to answer lightly, without betraying her plummeting mood, but she could hardly think what to say. "Really?" she said finally, hoping she didn't sound utterly stupid.

He admired her remarkable poise. "Certainly. If all goes well at my meeting tomorrow, I can be on a plane headed home by four. I thought I'd have to be at my most charming tonight, since I might only get one chance." He saw that she looked puzzled, so he clarified. "To erase whatever miserable first impressions of me you've been carrying around." She raised an eyebrow, inviting elaboration. "You know. Arrogant. Overbearing. Obnoxious. Blustering. Conceited."

"Amazing," she marveled, mock-seriously. "And *psychic*, too."

They both laughed at that. He patted her hand again briefly, a feather-light touch that sent tingles racing inexplicably up her arm. Startled, she looked at him, but he had already withdrawn his hand and was nodding at Martin, now playing a medley of Andrew Lloyd Webber tunes.

"He seems awfully good."

"He is." Amanda hummed along with the piano. "He knows everything, back to the Princess musicals that Jerome Kern wrote with Guy Bolton and P.G. Wodehouse before 1920."

"And they were called the Princess musicals because...?"

"Because," she said, knowing he was testing her, "the theater where they were produced was the Princess Theater. They weren't *about* princesses. They were more modern than the operettas Victor Herbert was doing at the same time. A lot of them were college musicals, like *Very Good, Eddie* and *Leave It to Jane*."

She saw approval in his eyes, but all he said was, "Not many girls your age know that."

"Not many people *any* age know it, not these days," she retorted, but she was smiling.

"Touché. You are a very special girl."

She looked up at him quickly—even sitting down, he was so much taller—but this time there was no irony in his eyes, no laughter. He looked straight at her, his eyes holding hers warmly, until finally she had to look away. Somewhere in the pit of her stomach, she began to tremble. What was happening to her? This had never happened before.

The plunge into the unknown abyss, so desirable a few minutes ago, now seemed suddenly so imminent and frightening that she had to tiptoe back from the edge. In a slightly louder voice, she asked brightly, "So how did your meetings go today?"

Immediately she could feel the atmosphere shift to a more casual level. He grimaced. "Don't remind me. I should have insisted on doing all the work in L.A. Here, they've got me at their mercy."

She laughed. "Sounds serious."

"It is! The wrong jingle for a new diet soda apparently could spell the end of civilization as we know it."

She wrinkled her nose. "Ugh. If that's the standard, maybe it's better ended."

He'd only meant to meet her for one drink, to convince himself she wasn't really as special as his fantasies had built her up to be. He'd intended this meeting to prove that his thoughts about her were baseless, that it was his need building her into a seductress, that she was like every other twenty-something girl of the '80s, thinking thoughts too foreign to his to ever meet on any plane.

Instead, he thought helplessly that he couldn't remember the last time he'd been so enchanted. In the dance of words he'd initiated, to cover his own overwhelming, immediate attraction to her, she'd followed him as fleetly and gracefully as a dancer turns in a tango, without missing a beat or breaking the connection between them.

He could talk to her forever.

He refused to allow himself to think of other things he wanted to do with her.

Thank God he'd deliberately made a dinner date with Hattie, in case meeting Amanda turned out to be awkward, and he needed an excuse not to prolong it. Now it would be his salvation. He'd have to say goodbye soon, so he wouldn't be late, but he was sure he had time to talk to her for a few more minutes...

"Excuse me, sir." Bruce, the maître d', appeared at their table noiselessly, nodded to Amanda. "Mr. Kellogg? Phone call at the desk for you, sir."

He didn't realize how far he'd lost track of time, until Hattie's voice said anxiously, "Beau? You did say 8:00, right?"

"Why? What time is it?" He glanced at his watch and cursed silently. It was past nine, and though he felt as though they'd just begun to talk, they'd already been together for two and a half hours. He didn't want to leave her, but he'd promised Hattie. And now that he thought of it, it was probably a good idea to break away. This was getting into dangerous territory.

"I'll be there in half an hour," he told Hattie. "Wait for me, will you? Sorry about this. I got—hung up."

He hurried back to Amanda. "I'm late," he said apologetically. "Dinner with Hattie—she's waiting for me. I have to go."

"Don't worry. I'll pick up the glass slipper on the steps."

He turned to her, startled. He knew the pull on his side was strong, but she was a lovely young girl, after all; it was hardly surprising. But it almost sounded as though—No. He was an old man. How could she find him attractive?

He dropped a twenty-dollar bill on the table, wondering if he should shake her hand or do something more in keeping with the hammering of his heart.

She smiled and held out her hand. He took both her hands in his.

"I've enjoyed this. It's been wonderful meeting the face behind the voice."

"Disappointed?" she asked, her smile glowing but her eyes strangely serious.

"Impossible," he said, suddenly serious himself. His eyes swept her face, the luminous gray eyes, the dark fringe of lashes, the soft hair brushed down to her shoulders. "I'll remember this always."

"I'm glad," she said, not moving. Her hands felt so soft and small and trusting, clasped in his.

He squeezed them once more and looked at his watch. "Oh, God, Hattie'll kill me," he said, already heading out the door. "Thanks again!" he called back to her as he reached the doorway. When he disappeared into the lobby, Amanda wondered why a sudden chill settled on her heart.

***

At 1:00 in the morning, she still lay awake, staring at the ceiling.

She'd gone to bed an hour before, so restless she could hardly calm down enough to undress and slide under the covers. Now she lay sleepless, her mind racing.

He was so different from what she'd expected, yet so much what she'd hoped he'd be.

Smart. Witty. Wonderfully energetic and vibrant. A marvelous conversationalist. She could listen to his stories for hours, wished their time together could have gone on and on. *I had fun*, she told herself. Time just melted away while she was with him.

She wished she could settle down enough to sleep.

She thought instead of the way his fingers had touched hers, remembered it as vividly as though it was happening again, and a sudden warmth spread from her stomach and blossomed into her throat, her face, the roots of her hair, down to her toes. Then she thought of his dark eyes dancing at her and the energy in his gestures and the way he smiled at her.

And suddenly, out of the blue, she began to cry.

Something about him just left her... completely undone. It wasn't entirely sexual, though she knew she was attracted to him. But there was something else... something that reached deep inside her. It was something about the slightly crooked line of his lips, the little hesitation when he slowed to think of the right word, the silver hair, the fine lines etched about his eyes. Something just twisted inside her heart whenever she thought of him—and she couldn't stop thinking of him.

Ridiculous, really. She'd only the met the man for a couple of hours—there'd been almost no physical contact, just wonderful talk—so why did she feel so open to him, so *connected*? Why did she feel as though she knew him better than people who'd been in her life for years, and that he understood her better than her own family?

It was silly. It was illusory. It was impossible.

And she didn't even know why she was crying, and yet she couldn't stop.

Then a thought rose from somewhere inside her: *There'll never be enough time for us.*

The tears began to fall faster. *What am I thinking? He didn't even ask to see me again. For all I know, he never will.*

She who never cried was now sobbing into her pillow. She cried for a long time, tears dripping onto the bed sheets, eyesight blurring. Just as she thought she had no more tears left, visions of his face rose in her mind, spurring her to a fresh bout. When the tears finally ended, her pillow and pillowcase were soaked. She got up wearily to change them, to rub a towel over her tear-drenched hair and gulp down a couple of aspirins to combat the headache slicing into her head and the sudden soreness in her throat. When she tried to speak out loud, she croaked. For the first time in nine months, she decided to call in sick to work. Part of it was her sore throat. The other was the fear that she would break down in fresh tears in front of the staff or guests.

By the time the aspirin had soothed her headache and she'd settled down on a fresh pillow, it was nearly three. Exhausted by the depth of her feelings, touching her on a level she'd never thought she'd reach, thinking again, *There'll never be enough time*, she fell almost instantly into a dreamless sleep.

***

Beau couldn't sleep. The Valium wasn't working. But this time it wasn't a lyric nagging its way into his mind. It wasn't Jean and what-had-she-done-this-time? It was his uncanny, unexpected response to Amanda. He had thought their meeting would end it for good, would prove he had mistaken her for someone of his own time. He was sure she would turn out to be just another disappointment, in a lifetime full of them.

Instead, he couldn't believe how much he wanted to pick up their conversation again. He wanted to watch that soft hand with its long slender fingers tapping a tall glass, wanted to hear that lovely voice in person again, wanted to ask her a thousand questions. He wished he'd thought to ask them earlier, but there had been so much to tell her, and she'd listened with such interest. Or was she just being polite?

Now he wished he hadn't been so damned self-centered, so eager to charm her with his conversation; she probably would never want to see him again, after meeting him in person. He wished he'd taken better care of himself the last few years, so he could have looked more attractive to her.

He drew a last long lungful of his fourth cigarette and stubbed it out, aware that he was being silly. At the height of his infatuation for Nancy, his youthful romantic passion for Jean, he had never paced back and forth and daydreamed and fretted like he was now. Over a hotel clerk! Christ! *Old age is getting me where it counts*, he thought ruefully. *Serves me right.*

He pulled up his wrist and squinted at the watch hands. Almost 2:30. Maybe he could call her at the switchboard.

Or would that be too much? They'd already spent a couple of hours together in the bar tonight. Only damn it, it hadn't been nearly enough time for all the things he still wanted to say to her. But maybe she would think it was too much.

Instead of reaching for the telephone, he lay still, thinking of her. She wasn't strikingly pretty. Nice-looking, in a quiet way. Well groomed, of course, but so was every woman in New York. You could put her in a lineup with a dozen other women, and the others would rank as outstanding, looks-wise, compared to her. Objectively speaking, of course.

But that was reckoning without the dancing light in her storm-gray eyes, the sweet upturned curve of her lips, the sparkle of her conversation, and her fair skin, so soft, so touchable. Somehow, he'd thought she was beautiful.

However, despite her joke at the end about the glass slipper (that's all it was: a joke), *she* may have found him repulsive, or at least wrong for her. Why wouldn't she? She dealt with old geezers like him all the time, as hotel guests; no doubt she had a boyfriend stashed away somewhere (he'd always been careful not to ask). Even if she didn't, which he somehow hoped was the case, what could possibly be attractive about a guy old enough to be her father?

Maybe she'd prefer not to hear from him again. Or maybe she'd just like to scale things back to where they had been before, just casual talk on the telephone. He hoped that no matter what happened, she would want to continue their conversations. He didn't want to think about how much they meant to him, at this point.

Well, if she doesn't want to talk to me again, it's better to know it sooner than later.

Bolstered by this thought, he propped the receiver under his chin and punched the numbers for the desk. A young, strange voice answered, heavy with sleep. "Amanda?" he asked, unbelieving.

"No, Amanda's not working tonight. Can I help you?"

"She isn't?" he repeated foolishly. "I thought she was."

"I'm sorry, sir. Would you like me to leave her a message? Is there something I can help you with?"

He was so busy with his disappointment that he didn't realize he hadn't answered until she repeated the question, more loudly. "No," he said slowly. "No, there's nothing."

He put down the receiver and stared at it. He wouldn't find out tonight how she felt. All at once he was bitterly disappointed. He hadn't realized how much he wanted to continue the conversation. He hadn't realized that the game had escalated. Now it wasn't going to be enough, talking to her on the phone. Now he wanted to see her again, and again. But he had no idea whether she would want to see him. He refused to ask himself why this was suddenly so important.

He didn't bother taking another sleeping pill. There hadn't been one invented that would chase away the thoughts now hammering through his brain. He knew that no matter what he did, he wouldn't close his eyes tonight.

***

He finally dragged himself out of bed at ten to seven, feeling weary all over, knowing he had to pack and check out before he left for his meeting. He could probably leave his luggage with the concierge until it was time for him to leave for the airport.

I could ask Amanda…

And he suddenly realized that no matter what, he wanted to talk to her again before he left, if only for a few minutes. He refused to let himself think how disappointed he had been that she had not been at the switchboard last night.

But when he phoned the front desk, hoping she had somehow come in early, the feminine voice that answered told him Amanda was not expected before 9:30.

Damn! At that rate, he'd have only a moment with her before he had to leave for his brunch. Still, it was better than nothing. He kept replaying their meeting in his mind, seeing again the glowing gray eyes under thick dark lashes, the smile on her wide, flexible mouth, the slender bones of her hand as her fingers played with her glass, and feeling the unnatural thump of his heart as he looked at her.

A few moments of that, and he realized he was getting hard all over again. *I need a cold shower*, he told himself. He didn't allow himself to think of what else he might need.

Still, before he went into the bathroom he packed his bag, carefully and methodically, concentrating on folding his shirts neatly, laying his pants lengthwise so they wouldn't crease in the wrong places. In twenty minutes he was almost finished. All that remained to pack were his shaving things, toothbrush and pajamas.

He took a quick shower, shaved and dressed, wondering all the while whether she would be downstairs when he returned, and if he could see her for a moment before he left. It would only be a moment, though... his flight was at four, he would need at least an hour to get to JFK from midtown Manhattan, and these jokers could conceivably keep him right up to the last minute.

Blast them! If they did...

He was startled when the phone rang. Were they changing the schedule on him again?

He grabbed it. "Yes?"

"Good morning." It was her.

"Well, hello!" He hoped he didn't sound too eager, but damn, he was glad she'd called. "This is a nice surprise. I just called downstairs. They said you wouldn't be in till 9:30."

"More like twelve, I think." Her voice sounded unusually husky, distinctly different from last night. "I didn't sleep too well last night."

"Do you have a cold?"

He heard her sniffing in the background. "Not exactly... I woke up with a little sore throat. But I've had some tea, and it seems to be better. I'm still at home," she added unnecessarily.

"Oh." He was disappointed all over again, and concerned that she take care of herself. Now there was no way he would see her before he left. "Maybe you should take the whole day off."

"Too much to do. I'm sure I'll be all right with a little more rest."

"You shouldn't even be calling me," he said sternly, though he was secretly delighted that she had. It was the first time he could remember that *she* had called *him*. It made him feel their relationship was somehow progressing. "With a sore throat, you should talk as little as possible."

"I just wanted to thank you again for last night. I really enjoyed it."

"You're most welcome. So did I." He hesitated and hoped she was not just being polite. But would she have called him from home—while feeling lousy—just to be polite? "Maybe when I come back, we can do it again."

Her voice dropped audibly. "You're really leaving today?"

"Right after my meeting."

"That's so *soon*," she said quietly.

His heart stilled momentarily. She'd said it involuntarily, and so softly it was as though she was talking to herself. Something in him thrilled to the unhappy tone in her voice. Would his leaving really affect her?

He composed himself. "My flight is this afternoon. But I have a meeting at ten and I'm not sure when it'll be over. Could I check out before that, but leave my bag here?"

When she answered, a beat later, it was as though they'd never had anything but a professional relationship. Her voice was completely businesslike again. Even the huskiness had lessened. "Certainly. The concierge will be glad to store it for you."

He paused slightly. "Fine. I'll ask him."

"Fine. Have a good trip back."

"Thanks." There didn't seem to be anything more to say. He put down the receiver, concentrating on Jean and his day-to-day activities in California, all of which were washed away in the sudden roaring tidal wave of anguish that ripped through him, telling him clearly he didn't want to leave. And yet why did he suddenly want to stay? Desperate for action so he could avoid that uncomfortable question, he grabbed at his neatly-packed suitcase and pawed through it, destroying the symmetry, searching, he told himself, for a fresh handkerchief. After he'd completely undone what had taken him some time to do, he found a clean white square in his pocket.

***

When he returned to the hotel at 3:00, he was seething. The idiots he was working for had outdone themselves with their moronic opinions at this meeting.

A complete lyric rewrite! Throwing out everything he'd done and starting from scratch. The senior vice-president had claimed he liked Hattie's music, though he felt there was still something 'not quite right' about it that he couldn't put his finger on. Beau had a dreadful urge to tell him exactly where he could stick that finger, but he'd bitten his tongue and clung to his calm, reasonable tone. And look what it got him.

They all agreed it was the lyric that was at fault—naturally—and set another meeting for Tuesday. He was to have a whole new lyric ready to show by then.

Which meant he couldn't go home quite yet. Which meant... that he would need his room back. And it hadn't occurred to him to ask them to hold it, because he'd been so sure he'd wrap things up today.

When he asked at the desk, though, there was no problem. He wondered if Amanda had anything to do with that. The desk clerk he spoke to, with round young face, pastel hair, multiple ear piercings and a name tag that read "Cherry", told him his room wasn't booked for the next few nights; he could certainly have it back. A bellman would bring up his luggage.

He thanked her and was starting toward the elevator when she said, "Oh, wait, I forgot. A package came for you."

"A package?" He couldn't think who might have sent it.

"I put it in the storage room with your luggage. Hang on a minute." She vanished.

Across the lobby, Amanda stepped inside and caught sight of him almost at once. She stood still for a moment, looking at him, then started toward the desk. His back was turned away from the front door; he hadn't noticed her.

Then Cherry returned and handed him a thick manila envelope. He stood weighing it in his hands, studying it. His brow was furrowed and he looked bewildered... but still didn't seem to realize she was now behind him.

As she came closer, a soft whiff of his cologne came to her nostrils.

It brought back all the emotions she had felt last night.

Her heart began to thump wildly.

He turned away from the desk and almost bumped into her.

His head snapped up. The sudden rush of warm feeling through his veins was so powerful it was a wonder it didn't lift him right off the ground. He tried to conceal it, even as he tried to act casual. "Well, hello! Sorry. I didn't see you."

"That's pretty obvious. Must be important." Her voice sounded much better; the huskiness of the morning was gone.

He looked at the package again. "I'm not sure. I—wait a minute." He suddenly remembered. The young cab driver he'd been impressed with had brought the pages of his work in progress. The return address meant nothing to him, and the name was unfamiliar, but that had to be it.

He told her about the incident, watching her eyes soften.

He's so generous with himself, she thought. *Kind even to strangers.* Somehow, that touched her; she could feel a stirring that could easily bring up tears. What was wrong with her?

"Penny for your thoughts," he said.

She smiled. "How did your meeting go?"

He winced. "Don't remind me, please."

"Didn't they like your idea?"

He shook his head. "They no longer trust me to work on my own. I have to stick around here for three more days. *At least* three more days."

Her eyes brightened, and her smile was genuine when she looked up at him. *What the hell,* he thought. *I might as well get some pleasure out of this farce.* "Have dinner with me tonight," he said impulsively. "I know a terrific place in Connecticut. It's a beautiful drive up there." When she seemed to hesitate, he added, "Come on. Do an old man a favor."

She had half-promised to take over the night shift, and she started to say so. Then she bit back the words. She knew she wanted to spend the evening with him, not behind a switchboard. For once, the staff would have to get along without her.

She smiled again as she thought how shocked they would be.

(HAPTER 13

They beat the traffic out of the city and sped over the turnpike, in the last light of the fading November day. The snap in the air was augmented by the rustle of crisp brown leaves fluttering down, and she drew deep, happy breaths, feeling rather than seeing the velvet tone of the darkening sky.

"Tell me about *The Life and Times*," she said suddenly, as traffic thinned and the wind gusted around them.

He smiled at the memory. "I'll bet you know every word of the score."

She shook her head regretfully. "Not anymore. I haven't heard the album in years."

"Neither has anyone else. It's probably at the bottom of some bargain bin in Idaho. But for awhile after the show closed, it was all over the place. Columbia thought we'd be a hit and made the mistake of issuing the record before the show opened. Jesus, were there ever copies floating around." He shook his head and turned off the turnpike, glancing sideways at her as he cut the wheel. "Go on, say it."

"What?"

"Slow down, or words to that effect. My driving bother you?"

"I like it." She did, too. She'd probably drive like this if she dared. But she hadn't had nearly enough practice; a couple of turns at seventy miles an hour, and she'd kill somebody, probably.

"In California you drive everywhere. It's the culture. What's really silly is seeing these fat women drive to aerobics class, sweat for an hour, then get in the car and drive home, when they could get better exercise and fresh air just walking a couple of miles."

She giggled at the thought, and felt somehow rewarded when his scowl lightened. "Tell me about the show."

"What exactly did you want to know?"

"I heard that—" She stopped, not sure how much to tell.

He glanced at her again, quizzically. "Yes?"

"There was a song you made up at some party, on a bet. Is that true?"

"Party? I never went to parties. Still don't."

His denial fueled her curiosity. "Jerry said you had. He told me about this terrific party you hosted when your book came out."

"Oh, that. I'd forgotten." He pulled into a dark driveway. She peered ahead, but could see nothing. A row of poplars—she could hear the leaves rustling—but no lights, no sounds. Then suddenly, the shadows yielded to a lantern swinging on a sturdy white pole, showing up as a golden flame against black velvet. Behind it, floodlights on the dark lawn lit up a long, low clapboard building, and she caught sight of the sign as it shuttered back and forth: "Wallarah Inn".

Inside, an inviting stone fireplace blazed warmth in all three dining rooms. Beau, winking at the hostess, secured a prime corner table close to the fire and a bay window, with an unobstructed view of the grounds. The cold wind against the glass made the warmth of the fire even cozier.

The tables were set with small intimate hurricane lamps, and the linen was stiff with starch, palest pink under white lace. The menu was crammed with simple old-fashioned dishes done superbly well. It was not a place, she saw clearly, to see and be seen or to show off one's taste in nouveau cuisine; it was a place to come for the pleasure and comfort of it. She was happy he had chosen it; it made her like him even more.

Over delectable hot chicken, crisp salad, warm rolls soaked in olive oil, and his favorite California white wine, she pressed him again about the party. "Why does this interest you?" he asked, amused. "It was such a long time ago."

"Maybe that's why. I wasn't here that long ago—"

"Thanks for reminding me."

"—and I'd like to know what it was like."

"Just like it is now, except no computers, no diet soft drinks, and nobody was afraid to smoke." He lit one of his own as he said this and glanced idly around the dining room, which suddenly seemed clear of other guests. How long had they been talking?

She regarded him with amusement. "Anyone ever tell you—"

"Yes. Constantly. Don't you start, too."

Her smile faded a little. He saw it; saw too when her nose began to twitch. "Does it bother you?"

She tried to shake her head, couldn't quite. He saw that, too. She knew that he had, so she tried to laugh it off, keep it light. "I've always been a little—well—sensitive to certain smells. And of course, I do coddle my throat."

"Of course. Say no more." He stubbed it out. "I promise, whenever I'm with you, not to smoke. Okay?"

Her smile burst forth again, but she said nothing. They gazed at each other for a moment, Beau looking rueful, Amanda smiling a little too brightly, but the flowing chemistry was too strong: she dropped her eyes to her plate and changed the subject. "How long have you known about this place? It's charming."

"Isn't it? It was a private home many years ago, and then the owners turned it into an inn and restaurant. Every room upstairs has its own fireplace and sitting area."

"It must be a lovely weekend spot. Very romantic." She glanced out the window as she spoke, and suddenly, electrifyingly, felt his hand on hers, stroking it gently.

"It certainly is." He was looking straight at her, and feelings started to churn up in the pit of her stomach. She put down her fork hastily. His hand remained on hers, lightly, but he went on talking easily, changing the subject, and she relaxed. The sensation was undeniably pleasant, though, and she felt a cut of disappointment when he took his hand away to point out some feature of the room. A moment later, when he casually clasped her fingers again, she returned the pressure of his hand, and answered his startled look with a small smile.

The waiter, who had known Beau for years, returned noiselessly with the wine bottle. He started to pour into Beau's glass, but Beau, glancing at Amanda's almost-full glass, shook his head. "No, thanks, Wes. No more for us."

The waiter did not allow surprise to alter his expression. "Very good, sir." He withdrew smoothly.

Beau wondered himself why tonight, he didn't care for a second glass of wine when usually, at the Inn, he was good for several. They had a wonderful wine list and he usually enjoyed it—sometimes a little too much, he acknowledged silently. For some reason, tonight he just wasn't thirsty. He refused to speculate on the reason.

Amanda prodded him gently back to the conversation. "You never answered my question, you know."

"Which question was that?"

"About *The Life and Times*. I think you're deliberately trying to avoid it."

"Why would I do that?" His voice had gone very soft; his eyes were straight on hers.

"I'm trying to figure that out." Hers was lower, too; her breathing was jagged. He looked at her plate. She'd hardly touched her dinner.

He pointed at her plate. "You don't like it?"

She shook her head. "I love it. The best chicken I've ever had."

"Then eat up."

"It's cold." He raised an eyebrow, and she went on hurriedly. "And I guess—I'm not too hungry after all."

Obviously he wasn't the only one feeling the flow between them.

He glanced at his watch. "I love this place, but the service can be very slow. Do you know it's past midnight?"

"No!" She strained for a glimpse of his watch; she'd forgotten hers in her rush to get to work. Smiling, he held his wrist close to her face so she could read the dial; she tried to ignore the vibrations leaping from his skin to her cheek, but she was sure he was noticing everything. "I've got to be at work at seven."

"On a Sunday?"

"One of the girls is on vacation. I'm filling in for her."

"Well, I hope you can make do on four hours' sleep. I can't get you home for at least an hour." He paused for a moment. "Unless—you'd like to stay?"

"Stay—" It took her a moment. "Here, you mean?"

"It *is* an inn, after all. And just as charming upstairs."

She thought of possible answers to that. He was married, she knew. That hadn't stopped her from allowing the relationship to grow. She'd told herself first that it was just business, then just friendship. Once they began talking, it just seemed... inevitable. And she was enjoying the physical contact, insignificant though it was, way too much. The feelings churning up in her were more powerful than any she'd ever felt. She knew it would be a mistake to take things any further. Still—

He laughed. "Separate rooms, of course. And I promise to get you back in time for work. But I thought you'd like the experience. It's much different from the Lorelei, you know."

Her sigh of relief didn't fool either of them. "*That* would be lovely."

***

A double verandah circled the house, one on each floor. The owners had wisely left well enough alone, deeming it unnecessary to split the wide, open area into cramped private cubicles. In any case, the upper level was a flowing public walkway for the inn guests, just as the lower level was for diners. As a compromise, the double doors that opened from each room onto the verandah were tightly curtained on the inside from top to bottom.

Amanda couldn't sleep. Her mind still swarmed with the singing sensation awakened at dinner with Beau. She had never had a better time on a date.

They had talked about Broadway—yesterday and today—for hours, and he'd told her stories about his early days in the theater, some of which she laughed at heartily. Others touched her oddly, and made her feel even closer to him. She knew, as he talked about his first tentative steps as a lyricist, that he was trying to amuse her, but the naiveté of that young theater hopeful of long ago moved her, and she could see that even as he talked, he knew what she was feeling.

At his urging, she'd told him about her family, her mother's ambitions to sing, her own tenuous relationship with Josie. She had told him things that surprised her, things she'd kept locked in her heart and hardly acknowledged all her life. But talking to him about these things was like talking to herself; he was attentive and comforting, and his dark eyes, following hers as she talked, seemed to see much more than she was saying.

She lay atop the soft, comfortable bed with its handmade quilt and fluffy pillows and thought that she had never felt less like drifting off to sleep. She hadn't bothered to undress, though the clock over the fireplace had already clicked past two o'clock. Beau had said a polite goodnight over an hour ago and told her he'd meet her in the lobby for the drive back at 5:30. She should probably strip down to her slip—it would be warm enough under the quilts and blankets liberally provided—but she had a strange urge to walk, and the verandah would certainly be deserted at this time of night.

It wasn't. He had bothered only to take off his tie, turn up his coat collar and light a cigarette, and the stalking figure in the moonlight seemed less menacing than comfortingly familiar.

They saw each other immediately.

He came to her at once, and smiling, conspicuously stubbed out the cigarette with his foot. She smiled back. Without a word, question or consent exchanged, they fell into step.

"I've been working on that ad campaign," he said, as though it was perfectly normal to be discussing agency business in eerie moonlight, chilled by a November wind, in the middle of the night. "Can't get it quite right, though."

"I thought you had it right before."

"So did I. Apparently I was wrong."

"What do they want?"

"Damned if I know. They asked for a slow song that moves fast, a simple tune with lots of notes in it, and a witty lyric with words anyone can sing after one hearing." He started to steam up again, just thinking about it. She walked beside him silently. "And in three days they want a whole new number, and they think they're being generous in giving us that! Christ! If I had any sense at all, I'd be writing real-estate ads for the *L.A. Times*. Why in hell did I agree to this?"

"Maybe—"

"This is the last time, do you hear? I'll never do it again, so help me. I don't care if their damned soft drink rots on the shelves. Stuff causes cancer, anyway. Probably more than cigarettes." He glared at her as he automatically snapped a cigarette out of the crumpled pack in his pocket and started to light it. Then he remembered, sheepishly put it away, and turned away from her, exhaling rage with each breath.

"If you could—" she started to say, but he cut her off impatiently.

"Three days, and that's it. If they don't like what we come up with then, I'm dropping the job and going home. They can get some local to do it. God knows, any idiot could." He gritted his teeth at her. "What's wrong?"

She had stopped and stood, hugging herself in the sharp wind, head cocked, eyes slanted with amusement. "Oh, of course. Any idiot could. God knows."

"For heaven's sake!" He tore off his coat and wrapped it around her. "What are you doing out here in the cold, anyway? It's late, and we've got a long drive back."

She stood exactly as she was, head still tilted, the sleeves of his jacket hanging off her shoulders and brushing her knees. She looked so ludicrous that he almost laughed. Then another blast of wind shook her frame, and he stepped forward to pull her out of the wind and tighten the coat around her. She turned her eyes up, startled, and he was conscious of liquid warmth shooting up his arms and legs and clenching at his throat. Abruptly, he released her.

"You'd better get inside now. Sleep well." He turned to go, but she held him back.

The wind was suddenly unimportant as they looked at each other, Amanda unable to find the words, not knowing what she wanted to say. But her hand still clutched at his shirt, until he reached over gently to loosen her grip.

Driven by an impulse she could hardly understand, she arched up to him, and the sound that finally broke free from her was a whimper. He stared at her for a long moment, fighting his own impulses, but when the wind broke over them again and a shiver convulsed her frame, he tossed aside his hesitation. Wrapping her tightly in the coat, shielding her from the blistering wind against his chest, he found her lips with his mouth, heedless of circumstances and other people. Her hair was icy to his touch, but her mouth was yielding, magnetic. And when she reached up to hold him closer, the coat slipped from her thin shoulders. Despite the rash of goose pimples that sprang at once from her wrists to her shoulders, neither of them noticed.

***

They slipped into his room, lit only by the fireplace, closing the French doors behind them. She tossed the coat on the overstuffed armchair in the corner and turned to him, and he could feel the intensity of the gray eyes on him without having to see them.

"Do I need to use a—"

"No." He felt, rather than saw, the wide mouth turn up in a smile, and pulled her down with him on the huge bed. And couldn't believe the rush of feeling as she began to kiss him playfully, on the nose and forehead and ears and cheeks. *God*, he thought, *maybe I'm not dead after all.*

He reached out to her slender silhouette in the darkness and swiftly loosened the buttons of her jersey dress, so he could slip his hand underneath. The unexpected warmth and fullness of her breast—and the rapid heartbeat below—made his breath come harder.

She blinked and swallowed hard as his hands roamed over her, exploring, caressing, registering shuddering waves of heat and pleasure. His touch was so gentle, yet her skin vibrated everywhere that his fingers moved.

For his part, he couldn't believe her lack of coyness. This girl who had seemed so cool and self-contained, who blushed at his jokes, wriggled out of the top of her clinging dress as naturally and impatiently as though she were alone, but her smile and the glow in her eyes included him in the performance. Then she moved toward him again and pressed against him.

Caution warred with his desire. *I've got to stop this*, he thought, *before it gets out of hand...*

She caressed his chest, her fingers moving swiftly and lightly, but he pushed her hand away, and with an effort, pulled himself up to look at her. "Amanda—"

She looked at him, startled.

He struggled to say what needed to be said, to tell her the truth, though his heart was hammering against his ribs and every cell of his being seemed to sing at her touch. He said it flatly, so there could be no mistake. "You know I'm married."

She blinked but kept her eyes on him and her voice soft. "I know."

"I can't offer you anything. I'm never going to leave her."

He saw her head drop and her eyes squeeze closed for a moment, and it felt as though an arrow had pierced his chest, as though he felt the pain he had just inflicted on her.

"I wanted you to know. I didn't want to lie to you."

He reached out a hand to reassure her, which she seized and kissed, and he could feel his resolutions melting like ice cream in the sun. When he tried to pull back, she clung, and without his realizing how it happened, their mouths were straining together again. It was an effort to drag himself to one side of the bed and hold her away from him. "Don't—"

Then he made the mistake of looking at her. She was breathing hard, her eyes glowing with passion, her hair tumbled and looking so soft, her skin still pink from the wind. He wanted nothing more in life than to run his fingertips over every part of her and follow up with hungry, impatient, all-out kisses. She was so fresh and glowing, so lovely, and she felt so good in his arms…

No. It wasn't fair to her. It wasn't fair to Jean.

She was looking at him, her arms still reaching out to him, her hair falling around her shoulders, looking so vulnerable, so sweet. And oh, God, it had been so long since he'd felt this way. He wondered if he'd ever felt this way before.

No. He didn't care what was fair, or to whom. He was going to have her.

He groaned and reached for her. Her arms went around his neck tightly, cool as silk. He couldn't believe how good it felt to have her lips on his, and then to feel her tongue probing gently inside his mouth, seeking an answer from his. A warm rush of feeling prickled from his scalp to the soles of his feet.

Neither of them ever remembered how they shed their clothes, but shirt, shoes, and underclothes landed swiftly in a jumbled heap on the side of the bed. In what seemed like just an instant, they were skin to skin, jolted by the feeling as they connected, fingertips and then hands touching, caressing, venturing upward, downward, every which way. What made it so shiveringly intimate for Amanda was that Beau's eyes never left hers, even as he touched her, brushed his fingertips over her lips, her cheeks, her throat, her breasts. He kept looking at her, devouring her reaction, and the wonder and joy in his eyes was almost unbearable for her. She closed her eyes and tilted her head, and he kissed the side of her neck, his lips moving up and down the slender column of her throat, and then working his way around to the nape of her neck, and she felt the thrill go straight through her, shaking her to the pit of her stomach.

"Feel good?" he whispered.

She nodded, unable to shape the words. 'Good' didn't begin to describe it; nothing she'd ever felt came close to what she was feeling now. She reached out a trembling hand, brushing against the soft hair arrowing down his stomach, and then gasped a little as she accidentally brushed lower and felt him pulsing hard and ready against her fingers. His face was very close to hers, and she felt him smile a little against her cheek as he registered her reaction.

She seized him and kissed him, one arm holding him tightly, as her other hand closed gently around his pulsing flesh, and she heard him gasp. She felt his arms tighten around her, pulling her even closer, as their lips took each other's hungrily, their bodies beginning to move together unerringly, as though they'd done this many, many times before.

Time stood still as they gave and took from one another, rolling closer and closer together, every inch of skin connected, hungry eyes never leaving the other's, hands, hair, faces, hearts blending together. Every touch, every breath, every look brought them closer and closer, until suddenly he was inside her, pounding with wild urgency, she twisting and moaning with the thrill of it.

He thought in wonder: *It works. It still works. Thank God.*

She thought: *This is magic. This is what all the songs and movies and books are about. Oh, God, this is a miracle.*

Frantic moments later, they both felt the roller coaster of feeling begin to crest, carrying them to a peak neither had ever known before. For an infinitesimal moment, they clung together at the top of a deeply distant mountain, suspended between moonlight and valley. Then, still together, they plunged down into the velvety darkness.

It was over.

Slowly, heartbeats easing bit by bit, they began to drift down to consciousness of the feather-soft bed, the crackling flames of the fire, and their two separate bodies.

As his breath began to come back, Beau rolled over very gently, holding Amanda tight against him, still inside her, careful not to move and dislodge himself. He felt a strange urge, foreign to him until that moment, to stay as close to her as possible. She slid her arms tighter around his neck, smiling, knowing what he was doing and why.

He couldn't see her face, but the strength of her grip reassured him. "All right?" he whispered.

Her face moved lazily, up and down, against his shoulder, and he could feel the lovely wide mouth stretch into a cat-satisfied smile. Then, swiftly, being just as careful to keep him inside her, she turned and pressed her lips against his for a long moment. "Just wonderful," she whispered, and the glow in her eyes was even more dazzling than before. He pressed her closer to him, more contented than he could remember ever feeling.

They lay silent for awhile, still wrapped together, listening quietly to the crackle of the flames, their eyes still locked together. He stroked her hair and face lightly, just for the pleasure of touching her, obeying the strange new compulsion to stay connected to her. She put her hand gently on his as it moved over her, so as he caressed her, she was caressing him back. They smiled at each other, the currents still flowing strongly between them, even as they lay relaxed and at peace.

He couldn't believe how she had given of herself. He suspected she was not terribly experienced, yet she had given back every kiss, every touch, exchanged pleasure for pleasure, with a generosity of spirit that made his heart turn over. She had offered herself so freely, with such willingness and trust, that he felt humbled. While he'd known women who were certainly more creative (well, kinky) in bed, Amanda gave him a sweetness that soared above anything he could ever remember. Being with her was not just exciting, it was comforting; and in some unexplainable way, it was cleansing, too.

The room vibrated with a sudden loud snap and crackle as a log fell apart in the fireplace. It sounded like a gunshot in the quiet room.

The sudden sound made Amanda stiffen, and as she did, they finally came apart. For a moment, wide-eyed, she stared at him, and then they both burst into laughter and curled together, even closer than before, arms wrapped around each other, soaking in each other's warmth.

"I told you," Beau said softly, "it was just as nice upstairs."

"Nicer," she said, her eyes dancing. "Much, much nicer."

He settled her on the pillow and resumed stroking her hair. "Tired?"

She shook her head. "Wide awake, actually." She was restless, in fact, though she'd felt so languorous and satisfied a moment before that she could have purred.

He groaned. "Mandy, it's the middle of the night, and we have a long drive in the morning!"

She turned and looked at him. "What did you call me?"

He shrugged. "It's a nickname for Amanda."

She smiled. "Nobody calls me that."

He smiled back. "Good."

They held each other's eyes without speaking until she felt uncomfortable. The invisible thread between them was just too strong; she broke it with her voice. "Are *you* tired?"

He gave her a look. "Have pity on me, will you? I'm an old man."

"You sure are," she murmured, her hand trailing lightly down his chest.

He pulled away from her, laughing. "Stop it! Or we'll be up all night!"

"Suits me." Her eyes sparkled. "What about you?"

"Brat," he grumbled, but he couldn't hide the note of pleasure in his voice as he settled the blankets gently over them both. He lay back on the pillow, his mind finally relaxed, freed of the roiling resentment he'd felt from the afternoon onward. *Sex is relaxing*, he told himself reasonably. And it had been a long, long time. No wonder he felt unusually good.

A tiny niggling voice at the back of his mind said quietly but clearly that it was more than that; that while sex *could* do wonders, this time it was something else. He realized he was still stroking Amanda's hair, and she had snuggled in close to him. The fresh scent of her, combined with her warmth, so close to him, was invading his nostrils and making him sleepy. He couldn't remember feeling so peaceful... and so tired... so ready to drift off...

Amanda lay next to him, careful to make only tiny movements, her whole being alert to any sound or movement from him. But his breathing was so regular and even that she knew he'd fallen asleep. Given his habitual restlessness, this was a plus; she didn't want to disturb him. It felt so good having him next to her...

She gazed up at the dark ceiling and relived the last amazing hour, moment by moment, a kaleidoscope of impressions she knew she wouldn't forget.

What she couldn't get over was his tenderness. The gentleness, the caring. Despite the headlong rush of passion, he had been so clearly with *her*, so... so connected. It wasn't just two bodies; it was more. She tried to understand it, and suddenly she thought of her tears the night before, that tidal wave of feeling that welled up so unexpectedly and carried her to the depths of sadness. *And here I am now,* she thought, *standing on such a peak of joy...*

There was a connection, but she couldn't figure it out just then: suddenly she, too, was so tired that all she wanted was to drift off...

Confused, deliciously sated, she fell asleep, thinking of connections large and small, and miracles of all sizes.

CHAPTER 14

There was no discussion about whether they'd be together again; there was no doubt on either side. It was agreed that whatever time Beau could spend away from his work, he would spend with her. They didn't need to discuss whether she would spend every night in his bed. It was what they both hungered for.

Shamelessly, Amanda arranged to get the next three nights away from the switchboard, cajoling other girls to cover for her, reminding them unashamedly of favors she'd done for them in the past, making excuses, ruthlessly freeing herself from any obligation that could get in the way of her being with Beau. Where once she had routinely stayed late, now she was competing with Cherry to see who could clock out first. She would rush home, shower and change, and meet Beau at whatever out-of-the-way restaurant he suggested, the better to keep their relationship unnoticed.

He spent most of every day closeted with Hattie, trying to come up with something good enough to satisfy the agency people, and sometimes lunched with the creative team from the agency. He deliberately broke off all other social engagements, claiming work as an excuse. And it was true that as the days ticked down, he was becoming more and more worried about producing a lyric that would satisfy them. So far, nothing had.

On the second night after they returned from Connecticut, Beau was late to their rendezvous at a French bistro he liked on First Avenue. Amanda, rushing in five minutes late herself, almost laughed when she saw the traditional red and white checked tablecloths, which looked lacquered onto small round tables. The candles in wine bottles on each table were corny and old-fashioned. The lighting was dim to non-existent. She was the only customer.

It could hardly be called elegant dining, but she smiled as she realized that, elegant or not, the past few days had been the most romantic period of her life. It didn't matter what they did or where they went; the setting meant nothing. Being with Beau meant all.

She was just thinking that in these few days, she'd finally been experiencing the fulfillment of those many promises the nighttime had given her for so many years, when Beau hurried in behind her. She hadn't noticed, but it was starting to rain, and his jacket and hair were wet. The scent of his distinctive cologne clung to him.

He kissed her lightly on her right temple. "Hello. Sorry I'm late. More agency nonsense."

She was still shy about being affectionate with him in public, but she gave him a look from her glowing eyes that he could interpret for himself. When their eyes met, it was as though flashbulbs went off all over the room.

For a minute, his smile wavered. Then he stepped back and tried to assume a jaunty tone. "Hungry?"

They sat down at a booth in the darkest corner. Whenever possible, he preferred being close to her; booths were infinitely more desirable than tables, and dim ones were even better. He touched her fingers lightly beneath the table and looked at the hand-printed menu on the table while she looked at him, feeling desire well up in every cell of her being.

How did he do it? How, just by being in the same room with her and breathing, did he bring all her senses to a state of quivering expectation?

He looked up when he felt her eyes on him. "Well? Are you actually going to eat tonight? Or do I get to watch you push the food around on your plate again? That's *so* entertaining."

She laughed, but she couldn't help it; when she was with him she just didn't feel hungry... not for food, anyway. He, on the other hand, ate heartily and enjoyed it, though she had noticed surprise on the faces of the servers who knew him, when he refused a second glass of wine. She wondered if he had ever drunk heavily; when they were together, he never had more than one.

Instead of the middle-aged, blowsy waitress she half-expected, a six-foot dark-haired waiter in trim jacket and beautifully pressed slacks appeared promptly with a smile. "Welcome, good evening. It is a pleasure to serve you." He rattled off the dinner specials in a distinct accent which sounded more Italian than French. Neither of them paid attention.

Beau asked for a bottle of their top red wine; the waiter agreed it was an excellent choice and left to get it. They were alone again in the dining room.

Beau dropped his hand on top of hers. Just thinking about touching her soft fingers could start an earthquake of desire in him, and he was thinking of it entirely too often, especially in agency meetings. It seemed to be all he could concentrate on. At this rate, he'd never finish the damn lyric.

He caressed her hand under the table and watched her swallow, the gray eyes growing enormous in her thin face even as he himself began to grow warm. "So... what do you want?"

She turned her face up to his. The smile had fled from her eyes. Even in the dim light, he could see the urgency in them. "You *know* what I want."

He laughed. "I meant for dinner!"

But then she edged closer to him on the cracked leather seat, and the laughter died in his throat as he breathed in the delicate scent of her and held her eyes with his own. His fingers, which had been moving so lightly on her hand, now brushed accidentally against her thigh.

She stiffened, but never took her eyes off him. He could see a flush blossoming in her cheeks, and a pulse began to beat in his throat and spread down the length of his body. The warmth became heat. The heat became molten.

He moved his hand up her outer thigh, deliberately pushing his fingers under her skirt. She was wearing pantyhose, but he could feel her body heat underneath. He began to harden so quickly he didn't think he'd be able to move.

"You're driving me crazy," she whispered, leaning into his questing fingers. Then, with a sudden quick movement, she twisted toward him, so his hand was no longer at her side but between her legs, and the teasing abruptly became urgent.

He couldn't get at the wet warmth of her, not with the pantyhose and the table, and he made a sound of frustration. Yet they were both so maddened by lust, they couldn't sit there much longer without relief.

He withdrew his hand and pulled her skirt down. She looked up at him, mutely disappointed. He shook his head. "Let's go before the waiter gets back." At once, the flush came back into her face. Her eyelids were half-closed and her mouth half-open, which for some reason was making him even crazier.

He dropped a bill on the table and hurriedly, on trembling legs, they stumbled out of the booth and out of the bistro, where the streets were gleaming wet but the rain had stopped.

"Where's your car?" She didn't think she could wait till they got back to the hotel.

"I took a cab. I didn't want to bother parking." But the urgency in his face and his upraised arm must have been visible, because almost at once, a yellow cab swerved to the sidewalk and stopped with a screech.

She climbed in as he gave quick directions to the driver, of which all she could hear was "Hurry!"

They said nothing on the short drive but nestled together, his lips urgently taking hers, his hand pushing under her coat and blouse and into her bra, where he cupped her breast and caressed her nipple. Amanda thought she would faint before they got upstairs. She could feel the heat on her own face burning her, and the answering heat of his as he bent to kiss her mouth deeply, his tongue dancing provocatively until she caught it with her own.

When the cab stopped in front of the hotel, she got out first, leaving him to pay the cabbie, and hurried to the side entrance, where she let herself in quietly with a passkey and hoped no one would be lingering in the hallways. It was just after nine, but the lobby could still be crowded, and with her clothes in disarray and her hair and makeup mussed, she didn't want to run into anyone. It was better to use the side door, which led straight to the conference rooms in back.

Rather than take the elevator, she darted up six flights of stairs to his room, fortunately meeting no one on the way, and closed the door hastily behind her, kicking off her shoes and pulling off her coat. Her fingers were shaking so badly she could hardly manage the buttons on her blouse, but by the time Beau opened the door, she was down to her skirt and bra and wildly excited.

He threw her on the bed, kicking off his own shoes and shrugging out of his own coat, falling on top of her as she wrapped her legs around him. He pulled off her bra and skirt and tried to peel off her pantyhose, but he was so ravenous, his hands so unsteady, that he couldn't manage it, and she finally rolled away from him, lay back on the bed and pushed off her hose and panties, flinging them over the side with trembling fingers.

He was hurriedly discarding his own shirt and pants at the same time, and they came together in a flailing mass of arms and legs, his hand finally between her thighs, his fingers deep in the blazing wet heat of her as she opened her legs willingly to him and urged him inside her.

This time there was no linkage of hearts and souls, no teasing, no preparation. There was just the mindless, age-old instinct of bodies merging and melting together, driving each other to unbelievable heights of physical rapture. He pounded inside her, plumbing to her very depths, holding nothing back, his hands rough and urgent, pulling her hard against him. He never thought to wonder if he was hurting her. She cried out, but it was a strangled cry of pure pleasure and demand; she didn't care about anything but having him as deeply in her as he could be, touching all of her.

It seemed like hours that they rolled together, making muffled sounds neither heard because their mouths were glued together. Then the quaking started inside and spread outward, until they were both shuddering with an explosive release. Every quiver of one set off the other again, and it was several long minutes before they felt the final shiver and fell on their backs, sticky, spent and completely fulfilled.

For a few minutes, there was complete silence as their hoarse breathing slowed and quieted. Beau thought he was going to die of exhaustion right there, after the best sex of his life. *What better time to die?* he thought with an inner smile. Life didn't get more perfect than what they'd just had.

He wondered if she had experienced it the same way. He had been very gentle and considerate with her during their first two nights, thought of her comfort every moment. This was different: quick and selfish and coarse, yet infinitely satisfying. He hoped she had loved it—but loving it would expose an earthy side he hadn't yet discovered in her, if it even existed. He hoped fervently that it did.

With a great effort, he turned his head to look at her. She wore a smile like a cat lapping cream. He raised his eyebrows, mutely asking the question.

She leaned toward him to kiss his mouth and said softly, "Wow."

***

She was so exhausted she hardly registered it when he slipped out of bed in the middle of the night and quietly turned on the tiny lamp over the desk. She made a protesting sound deep in her throat, but when he said, "Go back to sleep, honey", she flopped over on her side. She was awake only long enough to notice that he was sitting in the desk chair, his pencil racing across a pad of yellow legal paper.

When she woke at 7:00 the next morning in his bed, she thought she might have dreamed the whole episode. The thought of the hot sweaty lust of the night before seemed incredible in the clean, calm morning light. But clearly it had happened; the crumpled heap of clothes thrown on the floor— his shirt and pants, her blouse and panties—were mute testimony that they had been anything but calm. Once, the thought of what they had done might have made her blush; this morning, it made her grin.

As she was picking up her discarded pantyhose, she noticed a page of yellow paper crumpled on the carpet. Curious, she reached down to pick it up.

He had balled the paper so tightly—like a clenched fist—that it was hard to read the scrawled lines on it; his pencil had raced across the page and the tight crumples in it ran down and through the words, blurring the almost-illegible letters even more. Still, once she smoothed it out, she could pick out the phrases jerkily.

She read through it once, and her mouth began to turn up in a smile. After she read it through a second time, she began to sing it aloud, making up a melody to go with the scrawled lyric. The words tasted wonderful on her tongue, and she sang it twice, just for the fun of it.

She hadn't heard the water in the shower stop running some time before, nor the soft footsteps padding behind her, until he said in her ear, "You sound pretty good."

She almost jumped then. "Oh!"

She turned. He was smiling, a thick white towel knotted around his waist. Droplets of water sparkled on his shoulders and neck; he must have come out of the bathroom without drying off when he heard her singing.

They looked at each other, and Amanda knew the night before had been no dream. The lust in his eyes now was the same as it had been last night, and fired an equal lust in her; it made her want to roll back onto the bed and open her legs for him again, right now. She couldn't believe how abandoned she had been, and how close to abandonment she felt right now.

Then his eye fell on the paper in her hand, and the lust faded from his face, replaced by irritation. "Another of my rejects, I see."

"Why did you throw this away?" she asked. "It's darling. It's everything you said they wanted."

"Which is why they're sure to hate it. I know it. Come on, throw it away." He started to take the paper from her, but she held onto it.

"No! I can't believe they'd hate this. You have to show it to them."

He grimaced. "I'm telling you, they'd hate it. They'd probably make me stay another full week writing even more useless garbage. Please, throw it away."

She tilted her head at him, a saucy smile growing on her lips, but the look in her eyes was hopeful. "You think they'd really insist on your staying another week?" Her hand reached softly for his cool skin; she began to caress the side of his neck very gently.

He drew her so close she could feel the rough texture of the towel between them, until he pulled it off and threw it aside, drawing her naked body even closer between his legs. She could feel herself beginning to melt toward him, her body tingling from his touch—

Until the phone rang.

They both groaned. But he grabbed for it anyway. "Yes?"

"Beau," Hattie said, "they've moved up the time of our meeting to 11:30. They want the new lyric by then." She paused, and then, not very hopefully: "Have you got anything?"

"Damn it!" He had just a few hours to come up with something else, and if he spent those hours the way he wanted to—with Amanda—he wouldn't have time to write anything. Besides, he really was out of ideas; he'd hoped for another session with Hattie where they could hash things out again, and something might inspire him. But instead of a 4:00 meeting with time to prepare, he now had one in mid-morning, and he didn't feel prepared at all.

"I'll come up with something," he told Hattie, trying to sound confident. "At least we know they already like the music. And how about speeding it up? Make it sound brighter."

Hattie sounded doubtful. "You think that'll make a difference?"

"To these bozos, yes. You just concentrate on playing very up-tempo, and I'll do the rest. Meet you there, okay?"

He hung up and turned to Amanda. Her hair was mussed and her eyes were shining; her skin seemed to radiate softness. He wanted the next hours alone with her, but he couldn't. He just couldn't. The professional in him raised the stick to his shoulder. He didn't miss deadlines, not for anything.

"I'm sorry, honey," he said, trying to keep his voice even. "They've re-scheduled the meeting for 11:30, and I'm just not ready. I've got to go back to work."

"You do not have to go back to work." She was advancing on him slowly, opening her arms so he could see her fully, see the beautiful breasts and the patches of red on her skin where he had grabbed her. He held his head back, trying to resist. "You have a wonderful lyric that's just perfect for that jingle. Take it to the meeting."

He groaned again, this time impatiently. "Mandy, I can't. The truth is, it hardly even mentions the product. It's just a silly song about a feeling, with little to no name recognition. It's a perfect example of how *not* to write a commercial."

"I don't care. I love it. I bet they'll love it too." She came closer, her hips began to wiggle suggestively, her eyelids closing halfway. For a girl who had been inexperienced, he thought, she sure knew how to vamp when the time was right. He was getting harder and harder, and without the towel covering him, she knew it, too.

She threw herself against him, spreading her legs so he could slip his hand between them. "Mandy, no!" he gasped, half-strangling. "I've got to go back to work."

"Show it to them... " she murmured, and then her arms locked around his neck and he was lost.

***

The first thing he saw when he'd finished singing the jingle was the smiles.

"Again," said the vice president, his usually gloomy face looking as though it might crack. He wasn't exactly smiling, but Beau thought he detected some upward movement of his mouth, and he was definitely tapping his fingers on the piano.

The others were beaming.

Hattie started it up again, and she'd never sounded more up-tempo. At Beau's suggestion, she was playing it twice as fast as before, and energy was flowing through the room.

Beau stood by the piano, using his best eye contact, and sold the song as he'd never tried to sell anything else:

"Snap— when the air feels so crisp and clear
Snap! Snap! All the glory of the morning's here—

It's a day when my life can't help but go just right—
From the gold-capped dawn through the moon-kissed night—
The glow in my heart feels so golden bright –

Snap, snap! What a day lies ahead!"

He sang both verses, proud of the interior rhyme he'd managed to work into the second verse, though he wasn't sure anyone else noticed. But when he stopped, the account executive all but leaped onto the piano herself. "I love this. I mean, I *really* love this."

Beau was startled. It wasn't like an account executive—one who intended to keep her job, anyway—to render an opinion before the client. But either she didn't care or she had extraordinary ESP, or maybe she was just betting on a sure thing, because anyone could see the client was grinning from ear to ear.

"Terrific," he said. "And I hate popular songs." He paused. "You know what it reminds me of? Remember that campaign song they wrote for JFK?"

"You mean *'High Hopes'*?" Beau asked.

"That's it. That's what this reminds me of—just a great, good-time tune people won't be able to get out of their heads."

Sure. It was a good-time tune now, *after* he'd put a perfect lyric to it and forced Hattie to speed it up. He didn't bother to mention that *"High Hopes"* had been a hit movie song before Frank Sinatra ever sang it for Jack Kennedy. To tell the truth, he was feeling too good at the almost tangible feeling of bonhomie in the room. It worked, and he knew it.

The meeting went at Mach speed after that. No one had any creative changes to offer; as one grateful executive said, it was so perfect that tampering with a word of it might drain all the magic out. Well, he was glad.

He was grateful to Amanda, too, who'd rescued the lyric from limbo and insisted he show it to them, even though he wondered how much she'd really liked it and how much she just wanted to take him back to bed. He began to flush, just thinking of those lovely hours with her, and hastily shook himself back to attention. He was a professional. If this was the last meeting, let him leave these people with a good impression.

There was talk about recording dates, and as a perfunctory courtesy, an invitation to Beau and Hattie to turn up to watch their creation being sung by professionals. Hattie said she thought she'd be able to make it; Beau declined politely, excusing himself with a fictional deadline in L.A. He couldn't get away from these people fast enough, and please God, let their check not bounce. If all went well, they would launch it in early January. Depending on the reaction, they might even ramp things up by buying spots during the Super Bowl. Expensive, but worth it, everyone agreed. Beau didn't care. He hoped they'd find good voices to sing it, people with good diction, who felt some obligation to the sense of the lyric. It shouldn't matter to him now. His job was finished.

Unlike the previous meetings, this one ended with sincere, hard-pumping handshakes, big smiles and genuine thanks. He accepted them as gracefully as he could, murmuring all the right things: how glad... he really hoped... best of luck... love to work with them again... (he shuddered inwardly as he mouthed that one).

On the street at last, he felt a sense of overwhelming relief, tinged with a strange sadness. He didn't understand it. The job he'd never wanted was finished, to everyone's satisfaction, and the final check was on its way.

He was going home tomorrow. Thank God. Thank God.

But the November afternoon *was* golden bright, just as his lyric said, the breeze just cool enough. New York looked to him like a fairy tale come to life.

Then the sadness rose higher inside him, choking out his appreciation of the golden afternoon.

He was going home. And leaving Amanda.

***

Over dinner at her favorite Chinese restaurant, Amanda's face was too bright, her smile too wide. She crowed with delight at the news of the afternoon. He'd not given her enough credit; her happiness over their reaction to his lyric was overwhelming. It hadn't been a rush to bed that prompted her enthusiasm this morning, but a genuine recognition of how good the lyric really was. Reluctantly, in his mind, he awarded her points for knowing what he himself didn't even recognize, and for her bubbling, incandescent joy, which was raising his own happiness level higher.

He couldn't help comparing her excitement with Jean's usual dry acceptance. It wasn't fair, though, it really wasn't, he told himself conscientiously, because Jean had had years of similar news from him; this was Amanda's first exposure to it. Still, the gray eyes were luminous, following his intently as he told her.

"I told you!" she cried. "I knew they'd love it. I told you it was wonderful."

"Yes, you did. Ten points for you." He smiled at her, oddly touched by her undiluted happiness. Then he added deliberately, "Of course that means I go home tomorrow."

Some of the joy faded from her face. "Yes, I thought so." She lowered her head, dipped her spoon in her tea, and fiddled with it. She raised the spoon toward her mouth and put it back in the cup. She stirred the tea, studying it intently.

"Mandy."

She didn't lift her head.

"Mandy." He waited. She continued to eye the teacup. "Look at me."

Reluctantly, she raised her head. The shine in the gray eyes had been replaced by wariness. She looked as though she expected him to kick her; he couldn't imagine why. "Let's make tonight as special as we can, and remember it until I come back."

The smile that came forth from her then was much more real than the one she'd brought to dinner. "I brought you a present," he said impulsively, "to remember me by until—well, the next time."

He brought up a paper bag and laid it on the table. It was from his favorite small bookstore in Greenwich Village. As she stared at it, her heart began to pound harder.

"Open it," he coaxed her.

With trembling hands she reached into the bag and drew out the tissue-wrapped bundle inside.

The gift was a small book bound in red, the cover faded, the dust jacket chipped a little on the bottom but otherwise in perfect shape.

Words for All Occasions.

Her very own copy.

She sat looking at it, turning it over in her hands, saying nothing.

"Open it," he said eagerly. "Look at the flyleaf."

She did. He'd written in a fresh inscription: "To Amanda--Who loves my words—With love, Beau."

"Well? What's wrong?"

She raised her head slowly, blinked away the shine of tears, and tried to wisecrack. "I'm just disappointed. I wanted the revised edition, with the new jingle in it."

He was disturbed to see the tears she'd managed to hide so quickly. "If I'd known you'd get this upset," he joked, "I'd have bought you a mink coat instead."

She tried to smile back, but he saw her fingers close protectively on the book, as though she was afraid he would take it back.

It meant that much to her.

It had never meant that much to anyone—except him.

They had been lovers for three days and he felt more contented with her—and more intimate—than he could remember ever feeling with anyone. He could say and be anything; she accepted it all. She accepted *him*, imperfect as he was. It was the most comforting feeling he'd ever known with a woman.

Very gently she replaced the book in the bag and folded it over carefully. "Thank you," she said softly, but the shine in her eyes seemed suddenly reflected all over the restaurant, so everything was unexpectedly brighter.

"Well. What would you like to do now?" He braced himself for anything—a visit to a nightclub, window-shopping on Fifth Avenue. He'd prefer to take her straight to bed, but this was her night. Whatever she wanted, he'd do. He just wanted to be with her.

She looked up at him fiercely, and all thought of joking fled his mind. "Let's go back to your room," she whispered.

"Why not your apartment?" He said it lightly but insistently. He'd wanted to come to her home, to see where she lived and what she surrounded herself with. Somehow, she'd always resisted.

Now she resisted again, her eyes darting around the restaurant, avoiding his. "I haven't cleaned in a week. It's a mess."

"I don't care. I want to see where you live. And it's not like you have a roommate we'd be walking in on." He'd ascertained that the morning after their first night.

"No."

"Then why won't you let me come? Are you afraid I'll judge you and find you wanting?"

She couldn't say what she really felt; it would sound so silly and childlike. But somehow, bringing him to her apartment—though it would keep them from the prying eyes at the hotel—would signal that they were no longer on neutral ground. It wouldn't be as romantic. It wouldn't be as magical.

She wasn't ready to give that up, and with one evening left to them, she didn't want to.

He had cupped her face with his hand; his thumb was stroking her soft cheek. And when she raised her eyes reluctantly to his, she found his had softened. "Okay," he said quietly. "Never mind. We'll do that next time."

Her heart lurched a little at the thought of a next time, and she smiled.

"So what will we do with the rest of tonight?" he asked again.

"Let's go back to your room," she said. "*Now.*"

***

He woke before the alarm went off. He'd set it for 4:30, so she could slip out unseen and go home to change clothes. They'd already arranged that she'd be at the desk when he left at 10:00 to catch a noon flight at JFK; they could say their final goodbyes innocuously, which he thought was best. No chance of tears or overwrought emotion.

He looked at her, lying beside him, and suddenly knew she was awake.

"How long have you been up?"

She shrugged into his chest. "Hmm. All night, I suppose."

He massaged the soft skin of her back gently. "You'll fall asleep at the desk."

"Better there than here," she said, and kissed him full on the mouth. He tried to resist for a moment but could not, his body coming awake and hardening at her touch. She kissed him again, holding him to her fiercely, before letting him go gently. In a minute he heard the shower running in the bathroom, and he lay back on the pillows until she reappeared.

He watched as she dressed swiftly and picked up her purse. "You'll be at the desk when I leave, won't you?" he asked, already feeling oddly bereft.

She smiled. "I'll be there. Though there are things I can't do in public—" Swiftly she caressed him, from his tousled hair down to his thighs, her fingertips igniting a trail of fire.

He debated momentarily whether to roll her back onto the bed and decided regretfully that they didn't have time. Instead, he drew her close to him, her soft blouse brushing his naked skin tantalizingly. He put his arms tightly around her and stroked her hair, looking down into the soft gray eyes.

There was really nothing more to say. He knew he was coming back. She knew it, too. He tried to think of the right words to say goodbye. He had a wild impulse to say *I love you*, but resisted it mightily. Where had that come from?

She made it simple, kissing him lightly on the mouth, brushing back his hair with two fingers, and then shrugging out of his embrace. "Better get going. I'll see you at checkout."

She stroked a hand over his hair one last time. He caught her hand and kissed it.

***

Jerry had taken him for a final, effusive breakfast in the coffee shop at 8:30, but begged off immediately afterward, claiming an urgent meeting uptown with new linen suppliers. A girl with a halo of wild curls around her head checked him out at the front desk, hardly looking at him. He'd returned the rental car to a midtown rental agency the day before and would take a cab to the airport: less hassle with rental clerks and a few more minutes with Amanda.

Checkout went swiftly and efficiently. Beau turned in his room key, received his itemized bill, signed where he was asked to.

Amanda materialized behind her, smiling professionally. "Hope you had a pleasant stay." Her eyes were dancing.

His were, too, he was sure. "Very pleasant, thank you. I'll recommend this to my friends. Such wonderful, personal service."

She smiled back at him. "We aim to please."

But instead of just nodding goodbye, she found herself taking his briefcase briskly and motioning to one of the bellhops to take his bag. The three paraded across the crowded lobby and out to the sidewalk, where the bellhop stowed the suitcase in a waiting cab and Amanda gave back the briefcase. The cabbie waited for him to slide in.

Beau held out a bill to the bellhop, who took it with a word of thanks and disappeared. He turned to look at Amanda, at the sun shining through her soft hair, the trim cut of her suit jacket, the smile on her lips.

God, he was going to miss her. He had a sudden, overwhelming urge to take her in his arms again. "Thanks for everything," he managed to say.

She smiled. "You're very welcome."

He looked at her. The ache to hold her was getting stronger, but the cabbie was already looking at them curiously in his rear-view mirror. He wanted an excuse to linger next to her for another minute and remembered something that he had wanted to ask her the day before. "Will you get in trouble for this?" She looked at him curiously, and he fumbled, trying to explain. "For—you know—fraternizing with a guest?"

Her smile became mischievous. "Jerry never mentioned it to me. I don't plan to publicize it, either."

"But you'll be here when I come back?"

She looked pointedly at her watch. "You'll miss your plane."

He got in the cab then. He didn't smile, but gave her a jaunty half-salute as the cab peeled out.

She smiled and waved until the taxi was out of sight, and thought, *So this is love.*

PART TWO

CHAPTER 15

December 1982—February 1983

As he flew west for the first two hours, Beau's mind had yearned east, remembering the sunbeams floating through Amanda's hair as they said goodbye. God, he missed her already. He could still feel the softness of her fingers entwined with his, the warmth of her lips and the twist of his heart when she smiled her final farewell.

But now, apart from her and flying closer to home every minute, he realized it was wrong, almost unbelievable. A girl less than half his age! What was he thinking?

A part of him didn't care, and longed for her unashamedly. The other, saner part of his mind scolded him. *What's the matter with you? How could you let things go that far? You don't do things like this!*

That part of his mind deliberately refused to remember the soaring delight of being with her. He stood back and looked at himself as he looked at other men who got involved with much younger women, to validate their fading manhood or flaunt a trophy in front of other men, and he was ashamed.

This was what other men did.

This was not what he did.

Yet this was also the first time he could remember traveling without Jean that he hadn't worried about her being alone. Of course, they were both older now; at this point, he wouldn't expect her to pick up a young stud in a bar the minute his back was turned. It seemed especially unlikely given how little interest she'd evinced in sex in the last few years. Most of her energy, as far as he knew, was focused on her responsibilities at the store and playing tennis at their club three days a week.

Still, he should have been eaten up by the usual anxieties, the never-ending catalog of wild possibilities she could have tried. He knew from bitter experience that she had tried everything, and he had to try to anticipate what she would do and prevent it. It was as ingrained a habit as buying cigarettes. Yet he'd hardly thought of her at all on this trip, other than his dutiful phone calls home. All his worries had melted away, for a short time.

It was a welcome respite, he reluctantly acknowledged. But that didn't mean he himself was blameless—or that the stupid, stupid thing he'd done was somehow excusable.

She isn't like most girls her age, he defended himself. *There was more between us than just sex. I have a right to feel the way she makes me feel—alive and excited and full of possibilities again.*

Beau held on to that thought as the plane flew west and touched down. He held on to it as he fought through the hordes of busy travelers to catch his bags off the luggage carousel. He held on to it as he found a cab and started home to Brentwood.

He held on to it until he walked into his house and found that Jean had tried to commit suicide.

***

He didn't realize till the cab was in his driveway and he was fumbling at his wallet that he didn't have enough cash on him to pay the fare. He was about twelve dollars short—had fares gone up in a week?—but he always kept around a hundred dollars in emergency cash in the house.

"Sorry," he told the driver. "I've got the rest inside. Give me just a minute." The cabbie shrugged and let him take his suitcases out of the cab. No way would a New York cabbie do that, but L.A. was more laid back.

He dropped his bags just inside the door and called to Jean that he was home. He didn't get an answer, though her car was parked next to the cab and the front door was unlocked, as it always was when he returned home from a trip. "Jean?" he called again, going into his bedroom. The extra cash was rolled up in an old sock in his underwear drawer. He got it and had started toward the front door when he happened to look toward Jean's bedroom down the hall.

The door was open and he caught a glimpse of something on the floor…

Without consciously knowing what was driving his heart rate up, he dropped the money and began to run.

Jean was lying on her side on the floor, fully dressed. An overturned water glass lay by her hand. She was perfectly made up and her hair was beautifully coiffed, but her skin was chalky and cold, and there was something dribbling from the side of her mouth…

"Hey!" he shouted, running to the cabbie still lolling in the front seat of his cab. "I need help here! Get us to the hospital, quick!"

Even in L.A., cabbies can be galvanized into action. This one saw Beau running out with Jean in his arms and threw the car into gear. They were at the hospital in 15 minutes. Beau hardly registered the moment when the cab stopped in front of the emergency room; he was already running inside with Jean in his arms, shouting for help.

***

Hours went by.

After the first rush of action, Beau was shunted off to the waiting room while doctors and nurses worked on Jean. A doctor came out to tell him she had overdosed on prescription sleeping pills, "probably accidentally," he added kindly. Beau knew it was no accident.

If it had been, why had she taken the pills just before he was due home? It was only 3:00 in the afternoon; why would she need to sleep then?

Oh, no. He had plenty of time to think this out as he paced up and down the tiny waiting room with its cheap uncomfortable chairs and small inconvenient ashtrays. She had done this to punish him, to frighten him (*she'd done a damn good job*, he thought grimly), to demand his attention. She had been breathing when he saw her in the bedroom; unless his flight had been unduly delayed, she wasn't in much danger of drifting away. She'd probably even phoned the airline to be sure his plane had landed before swallowing the pills.

And though he realized all that, he was still terrified.

She'd never tried to kill herself before.

Maybe she was segueing from her old habits to something new. It was certainly self-destructive, as her sexual escapades were. It was frightening; it was degrading. The doctors questioned him kindly but firmly after they got her stabilized and told him she would be fine, they'd managed to pump out her stomach in time. She'd need a couple of days to rest, and then they strongly recommended that she look into some kind of therapy.

He told them with great agitation that he had never known her to do something like this, that he couldn't imagine why she'd done it. And even as he spoke the words in a rush of sincerity, his heart sank into his stomach.

Could she somehow have known about Amanda?

Was that why she'd done it?

Oh, God.

He considered it when he was finally left alone in the waiting room. The place stank of cigarette ashes and body odor, and Beau, who had been smoking steadily since he first walked in, discovered late in the afternoon that he'd smoked an entire pack in about an hour and a half.

Did Jean know about Amanda?

He didn't think it was possible. How could she have found out? He himself hadn't really known what was happening between them until it happened, a bolt of lightning from a clear sky.

But if somehow Jean found out, or suspected... well, if she did, he was directly responsible for her actions. He didn't care what the stupid shrinks said.

His legs almost gave way under him as he thought about it. Suddenly, his feelings of happiness with Amanda turned rancid.

How could he have been so selfish?

***

They finally let him see Jean when she woke. He'd waited for four hours, jet lag and fear warring inside him. When he was told he could talk to her, he jumped up, but his legs trembled under him as he walked into the cool, sterile room. She was lying on her side, her eyes half-open, looking at nothing, when he came in anxiously. She didn't turn her head. She didn't speak.

"Hi," he said.

"I'm really sorry," she said. She didn't look at him.

"I'm just glad I got home in time." He couldn't think of anything else to say. There were things he wanted to scream at her: *Why did you do it? Why did you scare me half to death? What was the point?* But he couldn't say them now. The doctor had warned him to keep the talk brief and casual.

And now, in two seconds, he'd run out of conversation.

Jean seemed to sense this. She shifted slowly and laboriously onto her back. He sprang forward to adjust the sheet for her, and his sudden movement seemed to frighten her; she drew back, her eyes suddenly wide and blazing, the veins in her neck distended.

He stepped back, shocked at the fear in her face. "What's wrong?"

She breathed hard for a moment, looking at him. "Nothing. I thought—" Her voice died away.

He was taken aback. In all their years together, he'd never once raised a hand to her. Why, all of a sudden, was she afraid of him?

He'd grabbed up her prescription bottle on the way out of the house and knew she'd swallowed almost a hundred pills, but even more horrifying than that was the feeling he had that all their years together, all their shared experiences and common interests, seemed to add up to nothing. Now, facing him after one of the most traumatic events of their marriage, she seemed like a stranger.

It was one of the bleakest moments he had ever known.

He struggled to snap out of it and at the same time say something non-threatening. "I guess you could use some sleep."

She managed a wintry smile. "That's why I took the pills. Nobody here seemed to think it was a good idea."

He tried to smile back. "Well, the idea is to wake up again."

"I'm sorry, Beau."

That was all she would say. He stayed another two hours, watching her and making uncomfortable conversation, but she just said the same thing over and over. When he finally got wearily home alone, the drama and guilt and fear had drained him. He fell exhausted into bed and never once thought of calling Amanda.

***

Amanda hadn't stopped smiling in the three days since Beau left, even though she hadn't yet heard from him. He was probably insanely busy, that's all. He would call any time now. Nothing could dim her happiness, or her conviction that he would be back.

She caught the phone on the first ring and combed through her mail every day, but she also told herself sternly that she had a job and couldn't afford to moon around. She tried to focus on the hotel and also called her coach to resume voice lessons. She was glad to be busy. But somehow it seemed that a lot of the joy had gone out of the music for her.

She missed him so much it was beginning to alarm her. She wondered when he would call. It wasn't an adequate substitute for being with him, but right now she'd settle for it gladly. Just hearing his voice would lift her spirits.

She wanted to sign up for more night shifts at the hotel, hoping to intercept his call, but Jerry was out of town for a long weekend and needed her to spell him during the day. So she went home at five and badgered the operators for messages in the morning. There weren't any for her.

Then something curious happened.

She went up to the seventh floor to search for a lost earring for a guest. Room 704, down the hall from the search area, was still vacant. Though they had a respectable number of bookings, the hotel wasn't full, and Amanda couldn't quite bring herself to put another guest in that room, not yet; she still thought of it as Beau's room. Now she thought about him while she scanned the carpet for the missing earring.

Suddenly she detected a distinctive, faintly familiar odor. She stopped and sniffed. This wasn't the smell of the hotel's cleaning products. It smelled like... a man's cologne.

She looked up and down the empty hall. All the doors in the hallway were quietly closed. She listened. There were no sounds from the elevator, so no one had passed by in the last few minutes.

She sighed. She did love the women on the cleaning crew, but they did such a sloppy job when they thought they could get away with it. This should have been noticed and sprayed away. A lot of guests had allergies to perfumes and colognes. She had talked to the crew supervisor about air freshness before. Now she really had to crack down.

She used her passkey to get into 704 and called down to the desk.

Cherry answered. Amanda told her, "Send Lola up to Seven, will you?"

She sniffed the room: the scent of cologne was overwhelming. Lucky she *hadn't* put anyone in here; they'd have been screaming about it.

Lola, the heavyset head housekeeper, lumbered off the elevator a few minutes later. Her thick, shiny brown hair was tucked neatly under a net. Her blue uniform was clean and starched. Her thick lips broke into a smile when she saw Amanda, who had come into the hall to meet her.

"How are you today, Miss Amanda?"

"Fine, Lola. But we have a problem."

Lola looked around the hallway. "Here in the hall?"

"Smell."

Obediently, Lola sniffed. She sniffed again, uncomprehendingly. "Yes?"

"Lola, that cologne! Why didn't one of your girls spray disinfectant here?"

Lola's back straightened. "Seven is Judy, one of my best girls. She always sprays."

"Then she needs to spray again!"

"Spray for what, Miss Amanda?" Now Lola was becoming exasperated. "I don't smell a thing."

"That's ridiculous." The scent was filling all of Amanda's senses, and she realized in a heart-splitting second that it was the scent Beau used. *That* was why it smelled familiar. She tried not to sound exasperated. "Lola, it's all over the hall. Can't you smell a man's cologne?"

Lola lifted her head and sniffed ostentatiously. "I don't smell nothin'. Just air. *Clean* air," she emphasized, glaring at Amanda. "Now, can I go back to work? I have a new girl today. I shouldn't leave her alone too long."

Amanda couldn't believe it. How could Lola not smell it? The scent was so overwhelming it was giving her a headache. Lola didn't usually dissemble; still, she wanted another opinion. "Wait a minute," she said. She opened 704 again to use the phone and walked into what felt like a wall of cologne. "Come in here, Lola!"

Lola came in, her brow furrowed. Amanda wheeled on her. "I suppose you don't smell that either?"

Lola raised her hands to heaven. "Smell what? There's nothin' here!"

Grimly, Amanda dialed down to the desk. "Cherry? Send up a staff member to Seven... I don't care. Anybody with a nose... Thanks."

They waited in the hallway in silence until the elevator doors opened and Greg got off. He was one of the newer bellboys, a bright young guy with a ready smile who worked hard, had nice manners and picked up plenty of tips. Already guests were requesting him by name, and Amanda was relieved to see him. He was sharp; one of Jerry's better hires. He'd pick it up at once.

He smiled genially as he came up to her. "Can I help?"

"Breathe in," Amanda instructed him. "Breathe deeply."

Mystified, Greg did as he was told. He looked inquiringly at her. "What do you smell?" Amanda asked.

Greg exchanged a look with Lola. "Well... nothing. Am I supposed to?"

"Are you sure? Try again!"

Greg did it again, shook his head. "Sorry. Still nothing."

"Come in here." Amanda led the way to 704, which she'd left open. "It's really strong in here."

Greg tried again, closing his eyes, taking a deep noisy breath and letting it out slowly. After a minute he opened his eyes and shook his head again. "I don't know what I'm supposed to smell, Amanda."

"You see?" Lola's mouth, usually smiling, was a grim line. "There *is* nothing, Miss Amanda. We both smell nothing."

"But—" Amanda felt she could drown in it. And nobody else smelled it?

"Maybe you have allergies or something," Greg suggested uncomfortably.

"Or maybe you're just tired," Lola muttered.

Amanda's head snapped around to look at her. Had she seen Amanda with Beau?

But Lola didn't look sly or accusing, just motherly. "Too many nights on the switchboard—you should think about cutting back your hours. You're so tired you're starting to smell things. Now, may I *please* go?"

Amanda couldn't believe her senses were picking up something no one else noticed. Stubbornly, she followed Lola and Greg to the elevators. "Lola— send Judy back up here. I want this hallway and room 704 thoroughly sprayed."

Lola didn't argue. Defeated, she gave a tiny nod. "She's on Ten by now but I'll ask her to come and spray. *Again.*"

They both knew there was really no point.

***

Why hadn't he called?

Amanda didn't let herself ask the question until five days had gone by. She deliberately kept herself busier than usual, not allowing herself time to doubt—or to sit by the phone. Watched pots never boil, right?

Still, there were no calls, no notes. Nothing. She told herself he had jet lag or had gotten busy on a new assignment. She told herself a lot of things, while trying to push back the uneasiness that was overtaking her.

Finally, after a week had passed, she faced the nagging voice in the back of her mind. He was married. He had made no secret of it. Obviously, when he got back to L.A., his marriage had taken precedence over this sudden, silly infatuation. The fact that she found it breathtaking, overwhelming and wondrous, was her reaction, not his. For all she knew, this kind of thing happened to him all the time.

She told herself quick affairs were no big deal, that she was making a lot more out of it than he was, and that he had never promised her anything. He hadn't even told her when he planned to be back. And when he did, what made her think he'd want to spend time with her?

It didn't help her growing doubts that Josie breezed into town from Chicago and insisted on meeting her for dinner. As usual, she was wearing a hodge-podge collection of mismatched clothes and faddish jewelry that somehow fell into completely right lines on her. As usual, she was full of stories about her glamorous job at the Stock Exchange in the Loop, the many boyfriends vying for her attention and how frantic her life was. Amanda listened and said little about her own life. She could hardly get a word in edgewise. That was usual, too.

But her earlier exuberance had not quite been quenched, and when she thought of Beau, her heart still quickened. During a break in Josie's usual rattling on about herself, Amanda said tentatively, "I met someone at the hotel."

"You? You *met* someone? Another Steven, I suppose." Josie giggled and refilled her wineglass. She'd ordered a half bottle and was polishing off most of it herself. She had made no bones about her disdain for Steven during the one and only dinner they'd had together. Steven found her shallow, self-absorbed and egocentric; Josie thought he was boring, too introspective (what kind of man needed to think?) and not nearly attractive enough to interest her. She told Amanda when they broke up that she was better off.

Amanda flushed. "I meant—someone interesting. Sort of a celebrity."

"Oh, please. There's no such thing as 'sort of' a celebrity. You're either famous or you're not." But Josie looked at her narrowly; it wasn't like her little sister to upstage her, and she didn't like it. "Who is it?"

"Remember that Broadway show record Mom used to play for us, years ago? *The Life and Times*? I loved the songs on it. You broke it," Amanda added, partly to jog Josie's memory and partly because she felt angry all over again when she thought about it. Josie's carelessness had deprived her of years of enjoyment. It was the first time she could remember that she had ever deliberately provoked Josie.

Josie's pretty nose wrinkled. "No, I don't remember." She added spitefully, "And if I broke it, I'm sure I didn't mean to, but it couldn't be all that important. Mom never let me near anything she really valued."

Amanda was silent at that, until Josie said, "Well, what's your point?"

"The guy who wrote the lyrics for that show stays at the Lorelei whenever he's in town. He and Jerry are old army buddies, and—"

Josie hooted. "Old army buddies? You mean your boss and this guy are the same age? That means he's about a hundred years old! Jeez, Amanda, can't you find a guy your own age?"

Amanda flushed. "I didn't mean I—that's not what I meant when I said he was interesting!"

"And he couldn't be a celebrity," Josie went on, "because who ever heard of a song lyricist being famous?"

"All right, Josie!" Amanda said sharply. "I get the point!"

There wasn't much conversation after that. Josie was startled and faintly unsettled that her little sister was asserting herself; that was a first. Amanda resented feeling the way she always felt around Josie—inadequate and uninteresting. She knew that her fleeting impulse to confide in her sister was something to suppress at once. Josie was decidedly the wrong person to trust with this.

She told herself to calm down and wait until he called... whenever that might be.

***

The buzz about the Snap jingle started slowly, ten days after he came home, and when it did, he was unaware of it. He was back to the sleepless nights and endless anxiety that came from watching over Jean without seeming to. He had told himself that his first impulse was the right one: *Let Amanda go.* There was no place for him in her life. The disappointment of that decision made him sleep even less.

But one sleepless night he finally got what he'd hoped for: a knockout idea for a new musical.

Amanda's anecdotes about the Lorelei contained the kernel. In trying not to think about her (and not to phone her), he had hit upon the stories she had told him as a way to think of her without really thinking of her. And one night, staring at the ceiling and straining to hear any untoward sounds from Jean's room, he realized the vein of rich romantic irony and lyricism he could tap into by expanding on those stories.

The next morning, he phoned Jules and laid it out for him in a white-hot burst, telling him first about the history of the Lorelei and the stories it inspired. "An old-fashioned hotel—set it in both the present and the past—with the ghosts of old guests and hotel personnel and the stories interlocking. Romance, tragedy, and a happy ending for the current lovers, though the past lovers had to die or go their separate ways. Of course it depends on the stories and characters themselves, and how we develop them... "

When Jules finally managed to untangle the various threads of Beau's inspiration, he said slowly, "That's not bad. It's a little like *Grand Hotel*. You might really have the start of something."

Beau was hardly listening. He was mentally off and running, the firecrackers going off in his head as he pictured it all. Tie together the story of the little duchess and the modern lovers who sneak in and out, never meeting their own spouses—add in some comic relief—and a score full of romantic, melodic songs—what a show it could be!

He was so hyped up and talking in such rapid cascades of words that Jules was having trouble sorting it all out. Finally, he broke in. "Look, can you write something down? A short outline, or something?"

"I'll have it by tomorrow." He meant it. He was so fired up that he would sit all night at the typewriter getting it right. He hadn't felt so excited about anything in years. Maybe decades.

"Good," Jules said. "Come over tomorrow at 10. Let's get started."

Beau couldn't remember the last time Jules had been so interested in anything that he wanted to get going this fast. For a creative guy, he was unusually placid, even phlegmatic. "What about that movie score you're writing?"

"Come over at 10," Jules repeated. "This is important."

I got to him, Beau thought in satisfaction. If Jules could be moved to such excitement, his white-hot idea was better than even he had thought. Two hours later he was so busy typing he didn't hear the phone ring.

Jean knocked lightly on his door. "Jim," she called.

He didn't hear her.

She knocked again. "Hey, did you hear me? It's Jim calling."

The ideas, storylines, and bits of lyrics were racing through his head at such warp speed, he was having trouble getting them all down on paper. He continued typing furiously.

Jean stuck her head inside, her tone now unmistakably irritated. "Beau!

Telephone!"

"Take a message." He never looked up from the typewriter.

"It's Jim. He says it's urgent."

"Jesus!" He slammed a hand on the desk and turned on the phone by his desk, which he routinely turned off when he was working on something important. Without preliminary, his eyes still on the page in the typewriter, he said, "What, Jim?"

"Hey, buddy, how are ya?"

"Busy," Beau said in a tone of finality. "What's up?"

Jim recognized that genius was burning and gave it to him straight. "Good news on the commercial."

Beau was so absorbed in the ideas flowing through his fingers that for a minute he couldn't think what Jim was talking about. He hardly listened as Jim launched into an enthusiastic account of his conversation with the ad-agency president.

"They're nuts about the jingle, Beau. I mean crazy, over-the-moon nuts. They were originally going to use a five-piece band to record it, but Len told me now they're using a full orchestra instead. They're really highlighting it, trying to make it as memorable as possible, *and* the company's changed their ad concept to sixty-second spots instead of thirty, just so they could run the song longer."

"Sixty seconds?" Beau's mind was only half on the conversation. He was penciling lyrics swiftly across his notebook while still typing with one hand, trying to keep the whirling, fluttering bits of words from dancing off, out of his reach. They were so perfect, even if they were still just fragments. His heart was thudding and his mind was soaring. This one was a winner. He could feel it.

"Hey, don't you get it?" Now Jim sounded impatient. He'd called with the best possible news, and his client hardly appeared to be paying attention. "They're going to repeat the song *twice* in the ad, *and* they've bought spots at the Super Bowl—talk about exposure—but that isn't the half of it! Renny Marks heard about it and he wants to record it!"

Beau surfaced slowly, as he captured the last elusive pieces of lyric and put down his pencil. He wouldn't lose them now; he'd caught them in his scrawls on the page. He half-heard Jim's last words and repeated them carefully, wondering if he had heard correctly. "Renny Marks?"

Renny Marks was *the* singer of songs. He could sing anything—torch songs, beautiful ballads, but also comic songs with tongue-twisters. He rivaled Danny Kaye for personality, comic touches and silly accents, and Sinatra for his interpretation of smoky love songs. His body, short and squat, didn't match his soaring baritone, nor did his ugly face with its sour expression, but it didn't matter; Renny Marks could sell a song like no one else. Beau had wanted to work with him years ago; his agent said Marks had been too busy.

"What about Renny Marks?"

"Good, you're finally listening. Somebody sent him a tape from the agency; don't ask me how or who. But he loves it and wants to record it on his next album."

"You mean the Snap jingle?" Jim's words, unexpected as they were, suddenly registered with Beau. He stopped fiddling with his pencil. "He wants to record a *commercial jingle* as a song on his album?"

"Yeah, well, he says it sounds like a song to him, and he wants it."

Beau stared at the phone as though Jim had reported that Martians were landing. He couldn't believe it. That silly little lyric Amanda had rescued from the garbage had caught the attention of one of the premier singers in the country?

Unbelievable.

Come to think of it, it was all unbelievable—and it all seemed to be happening at once: the idea for the new musical, the wonderful lyrics he could already hear in his head, Jules' excitement, Jim's report... he couldn't remember a single day of his life that had ever brought more good news, career-wise.

And it had all sprung from one source.

Unbidden, his mind went back to New York.

He had told himself it was over, that he was not going to continue this silly infatuation, that the right thing to do was turn his back on her, cut off all contact, just let it die. It would hurt her less in the long run if she thought he was an unprincipled bastard, and he could feel benevolent about setting her free to find someone who could offer her his full attention and commitment. He would at least have given her that much, after all she'd given him.

But he had to tell her. He knew she'd love to hear it. And it just wouldn't be right that so many wonderful things were happening to him—all of which had started with her—and she didn't even know about them. She *deserved* to hear it, and from him.

He told himself it was simply common courtesy that made him pick up the phone that night to call the Lorelei.

***

When the line buzzed at 2:00, she didn't even realize it was an outside call. The sudden temperature drop must have prompted a lot of insomnia, because she found herself talking to more guests than usual. When she saw the red light blinking out of the corner of her eye, she snapped it down without consciously registering its origin, though she automatically gave the correct greeting for outside calls. "Good evening. The Lorelei."

"Hello there." It was him.

"Oh... hi!" She was so glad to hear his voice again. Her heart began to thud hard in her chest. *See?* she told herself. *He* did *finally get around to it.*

"I suppose you're wondering why I haven't called."

"Uh—well—" If she'd learned anything from Josie, it was that men liked girls who didn't appear too eager. She'd always been too eager with Steven, too pleased at his attention to do otherwise. It certainly hadn't worked. She tried to seem blasé now. "I've been so busy, I hadn't noticed."

The chuckle at the other end told her she needn't have bothered. She smiled into the receiver. "Well, I might have wondered a little."

"In between all those things which kept you busy."

"Right." Both of them could hear the smiles through the phone; the chemistry and sense of connection were as strong as ever.

He cleared his throat. "I know I should have called. I wanted to. I've been busy, too."

"An old man like you? What could be keeping you busy—putting your teeth in and finding your cane? Maybe rushing to those senior specials at Denny's?"

"You really are a brat," he said, but he sounded pleased. "You might be interested to know that it involves you."

He told her about the jingle, the Super Bowl spot, and Renny Marks. She hung on every word, and when he finished, her voice seemed to bounce through the phone. "I knew it! Oh, I knew it was a great lyric! How fantastic!"

He couldn't remember anyone, even one of his collaborators, being so excited over his career. It made his own excitement ratchet up even higher, but he tried to sound sensible and mature, even as he laughed with pleasure at her euphoria. "Oh, and there's more." He'd almost forgotten this, but it was really the most important thing.

He'd never discussed creative ideas for his musicals with anyone except his collaborators. Even Jean heard only the barest outline of his thoughts, until he had them securely down on paper; it was an old superstition he clung to, that telling a story to someone else would insure that it never got down on the page. Yet without a qualm, he told Amanda all about his idea for a musical set in a hotel like the Lorelei.

She listened avidly, and when he had finished, said, "That's fabulous," and he could hear that she meant it.

He smiled; his heart was soaring at the sound of her approval. "Well, you deserve all the credit, you and those stories of yours. They're what gave me the idea in the first place."

There was a silence on the other end of the line. After a moment he prodded her. "Hey? You still there?"

He heard what sounded like a sniff. "You have a cold?"

"No… "

Then he understood, and it sent a pang right through his heart. And though they stayed on the phone for another hour, he wasn't about to tell her that when he heard the sound of her happy tears, a tear rose to his eye, too.

***

"Today's Sunday," Jean said to him a week later.

They were sitting at the kitchen table, poring over the newspapers. Beau as usual was deep in the theatrical section; she was reading the sale ads, but he caught her words and looked up. "So?"

"Well—don't you want to visit Ben? You know he looks forward to seeing you."

He tried to sound casual. "I'd rather stay with you." He'd been very careful since her return from the hospital, aware that he needed to be kind and encouraging, always smiling brightly whenever he spoke to her. The effort had been draining.

"Oh, go on." Jean sounded petulant. "You've been hovering over me since I got home. Didn't you think I'd notice? It's getting really boring. And you don't have to worry; I'm not going to do anything stupid."

"Do you want to come?" He still felt uncomfortable at the thought of leaving her.

"Don't be ridiculous. Ben and I are like oil and water. When have we ever gotten along? He's your friend; go spend some time with him."

He looked uncertainly at her. He did want to see Ben; he wanted to tell him all the good news about the jingle, though whether that was a kindness was anyone's guess. This would have been Ben's assignment, if not for the cancer. On the other hand, Ben had passed it on to him, and he'd always had a generous spirit. *He would* want *to know what had happened*, Beau told himself. *It would be mean* not *to tell him.*

But he still didn't feel right about leaving Jean, and her pouting didn't reassure him at all. She'd sounded this normal many times, and several times he'd felt reassured and left her. Then when he came home, all hell had broken loose. He remembered the phone call from jail twenty years ago… she'd been picked up for soliciting a cop in a hotel lounge… God, what a nightmare that had been.

She began to gather the discarded newspapers into a stack. "Go on. I promise I'll be here when you get back, just like always. Go tell Ben all the good news so he can feel bad and you can feel guilty."

"What?" Now he was beginning to get hot under the collar. *Careful*, he told himself. *She's still in a fragile state.* But when had she not been?

"Well, you do want to tell him, don't you? And maybe take a few bows? And if he hadn't gotten sick, it would have been his good news."

"The lyric that started it all was mine!" Now he *was* feeling steamed, and couldn't stop himself. "Ben couldn't have written it. It's my lyric that did it all."

She shrugged. "Fine. Tell him that. I'm sure it'll make him feel a lot better."

He shut his mouth firmly before he could say anything further, wheeled and left the kitchen. The truth was, the way he was feeling, it was safer visiting Ben than staying with Jean. And God knows he'd enjoy it more.

***

It was one of Ben's good days, though the nurse warned that Ben was too tired even for a short walk. But he was jauntily dressed in a dark jacket, white shirt and slacks, a silk ascot tied around his knobby throat, and he sat in a wooden chair in his garden, next to a round table with a large green umbrella stuck in a pole in the center. His pale blue eyes were alert and sparkling. Beau told the nurse he'd take over for her and joined Ben on the lawn, where a sliver of weak sunlight was trying to peek through a slow-moving mass of thick gray cloud. It didn't help; even in southern California, you could tell it was close to Christmas.

Ben hardly waited until Beau sat down. "Well?" he demanded. "How did it go?"

Beau told him. He tried to stifle the pride in his voice when he explained that Renny Marks was going to record the Snap jingle as a cut on his new album. Ben, squinting sharply at him, pursed his lips so hard that his cheeks were pinched. "Congratulations," he said shortly.

Give the devil her due; Jean was right. Beau did feel guilty. But he couldn't think at that moment of anything he could say to alleviate the tension. So he said nothing.

Ben fiddled with his ascot. Beau watched him uneasily. Just when he began to think it would be wise to offer an apology and make a quick exit, Ben coughed and looked up at him. "Damn cigarettes," was all he said.

Beau looked uncertainly at Ben and started to rise.

"Oh, stop it!" Ben snapped at him. "I won't throw you out, even if you did steal my thunder. What the hell, I knew who I was recommending... you could at least tell me the details!"

He had permission to gloat. Beau smiled and sat down again, relaxing for the first time since he'd arrived; Ben's spirit was intact. Ben peppered him with questions about the size of the orchestra for the jingle recording, the recording date ("You mean you won't be there? Are you crazy?"), the airdates of the commercial (Beau didn't like to admit he hadn't thought to ask), and plenty of inquiries about the use of the jingle in the Super Bowl. Ben admitted grudgingly that though he'd written jingles for fifteen years after his Broadway career was over, he'd never written one that had appeared on the Super Bowl.

Beau was surprised at his tone; he sounded as eager and admiring as an apprentice songwriter, almost as admiring as a fan. Ben, the consummate Broadway insider, sounded like an excited... amateur. It disturbed Beau to see someone he had looked up to professionally behaving this way. The world felt out of whack.

Ben was so taken with the news about the Snap jingle, Beau almost forgot to mention his idea for the new show, but when he did, Ben nodded approvingly at his description.

As he watched Ben's wizened head bobbing up and down, Beau thought of Jean's bitter remark earlier: *If he hadn't gotten sick, it would have been* his *good news.*

He'd resented it when she said it, but he had to admit now, looking at Ben trying to smile, that she was right. *Maybe his jingle wouldn't have grabbed them the way mine did, but... Ben was one of the bona fide geniuses in the business. He probably could have done just as well, if not better.*

Somewhere deep inside, though, he knew the show idea could never have come to Ben, because Ben would never have stayed at the Lorelei, would never have met Amanda. And meeting her had set off this blaze of creativity. He had Ben to thank for that indirectly, as well.

That thought made him distinctly uncomfortable.

To cover his embarrassment, Beau said, "I brought a few of the songs I started for the score. Just sketches, really—" He didn't know why he was doing it—he never let anyone see his work in progress—but it was the only thing he could think to offer Ben for all the man had given him, knowingly and unknowingly. He laid the hastily-scratched lyric sheets in Ben's lap.

Ben held them in his lap without looking at them. He studied Beau for a long time, then reached over to the table for a pitcher of water. "Want some?" he asked Beau. Beau shook his head and bit back an offer to pour it for him.

Ben poured cool clear water, not too steadily, into a clear plastic cup, and set down the pitcher with an involuntary sigh, as though it were heavy. Beau fidgeted, wanting him to hurry and read the pages. Ben sipped slowly from the cup until it was empty. Only then did he read unhurriedly through the yellow sheets, nodding at a word here and there.

He finished and laid the sheets in his lap. His mouth was pursed thoughtfully. He was quiet for a long time. He seemed to be wondering how to say something.

Finally, he looked directly at Beau, and his eyes were speculative, and a little surprised. "This is good," he said. "Really good. Like your old stuff."

"Thanks. It felt good writing it."

Abruptly, the pale eyes intent on Beau, Ben said, "What's Jean doing these days?"

Beau was completely taken aback. Ben's inquiries about Jean were always perfunctory. In fact, he never mentioned her name if he could avoid it. Why of all times was he asking about her now? And why did he look at Beau so intently as he asked?

Beau opened his mouth to make a conventional reply, and was startled to hear himself say, "She's not too well. She—um—just came out of the hospital."

It was Ben's turn to say nothing. He gazed up at Beau and gave a short nod. Feeling cornered, Beau gave a quick, superficial account... an accidental overdose... lucky he got home so quickly... all was well now. He had never breathed a word of his wife's 'condition' (as he thought of it) to anyone else. Jean's behavior had forced him into a pattern of lies and evasions that was too deeply ingrained to change. To save what was left of his pride, he had learned to avoid the whole truth, even with his closest friends.

Ben nodded once or twice, looking troubled, then fell silent. After a few minutes, he said, "Sorry. Bad luck. Fact is, I thought you were looking... extremely well... and the lyrics sounded so much like the old you... romantic, sentimental... I just thought you two might be having a sort of... " he coughed, "well—a second honeymoon."

"Oh." Beau flushed. Was it that obvious? Were his feelings for Amanda actually making him look... better? Quickly, he said, "No, we've been taking it easy, until the doctors are sure she's fully... " He trailed off because he thought the more he said, the more Ben would guess. He couldn't stand it if Ben offered *him* sympathy.

Ben looked at him again. The faded blue eyes narrowed. The short stubby fingers tapped together. After a few minutes, not looking at Beau, he said, "When I was still married to my second wife, I got called in to do a quickie rewrite on a musical that was in trouble. *Up and Down the Ladder.*"

"I think I remember it."

"Well, you'd be the only one, then. I think it lasted a week, even though I put in a month on it, 20-hour days. What the hell, I was burning cash in those days—Gigi spent money in her sleep—and I took all the extra work I could get. The pay was good, and they promised to keep my name off the credits." He smiled grimly.

Beau waited for the punch line. What was Ben's point?

Ben looked away from him again. "There was an assistant stage manager, nice girl, not much to look at among all those gorgeous showgirls, and you know me, I liked the lookers—but whenever I needed help, she was there. And since I needed help a lot, we spent a lot of time together." He paused for a second. "Long story short, I fell hard for her. Huge mess. Gigi sued me for everything I had and left, telling everyone we knew I was a bastard. Most of 'em believed her."

"And the girl?" Now Beau knew why Ben was telling him this.

"Oh." Ben looked away from the lawn and finally met his eyes. "She and I had a long romantic honeymoon, of sorts. Wouldn't marry me, though; said she wanted her own career and didn't want to be tied down. But you know something? Even though she was twenty years younger and a helluva lot smarter than me, she was the only one who ever really loved me." He paused. "And I loved her. That's the only honest measure I have of what real love is."

"How long... ?" Beau began.

"Oh, we had about two years together. I was broke, of course, after Gigi took me to the cleaners. Just when I wanted to spend a fortune on someone! But it didn't matter to Lindsey. I took a small place in the mid-60s, and she moved in with me. God, we had fun. They were the best years of my life. Hers too, I think."

"And then she left."

Ben smiled, a lopsided smile. "Well, she got a job in Europe—Artistic Director at some theater in the Eastern bloc, something—I can't remember now. But it was exactly what she wanted. I had just gotten a movie job in L.A. that I couldn't afford to turn down. We both knew what it meant. She cried harder than I did, and I cried plenty."

Beau couldn't think how to ask what he really wanted to know, but Ben saw it in his face. "Go on, Kellogg, say it. Don't be such a wuss."

So Beau blurted out, "Was it worth it?"

Over the years, he had seen Ben in many moods, the leprechaun-like face mirroring all kinds of pleasures and sorrows. But never before had he seen such luminous joy in Ben's face. The flinty eyes softened, and the smile was no longer grim but real, and young, and passionately certain. "Oh, yeah. Worth anything. Those two years—in fact, every minute from the day I met her— are the only memories I care about. The best work I ever did, I did in those two years. Not surprising; Lindsey was my biggest fan." He said her name so softly, as though blowing a delicate bubble he wanted to preserve. "If anyone remembers a single word I ever wrote after I die, it'll be from those two years. I can't regret that it wasn't forever. Most people never even find it. Or if they do, they act conventional and stupid and let it slip away."

The next question was harder. "Did you ever—see her again?"

"Oh, she called a lot at first. I called her. Six-hour calls, sometimes." Beau thought of his endless conversations with Amanda. But Ben was going on, his eyes on the scudding gray clouds overhead. A cold wind was starting to blow. "Then... well, she got busier, and the time difference was tough; it was hard to talk when we were both able to. Long-distance relationships are hell." He was silent for a moment. "And I started to think, who am I to ask for paradise forever when all the other poor slobs never get it? By the time she came to L.A. on business, two years later, I was married again."

He gave a shrug that was eloquent. He didn't need to say more. And Beau didn't mention it again.

They talked in desultory fashion for another twenty minutes; then Ben began to look pale and tired, the nurse came out with a wheelchair, and Beau rose to go.

Ben handed him back the scribbled-over sheets. "Keep at it. You've got something there. And come back and show me more as you write it."

Beau nodded and stuffed them in his pocket.

"Well, ready for a nap?" the nurse said to Ben cheerfully. He nodded, the grumpy mask drawing down on his face again. Beau wondered if he had imagined the shining happiness in Ben's face a few minutes before, but he doubted it. The words were still ringing with conviction in Beau's mind.

He and the nurse helped Ben into the wheelchair and settled him under a blanket; the December chill was more apparent now than earlier, when they'd sat in the warmth of the sun.

As the nurse took the handles of the wheelchair and started toward the house, Beau called, "Ben!" Ben turned his head.

Trying not to say anything that would enlighten the nurse, Beau said, "Thanks."

Ben nodded. The radiant smile was gone, and his face was serious. "Just don't be stupid, and let it go," he said. "No matter how long you have... it's worth it."

Beau left feeling shaken, and wondered how soon he could call Amanda.

CHAPTER 16

Dinner with Jean was silent—as usual after he'd spent a day with Ben—and whether it was the fresh air in the garden or just the satisfaction of the work rolling along once more, he was very sleepy by 9:30 and in bed before 10. For the first time since he'd returned home, he fell into a deep, dreamless, unworried sleep that for once lasted all night.

It was just as well, because the phone by his bedside buzzed before 6:00 the next morning. He peered at it and at the clock, wondering who could be calling in the middle of the night. Usually he made it a point never to pick up calls before 9:00. But he felt refreshed and reasonably alert, so at last he reached out a hand to the receiver.

"Beau!" a deep male voice boomed at him. "Hey—good to hear your voice!"

Beau stared at the phone.

The voice didn't wait for him. "How's the smog out there? Still too thick to see the starlets through?" The voice subsided from a boom to a chuckle at its own wit.

But that smooth basso profundo did sound familiar... Beau rubbed a hand over the stubble on his face and wondered whether to hang up before or after he found out who was calling.

"Beau! Hey, you there?"

Beau settled for saying, "Yes. And you are... ?"

"Hey, Perry Fieldston, pallie. How the hell are ya?"

He should have remembered. Perry had the deepest bass he'd ever heard, even though he was only five foot ten and narrow-chested. Everyone on Broadway lined up to invest in his shows—Perry could always smell a winner—but he never bothered about simple common courtesy or the time difference between coasts. When Perry was excited, he wanted everyone else available right away. And he called everyone 'pallie', a holdover from the 1960s Rat Pack slang that Beau somehow found endearing.

It registered through his surprise that Perry was calling him directly, no secretary getting him on the line first. At—he squinted at the clock on his night table—5:35 a.m., which in New York was just after Perry usually strolled into his office.

Which meant Perry was excited. Something was definitely up. Beau's heart rate, which had been very calm up to that point, suddenly doubled.

He also realized that he could afford to play it cool, so he settled for some small talk, wondering how long Perry would keep him dangling. "Hi, Perry. How are you? It's been a long time."

"Way too long, pallie. I couldn't wait another minute to talk to you."

"I guess not. I don't take a lot of calls at 5:30 in the morning."

"What?" Perry hadn't heard him; he was already thinking of his own agenda, as usual. "Listen, Beau, I heard the song. Fantastic! Really. Your best in years."

Which song? Beau hated to ask. Not when Perry himself—not his stand-in nephew—was panting on the other end of the line. What had he heard? Something Beau had written recently? One of the movie themes? Whatever it was, Perry was excited. He decided to ease into it and hope Perry gave him a clue. "Well, we were pretty pleased with how it turned out."

"I'll say! Renny Marks! You don't fly a lot higher than that. Sinatra, maybe. Or Elvis. 'Course, he's dead." Perry gave a chuckle that sounded like the low end of an organ.

Beau sat up abruptly. His heart was pounding even harder. Perry was calling about the *jingle*. The jingle for Snap! The guy who was notorious for turning off TV and radio when the commercials came on was getting hot over a *jingle*!

God bless you, Amanda, he thought fervently. He stuffed the pillow over the phone for a minute to muffle the sound as he cleared his throat, then put the receiver to his ear again and said, as casually as possible, "I know. Unbelievable."

"You said it, pallie. Listen, I gotta apologize. I was off in Connecticut the day you came in here—hated to miss you." *I'll bet*, Beau thought cynically. But he said nothing as Perry rattled on, his speech getting more hectic by the moment. "That schmuck nephew of mine—listen, you forgive me, don't you? It was a choice between having you meet with Jason or turning you down altogether, and I hated to do that. Old times' sake, if nothing else. You know the door's always open for you at our place."

Beau didn't even bother holding the phone away while he cleared his throat this time; things were going too well. "Thanks, Perry. I appreciate it."

"Listen, Jason's a moron, but you know how it is: if I didn't put him on the payroll, I'd never hear the end of it from his father. And between you and me and the lamppost, Harlan's not much of a producer, but I need another pair of hands around here. And when I tell him *exactly* what to do, sometimes he manages to get it right. You know what I mean, pallie. You go through the same thing. We're surrounded by imbeciles, but somehow, we're supposed to pull rabbits out of hats."

The whole miserable meeting with Jason rose again in Beau's mind—the inane platitudes, the breezy unconcern about his own ignorance, the emphasis on flash and production value over book and songs—and most of all, his own humiliation at how far he'd sunk in the eyes of the Broadway moneymen. A flunky meeting him and giving him the brushoff, when he'd worked with the Fieldstons for twelve years!

And now this call from Perry, which was rapidly draining the sting out of that meeting. For sure, Perry wanted something. Beau waited, leisurely lighting his first cigarette of the day. You couldn't take a better phone call than a producer getting ready to beg. It didn't happen often.

Perry did a ten-minute tirade about the trouble of finding decent help these days (Beau thought of saying, "Why don't you put an ad in the classifieds instead of picking from your own dinner table?" but decided against it). Finally, though, he got to the point.

"Look, you know me. Eternally curious. That's why I'm a producer. I'm always looking for the next great thing. So I have to look everywhere, and okay, that means I have friends [*spies*, Beau silently corrected him] wherever I go.

"So okay, I've been asking around. Heard the jingle at the recording session last night, and I'm telling you, I was impressed. Last commercial jingle I liked was the—what do you call it?—the cigarette commercial with the cowboy, and that was some old movie theme, wasn't it?"

"'*The Magnificent Seven*,'" Beau said automatically. "For Marlboro."

"—Yeah, right." Perry hadn't paused for breath or to register Beau's interruption. "And what the hell, the best commercial jingles were always the cigarette ads, right? They got everyone buying cigarettes! You could never get the damn songs out of your head once you heard them."

Beau looked at the cigarette in his hand and almost laughed. Maybe that was why he was hooked. "I agree, Perry, but most of those songs weren't originals; they were already popular songs by good songwriters that the cigarette companies licensed."

"Same difference." Perry was still steaming ahead. "Look, here's the thing: I called Renny Marks myself after I heard the jingle. He's as excited as I am, and he's recording it in two weeks. Before the holidays, I think. New orchestrations, the works. And I'm telling you, he isn't just show-biz excited, he's *excited* about this song. On the level. *But...* I also asked what else he had on his plate. Guess what?"

Beau could guess, but he let Perry tell him. "What?"

"Nada. Zip. Not a thing. Can you believe it, Renny Marks with an open calendar? Of course, he won't do Vegas anymore—he says he can afford not to, he's got good investments. Good for him, I say. Every time I talk to my broker, I develop a new ulcer."

"Perry... " If he didn't get to the point soon, Beau was afraid he would fall back asleep with a lit cigarette and an open phone line.

"Right, I'm getting there." Perry wasn't Broadway's top producer for nothing; he could hear when creative talent was getting restless. "Point is, Renny would love—not like, but *love*—to do something on Broadway. I told him, sweetie, wouldn't we all, and can you believe it, he bursts out laughing, like I'm kidding."

"I would have laughed too, Perry."

"Yeah, well." He could hear the smile in Perry's voice, an acknowledgement of his own unbroken string of hits. "Look, anyway, I seldom if ever listen to Jason, but when he said he'd met with you I had to ask questions, right? And when he tells me he talked to you about *Cats*—my God—I almost smacked him right there. A 26-year-old schmuck! 'Have you learned nothing?' I bellowed at him. 'You talk to Beau Kellogg about *Cats*, that's like talking to Shakespeare about the Rotary Club play!'"

"I don't think they do plays at the Rotary Club," Beau said, but he was pleased nonetheless. Sure, it was bullshit, but it was a lot sweeter on his ego than his meeting with Jason.

"Listen, you know what I mean. But here's the thing." Perry shifted suddenly from aimless talk to the direct hit. "Renny wants to come back to Broadway in a new vehicle, not a revival, and he's crazy about your little jingle, and Jason did say you and Jules were working on something new—and once in a blue moon, who knows, things fall together, connections are made, and a miracle can happen. Renny on Broadway is money in the bank, and with you and Jules—what can I say, I've got a soft spot for you."

A soft spot? Beau and Jules' last show for Perry had earned him over a million dollars.

"So, on the level," Perry was asking, "whaddaya got?"

In ten seconds, Beau had shifted from being the one in control of the conversation to the one on the spot. How did Perry do it?

But this time, he felt confident. Jules was excited about the new vehicle. Jean had even said admiringly that it was the best idea he'd had since *The Life and Times*. He hadn't seen her so genuinely enthusiastic about his work in years. So he gave Perry a one-minute synopsis of the hotel idea.

Perry didn't hesitate when Beau finished. "Oh, Jesus, that's it! Big, beautiful, romantic—God, I love the old guys—you know what I mean, pallie, I don't mean you're old, I mean you know how to do the classic stuff, the good stuff. I'm gonna throw Jason in a dumpster with his whole collection of Lloyd Webber records—it's where they both belong—listen, when can you come back here with something?"

Beau was back in control again. Negotiation wasn't his specialty, but he knew that the minute someone else started asking questions, he had the power. "Well, look, Perry, I told Jason you guys would have first look—"

"Screw that crap," Perry interrupted. "I don't want to dick around and take a chance on losing out. We're in. Hundred percent financing."

Oh, sweet Jesus, Beau thought, his heart now pounding so hard he thought it would tear through his rib cage. How often had he longed to hear those words? And here they were—a prelude to production money, a guaranteed New York opening, cast albums, Tony Awards—the Fieldstons, for all their pushy manners and Yiddish homilies, always did things right. He felt as though a door that had slammed in his face had suddenly and invitingly opened before he even tapped on it. He had tumbled, like Alice, down the rabbit hole. The sweetness of it was dizzying.

"Hey! Beau! You fall out of bed? C'mon, answer me."

"Uh—yeah," Beau said.

"What?"

"I mean—look, let me talk to Jules and to Jim."

"Jim? You still letting that cheesy guy from Ohio represent you? When are you going to get in with the big boys at the big agencies? I'll introduce you; they'll be thrilled to sign you."

"We'll get back to you, Perry," Beau said, trying to close the conversation.

"Well, look, you got my number? Here, write it down."

"I've got your number. I've had it for years."

"I meant my home number. It's a new place. Croton-on-the-Hudson."

This was serious. Perry didn't give out his home number to librettists, even the ones he'd hired; he mostly tried to avoid talking to them or paying them.

Beau took down the number on the pad he kept at his bedside. Perry repeated it twice and asked Beau to read it back to him. "Take my car number, too. You never know." Beau took that down too. "And listen, Beau, I have nothing against Jim, and I negotiate with everyone, but you and me, we go back a ways. When you're ready to get in touch with me, you call me. Okay? I'll let Jim cross all the T's and dot all the I's, but let's you and me talk it over.

And Jules too. What a talent that guy is."

"He sure is."

"Take your time thinking it over."

"We will."

"Good. Call me tomorrow." Perry hung up.

Beau stared at the phone in his hand for half an hour. He didn't make a move to put the receiver back. He just sat and stared until Jean came in and asked what was wrong; she'd been trying to call the store and couldn't get a dial tone.

It didn't occur to him to tell her. He just put the phone back on the receiver and waited until she'd showered, eaten breakfast and left for work. And then he called Jules, his fingers trembling so hard he could hardly push the telephone keys, and shrieked into the phone that they had a deal, they had a deal... and he kept shrieking it until Jules, roused from his usual calm, was shrieking too.

***

By 2:00 he realized he'd spent the entire day on the telephone. He was exhausted.

His stock had clearly risen, and in less than half a day. Perry Fieldston waking him up, practically forcing Beau to take his private telephone numbers, begging to work with him, Renny Marks phoning an hour later, saying how excited *he* was at the prospect of working with Beau and Jules in a new musical, and wasn't Perry a dear? Various members of the agency's 'creative team' called, raving about the recording session and subtly probing for gossip about the Renny Marks album. Between taking and returning calls, he hardly had time for breakfast.

Jim had called three times. Each time Beau was on the phone and had said apologetically that he'd call right back, and when he finally did return the call, Jim all but leapt on the line.

I don't know what happens when it happens, but it sure does happen fast.

"Listen," Jim said without preamble, "I hate to sound suspicious, but did Perry Fieldston try to hook you up with another agency?"

Beau tried not to sigh. He didn't want to spend a lot of time coddling Jim. He hadn't yet been able to reach Amanda, and he couldn't wait to tell her the news. He was anticipating the joy in her voice when he told her he would almost certainly be returning to New York very soon. He was timing his call for 2:30 (5:30 in New York), to catch her before she left for the day.

Yet for all his impatience, he was glad that suddenly Jim didn't want to lose him as a client.

"Well?" Jim prodded him before Beau could answer. "Didn't he? Perry's notorious for trying to get all his creative people into CAA and ICM, where he still has a lot of power. You know that."

"Yes, and that might be one reason why I never signed with them," Beau said, trying to sound reassuring. "You and I have been together for years. If I'm thinking of going somewhere else, I promise I'll talk to you first. Okay?"

"Thanks. I appreciate it." Jim's voice sounded cautious, as though he'd just discovered a delicate bird (or more likely, a golden goose), which might fly away at any moment if its feathers got ruffled. Then, with no visible transition, his voice shifted into its usual business mode. "Look, I got a couple of other calls about you today. I wasn't sure how you'd want to play this. But the ad agency mentioned you to two other clients of theirs who want to use you."

Beau was genuinely surprised. With all the excitement over Renny Marks and the new show, it hadn't occurred to him that he might be offered more bread-and-butter advertising jobs. His first instinct was to focus on the show and not waste his time doing more jingles. On the other hand, it would take a while to mount the show, and who knew how Snap would go over? Better to have something in hand.

"What are the products?"

Jim named them—a floor wax and a new children's cereal. "Both national campaigns," he added. "The Parker Agency got a real feather in its cap with the Snap jingle—maybe even an Obie Award down the line— and they're playing it to the hilt with their client list. I can ask for the moon and pretty much get it."

He couldn't believe it. This day was turning out to be memorable in all kinds of ways.

Jim told him the accounts were with two different account teams, but they all worked for Parker, and he could structure both deals the same as Snap, at a substantially higher rate. It meant going back to New York sometime soon, though. Did he mind?

He said he didn't mind.

But to Jim's disappointment, Beau didn't want to sit there and throw around figures they would offer Parker. He excused himself hurriedly to make another important call.

"What could be more important than getting this nailed down?" Jim asked, but his client almost hung up on him in his haste.

Jim sighed as he called his secretary Sharon to bring him his telephone call list. "I don't know what happens when it happens," he said to her, "but it sure does happen fast."

***

She had a voice lesson at 7:00, but she couldn't leave her desk while Beau was telling her about Perry Fieldston and his offer to finance the new show. She couldn't just say abruptly, "I'm sorry, I have an appointment", when he was talking about the agency offering him two new ad campaigns and Jim's fear that he might fire him. She couldn't tell him haughtily she was too busy for him—not when he was speculating that he could be back in New York in a matter of weeks.

Besides, she was thrilled.

And though she tried to listen intently to everything he told her, once he said, "I may be back in town sooner than I thought. Maybe even before Christmas," her heart slipped out of her chest and danced up to the ceiling. At least, it felt that way.

***

Since his return to L.A. he hadn't allowed a sleeping pill in the house: too dangerous in case Jean took it into her head to try again. Ditto with alcohol, and he sorely missed his usual red wine nightcap.

But after this remarkable day—capped off by Amanda's ecstatic reaction to all his news—he couldn't sleep. Incredible. He'd started the day at 5:30 in the morning and here he was 21 hours later, unable to shut his eyes but too weary to do anything else.

Finally, too groggy to get up and too hyped up to doze off, he stumbled to the study and sat with the door cracked open so he could hear Jean if she needed him, but closed enough to block out the light of his desk lamp. He looked at his half-finished libretto and couldn't bring himself to do any more at the moment, and the agency work wouldn't come until Jim had finished negotiations.

His eye fell on the stack of mail Jean had placed as usual on his credenza. He hadn't even looked at it; he'd been too busy telephoning.

At this time of year, it was mostly Christmas cards. From Dave, from the Parker Agency (with a big scrawl in blue ink: "Thank you for your wonderful work!"), from Jim. The personal ones, from their friends, would come closer to Christmas Eve.

He looked at the cards, cheerful with gold borders and jeweled red and green ornaments or Santa Clauses, and wondered idly what he could get Amanda for Christmas.

He was aware that such thoughts were counter-productive; hadn't he just started the process of gently separating them? Still, it was the middle of the night, he couldn't sleep, there was nothing on TV and the speculation was at least diverting.

He wasn't going to actually *do* it. It was hypothetical, just a fantasy to pass the time until he felt tired enough to go back to bed. That being established, he settled down to think about it.

Whatever he thought about giving her, he would want it to be good. She deserved it. Something very personal. Something in gold—a watch, maybe, or a string of pearls—nothing too flashy or trendy. She looked good in simple, classic lines. She didn't wear a lot of makeup, so a compact or lipstick case probably wouldn't be right.

The clock ticked over to 4:00, but he still wasn't sleepy.

He thought of how she'd reacted when he gave her *Words for All Occasions*. He'd loved how she'd held it so tenderly, as though it was precious. That had been an inspired choice. It was personal and it would last.

He'd like to give her some of his favorite books. She had a quick mind and appreciative spirit, and they seemed to like the same things. She might enjoy the books he valued most. But it also seemed presumptuous; she might not like any of them and still feel obligated to finish them for his sake.

Besides, she didn't have time to read; she was a budding singer who used her spare time to practice and rehearse. She was busy and committed and young. What could he give her that was personal and unique and would last?

He knew the answer before he finished formulating the thought.

And hypothetical or not, he decided to get started right away.

CHAPTER 17

Jim's negotiations with the Parker Agency dragged out for weeks. By the time he finally finished the deal, there was no chance of Beau's getting to New York before Christmas.

On the other hand, he was getting the most favorable terms he'd ever gotten. With the extra clout of the Snap jingle and the news that Renny Marks was recording the song, Jim was right that he could up the ante considerably.

Beau didn't really mind. From the moment he'd decided on his perfect Christmas gift for Amanda (the hell with hypotheticals!), he'd known he couldn't ease off their relationship as swiftly and simply as he'd first thought. The problem was, he felt deprived without her company. It was a hardship staying away from her, even from a distance of 3,000 miles. So he knew he shouldn't tempt himself further by coming to New York and actually seeing her.

He did feel he had to wish her a Merry Christmas personally. He called ten days before Christmas and managed to sound both friendly and distant when he reached her in the manager's office.

"Hello, how are you?" she said, and her voice sounded warm and inviting. "Merry Christmas."

"Merry Christmas to you. And thank you for... everything."

"You're welcome."

The unspoken question hovered in the air between them. He decided to tackle it head on. "Jim is still negotiating with the agency. I won't be getting back east before January, I don't think."

"That's too bad." She sounded polite and professional, not distressed.

"When your agent is having this much fun squeezing someone, you hate to stop him in the middle. Let him get his jollies; I'll get twice the money and more perks for the next campaigns."

"Sounds wise."

"Plus, you never want your agent to think he's not important."

"God forbid."

He could hear the smile in her voice. Changing the subject, he told a small fib. "I wasn't sure what to get you for Christmas. So for now I'm just sending a card. You'll get your gift later."

There was a pause, and then a softening in her voice. "Well, thank you. I—I got you something, too."

"You did?" He was undeniably pleased; it hadn't occurred to him that she might get him a gift. "You didn't have to."

"I wanted to."

"Well, now I really feel terrible. I guess we'll have to exchange gifts after Christmas."

"Yes, I suppose so." She was back to being polite and friendly.

Suddenly there didn't seem to be much more to say. He had wished her a Merry Christmas, and she seemed to be fine with his not coming to New York for the time being. He was curiously reluctant to end the conversation. "Well—hope you have a good holiday. Tell me Jerry didn't talk you into working on Christmas."

She laughed, sounding lighthearted. "No, no. I'm spending Christmas with my mother and my sister on Long Island."

"Sounds wonderful. Merry Christmas, Amanda."

He hung up the phone feeling cheerful and somewhat relieved. What had he been worried about? She was a very sensible girl.

***

She hung up the phone wishing he'd said something more personal, something to let her know he was thinking about her. Of course, it was hard doing that in his situation. She was convinced the true test of their relationship would come when he returned. She had been thrilled when it seemed that would happen in December, but on reflection, it made sense that things wouldn't move that fast during the holidays.

She was glad she'd acted professional, instead of crying out, "I miss you!" If there was one thing she'd learned early in her life, and learned well, it was that emotional overtures were often not appreciated. In fact, based on her mother's experiences, it was clear that showing any kind of negative emotion—anger, tears, hurt—was a tactic that simply drove people away.

So she had learned to keep all her emotions under wraps. She thought of it as being cagey; you don't want to show someone how much you care early in a relationship. There was time for that later, if they stuck around.

She was happy that he'd even considered giving her a Christmas gift. Just the fact that he wanted to meant that there was *some* feeling on his side.

Christmas was the one real family tradition her mother kept, and this year, for the first time, Amanda felt equal to spending three days on Long Island. Most of that was her confidence that Beau did have feelings for her, though he'd only called twice since he left. For the first time that she could remember, she was going home with the warming belief that someone she cared for deeply cared for her too.

It was fortunate she had that assurance, as the one-two punch of her mother and Josie was enough to severely shake her equilibrium.

On the first day, Josie managed to rip a seam in Amanda's favorite skirt and said her job sounded 'tedious'. When Amanda protested that she loved her job, that it was never boring and always stimulating, her mother chimed in that Josie was entitled to her opinion, though Josie had never once visited the Lorelei or seen Amanda at work.

The second day was Christmas Eve, where Josie and Amanda followed the long-standing tradition of decorating the tiny fake white tree they'd had since childhood. Josie stood it on the little metal table that had served as a play table for both girls in turn, while Amanda carefully unpacked the boxes of old ornaments and handed them to Josie, who hung them carelessly on the withered branches while chattering in detail about her latest romance, which sounded suspiciously like all the others: a handsome, shallow guy who loved to have a pretty girl on his arm, but as soon as she raised the question of involvement, he was gone—that is, unless Josie left first, which she often did. Josie's romances were varied and many, but they all had one thing in common: they started abruptly and sexually, and ended in less than six months. She'd been flitting in and out of such relationships since high school.

Amanda had long since decided that she and Josie were two sides of the same coin: Josie got into situations (they couldn't be called relationships) where she could refine the art of leaving a guy before he left her. Amanda seldom if ever got involved, and when she did, bent over backward not to make waves, so the guy in question wouldn't get angry and abandon her.

Either way, they were each replaying facets of their mother's experience, and she for one was getting tired of it.

Their mother, in between baking fresh strudel and pound cake dusted with confectioner's sugar, checked on their progress every few minutes.

Each time, she had a smile for her curly-haired older daughter and criticism for her younger one, though Amanda was doing more of the work and more efficiently than Josie, another situation that hadn't varied with the years. But when they had finished decorating the tree and were sipping hot chocolate in front of the fireplace, Amanda hesitantly brought up the subject of Beau. She'd debated whether to mention it, but Josie's continual talk about her various boyfriends (though she didn't say much about her job, another bad sign) was beginning to irritate her. All these years, she had had nothing to say in response (Steven had made it clear he didn't like being discussed when he was absent, and of course, she'd acceded to his wishes). Now, finally, she had someone to talk about.

Her mother and sister stared at her when she finished, though she'd left out a great deal and mentioned only Beau's talents and kindness to her. "And so—what? This guy went off to California and you may never see him again?" Josie asked. "That's your idea of smart?"

"Josie—" Amanda began, but her sister broke in.

"Please! You're always telling me I don't know how to conduct a relationship. Sounds like the shoe's on the other foot now!"

Amanda turned to her mother, who was shaking her head. "Amanda," she intoned. "Josie's right. The guy goes off and you hear nothing from him, after you gave him *everything*? This is not the way to play the game!"

Amanda flushed. Her mother's emphasis on old-fashioned values was disconcerting. She had never been promiscuous; Steven and Beau were her only two relationships. For the 1980s, she was practically a nun. But more than her chastity, her mother seemed intent on teaching her to use her virtue as a bargaining chip, something that had always revolted her and that she flatly refused to do. Beau would come to her or not, of his own free will, not because she was luring him with sex.

She tried to explain that to her mother. "It's not like that, Mom," she said. "There were no strings on him. I—I wanted to."

Her mother shook her head. "Everyone *wants* to. The point is to *have* strings. If a man knows you're giving it away, why should he bother to come back? It was too easy the first time!" She pursed her lips. "At least I had that much self-respect, that I didn't give in to your father. Before we were married, I mean. And because he respected me, I could get him to marry me. But asking for nothing in return, that's a big mistake, even for you liberated girls."

"I don't think it's a mistake," Amanda said quietly. For a moment she thought of Beau, at the smile on his face when he made love to her, and her heart lifted. What she felt for him could never be a mistake. "I'm not sorry."

"Hah, not now!" Her mother scoffed. "But wait till you're pregnant and alone—then you'll be sorry you didn't have a way to control him!"

"I'm not pregnant, Mom!" Amanda flared. "And what I'm feeling isn't a mistake!"

She should have known better than to bring this up, even on Christmas

Eve, even when it seemed her mother had set aside petty vindictiveness for a few hours. Her mother's unquenchable rage against her own unhappy life could always be counted on to come back; it was the one constant in her life. The sense that she was entitled to more, that she'd been forced into an untenable position (a paid-for house on Long Island, two healthy, independent adult daughters), was the focus of her unending bitterness, and the topic around which her life revolved, the engine which drove her from day to day.

The rest of the holiday, all 24 hours of it, was unbearable.

Again and again her mother brought up the subject of Amanda's 'mistake', trying to get her to understand how stupid she'd been for getting involved. Amanda, trying to defend herself, said Beau wasn't like anyone she'd ever known, and she was happy she'd met him, a line that her mother attacked, both head-on and subtly, unendingly.

She constantly reviewed how terrible Amanda would feel when Beau decided he'd had enough. "One day he'll walk out of your life, and pow! No more man. No more life as you've known it. Because he's fed up. Because you wore the wrong color that day. Who knows why they leave? And then what will you have?"

"And what if he doesn't, Mom?" Amanda said on Christmas afternoon, finally driven to want to hit back. "What if it turns out he loves me?"

"Oh, and you think this is a good idea? A man his age and a girl your age? How in God's name would you build a life together?"

"It's been done!" She didn't go any further because she remembered Beau's warning her that he would never leave his wife. She couldn't bring herself to spin a fantasy, even to placate her mother, that he would really come to her unencumbered.

Her mother seized on this. "You think he'll ask to marry you?"

"We haven't talked about marriage!" Amanda shouted. "We've hardly even gotten to know each other! Give this a chance to grow into something more... something we'll both want to commit to!"

"You really think that, Amanda? Do you? Then you're a lot stupider than I ever thought. Book smart isn't the only kind there is, you know. There's common sense; there's understanding people. And your beloved Beau sounds like a selfish, self-centered man who wants everything in his life the way *he* wants it. Do you realize while he's spending time with you that he's turning his back on his wedding vows? You think he wouldn't do the same if he somehow pulled himself away and married you? In a heartbeat, he would! He's done it before and he'll just keep on doing it!"

Amanda left the house in Long Island three hours earlier than she'd planned, to get away from the constant nagging, and spent Christmas night riding a train into the city with a huge, throbbing headache. For years, she had seen her mother indulge Josie's on-again, off-again relationships, tell her soothingly everything would be okay, comfort her when Josie's latest relationship went south. *But she doesn't do it with me*, Amanda thought. *The rules are different for me.*

Until Christmas with her mother, Amanda had never really doubted Beau's feelings for her. She knew things would be different when he was at home; she couldn't expect the same open talk and freedom as when they were alone together. But two days of her mother's harping on Beau's shortcomings were damaging. While she didn't really believe her mother—she'd heard the same litany for too many years—it was hard to shake the doubts that were beginning to creep in.

She tried to tell herself there was no point in wondering about Beau's feelings until she saw him again. Only when they could talk freely would she know what was really going on. She resolved to table all doubts until then.

But it wasn't always easy. Her college roommate Doreen came to town and met her after Christmas for brunch and sale shopping. "How was Christmas at home?" she asked, her lanky five-foot-ten-inch frame encased in a new snowsuit and boots.

Amanda shrugged, trying not to show her uncertainty.

Doreen peered at her in the sharp morning light. "Well, come on. What did you get from your mother for Christmas?"

"Same thing I always get. Guilt, rage and a lecture."

CHAPTER 18

The negotiations for the two agency jobs were finally finished in mid-January, with Beau's price almost doubling overnight. The Parker Agency shipped him two enormous product information packages the next day, and he got to work on the new jingles.

Meanwhile, he had worked up the basic framework for the musical: story outline, character sketches and notations of where musical moments were needed. He also filled in the song sketches he had shown Ben and turned them over to Jules, and Jules had four songs finished by the time Beau began the agency work. They were beautiful songs, too, among his best ever. Beau sent the finished songs to Perry on a tape, and had his eardrum almost shattered when Perry called him to crow over them.

He couldn't remember a new year starting so auspiciously.

He just wished he could call the Lorelei as often as he wanted to. But he thought it the better part of wisdom to play things down. Friendship was one thing; anything else was out of the question. Jean had been unusually cheerful of late and working a lot at the boutique, an indication that she was at least temporarily stable. But he knew this was the exception, not the rule, and he would do nothing to disturb her equilibrium and propel her into a new episode. The older he got, the more traumatic they were for him to handle.

Then he had a new flash of inspiration.

Perry, in one of his almost-daily nagging phone calls, mentioned that the character of the hotel itself—the over-arching character of the entire show—seemed too bland, too generic. He wanted something distinctive and specific, something the audience could believe in as they believed in 221B Baker Street in London. He felt without that, the emotional resonance of the entire show was in question. Beau promised he'd sleep on it.

His relief over Jean's continuing progress led to three straight nights of deep, dreamless, refreshing sleep, and on the fourth morning, he woke with the obvious answer: pattern his fictitious hotel after the Lorelei, down to its ambience, furnishings and ghostly history, and even better, publicize the connection between them in all of the show's PR.

Perry almost had an orgasm when Beau suggested it to him.

"A songwriter thinking like a producer—except for Jule Styne there weren't any—God, Beau you've made my day! But will these people cooperate at the—uh—"

"The Lorelei. I think so. The manager is an old army buddy of mine. I stay there whenever I'm in New York."

"What's his name? I'll call him."

"No!" Beau said quickly. "Let me do it. He can be a little—er—touchy, at times. You never know how he's going to react. We don't want to blow this." He paused and added, "It's better to let me handle the whole thing."

"All right, fine." Perry backed away. "You sure you don't mind?"

"Not at all." He was already anticipating a dozen new excuses to call Amanda. And who knew? With the Fieldston people in and out all the time, it could end up boosting her singing career too. He hoped so, anyway.

Jerry was euphoric at the idea of linking the Lorelei to an upcoming first-class Broadway musical production, with all the attendant publicity. Phone calls flew between him and Beau for weeks.

Mrs. Sarandon had approved almost at once, but her terms were tough, and they included discounts on the show's ticket prices for Lorelei hotel guests, something that hadn't occurred to Beau. Her negotiating toughness—along with Jerry's—surprised him. Among other concessions, the Lorelei would offer a standing block of rooms for the producers' use throughout the show's run (for out-of-town VIPs), plus full cooperation between the hotel and show staffs during pre-production. The hotel would promote the show in the lobby and all public areas and on flyers in every guest room, much more so than their standard promotions for other current New York productions. Mrs. Sarandon got her guest ticket discount, credit in the show program and other financial concessions. Beau's favorite of her demands was that any hotel employee who provided musical entertainment to guests in the hotel could sing songs from the show without paying royalties, as long as they mentioned the show.

Perry, after initially balking (Beau suspected it was purely for effect), eventually gave in with grace. More contracts were drawn up, this time between the hotel and the Fieldstons. Beau assured him that he didn't mind the 'entertainment' clause at all, and laughed heartily about it privately. The only one who would sing at the Lorelei was Amanda, and he was warmed at the thought of her singing his new songs. She had inspired them, after all.

More importantly, as a result of his quick move to intervene between the hotel and the Fieldstons, he created an excuse to call the hotel constantly and talk to Amanda. Knowing Jerry, and his dislike of administrative detail and dependence on Amanda, he was sure Jerry would turn over most of the grunt work to her.

During late January and early February, he spoke to her an average of twice a day, and the warmth between them blossomed again. He was careful not to let the talk edge into flirtation, but the chemistry was still undeniable, and it seemed to give a new dimension to this golden time.

He also got something he hadn't expected: Perry was so grateful for Beau's intervention at the Lorelei that Jim persuaded him to grant Beau the title—and salary—of associate producer.

He was now talking constantly to the person he most wanted to talk to—and getting *paid* for it.

***

Ever since Beau's brainstorm led to the linking of the Lorelei and the new show, Amanda's job had become more hectic and demanding. She agreed with Jerry that he needed her for more hours and willingly spent more time at the hotel and curtailed her voice lessons (which were beginning to seem pointless, something she didn't understand).

Jerry also gave her a raise, which he said with a grin was probably overdue. With a higher salary and fewer expenses for coaching and lessons, she found her paycheck finally becoming more than adequate. *It was about time*, she thought happily.

She was now working five days a week, up to ten hours a day, from early morning to late evening. She worked only occasionally on the switchboard at night, which distressed some of the older, regular guests who loved her, but put her in the hotel during its busiest hours, when she was most needed.

As Beau had known, Jerry was temperamentally unsuited to dealing with dozens of tiny details. He had little patience for the precision necessary for a Broadway production, and he preferred creating and implementing strategies for new growth and direction, rather than overseeing the mundane matters that kept things running from day to day.

He was glad to leave the everyday matters to Amanda, which made her the ideal point person for the show. Perry was beginning to talk about staffing up for production, and he brought his own people over several times to go over the building layout and ask bread-and-butter questions about hotel management. Though Jerry always made sure to be on hand when they arrived, to schmooze the production team, they saved their questions for Amanda. She was sure they'd never use a quarter of her answers, but it was exciting to be part of the mounting of a new show and to take a break from her regular duties to work with them. Jerry delegated it to her with relief.

Best of all, she and Beau were talking again, more frequently than ever. Her uneasiness in December was washed away by his constant presence on the phone in January and February, and there wasn't a moment of discord between them. *See, Mom?* she thought more than once. *You were wrong.*

***

In the second week of February, it began to snow. Within days, the city streets were dark with depressing wet slush. It was a far cry from the bright skies and vivid colors of autumn, when Beau had last visited, but Amanda, trudging the icy streets, felt almost as buoyant now as she had been then.

He usually phoned in the early afternoon, New York time. They often didn't have a lot of new business to talk over, but still would spin out a call for half an hour.

At 1:00 on a dingy Thursday, the lobby was crowded with guests, most hesitant to go out in a sudden unpredicted sleet. Everyone was wrapped in warm coats, gloves, hats and boots, and Amanda, returning from the dining room after lunch, saw that the lobby floor was soaked and discolored from the tramping of slushy boots and shoes. She reached for the phone to ask Housekeeping to mop it up.

Instead, the phone rang under her hand. It was her private line. She picked up. "This is Amanda."

"Well, hello." It was Beau.

She glanced at the clock. "Hello! You're early. Something must be up."

"It is." He paused. "The agency finally called about the ad campaigns. They're ready to see what I've done. And Perry and I need to sit down and talk." He paused. "I'm coming back to New York this weekend."

So soon!

Her heart stilled, then began to bang against her ribs until it was almost painful. Dazed, hardly able to process anything except her overriding delight, she took down his request for a double room for Sunday. *Sunday was Valentine's Day.* But she shook off that thought. "For how long?" she asked.

"I'm not sure. I'll probably find out at my first meeting. Can I let you know then?"

"Yes, sure." She hoped it would be a week, at least. She wanted as much time with him as possible, after waiting this long. "How about Room 704?" Her tone turned mischievous.

For a moment there was silence. At length he replied, "Any nice double room is fine."

She refused to read anything into that. "Do you need to rent a car?" If so, she hoped they could sneak off to the inn in Connecticut again.

He hesitated again. "Not this time. I hate driving in snow and ice. I've gotten out of the habit of it."

"I don't usually work on Sundays. Would you like me to be here when you check in?"

This time, the pause was longer. "If you like," he said finally.

Something was wrong. She couldn't ignore it anymore. But before she could ask a question, he yelled something to someone in the background and said hurriedly to her, "Sorry. I've got to go. I've got an appointment in 20 minutes. See you when I get in."

She wanted to say something lighthearted and casual, but before she could think of anything, he had hung up.

***

He didn't call her again before Sunday. He was busy, of course, wrapping up his work and preparing to travel. He thrived on the pace; he hadn't felt so stimulated in years. But even talking to her about the mundane business of making hotel reservations, he'd felt the pull toward her grow stronger again, and automatically tried to extricate himself.

He couldn't do this. Not when he finally had his life in balance once more.

Jean was doing so well. She had finally agreed to go to therapy, if he went with her to appointments and sat in the waiting room, and he couldn't refuse her. She'd been twice and promised to continue while he was away.

His career was more promising than ever—at his age! The Snap jingle had sounded great on Super Bowl Sunday (they'd had a chorus of children sing it, backed by a string-heavy orchestra). Renny's new album would be out in March, with a longer version of the jingle and a great new arrangement. The tape he'd sent was a revelation.

The new ad agency clients were more deferential than anyone he'd worked with in the field; they were glad to work with him and he appreciated his new status. Parker was already hinting at more work coming his way.

No, he wouldn't do anything to mess it up.

He'd managed to keep his conversations with Amanda friendly but not intimate, even if they were still ridiculously long and frequent. He told himself it was just business, and it meant nothing. He was sure he wouldn't have the same reaction to her this time.

It had been a combination of things that led to their intimacy: his standoff with Jean, the humiliation at Jason's hands, irritation with the ad agency, frustration with his own personal writing. Now he was busy, productive and respected.

A quiet voice inside said, *And whose doing was that?* But he refused to acknowledge it. She was a sweet young girl, unusually professional and efficient but otherwise perfectly ordinary. What happened between them before was inexplicable, and something he was vaguely ashamed of. He didn't want to hurt her feelings, of course, but the idea of anything more between them again was impossible.

His life was back on track now. His circumstances had changed significantly. He wouldn't be vulnerable again.

He was absolutely sure of it.

CHAPTER 19

Despite his lukewarm parting words, she intended to be at the hotel when he arrived Sunday.

She threw open her rickety closet door. She should choose one of the simple skirts or dresses she wore to work, but she didn't want to; she wanted to knock his socks off. But with what? She didn't own anything really special or provocative.

Then her eye fell on a tissue-thin long-sleeved scarlet dress with a deep V-neck, one of Josie's cast-offs. It fit her but had never suited her—but everything else she owned was so dull…

It still didn't suit her, closed and zipped up, until she scrounged in her accessories drawer for a long black rope belt that nipped in the waist and tightened the bodice. She looked askance at the gold earrings—were they too blatant? *Love knots*, after all—"Oh, the hell with it!" she said aloud. She didn't have much to choose from. He probably wouldn't even notice.

***

He sank into three inches of slush as he stepped from the taxi in front of the Lorelei. February in New York—no, thank you. He thought of the warm inviting skies in the west and groaned. What was he doing here? Nothing was worth it. As he mentally patted himself on the back for his self-sacrifice, he sneezed.

The lobby, as usual, was five degrees too warm. Jerry always complained about the cold and took special pains to be sure his guests were kept close to broiling. The only way you could get cool air, Beau thought resentfully, was to stay here in the summer, when the air conditioning in the lobby hovered around the temperature of a meat locker. Christ, why had he come back?

Then he saw the vivid flash of scarlet. It was so striking, his eye would have followed it in any case. When he realized that the girl in the slinky dress was Amanda, his pulse sped up. In a moment, everything he had told himself conscientiously back in L.A. had become irrelevant.

All he wanted was to look at her and be with her, and damn it, he knew he couldn't.

His eyes followed her, hypnotized, as she crossed the lobby swiftly, her high heels tapping lightly on the shining floor. She hadn't seen him. He watched her speak to a bellman, hand an envelope to the desk clerk, stop to answer a question from a guest. When she knelt to speak to a little girl who was no more than five, and he saw the shimmer of scarlet slide up her legs, his heart rate tripled.

A bellman spoke to him, and he swung around to answer. When he turned back, he couldn't see her.

Then suddenly she was next to him. "Good afternoon. Have a good flight?"

He fumbled for an answer, but it didn't matter; she wasn't really listening. He noticed her head had lifted higher; her cheeks were slightly flushed. There was a faint scent of cologne in her hair.

When she tilted her face slightly toward him, he thought he was going to grab her right there.

How could he ever have thought he was immune to her?

Without quite looking at him, she led him to the front desk and stood beside him as he registered (for room 704). She didn't move a muscle, and he hardly glanced at her, but he could feel the energy trembling in the air between them.

Then he was registered and the bellman took his bags and rang for the elevator. Beau could feel her breathing quickening and knew she was waiting for him to speak.

"Is Jerry in?"

She looked at him directly now, the brightness fading from her eyes. When she answered, he could feel the chill beneath her professionalism. "Not till tomorrow. Shall I have him call you then?"

"That's fine." He watched as the joy drained from her face, and knew that even though he was just trying to be circumspect, the casual greeting had hurt her.

The elevator doors opened, and the bellman carted the bags inside and waited for Beau to cross the lobby. He looked at Amanda, who stood ready to take the message. They were momentarily alone. "I'll call you later," he said quietly.

And left her as the shadows lifted from her eyes and the color in her cheeks began to rise.

As the elevator door closed, Cherry hurried into the lobby, at a gait Amanda had never seen from her before. "Hey, 'Manda! Look what Bobby gave me for Valentine's Day!" She waved her arm, ornamented with the ugliest link bracelet Amanda had ever seen. It weighted down her wrist as though she were half-manacled.

Amanda glanced at it and smiled a brilliant smile. "How beautiful!" she said sincerely.

***

By late afternoon, he still hadn't called, though she had not left her desk. Dark gray clouds were scudding across the winter blue sky by the time she finished the filing—*might as well get something done while I'm here.* She stuck the last letter in her Maintenance file and stood up, stretching her cramped back wearily.

Some Valentine's Day, she thought bitterly. There were hearts and streamers around the lobby, and Jerry had cheerfully strung up some leftover Christmas mistletoe in his office—"To encourage the right spirit," he said—and Amanda thought of the present hidden away in her nightstand at home. It had been meant for Christmas, but she was beginning to feel as though both she and it were leftovers. How stupid to be giving a present to someone who promised to call and had obviously forgotten. And it had been extravagant—she'd had to work overtime for a month to pay for it.

Her nerves had been strung so tight since he called to tell her he was coming that she wasn't sure anymore how she felt or what she wanted him to do. The one thing she knew was that whatever she had hoped for from this day, it hadn't happened.

A delivery boy stopped at the doorway of her office with a huge splashy bouquet. "Can you sign for this?"

"Ask at the lobby desk, please."

"They told me to come here," he persisted. "They're for—" He looked at the card—"Amanda Harary. Is that you?"

Amanda gazed at the gorgeous cluster of flowers in the heavy glass vase, signed the form hastily, and fumbled at her change purse for a tip.

He took it, mumbled thanks, and fled.

It was a beautiful arrangement, a dozen extravagant blossoms representing every shade of purple from palest violet to flaming amethyst. The little white envelope stuck between the flowers looked very intriguing. Quickly she pulled the envelope out and ripped it open. All it said was "Happy Valentine's Day". No signature. No endearment. Not even her name.

She stuffed it in her purse, disappointed at the lack of sentiment, but cheered by the flowers. They were beautiful, and more importantly, he'd taken the time to send them. That counted for a lot.

She picked up the phone and dialed his room.

He had been napping. Lazily he rolled over and dangled the receiver by his ear. "Yes?"

"They're beautiful," she said simply.

"Oh! Well, I'm glad." He had ordered them immediately after he arrived, as soon as the bellman closed the door behind him.

"Aren't you interested in getting yours?" she asked teasingly.

"You shouldn't have spent money on me!" He sounded gruff but pleased underneath. "You work too hard for it."

"It's a belated Christmas present. And who knows? You might like it."

"It's probably much too expensive. And frivolous. You shouldn't have done it."

She was silent. It *was* frivolous, she couldn't deny that. Maybe he wouldn't like it. She couldn't return it, either. Moreover, he actually seemed irritated that she'd done it. Heaviness settled over her spirit. This wasn't going at all the way she'd hoped it would.

"Are you there?"

She choked back the hurt that had risen, unbidden, to her throat. Things that should have been so simple were getting so complicated. "I'm here."

"Why don't we have dinner tonight? You can give me your much-too-extravagant present and we'll have a chance to catch up before I leave."

She hadn't expected that. "When—when are you going back?"

"I'm not sure, but I'll be busy every other night." He figured it was safer that way. No chance—or time—for temptation.

She said nothing.

He could hear her hurt in the silence.

Damn it, he hadn't thought it would happen again. The last time was an aberration, wasn't it? But from the first moment he'd seen her in the lobby in that scarlet dress, he'd known it *wasn't* an aberration, and it was more than just sex: as the silence stretched between them, he actually *felt* her aching at the other end.

He didn't think that had ever happened to him before, with anyone.

When she finally roused herself to speak, he heard disappointment coating her words. "I suppose I should be grateful you could find any time for me at all."

"I'm glad it could work out." He sounded pleased with himself. "How about 6:30?"

"That's fine. Why don't you come to my apartment?" She gave him the address and hung up, feeling suddenly wilted, limp and foolish.

***

She'd wanted to change, but he told her the scarlet dress was too striking to put away. So they compromised; she brushed out her hair, freshened her makeup and added a gold choker around her throat while he waited and looked around, curious about her home and feeling strangely triumphant that she'd finally invited him here.

There wasn't much you could do with a studio. But she'd tried. There was no room for real bookshelves (and probably no money, either, he surmised), but the sturdy crate that held a row of faded classics and girls' series books had been covered with a cheerful patterned chintz material inside and out. The bare spots on the old couch were hidden under well-placed needlepointed pillows. The standing studio lamp was carefully directed at the plumpest, lushest portion of the scuffed carpeting.

Bare as it was, the little apartment looked neat and warm. Just like Mandy.

She came out of the dressing area looking fresh and vibrant, and beamed a smile at him as bright as the studio lamp. He tried to tell himself it was sympathy for her circumstances that made a lump rise in his throat.

But he managed to match her smile as he rose.

"All set?"

Shyly, she thrust a package at him. It was a heavy gift-wrapped box from one of the best stationers in the city. He'd never expected anything like this. He tried to put on a stern air, and failed completely. "Mandy? What is this?"

"Why don't you open it and see?"

He stood a moment, staring at her, strangely touched. That she had gone to this kind of time and expense meant more to him than he was willing to acknowledge. The hell with keeping his distance; this demanded an answer from him. Deliberately, he set the box down, caught her in his arms and kissed her, drawing her deep and close, enough to feel the trembling in the slender body and the tender clasp of her arms around his neck. And he knew she could probably feel his own body trembling, too. He had promised himself to forego this, but it felt so good to hold her, and he wanted somehow to convey how moved he was at her thoughtfulness.

She was the first to step back, composed and merry. "Well? Aren't you going to open it?" She reached to hand him the package again, and he saw her fingers shaking.

He was careful not to tear the bright paper, to untie the ribbon slowly instead of ripping it to shreds, as he did with Jean's packages. She watched him as he examined the gift box, the store name stamped in gold lettering, as he read the little card and smiled, a bit wistfully. Neatly, he folded back the tissue paper.

The gift was exquisite: Functional, practical and beautiful. The clipboard was fashioned of heavy, well-grained wood, about nine by twelve inches, and the clip on top was coated with gold. Even the paper clipped into it was distinctive, heavy cream backed with a special watermark. His name was lettered in gold leaf on the bottom.

He loved it at once. Turned it over, examined the beautiful wood, ran his fingers over his name etched into the board. He knew at that moment he would keep it forever.

She looked at him anxiously, ready to explain her choice. "It's for your lyrics. You can carry it around and write them down whenever you think of them."

He'd never been good at receiving presents, never knew exactly how to pretend enthusiasm, or worse, express his real delight. Every exclamation seemed forced, every hug and kiss slightly phony. She was waiting for his reaction, though.

He looked up, his lips framing the words, but she stopped him with a soft kiss on his cheek. Apparently, his reaction was perfect, because her eyes glowed as she brushed a tear from his.

***

She'd wondered how he would get a reservation for Valentine's Day, when every restaurant in the city would be standing room only. When she saw the tiny Italian restaurant literally tucked away behind Grand Central and heard the maître d' call him by name, she understood.

The maître d' shook hands with the fervor of a religious convert, exclaiming his delight in indiscriminate streams of English and Italian, though Beau, from long acquaintance, understood every word. Wisely, the man made no mention of Jean, whom he'd seen many times over the years. Instead, he complimented Amanda's youth and charm, and just before she slid into the booth next to Beau, kissed her hand elaborately.

"No menus, Gabriel," Beau told him. "Just bring us the works."

He sat back and looked at her. The bright smile pinned on her face almost hurt to look at; it was so vulnerable, so sweet. Or maybe it was just the extra dimension of *seeing* her, after all this time of just hearing her voice, seeing the wide gray eyes framed by those inky lashes, the softness of her wide trembling mouth. And that scarlet dress didn't hurt, either... it was so vivid, and the deep V which showed off her cleavage made her look so lush and desirable...

Part of him wanted to run. The other part wanted to bury himself in her. The contradictory impulses kept him frozen and silent.

She was quiet too. She had forgotten the amazing contrast of his dark eyes and silvery hair; the slightly crooked line of his mouth, the way his tweed jacket hung on his long slender frame, the paper whiteness of his skin.

She wished she could nestle into his arms and feel them closing tightly around her, feel his mouth taking hers with the same hard, hot, demanding flavor as before. She wondered if he cared enough after all this time even to try.

They looked at each other for a long moment, a half-smile on their faces. "Since when have we ever been at a loss for words?" he asked finally.

She answered at once, a smile quirking her mouth. "This might be a first."

Ten seconds later, they were talking so intensely, leaning forward, their eyes locked together, that when their waiter brought a pitcher of water and a basket of bread, they didn't notice him. He had to clear his throat twice before they looked up.

Beau told her about the contrast between his first meeting with Jason and Perry's now twice-daily phone calls, demanding updates. The meeting with Jason had been so humiliating at the time that he couldn't bear to talk about it, but somehow he could laugh about it now. "Of course, it's easier now," he added, "since I'm no longer treated like something that's staining the rug."

She told him about Jerry's pride in the connection between the show and the hotel. "He dines out on it. There isn't another hotel in town that has anything like this, and he's playing it up like crazy."

By the time the main course arrived, Beau was talking about his most recent musical flop, twelve years before. "And when the producer called, we all decided just to let the phone ring. There was a rumor that he was going to ask for a major revision and throw out six songs. So the phone rang and rang, while we sat around the suite watching it. Seven of us, the whole creative team."

He stopped only when the waiter and his assistant set down identical steaming plates of pasta seasoned lightly with garlic and oil, oozing melted cheese. It smelled delicious.

The waiter made an elaborate show of adding fresh grated parmesan, then bowed himself away from the table. "Enjoy, enjoy."

"It's the best pasta in New York," Beau told her. "Go on, dig in."

Four hours went by, consumed in puffs of talk, sips of tart red wine, and for Amanda, a short lifetime of toying with the food on her plate, but hardly tasting it. She was too busy laughing at his stories, feeling the flutter in her throat spread into warmth in the pit of her stomach. But though the meal looked and smelled delectable, she couldn't get a bite past her lips.

She couldn't keep her eyes off him, off the quick, nervous gestures of his slender hands, the energy and vibrancy in his snapping brown eyes, the passion in the rise and fall of his voice.

She could have listened to him forever.

She didn't realize that the other patrons had left, that their waiter had taken to hanging around, pouring more water unnecessarily, eyeing them meaningfully. Dinner had gone; dessert had ended; the check lay on the table and Beau was taking the last sips of his cooling coffee.

And when he set down his spoon purposefully, she knew something decisive was coming. "Mandy." He took her hand, but the touch was meant to be comforting, not lover-like. His eyes were calm but not eager, as they had been.

Something cold started at the pit of her stomach. She steeled herself to hear something she didn't want to hear.

"We can't continue this." He smiled, self-deprecatingly. "I kept trying to think of another way to say it, all the way across the country. And all the old clichés kept creeping in." He paused, and when he spoke again, his face and voice were serious. "It's got to end, Mandy. I can't ever be...with you... again."

"I suppose I should be flattered. At least you were thinking of me." It was a quick, flat retort, made to ward off his pity, though inside she felt as though she were drowning.

"Honey, there just isn't any easy way to do this. Last time was... " He hunted for a word that wouldn't sting and couldn't find one, so he settled for, "It shouldn't have happened. We both know it." She said nothing. Uneasy, he plunged on. "It was my fault. I admit it." Her eyes were enormous and still, focused silently on him; they made him even more uneasy. "Look, we know it couldn't work out. It just wasn't in the cards. We live so far apart, and the age difference— " He wanted to hammer home that point, but the problem was, he couldn't make himself care about it. He never had. It just seemed irrelevant.

He swung about and tried another tack. "But you're a lovely girl, and you've been wonderful to me... "

This is really happening, she thought. *It's a nightmare, and everything he says makes it worse. I can't block it out or try to pretend it isn't real. He's dropping me, just like that. Just-like-that, while I'm feeling so much for him...* She struggled to maintain a blank expression, and to blink back her rising tears.

He was talking rapidly, soothingly, patting her hand, trying to make it less hurtful. "You couldn't possibly love me, you know. I'm so much older than you—it just would never have been right for either of us."

"Have *you* ever felt an age difference between us?"

He stopped, disconcerted for a moment, then charged ahead. "That's not the point."

"That's exactly the point. There never was a difference, not for one minute. You've never had to explain anything to me, have you? Haven't I always understood what you were talking about? You're trying to—"

She couldn't explain what he was trying to do, because the unshed tears were rising into her throat, threatening to choke her. Her lips were trembling.

Meanwhile, he kept raining out a hurried stream of words that was meant to be soothing. "Look, you're a sensible girl. There'll be someone else, someone terrific, who's right for you... "

She struggled to compose herself enough to ask the question that was strangling her. "Are you—are you trying to say you don't—don't... like me?"

His eyes widened. "My God, of course I do. But you have to understand—I'm in love with my wife. Always have been. It's not the same with us. I don't know how all this—" he gestured helplessly, "even happened last time. But I'll never leave her; you have to realize that. I never want to mislead you." He began to talk rapidly, as though seizing on a familiar topic relieved the anxiety. "Have I ever told you about my wife? She's one of the most beautiful women I've ever seen... "

This is all I need, she thought.

"There was a party once, at Merrick's house, two nights before *The Life and Times* opened—"

"I thought you never went to parties."

"This was an exception. We were celebrating. Don't interrupt." Beau warmed to his topic. "And around 2 a.m., we decided to play charades, and the other team wanted to do a beauty-pageant thing as one of them. They insisted on having my wife as the pageant winner. They got her to drape a sheet over her evening gown, so it looked like she had a tunic on, and they put a little crown on her head... everyone laughed, but I could see all the women envied her, and the men, well, I'm used to how they look at her..."

I can't stand it, she thought. *I know I'm no beauty, but he's discarding me for his wife! Is this supposed to happen?*

He gave her an abashed smile. "I know I'm bragging, but she really is that glamorous."

"Then why," she said quietly, "are you here with me?"

His smile dimmed. "What?"

"You heard me. If she's so marvelous, then why are we here? Why did you even ask me to dinner?"

"The clipboard," he said fumblingly. "I wanted to thank you—"

"You did that already, at my apartment."

"Well, I thought—"

She was on her feet, although she found herself swaying and feeling unsteady. She looked at her untouched dessert, some kind of chocolate cake with orange peel, and thought of the almost untouched pasta she'd sent back to the kitchen. "Thanks for dinner. It was delicious." And she was gone.

It took him almost ten minutes to understand that she hadn't gone to the ladies' room to cool off; she'd simply picked up her coat and walked out the front door, with no intention of coming back.

"Shit!" Beau muttered through clenched teeth. He tossed down five twenty-dollar bills, hurried out, shrugging his coat on, and instructed the weary doorman to whistle for a cab.

***

She didn't feel really safe until she had trotted 20 blocks through the slushy streets. Even then, she reminded herself she wasn't *safe*; this was New York at night, remember. But she felt the need to stretch her legs, to burn off her pain in action. And she felt better as she got further away from the restaurant. She made a mental note to go back someday and actually try the food, when she could swallow again.

She kept herself occupied with such inconsequential thoughts until she unlocked the door of her apartment. Then she broke down and sobbed. The hurt went right through her. She couldn't even summon the strength to rage at him. She was defenseless against his calm, matter-of-fact declaration of non-interest. *I'm crazy about him*, she thought, pushing away the streaks of wet mascara and ruined eye shadow. *And he thinks I'm...* expendable!

Beau gave the cabbie her address and told him to hurry. "Whatever you say, boss," the cabbie said, unruffled. His willingness to please did not extend, apparently, to raising his cab's speed. Beau asked him, as civilly as he could, to step on it, it was terribly important. "Sure thing," the cabbie told him, and kept the speedometer at a serene thirty-five.

Beau clenched his teeth.

Why didn't I realize she was walking out? he berated himself. *Dumb! I might have known she wouldn't want to hear it. But how could she just leave me like that?* And then, worried—*God, I hope she had cab fare.*

He jumped out half a block away, tossing the fare blindly on the floor of the cab, worried now that she hadn't gotten home safely. A distraught young girl on a bus—or God forbid, walking—in New York, anything could happen. He shuddered.

There was a phone booth on the corner. He hesitated a moment, then reached for some change. It would be kinder to phone first. If she was still upset, and he was sure she was, then he would just make sure she was okay, and leave her in peace. They could talk in the morning, before he left, if she was still speaking to him.

That thought somehow made him cold inside. He dropped in a coin and dialed. The line buzzed—ten times, twelve times. No answer.

He stood thinking. Where could she have gone? She had mentioned a mother living on Long Island, but he'd never questioned her about it. He wouldn't know where to look. He didn't know her friends, or to whom she would turn for comfort. But he hated to think she was alone tonight. He phoned the Lorelei, clinging to a faint hope, but the hotel operator told him Amanda had left at five and not returned.

He had no idea where she might be now.

I'll wait here until she gets home, he figured. *Just until I know she's all right.*

He tried the outer door. To his chagrin, it was cracked open. *Is she crazy, living in a building like this, without any decent security, where any lunatic could get in without half trying?*

He went inside and up to her apartment. Maybe he could leave a note on her door.

She hadn't answered the phone, but he touched her doorbell lightly, just to be sure. And was startled by a shouted, anguished, "*Go away!*" from inside. Stuffy with tears, swollen tones notwithstanding, it was Amanda's voice.

He pounded on the door. "Let me in, Amanda! I've been worried sick about you!"

"Get out of here!" she shouted back. "Leave me alone!" He could hear what sounded like muffled sobbing inside.

"I will not go away!" he shouted back. "Let me in! Damn it! I'm trying to be sure you're all right!"

"If you cared—" she caught a sob in her throat and swallowed painfully, "if you cared what happened to me, you'd never have come here to begin with."

He didn't know what she meant, and the confusion added to his anger. He kicked the door. "God damn it, let me in!"

The door jerked open so suddenly and violently that he almost tumbled to the hardwood floor and had to catch the doorframe to stop himself. In front of him, Amanda's face was tear-stained, but her mouth was set in a hard line.

"Okay! You're in!" She slammed and locked the door. "Happy now?"

Her face was puffy and swollen from crying, her nose pink and white in spots. She had discarded the scarlet dress on the double bed behind her, and loosely tied on a long pink bathrobe. There were still droplets on her eyelashes, and her eyes were a deeper gray than he'd ever seen, the color of rolling thunderclouds.

"Mandy—"

She stared back, arms folded, lower lip pushed out stubbornly. "I'm here. I'm all right. As you can see."

"You are *not* all right!" She didn't reply. Turmoil twisting inside him, he demanded, "How did you get home?"

"I walked. Okay?"

The knot in the pit of his stomach was blown away by his rage. "What? Are you crazy? Thirty blocks? This is New York! Nobody with half a brain, especially not a young girl the goddamned *wind* could blow away, walks alone in New York at night!"

He wasn't expecting the jolt. But suddenly Amanda was shoving him toward the door, fire in her tear-stained eyes. "Fine. I'll keep your sage advice in mind. Now get out, damn you!"

For an instant, his surprise stopped him cold. Then anger took over again. "The only reason I'm even here is because I was worried about you! Which, I can see, is all wasted!" He couldn't think of anything else to say, and for a moment they just stood looking at each other, sparks of rage in his eyes, hurt and anguish in hers. They were both breathing heavily.

He could feel the doorknob in his back, but he held his ground. He wasn't leaving. She would have to physically throw him out, and even in her fury, he knew she couldn't. She tried to reach behind him, to unlatch the door, but he took a step to block her. His face was implacable.

Finally, clearing her throat, her eyes still stormy but her tone quiet, she said, "Go away. You've made your choice."

"I can't turn my back on her. I won't abandon someone I promised to love, honor and cherish." His voice was getting quieter too, but they still eyed each other warily.

"You're right." The tears were trembling on her lashes again. "And it wasn't me. So why are you here?"

He got angry all over again, just thinking about it. "My dates don't usually abandon me at dinner!"

"How many of them have you *dumped* over dinner?"

He started to say he'd done no such thing. Then he stopped. She was right; he'd taken her to dinner so he *could* let her down gently. It hadn't worked. "Look, can I sit down?"

"No." Her eyes were like lasers. She tried to reach the doorknob again.

He still refused to move.

"Just tell me one thing," she went on. "Because I'm curious. You've been married to her for... how long?"

He hesitated. "Thirty-two years."

"And in all that time, she's been beautiful and wonderful, I assume.

Jerry said she was."

He flushed. "What's your point?"

"If she was beautiful and wonderful before you met me, and she was beautiful and wonderful while you were getting to know me, and she's still beautiful and wonderful and everything you ever wanted... then why did you get involved with me?"

He looked at her, at the absurd fluffy pink bathrobe that suddenly seemed so soft, so inviting, at the tears that rimmed her extraordinary eyes, at the disheveled hair he suddenly wanted to touch so much it stopped his breath.

Trying to pull himself together and calm down, he said, "Why are you asking?"

"Because I don't understand!" she cried. "If she was everything you wanted, why did you have to go looking? What was the point? Did you just need a *change*? And why me? I'm not the kind of girl men go crazy for. Or was I just the best you could do?"

Her voice broke on the last word, and when he continued to block the door, she turned away from him, dropping her face into her hands, her shoulders shaking.

His heart went out to her. He knew he had hurt her terribly, saying what he felt he had to say in the restaurant. But he'd had to be clear about their relationship, not give her any false hope. He didn't know if she knew what it had cost him to say it. But it had broken her heart, and he couldn't stand to watch her.

He reached out a hand to touch her shoulder. "Mandy—"

She shook his hand off furiously without turning around or lifting her head. "Don't call me that! Don't you *ever* call me that! And why are you still here? Why don't you go back to your beautiful, wonderful wife? I'm sure she's much more fun!"

"Stop it, damn you!" he shouted. "Do you have any idea what this is doing to me?"

She turned her head at this, and the look on her face was indescribable—incredulous, outraged, even—could it be—amused? "Doing to *you*?" She almost choked on the words. "To *you*? Does the whole world revolve around *you*, Mr. Kellogg? Or are you really the spoiled baby I first met at the switchboard, and I was seeing a prince where there was only a frog?" She averted her face again.

"Stop it," he said suddenly, and the harsh tone was the one he'd used in the trenches in France during his army service, forty years before: a voice that brooked no nonsense, that commanded respect.

Suddenly they were on another level.

Amanda's shoulders stopped shaking, and though she didn't turn around again, her head stilled.

He addressed the back of her rumpled head.

"All right. I hurt you, and I'm sorry. But this relationship has no future, and trying to pretend it does would make things worse in the long run. I wanted to tell you the truth. I thought it was fairer, even if it felt lousy. I didn't want to be like most men, stringing you along and taking what I could get." He saw her flinch, and added, "Wouldn't you *rather* know the truth?"

After a moment, in muffled tones, she said, "Is this the whole truth?"

He sighed. "It's all I can tell you, Mandy. There are things I just can't talk about."

"Why?"

"Because talking about it isn't—honorable." He bowed his head, feeling all the humiliation of his connection with Jean, and added silently to himself, *Because talking about it would make me feel less than a man. Because I don't want to see disillusion in your eyes when you look at me. Because even if you end up hating me, I still want your respect.*

To his surprise, Amanda turned around and regarded him for a long minute in silence. Her eyes were still wet, but her face was calm. Finally, she said, "For most people, honor isn't very important these days."

"It is for me. Even if—even if it doesn't seem so."

As angry and loud as they'd been before, that's how quiet they were now. The nonstop chatter of their dinner conversation had been replaced by short significant sentences and long silences.

He looked at her and sighed. "You look better. Are you going to cry anymore?"

She shook her head silently.

"Good. I'm not worth it. You'll see that someday." He buttoned the top button on his coat. "I'll be going now."

"The only thing I regret—" she started.

"What?"

She didn't look at him. "I don't mean that I think you should have done wrong—but I wish that I'd been—" She hesitated, and then forced the words out, "I wish I'd been... *tempting* enough... for you to want to... to spend more time with me."

He looked hard at her. Her gray eyes were lighter, but still rimmed with tears. He put a hand under her chin, lifting it up firmly to face him. "Listen to me. You are the most tempting—the most desirable—woman I've ever known, bar none. I've been *tempted* so many times tonight, I may have to take a cold shower. In February!"

A little laugh escaped her. But the gray eyes had brightened, and he managed a crooked smile himself. "If there's any man out there who thinks you aren't tempting, he needs his head examined. There are movie stars and models who haven't got this much sex appeal. Trust me."

He turned to go.

"Beau?"

He looked around. She was holding out her hand, a little wanly, trying to smile. "I wish things hadn't turned out this way, but—I guess—I'm glad you're trying to do what's right. I know I won't see you again, even if we talk on the phone, but—I'm glad I knew you."

He took her hand and tried to smile. This is what he'd wanted, wasn't it? Her acceptance, her understanding? He'd gotten it all, and caused her untold anguish in the bargain. Yet she was letting him off the hook and offering him her hand in truce.

He didn't want to take her hand. He wanted to take her in his arms. Right this moment, when she was relinquishing their relationship once and for all—at his insistence—he wanted her so fiercely he seriously considered throwing her on the bed right then.

But he didn't. Instead, he shook her hand gently. "Thank you again for the clipboard. I'll use it forever."

"I'm glad."

"We'll still have to talk about the show," he warned her. "You know I can't trust Jerry with all the details. Do you mind?"

"No. I think I'm flattered. I'm glad you trust me."

"More than you know. Sleep well, honey."

She shut the door gently behind him, and he stood for a moment in the hall, feeling completely bereft. He'd done what he promised himself to do—a clean break, ending it before it got out of hand. Better for everyone.

As he stomped out of the building, he told himself he'd considered everyone's feelings. He'd done the only thing he could, and it was honorable and upright.

So how did it feel?

It sucked.

CHAPTER 20

She was so exhausted from the tears and emotions of the night before that she fell into a drugged sleep and had to drag herself to work the next morning. Beau, she knew, had meetings from 8 in the morning till 5:30. She would have left work before then.

Deliberately, she didn't arrive at the hotel until 9 a.m., when he would be long gone. She had turned a corner last night. No point in dwelling on it. He had been very firm about his feelings, and all her wishing wouldn't change them. No matter how she regretted it, it was time to move on.

She concentrated on the notes she'd made for herself yesterday. She decided she'd leave the Valentine's Day decorations up for a few days— some couples might want to celebrate with the pink and red hearts for a little while longer. The chefs were still serving Valentine-related desserts. Maybe they should keep the champagne fountain one more week: it was beautiful in the dining room and might not cost much after the holiday.

She was looking up the telephone number of the caterer who had supplied the fountain when the phone rang. For a moment she dreaded answering it— it might be Beau—but common sense won over emotion.

She couldn't duck telephone calls, not in her job.

"This is Amanda."

"Amanda, it's Jerry." She started to greet him, but he talked over her, at twice his normal speed. "Look, I'm still in Connecticut at that hotel expo. I'll be back later, but I was wondering if you and Martin would do me a favor?"

"What?"

"Would you sing in the lounge tonight? Just a couple of songs? When the expo is over I'm bringing back some of the guys I've met here, and they'd really like to hear you. They like old show tunes. I'd consider it a favor, really."

"Well, if I can get hold of Martin," she said dubiously. Martin wasn't always easy to reach in the daytime. "If he says yes, I'll do it."

"Great. Find him and tell him to start your set at 8. You'll be finished before 9, but it's a big help to me."

"Okay. And Jerry, I went over those event receipts from last month. I found a big mistake in the math."

"Oh?"

"Yes. Six thousand less on the manifest than in the receipts. I changed it and put the revised one in your box."

"Thanks. But I'm sure I would have caught it before I recorded the final figures." He sounded rushed. "See you later."

By 1:00 she had set it up and had arranged to leave work early so she could wash and style her hair, do her makeup and press her lounge dress. She also decided to rehearse in the lounge during her lunch hour. She figured Jerry wouldn't mind.

She kept her mind on these details all day, because by carefully diverting her thoughts to those she could handle, it kept her from thinking of those she couldn't.

***

As usual with initial creative meetings, everything went long and nothing got settled. As Beau had expected, they requested that he attend meetings for two more days. He said he would.

Unlike his experience on the Snap jingle, though, the people he met with now were bending over backward for him. He was accorded the respect due a hit-maker, something he didn't mind at all. He also didn't mind staying over another night or two.

Now that he had everything settled with Amanda, he missed her fiercely. He didn't want to get on a plane without seeing her again—platonically, of course. Now that they knew where they stood, there was no reason they couldn't talk, was there? They'd parted amicably, after all.

But she wasn't there when he returned and requested his room back for two nights. He phoned her at home. No answer.

He didn't want to go out to a solitary dinner—what was the point? If she'd been around, he'd have asked her to go with him—as friends—to one of the better restaurants, but he hated eating out alone. The weather was lousy too: it was looking like snow again, and the temperature was dropping toward zero.

He decided to settle for the hotel dining room. He didn't mind; Jerry always hired good chefs.

He stopped at the desk beforehand; he'd forgotten to pick up his messages when he came in. The smoothly tailored brunette behind the desk handed him four pink slips, which he scanned hastily. None were from Amanda. The moment after he read them, he forgot who left them.

"Too bad the weather is so awful," he said in a conversational tone to the brunette. "I'd like some good music tonight, and there's a pretty good place not far away, right?"

"The Can-Can." The brunette nodded and smiled. "But they're not open on Mondays. Anyway, you can hear music right here."

He frowned. "Tonight?"

"Special program tonight at 8:00, with our lounge singer and pianist. They're really good."

He looked at her blankly, not sure if he was leaping to conclusions. "You have a lounge singer?"

The brunette laughed. "Amanda, our assistant manager. You know her."

"Yes." He couldn't think of anything else to say.

"Well, go hear her, then. I'm sure she'd appreciate a friendly face."

***

She had talent. It peeped through the rounded high notes and the careful enunciation, enough to narrow his eyes as he listened. The song was a standard, and God knows enough singers had interpreted it before her. It wasn't even something he particularly liked; he'd never thought much of Oscar Hammerstein.

But she really had a voice—sweet, clear and warm. He saw her imperceptible flinch when she jarred a note or didn't touch all the consonants. He also saw that she loved the song and enjoyed wrapping her voice around the music. She gave no sign of stage fright that he could see.

She was wearing a quiet navy silk dress, a far cry from the vivid scarlet of the night before. He was disappointed; he'd loved the scarlet dress and would have thought she'd have chosen to wear it while performing. The navy dress was nice to wear out to dinner, but it certainly didn't rivet attention. It was almost as though she was trying *not* to be noticed... which was foolish for a singer... wasn't it?

He sat way back, beyond the lights, so she didn't see him while she sang her set, accompanied by Martin. Only six songs, and she never got off the high bar stool she'd pulled near the piano. It was more like a talented amateur fooling around with the pianist than a performance.

She was finished before 8:30. The scattered couples and solitary drinkers at the bar clapped enthusiastically. She bowed and smiled, still sitting on the stool. Then, with a word to Martin, she got up and wandered toward the bar.

At once he abandoned his original idea of listening to her and leaving before she noticed him. He had to say *something* to her; they'd been talking about her singing for months. It seemed only fair to acknowledge it.

He started toward her, but hung back when he saw some guests walking up to speak to her. One, a tall, good-looking young man, put his hand on her arm and whispered something to her. Amanda laughed. Beau tensed. That guy shouldn't be grabbing at her—she wasn't some Vegas stripper!

Before he could make his way across the lounge, the young man patted her arm again, gave her a smile and left. Amanda went to the end of the bar, smiled to acknowledge the other patrons and waved at the bartender.

"Buy you a drink?"

***

She swung around, startled at the familiar voice. And wasn't sure whether she was delighted or chagrined when she realized, "You heard me sing!"

"You're very, very good."

"You think so?"

"Honestly. Your voice is very sweet—and fresh—and—"

'Sweet and fresh' didn't sound like code for 'superstar'. Besides, just looking at him dredged up both the hurt of the night before and the pain of wanting him and knowing he didn't want her. She'd had time enough to understand that his saying she was 'tempting' didn't mean anything; she clearly didn't tempt *him*. Not enough.

She thought of this as she broke in, "You don't have to fumble for the words. Really. It's all right."

She turned and started out swiftly. He had a hard time keeping up with her, but he caught up to her at the door. "Christ, what is it with you! No matter how I phrase it, you think I'm insulting you! I liked it, Mandy. You do have promise. And you work so hard. I don't see how you can fail to get somewhere." He shook his head at her. "Stop putting me in the wrong all the time. It's making me crazy."

She gave him an ironic look but said nothing.

"Beau! Hey, over here!"

It was Jerry, with two other men in tow. Jerry was sweating—not surprising, in the crowded, overheated lounge—and waving frantically as he hurried through the crowd to catch Beau's attention.

Beau sighed. There wasn't a chance of pretending he hadn't noticed. "Beau! C'mon over, have a drink!"

"Hi, Jerry." He shook hands and acknowledged Jerry's quick, almost unintelligible introductions of the other two men, both plump and balding. If Beau understood correctly, they were also in the hotel business and had been at some sort of hotelier's convention with Jerry earlier in the day.

He wasn't paying much attention. His entire being was keyed to the silent figure standing next to him.

Jerry introduced the men to Amanda. "Here's the singer I was telling you about. Isn't she great?"

One nodded disinterestedly. The other examined her minutely as though she were a piece of horseflesh. He bent too close to her, his eyes on her chest, as he said, "That's some nice voice you have." He put a plump hand on her shoulder, a hand that sported a thick gold wedding ring.

"Thank you," Amanda said, trying to move away.

"Let's grab that booth," Jerry said quickly, herding them toward a dark corner. "Beau, you'll join us, right?"

Beau could feel his temper beginning to flare up. He didn't like that Jerry was treating Amanda as though meeting these guys was part of her job. What was going on?

He looked at Amanda, whose mouth was beginning to curl with distaste. He wasn't about to leave her alone here. Who knew what else Jerry had in mind? "Sure, I can manage one."

He made sure he sat between her and the two hotel guys, which he could see wasn't Jerry's plan. What the hell—was he pimping for her?

His opinion of Jerry, never very high, was beginning to plunge precipitously. Old army buddy or not, what he was doing was beyond the pale. Asking her to sing in the lounge, even for nothing, was okay; it was good practice for her. This shouldn't be part of the package. He watched warily as they ordered drinks.

The conversation was desultory. After quizzing him about life in L.A. and advertising, the two men turned away and talked to each other about hotel business—a snore and a half. Jerry jumped in eagerly every few minutes with a joke (most of which fell flat), occasionally making a remark to Beau, to include him. They all ignored Amanda.

The two men and Jerry had ordered scotch, and seemed bent on some kind of macho competition; they were ordering fresh ones every ten minutes. Beau sipped one watered-down scotch and watched them. Amanda stirred her ginger ale and said nothing.

Within a half hour, the men had become boisterous and loose-lipped; they were making dirty jokes and slapping the table. Jerry had stopped trying to top their jokes and now contented himself with laughing at theirs.

The plump one who had looked Amanda over earlier now said to her, "Hey, cutie! How about singing a song just for us? We *love* show music."

"Thanks, but I'm kind of tired," Amanda said, trying to stand up.

The plump one wouldn't take no for an answer. He reached over the table, past Beau, and tried to put a hand on her wrist. "Hey, come on! It's just-friends time! Just a little tune—you don't need the piano, you can just hum it for us. Do you know *'By the Light of the Silvery Moon*?'"

"Uh, I don't think so," she said, jerking her wrist away.

"Ah, come on, sure you do. It's a standard." The guy stood up with a swiftness that belied the three scotches he'd downed, and in one swift movement he had her by the arm and was pulling her toward him. "'By the light... da da da, da da da... of the silvery moon ...'"

Beau had had enough. There was a thump and a splash, and suddenly Chubby was wearing his scotch. Amanda gave a little startled cry and pulled away. The guy stood frozen, his cheap crumpled suit now a puddle of dark stains.

Beau stood up quickly and elbowed his way out. "Ah, God, I'm sorry," he said to the guy. "I've had way too much. Always gets to me. Listen, send me the cleaning bill, will you? I feel terrible about this."

He leaned down to Jerry and gave him a look that froze him in his seat. "I'm putting Amanda in a cab," he said quietly. "You'd better never pull a stunt like this with her again."

Amanda, shocked into silence, automatically got her coat from the office and he helped her into it, glad to see his impulsive move hadn't splashed her dress as well as the bastard's suit. She was trembling.

Beau's eyes were dark with anger. "Has Jerry ever asked you to do something like this before?"

She shook her head. "Never." She took a deep breath. "It's okay. I'm fine. Nothing happened."

"It is not okay." He got her outside. It was bitter cold, and while she had turned her coat collar up, she wasn't wearing a hat or gloves. "You'll freeze before you get home."

"No. I'm really fine." She was edging away from him, too. Though she was grateful for his help in the lounge, she couldn't forget that he had rejected her just last night. She shouldn't expect him to comfort her now.

He hailed a cab and got her inside, then leaned in and gave the cabbie her address. He looked at Amanda, who was pale, her breath steaming. "You sure you're all right? Do you want me to come with you?"

Yes, I want you to come with me. I want you with me all the time. But do you *want to be with* me, *or are you just being polite?*

She wondered if all these thoughts were visible as she looked at him. Maybe they were, because he hesitated for just a moment and then swung onto the seat next to her. With a splash and a screech of wheels, the cab took off.

***

The cab wasn't heated, and it was cold as hell. The driver was wearing a thick jacket, but Beau could see Amanda shivering and pulling her coat tighter around her. Automatically, he moved closer to her, to warm her. He was cold, too—he'd jumped in the cab without a coat. Maybe they'd need to warm each other.

That thought reminded him of how they'd warmed each other in a cab the last time he was in town—oh, God, that night at the French bistro. He flushed. And from the look he saw on Amanda's face, he suspected she might be remembering it, too.

He took her hand in his and began to rub it briskly, trying to massage heat into it. She'd stuffed her other hand in her coat pocket and watched him warily as he used both his hands to warm hers. He wasn't acting romantic—more like offering first aid. But he saw her eyes warm as she watched him—it had to be better than when that bastard tried to grab her.

The cabbie got them uptown quickly; Beau saw the corners of her mouth turn down as the cab slid to the curb in front of her apartment house, and she made no move to get out. Did she want more time with him?

"Maybe you'd better come up," she said casually, when he seemed inclined to stay in the cab and return to the hotel. "I'll make you some coffee."

He didn't make a fuss about it. "Coffee sounds good." He paid off the cabbie and followed her inside.

It was freezing in her apartment, and she turned up the heat immediately. "It'll be warm in a few minutes," she said apologetically. "I always turn everything off when I leave. Con Ed is so expensive."

"That's okay. I could use some coffee, though, if the offer was on the level."

She raised her eyebrows. "Did you think I was going to lure you up here and then rape you?"

"Are you?" He meant the question to be light, but his voice sounded a little hoarse.

For an answer, she disappeared into the kitchenette. "How do you like your coffee?"

Served him right.

Twenty minutes later, they were sitting at her kitchen table, black coffee with two sugars in front of Beau, hot tea with lemon in front of Amanda, their chairs close enough to touch. The apartment had warmed up nicely, as she'd promised, and the sordid incident in the lounge seemed far away. Beau had discovered that one of the phone messages he'd stuffed in his jacket pocket was from his friend Alex, who ran a lyric-writing workshop uptown.

"We did revues together years ago," Beau told her. "Very nice guy, but— well, you know the expression, 'those who can't do, teach'? It doesn't surprise me that he teaches."

"That's mean." She was stirring the steaming tea, waiting for it to cool.

"Unfortunately, it's accurate." He looked at the message. It had said 'call any time'. "Could I use your phone real quick?"

She pointed out the phone on the hall table, and he went over and dialed.

When he came back ten minutes later, Amanda was reading some notes on a scratch pad, taking small sips of the cooling tea with an air of studied indifference. He was trying to suppress a flare of excitement.

But he couldn't help leaning over her, to see what she was scribbling. They looked like disjointed lines of poetry. "What's this?"

"What does it look like?" Her tone was light, but her eyes were tense.

He glanced sharply at her. "Like poetry... or a song lyric."

She shrugged. "I'm just... doodling."

"How long have you been 'just doodling'?"

She shook her head, trying to seem casual, but inwardly thrilled that he seemed interested. "I've always liked playing with words, and Stephanie's taught me a lot. Nights at the switchboard tend to be quiet, and the ideas started to flow in. So I just... wrote them down."

"Would it be okay if I look?"

She hesitated, not wanting to impose on him but worse, dreading that he might tell her to pack it in. She didn't really want to hear it, didn't want to be prodded into giving it up. She got enough of that from her family.

With the drift away from her singing, this felt like an anchor. She not only liked hearing the words in her head, she liked the feeling of *knowing*, somehow, what she was doing. When a rhyme fell into place, or she knew just how to say what she wanted to convey, it gave her a sense of confidence that the endless hours of voice lessons, theory and practice never had.

Besides, if he did look down his nose on her efforts, it would seem like yet another rejection from him. She didn't think she could stand another one.

Yet, who better to give her a professional opinion? She had thought about showing it to Stephanie, but knew that on some level, Stephanie would view it as rivalry. She was thoroughly insecure about her work. Amanda had never dared approach her about it. She had daydreamed about asking Beau, but had never dared mention it when they talked. And now he was *asking* to look at it.

As she tried to think out the conflicting thoughts crowding her mind, he watched, and unerringly knew what she was wrestling with. "No criticism. I'd just like to see what you put down. But if you don't want me to, that's okay."

He pushed back his chair, widening the physical distance between them.

Amanda looked at the six feet between them, and pushed the scraps of paper across the table. "Don't expect much."

He just smiled, and turned to the scribbled sheets. She got up to reheat the kettle and wipe down the counter.

Two minutes went by. Three. She turned off the re-boiled water and risked a quick look over her shoulder. He had finished reading her pages and was looking thoughtfully at them.

"Well? Is it hopeless?" She meant it teasingly, but he was tapping a finger absently on the pages and didn't seem to hear her. "Beau?" He finally turned to her, but still said nothing.

Exasperated, she said, "It won't hurt my feelings if you don't—"

"Of course it will." His eyes flickered to her face, and he nodded slowly. "This is good."

The unexpected response stopped her dead.

He looked at her and laughed. "Your face looks frozen. Did you think I'd tell you to throw it out?"

Cautiously, she said, "Well—possibly."

He shook his head, and the laughter left his face. "You're talented, Mandy. You really are. It's pretty clear."

"You really think it's good?"

"Good enough to get into a revue right now—if they were still doing revues."

She thought of her disastrous night at the Hot Grill, but said nothing.

"You need more experience, and a mentor, of course." Her eyes brightened, until he added, "Maybe your friend Stephanie. But if anyone can still make a living writing song lyrics, you can. If you want to." When she still said nothing, he patted her hand. "You've got it, kid. So rest easy." He glanced around. "Any more coffee?"

"How about scotch?" She'd bought it after their first few nights together.

He raised an eyebrow. "*You* drink scotch?"

"Uh—you know, to be sociable—" She felt suddenly foolish. "Never mind. Coffee's still hot." She brought the pot and poured for him.

"Thanks." He took a long sip.

"You don't want something—stronger?"

"This is fine." He smiled at her. "Usually I never turn down something 'stronger', but for some reason, Miss Harary, when I'm with you, I don't need anything else."

He knew he shouldn't have said it, but Amanda's heart, which had felt lacerated since he came back to New York, began to expand in her chest. When she raised her eyes to his face, his eyes caught hers—a tentative smile in hers, something rueful in his. They looked at each other, and suddenly neither was moving; the air was charged.

Then he stood up abruptly, forcing her to move back in the tiny space. The moment was over; she could see he would make some quick excuse and leave very soon. Trying to keep him there, struggling not to threaten his sense of fidelity, she said, "How did that call go? To your friend?"

She didn't know if he'd even reply, but the excitement that had fizzed in his face came back; he had forgotten the call in his surprise over Amanda's unexpected talent. "He asked me to speak to his workshop," he said in wonder. "Isn't that something!"

"When?"

"Tomorrow night. Forty students, and they all want to be the next Stephen Sondheim. He says they're huge fans of my work and they'd love to hear me. Flattering as hell."

"Will you do it?"

"Yes!" He looked surprised at his own decision, but elated. "I haven't done anything like this in years. Not even sure I can hold their attention. But it'll be fun, and maybe something I say will help someone."

"I'd love to hear you," she said wistfully.

He paused. "Why don't you come? It might make up for tonight." He hesitated, but felt he really had to say something, if only to protect her. "You really ought to reconsider this lounge singing business. I wouldn't trust Jerry not to pull something like this again."

She grimaced, and his hand moved involuntarily to touch her face. "You may be right. But I didn't think this was his intention at all. Maybe I'm just dumb," she said, as his hand gently caressed her cheek.

"Maybe you're just sweet, and you can't imagine people doing something like this."

"Not Jerry. I would never have believed he'd do this to me." His hand felt so good, stroking her skin. She put her hand on his, moving lightly with him, so as he was stroking her cheek, she was stroking him too.

A shock wave went through both of them at the same time.

His eyes riveted on her face. "Be careful, Miss Harary. I'm too old to fall in love."

Her eyes caught his, just as his words had caught at her heart. This time, the look in his face was as soft as his words. "Are you sure?"

He smiled and looked at her for a long moment, seeing the soft hair framing her sweet face, the upturned lips, the whole wonderful package he'd almost thrown away. And for what? What was supposed to be his compensation? A life of disappointment and sterility? Hauling Jean back from the brink, again and again?

"The hell with it," he said finally.

"With the workshop?"

"No. With everything else. Ben was right."

"Who's Ben?"

He turned her face up to his, knowing that telling her this was telling her everything. "He's the guy who said to me, 'Just don't be stupid, and let it get away.'" He kissed her mouth deeply.

She leaned back and gazed up at him, her face serious. "Last night you said you didn't want this."

He looked down at her. He could almost *see* the radiant threads of feeling connecting them, and for sure he could feel the luminous warmth emanating from her eyes. It was like being wrapped in a velvet cocoon. All he had to do was say yes to it.

He couldn't turn his back on her. He knew he was being selfish, but how could he deny the beauty and perfection between them? Nothing in his life had ever been so flawless. To give it up for the splintered empty fabric of his life with Jean was more than his aching soul could bear.

He drew a quick breath. "I know what I said."

"Then why the change of heart?" She wasn't flinging his words back in his face. But her troubled eyes begged for answers.

He answered as honestly as he could. "Because being with you feels like home."

She could feel her heart twist in her chest at the aching sweetness of his words. The kiss she gave him in answer was warm and gentle, and her arms when they closed tightly around him were soft and comforting, not wild and passionate.

Oh, yes, this *did* feel like home. They both felt it at the same time. He knew, in the deepest recesses of his soul, that he'd never felt this way before.

"Will you stay here tonight?" she was asking, the soft gray eyes turned up trustingly to his.

He managed a wry smile to cover the surge of joy he felt. "I was kind of hoping you'd ask."

It was like the first time all over again—only this time, instead of an impersonal bed in an inn, it was her bed, her home. He loved being there, seeing the little knick-knacks on top of the bookcase, smelling the scent of talcum powder that lingered around the room, lying on pillowcases she had chosen, on sheets she had slept in.

All their movements were slow and gentle, but nonetheless profound and moving. They moved together lightly, every inch of skin aglow, feeling the shock waves together from the curve of her cheek to the side of his foot. Exciting as some of their times together had been, nothing was better than this. When he came inside her, he was so deeply imbedded that he thought he could feel the beating of her heart inside the soft wet warmth. And when they took each other to the highest of heights, she heard his groan and the next moment, a whispered word.

She thought for just a moment that he said, "Home."

CHAPTER 21

W hen they woke the next morning at 7:00 to the buzz of the alarm, a dull gray sky arched over the city, and a few stray snowflakes tumbled over the wakening streets.

Beau groaned.

Amanda leaned close to him. "It's not really snowing. It's not even supposed to snow today. Just flurries. No big deal."

"I hate snow," he said.

Her hand, which had begun to stroke his chest, stopped suddenly. She looked at him without moving. It never snowed in L.A.

He pulled her hand back and covered it with his own. "And to make matters worse, I have to leave this nice warm bed in about three minutes to go back to the hotel, change and get to my meeting. And I know it'll take all day with these jerks. I won't be able to see you till much later." He began to kiss her.

"No," said Amanda impulsively. "Let's steal today."

He stopped nuzzling her. "What?"

She pulled away from his lips and faced him. "Beau, listen. The workshop lecture tonight is important. Nothing else is. Why can't we have a whole day to ourselves?" She didn't want to plead, but she felt the relentless walls of time pressing in on their idyll. Suddenly it was forcing out hurried, desperate words she didn't even know she'd wanted to say. "I know your life doesn't include me. We'll never have much time together. So let's have today. I'll call in sick and you call in—whatever—to your meeting, and let's do something together."

"Stop tempting me." He kissed the top of her head. "That sounds more enticing than anything you've offered me yet."

He didn't sound completely convinced, though, so she wiggled down the length of the bed and bent her head between his parted legs. Twenty minutes later, he told the president of the ad agency that he'd awakened with a migraine and had to spend the day in bed. Amanda called the front desk and told them she'd caught the flu and was turning off her phone so she could sleep.

They returned to bed but not to sleep: they had a delicious, passionate interval before they dropped off to nap and then finally rose and bathed. Together.

The flurries ended around 8:00, and a watery sun emerged from behind the gray clouds. For February, it was a lovely day, and after Beau insisted on going back to his room to change (Amanda waited for him at a coffee shop around the corner, to avoid the prying eyes at the Lorelei), they went out together.

"I am not going to skate," Beau said to her sternly an hour later. Skaters wrapped in heavy coats and scarves or encased in woolly tights and pleated skirts were already whirling around the rink in Rockefeller Center, and Amanda was looking at them longingly. "I haven't done that since I was a kid in Chicago."

"No kidding. They had ice skating when you were a kid?" Her eyes were dancing. He glared at her, even as he knew that it was all for show: he'd seldom in the last few years ever felt so joyous. "Thank you. That definitely makes me want to skate now."

She wanted to press the point, but the look in his eyes was decisive. Instead, they huddled together at a ringside table, ordered hot chocolate and watched the skaters, depending on their skill level, glide past confidently or take a tumble and laugh. Amanda could have watched them for hours, her fingers clasped in Beau's, but when they'd finished their hot chocolate Beau said, "Come on. I'm taking you to one of my favorite places."

She followed him obediently to the Fifth Avenue entrance, where he hailed a cab and gave directions. A few minutes later they drew up to a small building in the middle of a quiet West Side street.

"The Museum of Television and Radio," Beau told her, pulling her out of the cab. "Have you been here?"

"No."

"Good. It'll be a first for you, then."

They went inside, and Amanda looked at printed announcements of upcoming programs on costuming, television documentaries and a special on Orson Welles' *War of the Worlds* radio broadcast. Here was a real comprehensive repository of the history of radio and television, from the earliest Amos 'n Andy to current newscasts.

Beau led her downstairs to the computer stations, where more than a dozen cubicles were blocked off. He told her visitors could call up any TV show they wanted, from old Huntley-Brinkley newscasts to the most recent presidential inauguration, and to prove it, had her close her eyes while he chose something from the extensive catalogue. A few minutes later, the TV monitor in front of them began to stir to life.

"What did you pick?" Amanda asked.

Beau just pointed at the screen and motioned her to put on the headphones plugged into the set, so they could listen in privacy. "Watch."

She heard before she saw—and what she heard, unmistakably, were the opening notes of the overture for *The Life and Times*. "Television?" she whispered, though the closest patrons to their cubicle were across the room, watching their own picks, and couldn't hear them.

He just smiled, listening through his own set of headphones.

Watching, enchanted, Amanda saw a shortened but compelling version of the stage show, filmed in black and white. They'd done it in less than an hour, but the major songs remained, sung by the Broadway singers who had sung them on her old album. She marveled at seeing the full scenes where the songs were set, hearing dialogue she'd never heard before, finally understanding the context of lyrics she'd first heard when she was six, and she didn't notice Beau's eyes narrowing as he watched, or see the disappointment in his face as a line fell flat or an actor muffed a lyric.

When the credits rolled at the end (she watched carefully for his name, which was listed under Libretto and Lyrics by), she turned to him, eyes brimming over. "Thank you."

His answering smile was weak. "You liked it?"

"I loved it! I didn't know it was ever on TV."

"Yeah. Just once." He sighed.

"It was never rerun?"

"No. Lousy ratings." He started to say something else, but stopped.

"It was so good... I can't believe it wasn't a hit."

"I can. I look at it now, and all I see are the flaws."

"Not the songs!"

"No, not the songs. But the story... " He shook his head. "That was my fault."

She refused to believe that. "It was wonderful."

He kissed the top of her head lightly. "Keep thinking that." He looked at his watch.

"Let's have an early dinner, since we're meeting Alex at seven. I'll put you in a cab, go back to the Lorelei, change and pick up a few things for tonight.

Then I'll pick you up at your place around 5:30."

She smiled. "I'll be waiting."

When he dropped off a small case of overnight things at her apartment (she loved the new intimacy of his staying at her apartment), he announced that they'd have dinner at the Oyster Bar, one of his favorite restaurants since he first came to New York. When she admitted she'd never been there—because everyone she knew said the Oyster Bar was for tourists—he laughed. "That's the point! You go to the Oyster Bar when New York looks brand-new and glittering, and if you're only here for a week or so, that's how you remember it forever. When you live here it stops looking like a bright new penny, the streets are filled with garbage and crime and the people are pushy and rude and ugly—"

"Hey—"

"It's true. Who wants to be reminded of that? So let's go somewhere that makes New York look magical. OK?"

He gave her a wistful smile, and she saw the hope shining in his dark eyes.

She gave in without a word.

***

By the time Beau introduced her to Alex, a pleasant fiftyish man a head taller than her with a thin mustache and a quick smile, she had a thousand new memories to store up and cherish. After shaking hands with Alex, she sat in one of the plush red seats in the last row of the small auditorium and waited to see if Beau could captivate an audience, or whether he only captivated her.

In front, on the small stage, stood a lectern, lit by a single work light. Amanda saw dozens of people walking in, singly or in pairs, and taking seats, far more than forty people here—it had to be closer to ninety. Beau didn't seem to notice. He was talking quietly with Alex by the back door.

When the clock clicked over to 7:00, Alex strolled to the lectern and said without preamble, "Good evening. I passed the word about tonight's session and I see our class enrollment has temporarily shot up." He waited for the laughter before adding, "I'm pleased tonight to welcome an old friend whose work you all know and respect—and therefore I see no reason for further introductions. Ladies and gentlemen, Mr. Beau Kellogg." The students' faces brightened as they broke into a round of genuine applause. Amanda, clapping hard behind everyone else, saw Beau's startled face as he made his way to the lectern, as the applause grew louder, accompanied by a few cheers.

Beau waited until the room had gone silent. He seemed not to know what to say. Amanda leaned forward, hoping he wasn't having an attack of stage fright like hers. Would he even be *able* to speak?

Then suddenly, he said, "Wow." The audience laughed.

"Thank you, all. I'm very flattered." He made a short bow in Alex's direction. "When I think of illustrious lyricists, I think of Alan Jay Lerner, Larry Hart, Cole Porter. It's nice to feel I'm in their company... in this class, anyway." He paused. "Alex and I set this up at the last minute, and I really don't have anything prepared to say to you, but if you have any questions, I'd be glad to answer."

"How do you get rich and famous?" called out one guy with a mane of wild black hair frizzing around his forehead and a pair of black-rimmed glasses.

Beau laughed. "When you find out, let me know."

A girl in the front row with long red hair and a tight lilac sweater said, "Are you working on something now?"

Beau smiled. "Yes. I'm doing a show with the Fieldston Organization, with music by Jules Hamner." There was an intake of breath all around.

"What's it about? When will it be on? Are you writing the libretto?"

Beau held up his hands. "Yes, it's my original libretto. No title yet. It should be on in the fall. You want to know more, buy a ticket!"

From that moment on, the students wouldn't let him alone. Eventually they stopped asking about his career and began to ask about the craft of lyric writing. Alex, leaning against the side door, watched without interrupting (Amanda thought it was nice of him) as his students peppered Beau with questions and demands that he name his favorite lyrics by others, which he finally, reluctantly did: *"The Love of My Life"* from *Brigadoon*, for the wit of the lyric, *"The Ladies Who Lunch"* from *Company* for its revelation of character, and *"Ol' Man River"* from *Show Boat* for its timelessness.

"What about straight love songs?" asked the guy with the frizzy hair. "Which ones do you like?"

"There are no straight love songs," Beau answered. "None that last for very long. The really good ones still have an original angle. The great ones have that *and* passion."

He glanced up at Amanda, and as their eyes met, the words seemed to move in the air between them.

He went on to explain why many Cole Porter lyrics were dated, because the details referred to the time he wrote them for, but songs like *"Night and Day"* and *"Begin the Beguine"*, which had no such references, were still classics.

"What about Lloyd Webber's shows?" someone called.

He grimaced. "What about them?"

"What do you think of *Cats*?"

"My opinion isn't important. I'm not an authority on pornography." That got the loudest laugh of the night.

The guy with the frizz persisted after the laugh. "Why are you against him? The money he makes? Isn't that like penis envy?" Even as he said it, Amanda could see distaste on the other faces in the audience.

"I don't know him," Beau said. "I'm against his shows because they're all production and very little substance. You don't walk out of the theater moved; you walk out overwhelmed by the special effects and the huge orchestra. But you don't remember the stories or characters; you remember the spectacle. That's not what musical theatre should be."

Amanda looked at the round clock on the left wall. He'd been talking nonstop for over fifty minutes, and still hands waved all over the auditorium. Students asked facetious questions and overly earnest questions, but Beau gave a polite and considered answer to all.

When they demanded he define a great lyric, he finally said, "Look, the essence of a lyric is poetry, and the essence of poetry is saying something profound in a simple, beautiful and original way. Great lyricists take a universal emotion—something everyone's felt and other writers have written about—and *say something new about it, in a fresh way*. That's the whole secret." He looked around and added, "And it's not easy to do."

"Example!" called a beefy guy from the third row who looked like a football linebacker.

Beau nodded. "How about *'Both Sides Now'*?"

"Since when is that a show song?"

"It's good enough to be. And it's a great example of what I'm talking about."

When the rustle of protest died down, he explained. "Our stock in trade is love, right? Love wanted, love gained, love lost. This song isn't about that. It says that as you grow and change, the way you look at things changes. Yet, even when you know better, you'd still rather believe in the fairy tale. It's about love, sure; but it's also about life and truth."

All around the room, students were scribbling notes. Beau looked around and concluded, "This is a great song lyric, and it will last. Joni Mitchell, who wrote it, gave us *timeless* specifics—they won't date like Porter's songs, so this song will be relevant forever."

He glanced up at the wall clock. It was past nine, and the class was supposed to end at 8:30. "Sorry," he said apologetically to Alex. "I didn't think I had that much to say."

Alex pushed himself off the wall and came to stand next to Beau. "You should be teaching here, not guest lecturing." He led the applause.

Beau was the most surprised person in the house when these kids in their teens and twenties gave him a standing ovation.

CHAPTER 22

B eau took his last bow at 9:15, but students still crowded around him with questions, eager to shake his hand, thank him for his insights or tell him which of his songs they loved most. (Beau was genuinely astonished—and moved—that they actually knew his work.)

Alex, Amanda and Beau were the last ones out of the auditorium, and as they walked toward the exit, Alex, shaking his head, was laughing. "Damn, you did it again!" He turned to Amanda. "Look at this guy—he comes in here and teaches my students more in one night than I do in a semester." But Alex sounded rueful rather than envious.

"They're nice kids," Beau said, but his eyes were shining, he was beaming and Amanda saw that he was feeling all the excitement of a successful performance.

As they reached the outside doors, Alex said, "How about a drink? I owe you that much."

Beau glanced at Amanda. "Next time, Alex, do you mind? We have an appointment, and I yakked so long, we might be late."

"Hope not. This was brilliant, Beau. Come back again, will you? You've got knowledge to burn, and they loved hearing it." Alex waved cheerfully and headed toward the deserted parking lot.

Amanda was still high on Beau's unexpected skill as a speaker and the class's response to him. "We could have gone for a drink with him," she protested. "I'd love to hear more."

They came out into the bitter February night, and before Beau could reply, she exclaimed, "Oh, look!"

She gazed up at the shining full moon that was itself surrounded by a huge, perfectly formed circle that glowed in the dark night sky. "What is that?"

she asked. "It's so beautiful—I've never seen anything like it."

Beau wrapped an arm around her shoulders and pulled her against him. "It's a moon ring."

"A what?"

"That huge ring is made of ice crystals in the atmosphere, and if I remember right, there's some old expression about 'Ring around the moon, snow coming soon'."

"Oh, no!"

But she couldn't take her eyes off the ghostly ring silhouetted so clearly among the stars. The perfect circle shimmered in the cold air. *Another first*, she thought. *Like all the things we've done today.* Beau pulled her close to him and spoke into her hair. "Take a good look. It won't last long."

"No?"

"A moon ring is beautiful and rare. It makes its impact and disappears."

She looked at him, at the knowledge in his face. And suddenly she knew, and a lump of lead began to descend into the pit of her stomach. "You're going home tomorrow, aren't you?"

His arm tightened around her waist as they looked upward together at the moon ring. "That's why I didn't want Alex tagging along tonight."

So soon! But he'd just arrived! How long would he be gone this time? How many memories could she nurse in her heart until she saw him again?

She took a moment to compose herself. She didn't want to cry. But the thought of his leaving was hard to take, when they'd just begun to find each other again. "Where—where are we going?" she managed to ask, her voice unsteady.

He hailed a cab and bundled her into it. "You gave me my Christmas present, but I didn't give you yours."

That was all he would say until they reached her apartment. She took off her coat and sat on the bed while he snapped open his briefcase and took out a plain manila envelope. She eyed it without speaking, but her heart was thudding almost painfully, she was so curious and excited.

"Merry Christmas," he said genially, apparently not noticing her nervousness. He leaned down to kiss her cheek, and in her fumbling tension— or perhaps for some other reason—he got her lips instead. The tension began to seep out of her as their mouths pressed together, and her hands moved hesitantly over his chest.

He broke the embrace abruptly. "Don't you want to open it?"

She opened the envelope gingerly and slid out the single sheet inside, filled with musical notation and inked-in words.

Scrawled across the top was *"Being There"*. Underneath, in the same scrawl: "To Amanda".

She sat very still. It was the most personal kind of gift she could imagine. "You wrote a song for me?" She looked up, astonished.

He bowed, half-mockingly.

"Is it from the new musical?"

"No."

She looked closely at the music sheet and began to hum and then softly sing the song. It was beautiful—and like the point he had made in Alex's class, it was about more than just love, love, love.

He raised an eyebrow. "Did you see the most important part?"

She scanned the sheet. "You wrote the music! I didn't even know you wrote music." His name alone appeared on the credit line.

"That's not what's important."

Impatient, he pointed at the bottom of the sheet, where a tiny circle enclosed the letter c—the symbol for copyright.

Next to it was her name.

"It belongs to you. I registered it that way. You can sing it, record it, let other singers record it, whatever—but all the royalties are yours. Forever."

She didn't know what to say. The tightness in her throat prevented her from speaking. She knew that he cherished his songs perhaps more than anything in his life. To write something completely—music *and* lyrics—and then gift it to her—it was a gesture that spoke millions of words.

She understood at that moment that he loved her. Had to. Nothing could have said it more clearly, no matter what he might say—or think—to the contrary.

He was giving her a piece of himself, and she knew without needing to hear it that he'd never done such a thing before, for anyone else.

She could never again doubt how he felt about her.

The silence as they looked at each other grew deeper and deeper, as their eyes met. His eyes were warm, hers overflowing with tears.

Finally, as though by silent consent, they both looked away.

The moment, full of unspoken but overflowing emotion, was gone.

She started to go to the piano, but Beau stopped her. "Let me." He sat down on the bench and rippled through a couple of scales to warm up. She stood unmoving, watching, startled at this unexpected side of him.

He looked up. "Don't worry. I can play a little." He patted the bench. "Come and sing it. You'll be the very first."

She put the music in front of him, though he didn't seem to need it. He played the eight-bar intro and nodded her into the song.

"It's not enough to remember
Dust motes floating on golden air.
How your smile moved and melted me
How contentment turned into ecstasy
When I reached out to touch your sunlit hair.
There's always a wall that divides us
From the seconds that made our lives real
And summoning back a bright memory
Only echoes what once we did feel.
That's why I won't keep a scrapbook
Photos freezing joy once in the air
For nothing can capture the moment
Of being there.
No picture can bring back my heart's swell
The first time we met in a kiss.
No diary, no matter the words that I write
Could ever contain all my bliss.

For me, the joy ever is fleeting
But I'm happy, no matter it's rare.
For no one can relive the moment
Of being there."

She sang it through twice; then Beau let the piano go silent. They looked at each other, their faces only inches apart.

"Beautiful," he said softly.

Oh, Beau, she thought. *How I love you.* But all she said was, "Thank you."

***

They woke up before the alarm went off on Wednesday morning. There was frost on the windows, and snowflakes drifted down the outside walls. Outside, an inch of snow had piled on sidewalks and silent cabs. The moon-ring prediction had been accurate.

Amanda lay with Beau's head pillowed on her shoulder. She didn't want to get up and set about this day. At the end of it, he'd be gone. She could already feel the loneliness of it.

He opened his eyes without moving his head. "Good morning." She bent down and kissed him on the mouth. He reached up and took her in his arms, and they slid down together to nestle close, arms, legs and naked torsos intertwined.

Though they were both just awake, the feel of their skin touching was enough to set them both off. She got on top of him, opening her legs to take him in, and slid down and then up again, both of them groaning with the electric thrill of it. They quickened the pace, each of them driving the other, thrusting and taking, the red-hot lust throbbing in the air around them.

When they finished, the blood was pounding so hard in their ears that for a moment, neither heard the alarm buzzing. "Seven o'clock," Beau said, trying to control his breathing.

Amanda reached over and turned off the alarm. They looked at each other, faces flushed, eyes shining in the afterglow of hot, raunchy sex. Each of them could see what the other knew: this was the end.

"I'll shower first," Beau said, trying to sound normal.

"Okay." Amanda waited until he was behind the shower curtain and then scrubbed her face and brushed her teeth at the sink, sharing the bathroom with him. It was the only gesture she could think to make, to remind herself that on some level, he still belonged to her.

But she knew that warm cozy sense would fade fast, once he was ready to leave.

You do have to come back to real life. The trouble is, real life can really stink.

By the time he had dressed in fresh clothes, it was almost 7:30. He called the ad agency and asked to push the meeting back to 9:00. "It'll give me time to get packed and change," he said to Amanda with a smile. She tried to smile back, but it was an effort.

He sat down on the bed and pulled her, still naked, onto his lap. "No tears, all right?"

She shook her head. "No tears."

"I'm not sorry about this," he declared. "Are you?"

"Absolutely not. I love my new song."

"And I love my clipboard." He pulled her closer. "And in case you're interested, I love you too."

She sat very still on his lap, her throat tightening again. Here he was, saying something she never dreamed he'd say. *Oh, God,* she thought. *If he's saying it, it really* is *the end.*

She wished that somehow that wasn't true, but she was very much afraid it was. A cold knot settled in her stomach.

He shook her a little, when she'd made no response. "Well?"

She tilted her head against his chest. It was easier to talk intimately when she wasn't looking into his eyes. "I've always known that. Sometimes, it's all that gets me through the day."

It was his turn to feel a spike in his throat, a liquid pulse that threatened to dissolve him into tears. *Ridiculous,* he thought. *I don't cry.*

He braced himself against the wash of sadness inside and went on. She had to hear it, even if only this once. Even if nothing ever changed in his life. She deserved it.

"You're the girl I never expected to find. A great, unexpected bonus. And to think I had to wait till almost the end of my life to meet you." He stroked the tousled hair, pale in the wash of morning light. "You were worth waiting for."

Now the tears were running heedlessly down her face, but they were happy tears. She put her cheek against his. "And you," she whispered, "you're the prince I thought you were."

He almost crushed her fingers, squeezing them in response.

She agreed not to go with him to the Lorelei by cab, but insisted on coming down to the street to see him off.

It took ten full minutes to flag down a cab; the snowy streets were already jammed, and cabs were at a premium. The cab that finally pulled to a stop for Beau was battered, with paint flaking off several scrapes and dings.

Beau gave the cabbie the address of the Lorelei and turned to Amanda, who had thrown on a coat over heavy slacks. "Okay, my darling," he said quietly. "I guess this is it."

There were no promises, no questions, no commitments. He didn't say this time that he would return. He had explained all he ever would to her; she understood that. Someday, perhaps, he'd trust her enough to explain it all.

She seized him in a bruising kiss and felt his arms tighten painfully around her back and shoulders. But there was no time for more. He climbed into the back seat and looked at her. This time there was no jaunty salute. But she thought she could see a shimmer of moisture in his eyes as the cab pulled into the early-morning traffic.

***

Beau caught a late-afternoon flight back to Los Angeles, thinking of Ben and his advice and his own deepening feelings for Amanda. "Don't be stupid," Ben had said, and he knew now how wise that advice was. Walking away from Amanda might have been the moral thing to do, but the only thing that would ease the anguish in his heart was having her at his side. Thank God Ben had understood that. Thank God somebody did.

Jean had taken no pills this time, which for a sickening moment at the L.A. airport he had thought she might. But when he came in and gave her a perfunctory kiss, she handed him a folded copy of the *Times* and told him he'd probably want to read it right away.

He did, because it contained all the details about Ben's funeral.

PART THREE

(HAPTER 23

February—September 1983

The little church off Doheny was surprisingly crowded, Beau thought, looking around three days later. Ben had known a lot of people slightly, and because of his sterling reputation as a lyricist, many of them had turned out to pay their respects. Few, if any, had visited him in the last five years, but apparently there was some cachet involved in attending his funeral. Typical.

Jean had declined to attend, though she usually accompanied him to funerals. That she didn't attend this one gave Beau a pretty good idea of just how deep her animosity toward Ben had been. It also made him wonder about Ben's animosity toward Jean, and if Ben would have given him the same advice about Amanda if Jean had not been involved.

The service was simple and to the point. There were a couple of Catholic prayers (Beau hadn't even known Ben was Catholic, but with his being Irish, it made sense), and then two of his lifelong friends rose. The first read a selection of Ben's favorite poetry and his best song lyrics. The second eulogized him as a man who recognized truths that others ignored and spoke them in eloquent words.

The whole service was over in forty-five minutes. It was quite enough, Beau felt, and he figured he'd be lucky if someone had as much to say over him. He was sitting close to the front and made no effort to rush out once the casket had been pushed down the aisle. A crowd of elderly people was hobbling after the coffin. He was content to let them go ahead.

As he walked out of the pew and into the center aisle, he almost bumped into a much younger woman wearing a smart black dress and black pumps. She made a little moue of apology.

"My fault," Beau said. "Please." He bowed his head to let her go first.

"Thank you," the woman said, with a nice smile. She looked to be in her late forties, attractive, slim and self-contained. Something in her oval-shaped face and slightly tilted lips told him she had a sweet nature. Next to the other women in expensive hats and designer dresses, she was quite inconspicuous.

Beau looked after her. She walked briskly down the aisle, clearly alone. Most of the other guests had gone. He had a sudden strong hunch about her.

He hurried down the aisle and caught up just as she reached the front door. "Excuse me," he said, "I didn't recognize you at first. You're in from Florida, aren't you? Rose Stevens?" He'd picked the name and the place out of thin air.

She looked startled. "Why, no."

He tried to look chagrined. "Oh, my God! I'm sorry. You could be her twin, honestly. But you do live in Florida?" He looked self-deprecating. "Tell me I got that much right."

"Why, no." They were the last ones left in the church. She looked at him; the sunshine slanting in the open door was making her squint. She took out a pair of sunglasses. "I've never even been to Florida."

This was as he'd hoped. He held out a hand. "Well, I have made a mess of it then. I'm Beau. I live here in Brentwood."

She smiled and held out her hand. "Hello, Beau. I just flew in from Prague. My name is Lindsey."

***

The church had been crowded, but the luncheon afterward in the private dining room of a posh Beverly Hills restaurant was packed.

Beau saw dozens of people there he hadn't spotted at the church. He hated to be cynical, but did they only show up for the free lunch?

This *was* Los Angeles, after all.

He was surprised to see Dave Callahan there. The last time he'd seen Dave was at his own birthday party in September. From a birthday to a funeral—a natural progression, he supposed.

Dave greeted him with relief. "Jeez, will you look at this turnout? I'm not sure I've known this many people in my entire life."

"Ben did get around."

"I'll say. Studio executives, music executives, producers, songwriters, ad men... he worked with everybody." Dave shook his head. "C'mon, the buffet looks good. Let's grab before everyone else does."

Beau wondered if this was why Dave was always on a diet. Trying to beat out other people to stuff yourself at a funeral? He himself wasn't hungry. He could definitely use a drink, though.

Ten minutes later, Dave had a full plate and Beau had a glass of red wine. They wandered over to an empty table and watched people drifting by, chatting in low tones, as Dave methodically ate his way through three hors d'oeuvres and a thick sandwich.

Beau was beginning to wonder if he would go for seconds, when Dave nudged him. "Don't be obvious about it, but turn your head very slowly to your right."

"What am I looking for?" Beau asked, beginning to swivel his head slowly.

"The old guy and the young girl."

Beau scanned the room and finally noticed a silver-haired man in a navy sports jacket. His shirt was unbuttoned halfway down his chest— not exactly appropriate for a funeral—and he sported a couple of gold chains instead of a tie around his deeply tanned neck. Next to him, in a black leather miniskirt and an off-the-shoulder clingy top, was a girl who couldn't be more than twenty. Her long straight unkempt brown hair tumbled over her shoulders as she talked animatedly to the older man. No one else was nearby.

"That's Mick Watters, our art director. He's 58 and she's 19," Dave reported in Beau's ear. "Oh, and he left his wife and four kids to shack up with her. As you can imagine, we're all thrilled about it."

"It's your business?"

"Well, yeah, when he comes to client functions dragging that infant. You think this makes our clients value his professional opinions?" Dave's face and voice were full of contempt.

Beau threw another quick glance at Mick Watters. He was laughing with the girl, and his hand was edging around to her leather-covered ass. She was leaning forward, so her unbound breasts, outlined clearly in the thin black top, just touched his chest, seeming not to care if anyone else noticed.

Unbidden, the thought floated into Beau's mind about the greatest gift being the gift of the poet: to see yourself the way others saw you.

But looking at the ad man eyeing his nubile young girlfriend made him suddenly feel like vomiting.

Dave never did understand why Beau abruptly excused himself and fled from the restaurant. Five minutes after he'd first seen Mick Watters, Beau's MG was screeching out of the restaurant's parking lot.

***

Four hours later he felt calmer and more reasonable. He wasn't another Mick Watters. He knew he wasn't. And Amanda was nothing like that girl.

But facts had to be faced. Ben was gone. His own life was here. He had neither the desire, nor the energy and the money to start over again, even if it meant returning to live in New York, which he loved. He didn't mind being ostracized by his social circle or enduring a divorce. And he suspected if he lived with Amanda, he would be more than happy. In theory, it was right.

But in practice, he just couldn't do it. He couldn't uproot his life, destroy Jean's, break apart the structure they'd built together, even if the foundation had been rocky for thirty years.

Yeah, he understood Ben's point. Love like this is rare and special; you had to grab it if you were ever lucky enough to find it. But what if what he thought was love today nudged him tomorrow into an open shirt and gold chains, dating a teenage girl in a leather miniskirt?

Maybe Ben was just the lucky one in a million. Lindsey had come all the way from Prague to say goodbye to him; she looked like a good woman. He could believe that Ben never loved anyone more than Lindsey. Even so, they'd broken up. She'd been there for his funeral, sure. But where was she all the years that he was growing old and sick?

No. He just couldn't take a risk like that—even assuming Amanda would be willing to live with him. His life was looking after Jean, taking care of her; he'd done it for too many years. It was a serious responsibility. He couldn't just dump her and expect her to function without him. As it was, she was barely functioning with him.

This wasn't a decision Amanda could be part of. He had to decide for them both.

And he knew that despite the very real passion he felt, he had to let her go. For good. The only real mistake he'd made, he concluded grimly, was in telling her about it, trying to minimize her hurt. She had tried to keep her feelings to herself, but it wasn't possible, and between lust and sympathy for her, he'd ended up falling right back into the relationship.

No, he told himself. It was over now, and if he had to break off the relationship entirely, to avoid being tempted by her sweet silvery voice on the phone and ongoing thoughts of her, he would do it. He couldn't have it all. He'd chosen Jean years ago. That meant he couldn't have Amanda now.

He regretted it, but told himself to do the right thing. It would hurt for awhile, but the longer he was away from her, the easier it would be for both of them. He was finally prepared to pay the price.

***

Amanda could not get the figures to come out right, and she'd added them three times. They were the numbers that the Fieldston office had faxed over, but when she compared them with the hotel's figures, there was a discrepancy.

Obviously, she wasn't concentrating. She took a deep breath and was about to re-start the process from the beginning when the phone rang on

Jerry's private line. She picked it up. "Jerry Wrightman's office."

"Amanda?" It was Beau, sounding incredulous.

A happy smile flickered over her face. It was the first time he'd called since he left, five days before. "Hi!"

"I thought you weren't working today."

She smiled mischievously into the phone. "Is that why you called?"

"No... " He sounded distracted and far away. Obviously, he wasn't going to banter with her, as he usually did. "Look, I'm in a rush. The Fieldstons just called and they want a whole new outline from me and some photos of the interior of the Lorelei, for their set designer. I think they're looking for photos of the lobby and some of the upstairs rooms—the ones you don't use for guests. Can you help with that?"

"Yes, sure." She was a little bewildered. Before, even on his busiest days, he had always made time to say something personal to her. This call, apparently, was all business. She forced herself to speak calmly. "Are they sending a photographer?"

"I think the set designer wants to come over himself, with a camera and a sketchbook. Can Jerry show him around today?"

"Jerry's at a meeting downtown. From there he's going on to a dinner." She paused before saying, trying not to sound hurt, "I can show him around, if you like." Why hadn't he just asked her?

"Would you?" He didn't seem to notice her tone. "That would be very helpful." He read out the designer's name and phone number.

Automatically, feeling dazed, Amanda wrote it down. Why wasn't he treating her as he usually did? What was wrong?

"Tell Jerry thanks for me," he was saying as she tried to stem the disquiet flooding her heart. "And sorry if we're disrupting his usual routine."

"I'll tell him—" she began.

But she didn't get the chance to finish, because Beau abruptly hung up.

***

In the next two weeks, he phoned no less than six times—each time to Jerry's office, never to the switchboard at night. Each time, Amanda answered the phone, expecting him to revert to his old teasing and intimate personal tones. He never did.

Instead, he always asked brusquely for Jerry. Jerry always closed his door during these conversations, making her feel shut out. If Jerry wasn't in, Beau asked for him to call back, and specified that Jerry should return the call from home.

At first she was surprised, then bewildered, then hurt. What had happened?

She kept expecting him to phone the switchboard and explain. He had been tender and warm with her when they said goodbye. It had been wonderful.

Suddenly, in the space of a few days, he was behaving like a stranger.

In the third week after Beau left, she had to send him a packet by Federal Express. She assembled and copied the photos and charts Jerry gave her and took the opportunity to include a brief, urgent note: "Anything wrong? Can't we talk?"

There was no reply.

Jerry seemed to notice her despondency. One day, after yet another phone call in which Beau asked in a rush for Jerry and virtually ignored her, Jerry saw her downcast face as he hurried out to deal with a booking for a big wedding. Instead of continuing out the door, he stopped. "Amanda—I hope it doesn't bother you that Beau has been—well—not too cordial. He's really under the gun with this show. I mean, I hope you're not taking it personally."

Startled, she looked up from the typewriter. She hadn't thought it was that obvious, but Jerry had known her for a long time. He was looking at her with concern on his round face. She managed a laugh that to her ears sounded fairly natural. "Jerry! Why would I? We all get busy."

"Yeah, but when Beau's writing, he can really be a bear. He's so involved with creating that he seems to forget about people."

"We get our share of creative people here. I'm used to it." She hoped her tone was casual and unconcerned.

He looked at her, uncertain. "Well—I knew you two were friendly. I just thought you might have felt—I don't know—unappreciated."

She smiled, but it was an effort. "How could I possibly? You're my boss."

He smiled too, and hurried out, but once his footsteps echoed away on the marble floor, the hurt returned to her eyes. It was one thing to get wrapped up in work; it was another to brush aside someone you'd been really close to. Somehow, when she thought of his behavior—and she thought of it constantly—the tingle of uneasiness at the back of her mind grew.

In fact, by now it was more than a tingle; it was a heavy, weighted presence in her throat and stomach.

But she could handle it. She knew this relationship required stamina and discretion. She would tough it out until he called her—and if after a reasonable time he didn't call, she'd get in touch with him and ask what was wrong.

Would he really not call her for weeks? They hadn't been out of touch for that long since their first phone conversation, back in the fall. How would it feel not to talk to him for that long?

***

In the lobby, Jerry waved and smiled automatically at the couple settled in comfortable chairs by the front door. But as he began to cross the fifty feet toward them, his mind wasn't on their wedding plans and whether he could sell them his most lavish event package.

It was on Amanda's face, getting paler and thinner day by day, and on the strange need Beau seemed to feel now to deal with him personally, instead of letting Amanda handle most details, as he had before. Of course, bringing top show people into the Lorelei did mean getting all the arrangements right, but Jerry knew—and he knew Beau knew—that Amanda was as efficient as he was.

He wondered if they'd had some kind of falling out. Amanda wouldn't tell him; Beau was a very important client now, and angering him would be a serious misstep. On the other hand, she had always been wonderful with the hotel's clients; they adored her and often asked for her rather than him. Beau had said nothing to him. If there was a problem, Beau wasn't the type to keep quiet.

What if their relationship was more than just professional? Jerry hated to think about that, but he remembered the ill-starred night in the lounge when Beau had spilled the drink on one of Jerry's most important contacts who was making a pass at Amanda.

He had no idea why Amanda would find *him* attractive, but he could see why Beau would be attracted to *her*. He himself could conceivably—he tamped down on the thought rising involuntarily in his mind and the sudden resentment toward Beau that went with it. No!

To block it out even further, he quickened his pace to the chairs where a young man and woman sat, in expensive casual clothes. "Hello!" he said enthusiastically, extending his hand, brushing the unwanted thoughts from his mind. "Good to see you again. Now, how can we help you?"

***

It was easy to keep busy during the day. There was plenty of pressure from the agency on the two ad campaigns, plus relentless nagging from Perry to finish the libretto and the songs. The pace was maddening; he hadn't worked so hard since he was twenty-five.

The nights were a different story.

He *needed* to talk to her, damn it! He needed just to hear her voice. Hear the sparkle, hear the banter. Laugh with her. Tell her what he was thinking.

And every time he wanted to pick up the phone and refused to do it, especially when the urge was almost unbearable, he knew he was doing the right thing.

But he couldn't sleep through the night anymore, couldn't manage more than a short nap. Where before he couldn't remember her features distinctly, now he could see her face in front of him, clear as a snapshot, at all hours of the day and night. He was awake more dawns than he wanted to count, and waved out too many midnights in between.

He was drinking again, a couple of shots with dinner, and sometimes a pick-me-up when he was writing in the middle of the night. His smoking had gone up from two packs a day to two and a half, and within a month, to three.

But he didn't reach for the phone, no matter how often he wanted to. He told himself this was the right choice, the *inevitable* choice. That thought— and persistent distasteful thoughts of Mick Watters and his young bimbo— helped him walk away when the desire to dial became overwhelming.

But every time he managed to conquer the urge to call her, he found himself reaching for a cigarette—or a bottle of scotch.

CHAPTER 24

Amanda finally, reluctantly, faced the relentless truth: though he'd now been gone for a month, Beau had never phoned her once. When she happened to pick up his calls to Jerry, he was cold, impersonal, and quick with her. She couldn't find the right way to ask what was wrong, and she couldn't—though she tried—affect casual indifference. When she heard his voice, so standoffish and brisk, so different from what it had been just a few weeks before, it shriveled the words inside her.

The days, she noted listlessly, were becoming gray. Exhausting. Worthless. Day after day, she dragged herself out of bed and faced uninteresting chores that repeated themselves over and over. Unendingly. Nothing seemed worthwhile.

She was losing weight, she realized without interest. Her clothes were hanging on her, and she couldn't seem to work up an appetite for much more than toast and tea these days.

When the phone rang, her heart began to pump harder, not in anticipation, but in dread. She wanted so badly for things to go back to the way they had been, but it seemed as though every day, he was drifting further and further away from her.

And she didn't know why.

Couldn't even find a way to ask.

"You have to say *something*," Doreen said six weeks later, watching Amanda listlessly spoon up some yogurt in her tiny kitchen. It alarmed her how little Amanda was eating these days. She was fading visibly week by week, and didn't seem to care. "You're in this relationship, too. You're entitled to ask. Just *ask*, Amanda!"

Amanda contemplated *just asking* why he didn't seem to give a damn about her suddenly. Involuntarily, what rose in her mind was the picture of her mother screaming at her father, "You're no good! You're *useless*! Why don't you ever give me what I want? I'm *entitled* to this vacation!"

Demanding, always demanding. Sitting on her ever-fattening bottom at home, insisting her stick-thin husband work even more hours to provide even more dollars she could squander on shopping trips that never made her happy, because *things* were not the answer to her unhappiness, so more *things* would not solve the problem.

This time, she shrieked that she *deserved* so much more. Shrieked for hours, until she was hoarse, and Josie and Amanda were cowering in their rooms, their heads buried in their pillows to shut out the shrilling.

Her father had left a week later.

The thought of *demanding* like that made her stomach clench. She'd learned early in life exactly what happened when you demanded something from a man.

She pushed the yogurt away and met Doreen's eyes defiantly. "I'm full."

Doreen glanced at the yogurt. It looked untouched. But she said nothing. When Amanda made up her mind, reasonable, logical arguments went nowhere.

She'll figure it out, Doreen thought. *Amanda's really smart.* But she was also, Doreen thought regretfully, head over heels in love. And that meant she was in for a lot of pain.

***

She wished she could just forget. Yet she couldn't. Once more, the smell of his cologne was driving her crazy. She smelled it everywhere—in her apartment, at the hotel, sometimes even outdoors. At times it was so strong she found herself turning around, trying to spot him.

He was never there.

She'd asked others several times if they smelled anything. They never did. Her questions were first forthright, then circumspect. Finally she stopped asking. But she never stopped smelling it.

She thought about seeing a doctor, but couldn't figure out how to explain her problem.

The only thing that seemed to help was constant motion. She found that though there seemed to be a weight dragging at her heart all the time, though the days seemed gray and dull, she could bear it all if she kept moving. She went back to double shifts at work and found some relief in answering phones at night, once she accepted that the calls she picked up would never be from him.

Alone in the dark hours, thinking of his praise, she went on scribbling her verses, on the scratch pads Jerry always provided at the switchboard. It was habit as much as his encouragement that drove her, and now she had another motivation: as she wrote, it gave her an outlet for her hurt and allowed her to put down some of what she felt. With her singing becoming every day something she cared less and less about, she needed something positive in her life. Beau was making it more and more clear that he was no longer in it.

She found the brochure in her mail one night when she came home, exhausted, after a late evening at work. Bill... bill... notice of insurance policy change... folded notice of a tenants' meeting in her building. And a tri-fold glossy brochure with *"Musical Lyricist Workshop"* in iridescent green splashed across the white exterior.

The return address came from the school where Beau had spoken. They'd had to sign in that night... that's how she must have gotten on the mailing list. Curious, she slit it open and read down the three inside pages.

The school was presenting a six-week workshop for beginner musical theater lyricists, with the foundations of lyric writing, examples of great musical lyrics, introduction to types of musical theater lyrics—expository song, ballad, comic song, torch song—with discussion of their structure and history.

She scanned it once with casual interest, hoping for mention of Beau's name or the class where he'd lectured. She read it again, when she put the water on for tea, with more attention. By the time she read it for the fourth time, over her second cup of steaming tea and the buttered toast which was all her stomach could handle these days, she'd pulled out her calendar. And for the first time since she'd worked for Jerry, Amanda decided to cede the night shift to someone else—for good. She wondered, with a touch of her old mischievousness, whether he'd faint when she told him.

***

The voice on the line was courteous and intelligent, but unfamiliar. "Is this Amanda Harary?"

"Yes." It was early the next morning, and she had just dropped her handbag in her desk drawer when Tiffany put through this call from the switchboard. She glanced at the clock—it was ten to eight—yet the young man's voice sounded alert and very professional.

"My name is David Puffen. A few months ago I left a package for Beau Kellogg at your front desk." He paused. "Mr. Kellogg had asked to see some pages I wrote."

Oh, God. Her heart pounded furiously at the unexpected mention of his name from this complete stranger, but kept her voice calm and polite. "Yes?"

"I just spoke to Mr. Kellogg. He's sending my pages back. He suggested it would be best to overnight them to you at the hotel, since I don't have a permanent address at the moment. Will that be convenient?" She choked back the thought that popped unbidden into her mind: *Why me? Why do I have to be involved in this? I'm not a library where you check things in and out.*

But she never blew up in front of a guest, so after a brief pause, she said evenly, "That will be fine. When will the package be here?"

"Tomorrow by noon. I'll swing by in the afternoon to pick it up."

"I'll leave instructions at the desk to turn it over to you."

"Oh, no. Please." Suddenly the voice turned anxious. "They're my only copies. Would you hold onto them for me?"

"Why me?"

"Mr. Kellogg said you were absolutely reliable. I'd feel much safer if you kept them."

She hesitated for a moment, but it really wasn't a big deal. And though Beau wasn't speaking to her, he still seemed to hold her in some esteem, at least professionally. She wanted to justify his faith in her. "All right. But I have to leave here at 6:15. Can you be here before then?"

"Easily," David Puffen reassured her. "Thanks so much."

***

He was late. She tapped the bulky white and purple package in her hand and glanced at the clock. He'd said afternoon. It was now 6:21. She had to register for the lyric workshop at 7:00. Just how long was she supposed to wait?

She could leave the package at the desk. It would be safe enough with one of the clerks, she tried to argue with herself. If she attached a note with his name on it and left very specific instructions...

No. She couldn't just walk away, not when Beau had recommended her. She wouldn't see him again—she knew that now—but he still trusted her. She told herself she owed it to him to see it through.

By 6:40 she'd decided she had to leave. By 6:51 she was still there, fretting and irritated.

She couldn't miss the chance to sign up for the workshop. It was one of the few things in her life now that she thought she might really love.

As much as she loved...

No! Forget him. Concentrate on now.

But concentrating just reminded her of how irritated she was. She had no phone number for this guy, and he'd said himself he had no permanent address. Perfect. Any sensible person would just leave the package at the desk and go.

No. Beau trusted me... but where is this jerk? He'd seemed the type to keep his word... though the clock on the wall now read 7:30.

She sighed. Too late to sign up for the workshop tonight. She prayed there would still be a place open tomorrow.

***

He finally showed up at 8:32, a tall, slender young man in hornrimmed glasses, who came through the revolving doors, glanced around and headed unerringly for her across the shining floor of the lobby. "Are you Amanda?"

She wanted to throw something at him. "David Puffen?"

He smiled at her engagingly. "Yes, I'm David."

"You're very late," she told him crisply, thrusting the package at him.

He looked up at the clock above the reception desk in sublime innocence, which made her even angrier.

"You *said* you'd be here this afternoon!" she practically hissed at him. "And I had things to do tonight!"

"Oh, I'm sorry." His chagrin was real. He took the package, glanced at the address and gave her a relieved smile. "I should have called. I'd have been here long ago, but I had a fare out to the airport, and there was an accident on the way back. Traffic crawled for forty minutes. I really appreciate you waiting for me."

She grimaced. "I should have left long ago."

"I really am sorry I held you up."

It was hard to stay furious at someone who was so genuinely apologetic. "Well, at least you showed up," she said grudgingly. "Some people never do. And now, if you don't mind, I'd like to go home."

"Can I take you to dinner?"

The invitation was so unexpected, so out of the blue, that Amanda just stared at him for a moment, not sure she had heard correctly. "What?"

"Well... it's the least I can do... and if you waited for me all this time, I'm sure you haven't eaten. Have you?" When she shook her head, he went on, "Really, I'd like to show my appreciation. I know a great Italian place near here."

Her mind flew at once to the little Italian hideaway where Beau had taken her, months ago, and broken her heart. She felt a little sick at the memory. How had they moved from such intimacy to not speaking? What had happened?

David saw her downcast face and misinterpreted it. "It doesn't have to be Italian. You pick it. I caused you all kinds of grief, so we'll go wherever you want."

He gave her another smile, warm and open.

She hesitated. "Thank you, but I really just want to get home."

"How about another night?"

He was asking for a date. Openly and rather insistently. She looked up at him—he was at least Beau's height, six two or taller, while she was only about five four, even in two-inch heels—and wondered why. She certainly hadn't been warm and inviting, and she had been on the go all day; her face and hair were wrecked. Not one of her more appealing moments.

So why was he asking?

It didn't matter. She wasn't even particularly curious. Something inside her said silently that accepting a date with anyone else was akin to admitting in her heart of hearts that there was no hope with Beau. Even though she *knew* there was no hope—something her friends never failed to remind her of regularly, lest she fall back into old habits—some final reservoir of longing still lingered.

And as long as it was there, she dared not accept a date with anyone else. Once she did, she would be shutting the door on the most important relationship of her life. She just wasn't ready for that yet.

She knew without allowing herself to frame the words, even in her mind, that she would never feel this sense of connection so strongly with anyone again.

It was worth trying to hold onto, somehow. Somehow there had to be something more, some finality, not this... dangling, this lack of closure.

Whatever it was, it was well worth turning down a date with a man she didn't even know.

David was still waiting, a faint smile on his face. He had nice skin, she noted disinterestedly, with a few freckles scattered attractively over his nose, and thick dark eyelashes framing hazel eyes. Before Beau, she decided, she'd have been surprised and flattered that a David Puffen would ask her out.

Now it didn't matter.

She drew herself up straight, but her voice was much gentler when she answered. Though she was still furious at his thoughtlessness, she couldn't hate the guy, and she didn't want to hurt him. "Thanks," she said, "but I'm starting a night class on top of my job. I'll be really busy for some time."

"What kind of class?" He looked interested.

She hesitated, then told him.

He raised his eyebrows and shifted the package into his left hand. "Sounds exciting. Tell you what. Why don't you give me your phone number, and I'll try you in a few weeks? You might not be as busy as you think."

She wondered how she would have reacted if Beau had been this persistent. Well, he *had* been... in the beginning. Her stomach cramped at the thought.

"You can usually reach me here," she said hurriedly. "Just ask for Amanda, and if I'm not in, leave a message."

Just thinking of Beau was making tears sting her eyelids. She really had to end this conversation. "Look, I really have to go," she said, no longer trying to be polite. "I'm sorry I snapped at you." The unshed tears were already making her cheeks ache and her throat hurt.

She ducked her head by way of farewell and almost ran back to her office. She had a good cry in the deserted office and took some minutes to calm down afterward before she finally left—by the back exit, in case the persistent David Puffen was still hanging around the lobby.

CHAPTER 25

I can't *believe* you're putting up with this!" Stephanie exclaimed.

She and Fleur had listened silently for an hour as Amanda finally poured out her heart about Beau and their relationship. She'd told Doreen and a few of her other friends some time before, but she'd always hesitated to tell Stephanie and Fleur—especially Stephanie, whose lyrics were loquacious and cutting, and whose opinion of personal matters was seldom less. When Amanda had reluctantly explained, in answer to Stephanie's emotional demand, why she'd been forgetful and overwrought for months, Stephanie had launched into a diatribe. "Amanda, he's twice your age and unavailable, in every *possible* way, and he's treating you like—" She flapped her hands, for once at a loss for words. She stopped and put her hands on her hips. "Why you are putting up with this?"

"Obviously, because she loves him," Fleur said mildly.

Stephanie glared at her. "Please! Whose side are you on?"

"Same side you're on—Amanda's. But she's in pain and I'm trying to help."

"Well, you're not!" Stephanie snapped.

Amanda could see the two women were headed for their own lovers' spat, and she felt vaguely guilty about it. "Please stop!" she broke in. "Don't you two get mad at each other over this."

"We aren't," Stephanie insisted, at the same moment Fleur said, "So what if we are?"

The three girls looked at each other and burst out laughing.

Stephanie, her face rosier after the laughter, put a gentle hand on Amanda's arm. "Look, this is said with love, okay? You know you're better than this, that you *deserve* better than this."

In spite of her pain, Amanda managed a smile. When Stephanie let in the emotions that could overwhelm her, she could be so sweet, so caring. It made Amanda feel better just looking at her.

Talking about Beau wasn't the reason she'd come to the loft, though; she had an idea she wanted to run past them.

"I came because I want to know what you think," she said carefully. "Honest opinions, okay?"

"He's a dick," Stephanie said at once.

"Steph—"

"You said be honest."

"Not about that. Something else."

"Not another guy!" Stephanie looked dumbfounded.

"No, no, no." Amanda reached into her purse and brought out the brochure for the lyric-writing workshop. She handed it to them.

The girls looked it over carefully. "Alex Graham-Munroe," Fleur said, obviously impressed, pointing at the name on the bottom. "He's the guy who mentored a lot of the new kids writing stuff for the Hot Grill. He's supposed to be good." Then she looked curiously at Amanda. "How do you know about him?"

"I got this in the mail. I was at one of his workshops with Beau."

"Ah! The plot thickens!"

"Cool it, Steph," Fleur said. Her wide forehead was creased in puzzlement. "But Amanda, why are *you* taking a lyricist's workshop?"

"Tell me you're not trying to *understand* that bastard," Stephanie groaned.

"Stephanie, stop! I'm really enjoying it. It seems like it's just what I always really wanted. The fact is... I'm thinking maybe I... don't want to sing anymore."

Now they were both dumbfounded. "Not sing?" Stephanie finally croaked. "After all that training? All that work?"

Amanda shrugged her shoulders. It had come to her during one of her many sleepless nights ("white nights", the French called them—she loved the phrase even if she hated the experience) that her stage fright was an obstacle she might never overcome, and at this point, she no longer cared. She had dropped the gig at the Lorelei lounge after the incident with Jerry's hotel friends, and she was tired of endless scales, hours of repetitive practice and the prospect of constant auditions against much better and better-looking singers than she would ever be. Despite her love for the theater, standing on a stage wasn't really where she wanted to be; that was her mother's dream, not hers. It had taken her years to recognize it.

"Have you done any lyric writing before?" Fleur asked skeptically.

"A few things, here and there." Amanda reached into her purse, brought out her pad and handed it to them. Fleur looked over Stephanie's shoulder as Stephanie flipped through, reading each page until they both reached the end.

"Well?" Amanda asked.

"Raw," Stephanie said. "But... not bad. There might be something there."

Amanda reached into her pocket. "As a sample—not an insult, Steph, ok?—I re-wrote a couple of verses of '*The Girl with the Basket*'. Just to give you an idea of what I could do with meter and rhyme."

"I promise not to be insulted," Stephanie said as she took the paper.

There was silence when she finished. "It's good," Fleur said, looking questioningly at Stephanie.

Stephanie nodded reluctantly. "It is good." She handed the paper back to Amanda. "Welcome to the other side of the footlights."

***

Amanda was relieved that Stephanie hadn't been upset about her new aspirations: she could be touchy, as Fleur could attest, but she was also brilliant. If she thought Amanda had something going for her, then her crazy plan to leave the performing side and move to the writing side wasn't so crazy after all.

It was bleak comfort, even though it meant the end of expensive voice lessons and coaching and more time at home, doing the assignments for the lyric workshop and scribbling her own original work. These days, she couldn't find much comfort in anything else.

She spent her free time seeing friends, killing time, keeping endlessly busy. It was becoming a game to look at a weekly calendar and fill it in, use it up. Time was not of the essence; what she could cram into it was. And the more she could engage her mind and stop thinking about painful subjects, the better off she'd be.

She went to lots of art galleries, because they were free or very inexpensive, and there was a lot to see. Never mind that five minutes after she left it she couldn't remember a single painting. She agreed enthusiastically to meals with friends which she couldn't bring herself to eat. She went faithfully to aerobics classes four times a week.

She hated the exercises, loathed the instructor, and felt horrible during the workout, but it kept her from thinking of anything more complicated than which leg to lift. She went to movies, as long as they were funny. Sad films might open the floodgates, and she was too close to tears every day, as it was. She would gladly sit through a Marx Brothers double feature, or a Buster Keaton retrospective, but no Chaplin. She went to enough Burt Reynolds films to write a book about his career.

In short, she had never been so busy. And later, when she looked back on this period of her life, except for the lyric workshop, she couldn't remember a single thing about it.

(HAPTER 26

Beau was figuring with a calculator and a piece of paper, and the figures didn't match. Since he kept the checkbook and paid all the monthly bills at home, he'd thought it would only take a few minutes to reconcile the figures from the Fieldston Organization (in his role as associate producer) with those of the Lorelei, for the producers' payments to the hotel.

Except the numbers weren't working out.

For some reason, the hotel accountant listed the amount received from Fieldston as far less than the amount Fieldston insisted they had paid.

He had agreed to look into it, because he was the official liaison between the two parties, responsible for keeping everyone happy until the show opened. Perry wasn't giving a specific opening date at the moment, which was driving him crazy, as he and Jules were almost finished with the score and more and more convinced this could be their greatest show ever. They were willing to attend backers' auditions and jump through all the usual hoops—but Perry was for some reason shying away from setting them up, and it was making Beau uneasy.

The agency work had finally been completed, and though he had done his best, as always, neither campaign ended up with what they'd hoped for: an unforgettable song like the Snap jingle. They'd thanked him and paid him, but he could see their disappointment. Well, what did they expect? A song like that was a freak; it came along once in a lifetime, if you were lucky.

Beau couldn't understand why, but the damn thing was being played everywhere. Renny's album had come out in March, and DJ's all over town had seized on that song and played it incessantly. Even more unbelievable, it had become one of *the* big hits on the album. People were humming it—even more incredibly, they were *buying* it. It was not only boosting album sales, but Renny had put out the jingle as a single, and *that* was selling like hotcakes too.

The agency reported on the QT to Jim that Snap sales had gone through the roof, and the company attributed it in large part to the jingle.

None of that, though, had anything to do with these figures. He stretched and yawned. He was no accountant, but a suspicion was beginning to form at the back of his mind. He thought of Jerry and his lackadaisical attitude, his enthusiasm that often overrode precision, and how he always managed to have amazing staff—like Amanda—to dot the i's and cross the t's, so *he* looked good.

Wasn't it possible that Jerry had made the mistake?

If so, Beau wanted to know it.

He wondered how he was going to phrase it, as he dialed Jerry's office.

But it was Amanda who picked up the phone. "Hi," he said quickly, forestalling any personal comment. "Is Jerry in?"

He could hear her hurt in her answer, which came out a little too cool and precise. "He's on the other line. Should I have him call you back, or do you trust me to take a message?"

For just a minute, it flashed through his mind that Amanda could have screwed up the figures. Then he thought: *No, she's too capable.* Besides, Karen, the bookkeeper, handled all the funds; Amanda didn't.

"Listen," he said to her, "you should know by now that I trust you with everything."

There was a pause. "Funny, you could have fooled me."

She was definitely hurt. "That's ridiculous," he went on. "I know what you're capable of."

"Do you?"

He was taken aback; she had never talked to him like that before, and he certainly didn't like it.

"You must be having a bad day," he said, trying to give her the benefit of the doubt.

"Actually, I'm having a wonderful day. It's looking like spring here and things are going great." She still sounded snotty.

"Then you must be mad at me." There was silence at the other end.

"Well, look, I haven't got all day to play guessing games. Would you tell Jerry I need to talk to him today? Have him call me as soon as he can." He hung up, steamed at her. It didn't occur to him that she was simply giving him a taste of his own medicine.

She was being rude and snippy, and he hadn't done a damn thing to deserve it.

***

Amanda glared at the phone she had just hung up. She'd never let her anger show before while talking to Beau, but to call and hardly even acknowledge her after all this time made her furious. And he'd acted like *he* was the injured party!

But what really made her furious was that he never even asked her *why* she was mad.

***

The lyric-writing workshop ended in mid-April, but a more advanced workshop began a week later, and Amanda signed up for it eagerly. Alex had been very friendly when she joined the class, because he remembered she had accompanied Beau to the class in February. Now, though, he was friendly because she was turning out to be one of his best students.

Despite having a much later start than the others, she had two advantages that he believed would push her to the head of the pack: a natural feeling for words and word patterns, and her experience as a singer, which helped her understand what a singer needed from a song. Plus, all those years of singing show songs had given her a familiarity with Broadway music—including the obscure stuff—that was invaluable.

He encouraged her to do extra assignments and allowed her to range farther than the other beginner students. The truth was, she was more advanced the night she walked in than the others, and he recognized it. He also encouraged her to work with both Fleur and Steph on pieces for the Hot Grill. While the girls complained good-naturedly that she'd forced them to find a new singer, they were glad to have her join them on the songs. In fact, they were planning to audition for the next Hot Grill revue in May.

David Puffen had called again, as he'd promised. Amanda had talked to him at length several times and enjoyed the conversations, but demurred at going out with him. She still felt that accepting a date with anyone else meant turning her back on Beau, even though she felt deserted by him. She was sure when his show opened, there'd be some kind of resolution between them. After all, he'd have to come to New York for the opening, wouldn't he?

***

Beau's drinking was getting out of hand. He'd never drunk in the morning before, but as summer came in, he was taking a shot around 11:00 a.m., so he could get through his work until noon, and then a couple of shots in the early afternoon until he could have a drink before dinner. He was also smoking more than ever, and whenever he thought of Ben, his cigarette consumption went up. For some reason, after his last two jingles, Jim wasn't getting the kind of agency interest that he'd had before; the ad jobs weren't falling in his lap as they had after the Snap jingle. He knew his work had been as competent on those as on all the campaigns before it, but the clients just weren't that impressed.

He'd called Renny Marks, hoping to interest him in collaborating on something else, but despite the fact that the song was still in the Top 40 (a *jingle*!), Renny had said vaguely that he was just waiting for the show material; he wanted to rest his voice until they started rehearsals.

It didn't matter, he told himself. The important thing was to finish the show. There'd be no money from Fieldston until they were done, but Perry demanded progress reports almost every day, and though he seemed to be elusive about answering Beau's questions, he was not shy about demanding that Beau answer his.

As the California summer waned toward fall and his 61st birthday, he had plenty on his mind. He was concerned about the discrepancy in the hotel account and uneasy about Perry, who still had scheduled no auditions. He was always on guard for what Jean might do, and he missed Ben, the little leprechaun, more than he would have believed.

Most of all, he was really nettled that Amanda was being so cool to him.

27

On the last day of September, Beau looked at his life and wondered how it could all have turned to such shit.

He and Jules had finally agreed, in the interest of pushing Perry into action, to let him see some of their work. Jules had made a tape of six completed songs and Beau had sent along a carefully structured libretto, so Perry would know where they fit into the overall scheme. They'd overnighted the package to Perry's office, and promptly heard back that "This ain't exactly what we had in mind, fellas", which for Perry was being diplomatic and in any language meant 'rewrite'. If Perry didn't like their new stuff, it almost certainly would mean postponing mounting the show.

Jim had gone looking for more ad work, which Beau felt was prudent, since Perry was paying nothing but his (insignificant) associate producer's fees until the material was finished and approved. But the jobs that had come before with relative ease were now drying up. Jim told him grimly it was a good thing he had royalties coming on Renny's song, because word was—he was sorry, buddy, but here it was—the clients weren't all that excited about working with him. They felt the success of the Snap jingle was a freak (he agreed; of course it was) and that the younger guys knew what they wanted and could deliver it more effectively (and cheaper) than he could. Of course he'd keep looking…

He was feeling tired and sluggish a lot of the time and didn't know why. It didn't occur to him that the empty scotch bottles and his lethargy could somehow be related, but he found himself needing more pick-me-ups than usual. No, he didn't need a nap or a vacation; just another drink would be fine.

Jean made noises about his attending an AA meeting.

She didn't know what she was talking about.

And he was *not* being unreasonable; it just seemed like the people around him these days were getting a lot stupider!

It occurred to him that at this time last year he'd just begun to talk to Amanda on the phone. He thought about how promising *that* had been, until she started getting high-strung and unreasonable too. (He'd managed somehow, in the ensuing months, to forget that he'd made a point of distancing himself from her.)

You'd think being a performer, she'd understand about his need for quiet contemplation. But she was suddenly all cold and haughty with him. Mrs. High and Mighty: who the hell did she think *she* was? A clerk at a hotel, for God's sake!

But every time he called the Lorelei now, she was always the one who answered; he never seemed to catch Jerry in, and always had to leave messages. And most of the time, the dumb bastard didn't return his calls. He didn't know which rankled him more, not being able to reach Jerry or having to talk to Amanda.

Well, maybe he should try Jerry at night. The guy had to be in sometime; he had a job, didn't he? So if he wasn't in during the day, it stood to reason he was working later.

Fine. He'd call him later and dress him down for not returning his calls.

But most of all he'd dress him down because he'd finally figured out why the hotel figures and the Fieldston's figures didn't match, and unless he was very wrong, he knew that his old army buddy, whose life he'd saved in France forty years before, hadn't just made a careless error, as he was so prone to do. No, Beau would stake his life on the fact that Jerry, who'd been with the Lorelei for more than ten years, was skimming funds from his own hotel.

***

Jerry had left more than an hour before, but Amanda was still working at 8:30. The days were getting shorter, and it was already dark, but there was a wonderful snap in the air that reminded her again of the promise of such nights.

And what did that promise ever get me, she thought, *except a heart broken six ways to Sunday?* She tried not to remember her optimism and uncomplicated happiness just last year.

The phone rang in Jerry's office, and she left the front desk and went back to her office to pick it up.

It was Beau, and she stiffened. "Yes?"

He didn't bother saying hello. "I was wondering if Jerry was in." He sounded—well, not quite sober. The words were a little slurred, and she was surprised. Had he been somewhere and had too much to drink? *At 5:30?* she wondered uneasily. *Who can manage to get drunk by 5:30?*

"He left early," she said carefully.

"Well, where is he?"

Amanda knew he was on his way home, if he hadn't arrived already. But she said, "I'm not sure."

"Well, why don't you find out?" He sounded belligerent. "Do you know how many times I've called him in the last few weeks? Why the hell isn't he returning my calls—or are *you* just not passing on the messages?"

She began to steam. These days, it didn't take much. "I always pass on messages. What did you think I did with them?"

"Why don't you tell me?"

"I don't know," she said coolly. "I've just been doing my job."

"That's a laugh! You've been doing a lot *more* than your job, and I don't like it!"

"What do you mean?" There was a bizarre note in his voice, and it was causing a cold sensation in the pit of her stomach.

"You know damn well what I mean!"

She sat very still. "What are you accusing me of?"

He almost sputtered in his rage. "What *should* I accuse you of— screwing up communications between me and the hotel? Messing up my friendship with an old friend? Or just being generally nasty and bitchy when I call?"

"If I'm being bitchy and nasty, maybe you should ask yourself why!" she shouted. "Or do you think it has nothing to do with you?"

"No, I *don't* think it has anything to do with me!" he shouted back. He was no longer slurring his words; he was so angry he'd gone cold sober in a split second, and all the disappointment and rage of the past months was coming out. "The truth is you've *always* been a bitch, from the first time I ever talked to you! I don't know how you keep your stupid little job, with the way you talk to guests!"

"I happen to be very gracious with guests!" she yelled. "I've been commended repeatedly on how *well* I handle guest relations!"

"That's a laugh!" he shot back. "But maybe I'm just one of the few who got to know you better—so I found out what a loser you are! Do you know why I even had sex with you? Because I figured no other guy would ever look at you twice! It was the ultimate mercy fuck! And don't kid yourself it ever meant anything. It was just like you were—a cheat from the beginning! It was so lousy I wondered why I hadn't just paid a hooker!"

His heart was pounding so hard his ribs hurt. His head was beginning to pound too.

She was sitting motionless in her chair. Her eyes were wide with shock. She could hardly breathe and couldn't even form words. Her voice had disappeared somewhere into the icy pit in her stomach.

He breathed hard for a few moments, then said, "You're never to speak to me again. I don't ever want to call this hotel and find you there. Make sure somebody else picks up in Jerry's office, or the Lorelei will lose a lot more than just a client."

There was dead silence for a moment, as the telephone lines hummed, three thousand miles apart, with betrayal and pain and shock. For those few seconds, neither of them could think of anything to say.

Then Beau cut the connection forever.

He hung up.

***

He didn't know how long he just sat there, breathing hard in his chair. He knew he was still drunk, and he knew he'd shouted at Amanda, but he wasn't even sure now what he'd said. He knew it was bad, though— to make up for all the times she'd been cool to him on the phone, had treated him offhandedly, had spoken to him with disdain. She'd never try that again. He'd never let her.

It occurred to him that he'd taken out some of his anger and rage at Jerry on Amanda, though he still felt she had some of it coming to her. But what the hell? It didn't matter. In about five minutes, his connection with the Lorelei would be finished. Perry would be disappointed, but Perry could kiss his ass— six great songs and a great libretto, and all he could think of to say was, "This ain't exactly what we had in mind."

That was a joke!

Beau looked for his address book, where he'd written down Jerry's home phone number. It was time to confront him. He knew what Jerry had done, and this was his night for laying down the law to those who crossed him. He knew also why Jerry wasn't returning his calls. Jerry was going to find out it wasn't that easy to avoid him.

***

Fifteen minutes later, Jerry slowly hung up his home telephone. Behind him, he dimly heard his eight-year-old granddaughter and five-year-old grandson shouting in the den. They were probably playing airplanes again, making engine noises as they swooped over the thick carpet. For now, he didn't want to see them, or his wife. Didn't want to see anybody.

He had known Beau Kellogg for forty years, seen him in good moods and bad, seen him impatient, seen him angry. He had never heard Beau like this. He had never heard him spew out such venom, or such vile language. He shivered as he thought about what Beau had said, in a tone of icy rage: "Fix it, or I'll ruin you." It hadn't been a joke.

For the first time, Jerry perceived that his career was in Beau Kellogg's hands, and it wasn't a very safe place.

He hadn't thought it would be tough to juggle the accounts—he could always claim he'd made a mistake and deposited the check from the Fieldstons in the wrong account and then had spent some on—whatever—linens, dishware, extra staff for events—and he would correct things by apologizing and transferring money back.

There'd never been a problem before with his quietly skimming other funds. He'd never even had to apologize and try to gloss things over.

Mrs. Sarandon didn't keep that close an eye on the books, and she'd relied on him and trusted him for twelve years. And he had conscientiously not accepted a raise from her in five years, either—what he skimmed from the hotel receipts made up the difference. It also convinced her that he had the interests of the hotel at heart, and she would always believe him over other staff. The fact that he made sure to change bookkeepers regularly also helped.

Damn this show! He shouldn't have tried to mess with that money, because it was being watched like a hawk! But it just seemed like such easy money, and expenses at home were getting higher and higher…

Amanda had noticed some inconsistencies, and his current bookkeeper Karen had mentioned something once or twice. But how could he know that Beau, who knew him so well, would end up doing producer's work and thus have a reason to dig into his accounts?

He'd figured it out, without saying a word to the Fieldstons or to Karen, but he hadn't confronted Jerry with it before now. Why not?

Jerry thought about this and then, realizing the answer, began to smile. Because he cared about *Amanda*. Beau had held his tongue and kept his connection with the hotel because *she* was there. But now they'd had a fight and he no longer cared.

He had already told Jerry he was going to break the Lorelei's ties with the show. Mrs. Sarandon wouldn't like that at all; she was bragging to all her friends about the additional publicity for the hotel and the excitement of opening night.

Losing this deal meant losing a lot more than just a longtime guest. Jerry knew if he were held responsible, at best he'd lose his job; at worst, if they could prove the financial irregularities, he'd be prosecuted. And he had a wife and household to support; he couldn't go to jail!

But he *would* face all those penalties… unless Mrs. Sarandon believed it was *someone else's* fault.

Well, what if Beau just left the hotel in a snit because of a fight with an employee? He'd had a fight with Amanda, though Jerry didn't know what it was about. But Beau was high-strung and creative; it would be easy to persuade Mrs. Sarandon he'd just gotten irrationally furious with Amanda and flounced out. Amanda would get canned, and that would be that.

There'd be no need for anyone to dig any further. The contract Jerry had signed with the Fieldstons provided that any monies they gave the hotel were non-refundable, so if the deal ended, the hotel still profited. No one would look at those figures again, once they were persuaded Amanda had lost the valuable tie-in. They wouldn't suspect her of dishonesty. Amanda was so squeaky-clean no one would ever think she had skimmed money from the hotel. She'd be reprimanded for lack of tact, but that was all.

In the scheme of things, it was easiest for him if she were fired. In a few months, it wouldn't matter at all. She'd get something new, and he'd be off the hook.

He felt a small twinge at the thought of Amanda's leaving; she'd been a fabulous employee and his right hand, almost impossible to replace. But she was young and single and could get another job easily. He'd even offer to help her; anything to be sure his own interests were protected. Losing Beau and the show in one stroke would be the end for him; and Jerry was unusually creative himself when it came to protecting his own hide.

PART FOUR

CHAPTER 28

October 1983

For the next few hours, she never stopped trembling.

She couldn't stop thinking of the things Beau had said to her, and the ugliness and the shock of it made her feel weak and sick.

When she heard the click of the phone in her ear, after he'd shouted all those mean and horrible things at her, she'd just sat there. She couldn't move her arm to replace the receiver. The hurt she'd felt before was a pinprick compared to the tidal wave of pain that washed over her now.

She couldn't bring herself to believe that all the hideous things he said to her were true. That *he* believed them.

Did he? Was that what he'd always believed? Was that what had really happened between them? Was all the beauty she'd seen between them just an illusion?

Sleep was impossible. She borrowed Valium from Doreen, who offered to supply more "whenever", but she was afraid to take more than one, and that one didn't help.

The next day, the knot in her throat made eating impossible. She forced down a cup of tea, and managed to dress and get to the hotel, trying to ignore the drowning despair and the cramping in her stomach.

"Amanda, can I see you, please?" Jerry walked through the anteroom without looking at her, straight into his office. He didn't toss his hat at the hat rack, either, which had been his morning ritual for as long as she could remember.

The knots in her stomach tightened, but she managed to get up on trembling legs and follow him. He sat down at his desk and motioned for her to sit. She sat down, her back straight, not touching the chair.

Jerry was unusually ill at ease. He fiddled with the paper clips on the desk, eyes darting around the room. He looked awful. His face was paler than she'd ever seen it, and she thought she saw dark lines cutting under his eyes. She was really worried about him. "Jerry?"

"Amanda, we have to talk," he said gently.

She had been trembling, limbs shivering under her clothes, but something ominous in that soft tone ruffled her jangled nerves. *This is going to be bad.*

Then she noticed that Jerry looked really miserable; she felt sorrier for him than for herself. "Beau called me last night," he said quietly, when he saw her eyes on him. "He was very upset. He said unless we made a change in staff right away, he—he was going to break all ties between the Lorelei and the show."

Amanda sat stunned. She could actually hear the silence echoing in her ears. Her eyes began to blur, and she realized that she wasn't breathing. Deliberately, she inhaled deeply before she tried to speak, but her voice still came out hoarse. "What—did he say?"

"He said you'd—uh—been rude to him, that for months you've been difficult when he needed help—" The months, she thought, sickened, when she was trying to suppress her own aches and yearnings, to say nothing of her own hurt, and so had gradually shelled herself off from their previous relationship. She forced herself to listen to the rest. "He said last night you insulted him and impugned his professional reputation, that he had tried to overlook it because of your previous helpfulness and his friendship with me, but he has finally decided he will no longer deal with you. Or with us, if we retain you." He said the last words as though reluctant, and dropped his eyes to the desk as she stared at him.

A curious languor began to descend. She didn't feel like moving, while at the same time she didn't believe any of this was happening. "So am I fired?" she asked. Rudeness to a guest always resulted in firing; it was hotel policy. She'd just never thought she'd lose *her* job because of it; she'd gone out of her way to be gracious and received universally excellent feedback from guests.

"Amanda, honey—" Jerry shifted uncomfortably as she looked at him. "I'm sorry," he mumbled.

Amanda put a hand up to push back the loose hair falling in her face and was surprised to feel tears on her cheeks. She reached for the box of Kleenex on Jerry's desk, but he beat her to it, tucking a clean tissue into her hand. She nodded thanks and pressed it to her eyes. Jerry sighed, watching the tissue shredding as it grew wetter. "Amanda, I'm sorry. I talked to Mrs. Sarandon this morning. I told her you were an exemplary employee. She said no amount of exemplary service could excuse this kind of damage."

"Is that a direct quote?" Amanda sounded stuffy behind the tissue.

"Word for word." He looked at her helplessly. "I don't want to do this, Amanda, believe me."

It was up to her, she thought. Always up to her, to smooth things over, make things easier. Even now. Holding tight to the arm of the chair, she stood up unsteadily. "It's okay, Jerry." She met his troubled look full on, her lips still pressed tight but otherwise calm.

"I'll make some calls," he said, as usual taking refuge in action. "I have friends at other hotels—I'm sure I can help you find something else. One guy, in fact, told me he was *looking* for an assistant manager."

She nodded and tried to say thank you, as she left his office. But as she cleaned out her desk, her hands shaking, she felt sickened and alone.

***

"What a bastard!" Stephanie said grimly, two hours later in the loft.

She and Fleur had been silent while Amanda poured out the story of her firing. Fleur lolled in the brown beanbag chair. Her eyes followed Amanda's sympathetically, while Stephanie alternately fidgeted and paced the threadbare carpet, pausing occasionally to gulp down scorching hot black coffee from a thick mug.

Amanda told them everything that happened in the last twenty-four hours. The girls listened and said nothing.

When she finished talking, she was relieved: it felt so much better to lay the situation in front of friends and ask their advice. No matter what they said, at least she wouldn't face it alone anymore.

Fleur looked at Stephanie. Stephanie looked at Fleur.

Neither of them said anything.

"Well?" Amanda said finally. "I thought you wanted to help."

"Bastard!" Stephanie said again.

Amanda jumped in her seat.

"I didn't mean you," Stephanie said to her.

"What she means is," Fleur elucidated, "this is not a good situation."

"I *said* that," Stephanie said impatiently.

"Yeah, well—" Fleur waved a vague hand.

In the midst of her pain and humiliation, Amanda felt a wave of love for them both. They were completely on her side, and that felt good, no matter how awful she felt otherwise. Even the mug of hot tea in her hands, which Stephanie had thrust at her ten minutes before, seemed to resonate with their concern for her.

Stephanie sat down in the hard wooden straight chair next to Amanda and leaned forward, propping her chin on her fists until she was peering directly into Amanda's face. "All right," she said. "What do you want from us? Sympathy or the truth?"

Amanda managed a faint smile and took a cautious sip of her tea. "I can't have both?"

"I'm serious."

Amanda looked at her and took a deep breath. "I don't actually *want* it, but I think—I need the truth."

Fleur and Stephanie looked at each other again. Fleur gave a short nod, then got up and went over to the piano in the corner. In a minute she was improvising, both hands sweeping over the keys. Amanda heard a lot of minor chords, which indicated that Fleur was upset.

Stephanie, as usual, took the direct route. "This guy is no good for you," she said, as gently as she could.

Amanda defended herself. "He did a lot for me. Because of him, I'm starting a whole new career—the right one, Steph, you know it is—and not repeating my mother's life."

"You did a lot for him, too."

"I picked a piece of paper off the floor!"

"—Out of which came a huge bump in *his* career."

"Because of a song he wrote, not because of me—" Amanda interrupted, but Stephanie rolled on implacably, right over her.

"He got as much out of this as you did, maybe more. But that's not even the point. The point is, he's not giving anything back to you."

Amanda was silent. How could she explain the crescendo in her heart when she looked at him? When he joked with her, when he called her? When he kissed her? How could she define in words how it felt when those dancing brown eyes, full of warmth, looked at her? When those slightly crooked lips smiled? When she knew what was he was thinking. When she *knew*, despite his denials, that he cared for her, that it swept him away as it did her.

None of it was logical. None of it made sense. So how could she tell them? How could she defend something so ephemeral?

Behind her, Fleur's playing became louder, indicating that she agreed with Stephanie.

"You can't have him, Amanda, *that's* the point," Stephanie went on, ignoring Fleur's playing. "He's given you nothing emotionally. Has he ever promised you anything? Or even said he loves you?"

Amanda hesitated. "Once. Mostly, he—said he was in love with his wife.

He said it... a lot. But I think—"

Stephanie's eyes became enormous, and she shook her head until her dark hair was spiking outward. "*He said he was in love with his wife*? What the hell, Amanda, what more do you need to hear?"

Fleur's playing rose to a crescendo of dissonant chords. She banged her hands on the keys the way a child does, just to make noise, the more piercing, the better.

"Calm down, Fleur," Stephanie called.

The banging went on for another few minutes. Then Fleur stopped and closed the piano.

Stephanie turned back to Amanda, whose lips were pressed tightly together, and whose eyes were enormous in her pale face. Stephanie saw her pain and said quietly, "What did he give you? Why could you possibly want to continue this?"

Fleur got up and came back to the beanbag chair, where she plopped down and picked up her coffee mug. Stephanie leaned closer to Amanda. "Come on. You know where this is going."

"He did give me something. He—" She didn't know how to say it. She couldn't even describe it. And more than anything, she wished for it back.

"Stop bugging her, Steph." In sharp contrast to her shrill piano playing, Fleur's voice was soft. "She needs support."

"She has to see this for what it is," Stephanie insisted. "How can we call ourselves her friends if we let her continue this illusion?"

Is that what it is? Amanda wondered. *Just an illusion?*

It hadn't felt like one. In fact, when she was with him, things had been so sharp, so clear, so *real*—never in her life had she felt that way before. She tried, fumblingly, to say it.

Stephanie cut her off. "Okay. So it was big and romantic and exciting. Romantic isn't real, Amanda." Her voice left its staccato tones and became pleading. "Can't you see the difference between an interval and a lifetime?"

She could. She really could. She just didn't know how to go on, how to get past it. She could understand now how people could lose themselves in drink or gambling or sex—anything to assuage the pain, to forget, if only for a little while. But that wasn't her style. Instead, she had taken on extra shifts, read until her eyes ached and written lyrics for the course until her fingers cramped.

It wasn't exactly going to the dogs, but it was the best she could manage.

Finally, swallowing hard, remembering her phone conversation with her sister earlier, she said, "Josie thinks I ought to tell everyone *I* dumped *him* and get on with my life."

"It's hard to believe," Stephanie muttered, "but for once I agree with Josie."

Amanda gave a wan smile.

They offered her wine, cheese and crackers, but her throat had closed up. So had her heart. It was one thing to ask for advice; it was another to react well to what she knew she would hear. Either way, there was no longer any point in talking about it.

Stephanie and Fleur saw the change in her face and wisely didn't mention the situation again. Stephanie read over the new lyric Amanda had written the day before and grudgingly admitted it was 'pretty good', while Fleur took it to the piano and began noodling around with clusters of notes. On a professional level, things were progressing very well. But the reason she had come to them was no longer relevant. She had asked for their advice and they had given it, knowing she would eventually accept it, though she wasn't ready to now. They knew Amanda would be sensible; wasn't she always?

***

Marvin didn't look remotely like Jerry. Or sound like him. Or, she thought wryly, display any of Jerry's warmth and sympathy. He was a tight-looking man about five foot ten, wearing a perfectly pressed shirt and slacks. His tie, even at 6 p.m., was knotted tightly and smoothed down with a tie tack. What was left of his hair was combed neatly across his shiny scalp.

His meticulous grooming was reflected in the ambience of his hotel, Parkside, on the Upper East Side. While the place didn't look warm and inviting, it was impeccably clean, with shining floors, mirrors and windows, and staffed by employees who seemed to appear a split second before a guest knew he wanted something.

Three days after Jerry dismissed her from the Lorelei, Amanda sat in a gray business suit across the desk from Marvin, as he read through her resume, crumpling the edges with his fingers. Apparently, when Marvin examined a paper, he had to leave his mark on it in some tangible way.

"Well. Very nice." He didn't look up. The bright smile she'd brushed across her face by an effort of will was wasted.

She cleared her throat, hoping to startle him into looking up. The man didn't seem to realize there was another human being in the room.

"So, you worked for Jerry?" Marvin boomed out, looking at her.

Startled, she nodded.

"Knew him in the army. Good man." Marvin patted his crushed-velour chair. "Of course, the Lorelei doesn't begin to have the scope of operations we do." He gave another of those smug, tight grins. "But Jerry's done an admirable job, really, considering what he had to work with."

He examined her, running an eye over her neat business suit and smooth hair. "What kind of hours have you been working? We like employees who can put in a lot of time." He looked at her expectantly.

"I put in a lot of hours at the Lorelei," she said slowly.

"Overtime?"

"Yes."

"How much per week?"

She tried to count up on her fingers. "Well—a lot of double shifts. Toward the end, that was four days a week."

He cleared his throat. "One of those career people, are you?" He didn't wait for her answer; he had already made his decision. "We don't pay overtime. Should you—uh—choose to work a double shift, we'd pay all your hours at the standard rate."

"That's—that would be acceptable."

"Well, fine." He paused for a moment. Marvin had built a career on what he considered to be rational, placid thinking; his employees, if polled, would have described him as having the mind of an accountant, forever fussing with petty details. This girl seemed all right, he conceded. Nicely groomed. Young, but with manners. He suspected she'd work out fine, but he was none too keen to snap up someone Jerry had candidly told him was leaving the Lorelei. The Lorelei didn't lose employees often. So what was wrong with this one?

He decided to address that directly. "And—um—why did you leave the Lorelei?"

This was it. She'd known it would come sooner or later. She took a deep breath and decided, in a split second, to face the question head on. Either she'd be hired or she wouldn't be.

She met his eyes unflinchingly. "I was fired," she said matter-of-factly.

"I see." Now Marvin was slightly taken aback.

"Jerry fired me," she went on. *Well, if I'm going to develop what Steph calls brass balls, I guess now is a good time.* For the first time in months, her impish side reared its head. She did her best to tamp down an inner smile.

Marvin looked a little shell-shocked. His crisp facade had begun to wear away. "And—uh—why did he fire you?"

"Oh, it wasn't incompetence," she assured him brightly. "Jerry always said he was very happy with my work."

"How nice." Marvin was staring at her, dazed.

He couldn't believe what he was hearing. Was Jerry crazy—sending over a girl he'd *fired*? Was he crazy? And what the hell had she done—stolen from petty cash?

She smiled benignly, knowing what he was thinking. "It was nothing illegal. A dispute over a guest."

"Good God!" Marvin blurted out. "And Jerry recommended you so highly! What the hell happened?"

She lifted her head. Her eyes were level on his. "I stood up for myself," she said quietly. This was getting more and more surprising, Marvin told himself primly. In fact, it was becoming astonishing. That Jerry could have made a strong, enthusiastic recommendation of an employee he himself had fired for what sounds like rudeness to a hotel guest—if Marvin had had a paper fan at hand, he would have fanned himself vigorously.

And yet instinct, long repressed, reared its head at the sight of Amanda, sitting so correctly in the not-very-comfortable chair facing him. She hadn't flinched; she hadn't turned her eyes an inch from his. A long-dormant instinct whispered hoarsely to Marvin that there was some kind of exception in this girl's case: it would be worth it to have her on staff.

She looked back at him as he studied her, saying nothing, waiting for her to betray her embarrassment. She did nothing. He sat back. She remained motionless, watching him levelly. He tucked his fingertips together and surveyed them. "Well," he said, looking only at them, "it would seem we have a little problem here."

She said nothing.

"After all," he went on, trying to sound reasonable, "had I known that Jerry let you go—and I've always considered Jerry a pretty good judge of character—that would have precluded my even seeing you in the first place."

She didn't shift her eyes from his face.

"But here you are," he went on, trying to sound jovial, "and perhaps there's a good fairy watching over both of us. I've lost three employees in the last month." He sounded like he'd misplaced them. "I need to re-staff in a hurry, and I only want good people. Because circumstances are so unique, I'm inclined to think it was—what should I say—meant to be?

"Therefore—and understand this is most unusual—I'll give you a chance. I'll put you on the night shift, and give you—um—a two-week trial period. If at the end of that time I'm satisfied with your work, we'll— uh—see about a higher position."

"Excuse me." She couldn't have heard correctly. "What—uh—capacity are you—" Her voice failed.

"Well, we're not particular about titles here. Call it 'night operator'. After all, that's what you did at the Lorelei, wasn't it?"

She looked at him blankly, a child who didn't yet feel the sting of the slap she's been given. "I was assistant manager at the Lorelei."

"Yes, well, as I say, titles aren't big here. I'm sure Jerry handed out plenty of titles over there, to compensate for those low salaries. Now, we have a sliding-scale hourly schedule for our employees—" He went on in this vein, but Amanda stopped listening after a few seconds.

Night operator. That's what he thought she was worth, after all that time at the Lorelei. She shaded her eyes toward the floor, feeling as though she'd tumbled down a mountain and was craning her neck, looking up at what she had once almost touched.

My fault, she told herself. *I knew his temper. I knew what he'd do. I even goaded him into it.*

"All right, then," she broke in, "I'll take it."

"When?" He looked as though he thought she was going to try to slip in a vacation before settling down.

"How about tomorrow night?"

"Shift starts at ten."

"I'll be here." And she rose, extending her hand.

"I'd better warn you, Amanda, that in a probationary period, any infraction—"

"You don't have to warn me," she said quietly. "I know what probation means."

***

The call came as Beau was trying to climb out of a monumental hangover. "Yeah?" he mumbled into the phone.

"Hey, Beau, what's up?" Oh, God. Perry. Already it didn't sound like good news.

He tried to compose himself. "I'm fine, Perry. How're things in New York?"

"Well, you know, buddy, setbacks here, setbacks there. Though I am glad you got us out of the Lorelei thing."

"Yeah. Sorry it didn't work out." Beau had made clear to Jerry that unless he wanted to go to jail for embezzlement and fraud, he would quietly accept the Fieldstons' terms to get out of the contract; Beau thought it was the least he himself could do, to help them wangle advantageous terms for ending it. He was ashamed he'd ever recommended Jerry to these guys and concerned that it would reflect on his professionalism. But so far, it didn't seem to matter to Perry.

It didn't seem to matter now, either. But Perry was clearing his throat several times, which wasn't a good sign. What exactly was he calling for?

"Listen, Beau." Here it came. "I gotta be honest with you. Right now my people just aren't as excited about the libretto and score as I hoped."

Beau struggled to stay calm. "What do you mean, Perry?"

"I mean, nobody's jumping up and down in this office. You remember how excited I was when you told me the story—"

He sure did. It was one of the best days of his life.

"Well," Perry went on, "somewhere between what you told me and what you've turned in is a world of difference. And it's not an improvement."

Beau warned himself to stay calm. *Don't blow it by getting mad.* "What do you think I should do, Perry?"

"Personally, I think you should come here and meet with my people. Tell them the story the way you told it to me, and let's work on it a little—taking your *original* concept, which was so great, and building the show around that."

"Is that all?"

"No. I think while you're here, you need to meet with some agency people—I know, I know, you're loyal to Jim and that's admirable, but at this point I think it's hurting you. Come let me introduce you to these agency guys and let's see if there's a match."

He didn't have a lot of choice, and he knew it: if Perry thought he was resisting, the deal was dead.

On the other hand, he didn't have to *sign* with CAA or ICM; he could just talk to them and vacillate until the deal was set, then tell Perry he'd changed his mind. But he had to look like he was cooperating.

After a moment, he said, "That's no problem. When do you want me there?"

He could hear Perry flipping the pages of a calendar. "Well, hm—not next week. I'm booked back to back. And the week after we're out of town... say, you come out in about three weeks. Close to Halloween. That work for you?"

Anything will work for me, as long as you don't kill the deal. "Sure, Perry, that looks good."

"Wonderful. Plan on staying a week and we'll really get down to brass tacks on this thing. Should Jules come with you?"

"He'd probably prefer to stay here. I'll discuss all the changes with him."

"Fine. See you at Halloween, then. Trick or treat." Perry hung up.

Beau exhaled as he slowly hung up. His head felt like ice picks were being jammed into it on all sides, and he felt slightly sick to his stomach. He knew the deal was hanging by a thread now, and everything hung on this trip. He had to pull out all the stops to make sure Perry didn't close his mind, *or* his checkbook. He had to dazzle the people in the Fieldston Organization and the agency guys Perry wanted him to meet. He had to persuade them all that what he had was a solid moneymaker.

And while he was at it, he also had to find a new hotel.

***

Just don't blow it, she found herself thinking. *You got a second chance; stay out of trouble! You're not Judy Holliday in* Bells Are Ringing. *You're a night operator— again—in a job you can't afford to lose.*

The scope and glitter of Marvin's hotel was a far cry from the small, elegant and old-fashioned Lorelei. The equipment was more modern, the systems more efficient. The staff was, by any objective standard, better trained and better supervised. But the job was essentially the same, and she handled it—she couldn't help it, it was her nature—essentially the same way.

Within a few days, Marvin began to notice the difference. She took such an interest in the guests who called the switchboard at night that a few actually stopped by his office to thank him for the warm personal service. He was amazed at the number of insomniacs—men and older women—who raved about the new night operator.

Marvin finally called her into his office at 9:00 one evening. She perched gingerly on the edge of a divan as he shrugged into his coat; obviously the interview wouldn't take long. The divan, she noted, wasn't very comfortable; Jerry would never allow that.

"The guests seem to like you," he said gruffly. "You've caught on to the routine pretty well, I see." He was scanning what looked like some kind of report. "Oh, and you've been checking in on time." He nodded approval. "A very good sign."

She gave a tight smile.

"I think we can safely discuss a full-time position." He shuffled more papers. "Let's say next week we put you on full-time, forty hours, schedule to be determined, um, tomorrow."

"As assistant manager?"

"Well, for the time being, as night operator." He saw the look on her face. "All right, in view of your record, night-shift *supervisor*." He could move Gladys, his current supervisor, to weekends; she wanted to change her hours anyway.

"I applied for the assistant manager's job!"

"And this is the program we put you through to get it," he said soothingly. "I can't just jump you from night operator to assistant manager... I have staff who'll be screaming about it. But look, in two weeks I've made you a supervisor on the night shift. You'll still have operator duties but you'll also run the entire night side. In a few months, if I'm satisfied with your progress, we can discuss shifting you to the day side, and then—"

She sighed. She might have known Marvin would be stingy about promotions, since he was so stingy about everything else. But what was the alternative? Go out job-hunting again? She was getting used to the routine here, and it gave her lots of time during the day to work on her songs and meet singers and other songwriters.

The hell with it, she thought. *I've got to find a new home, put down new roots. I'm tired of feeling up in the air. Haven't I had enough of that in the last six months?*

She didn't wait for the rest of his little canned speech, though it probably would have been politic to do so. She just broke in. "All right, Marvin. You win."

***

Despite Marvin's penny-ante attitude, Amanda was comfortable at Parkside. She was efficient and professional, and she didn't think about the job when she was away from it, which was important because she was focusing so much on writing song lyrics. She, Steph and Fleur had written four songs so far that they'd auditioned at the Hot Grill, and finally on October 11th, they broke through. The same manager who'd given Amanda the coveted 9:30 spot to sing *"The Girl with the Basket"* now liked Amanda's first solo lyric. It was called *"Every Night at the Lake"* and he agreed to let them do it for the next revue, two weeks away.

They still hadn't found a singer who handled their material well, and Amanda had reluctantly said she'd sing it, if they couldn't find anyone better. But four days before she was supposed to sing, she picked up a cold, and it was the worst cold she could remember. Phlegm clogged her throat, choking her when she tried to speak, and her voice was scratchy, when it worked at all. She found herself talking aloud in her empty apartment just after she woke, simply to see how much voice she still had.

"There's no way you can sing on Saturday," Steph moaned when she heard Amanda. "We'll have to give up the spot."

Fleur agreed. "We'll audition it again for next month."

"No," Amanda said stubbornly, sounding like a cartoon character. "I cab do it."

It wasn't even worth arguing about; everyone knew she couldn't.

"You sound like Marlene Dietrich," Marvin greeted her when he heard her. "You sure you shouldn't be home?"

"I'm fine," Amanda said. It came out as 'I'b fide,' in a contralto that was just a shade off baritone.

Marvin shrugged into his coat and wound a wool scarf tightly around his throat. For October, Amanda thought that was unnecessarily cautious. "Take it easy," he told her. He wondered whether he should order her to go home. She looked bad and sounded worse. But she should know how to take care of herself, at her age. *I got my own health to worry about.* And continuing to do just that, he strode out, gloved fingers clenched on his briefcase.

Amanda settled into the high-backed chair in the telephone room and fixed the headset over her ears.

Suddenly, the board was alive with voices. She concentrated on connecting number to number, paying little heed to the quality of voice. There was no time. As soon as she disposed of one bank of flashing lights, there was another to contend with.

"May I help you?" The last light, thank God, and maybe then a few minutes' peace.

"God, I hope so. I want to leave a wake-up call."

She froze. It wasn't possible. Her voice, when it came out, was raspy.

"Just a moment, sir."

She noted the number of the room on the screen: 422. And scanned the guest list, something she'd neglected in her hurry to settle in.

There it was. Beau Kellogg, 422. Oh, God.

She sat looking at the flashing buzzer beside number 422. What were the odds? How had he turned up in her life again, without even trying? How was it possible?

She didn't need to ponder long. Another army buddy, of course. Marvin. The first call Jerry had made to help her, the "most logical place", he'd said, to continue a career. What happened? she wondered. Did he get mad at Jerry and change long-standing habit on a whim? And what would happen when he realized she was here?

She almost jumped when the light blinked again. *Keep calm, Amanda.* "Yes, sir?"

"I'd like a wake-up call at seven. Can you manage that?"

"Yes, sir, we can." Oh, God! Why didn't he recognize her voice? And then she sneezed, and understood. The cold that had taken away her voice had also disguised her identity. *Thank God.* Concentrating deliberately on the scratch pad in front of her, she scribbled a note. "7:00, sir. We'll wake you."

She heard the achingly familiar chuckle—flat, disjointed. "See that you manage it at seven, Operator. Not ten after, not half past." She felt the familiar irritation creeping up but struggled to subdue a tart reply. She didn't want to lose this job, too.

"Yes, sir. 7:00 on the nose. Have a good night." The phone clicked in her ear.

She didn't even reach for her book. She suspected she'd have enough to think about between now and dawn.

***

He was hungry again at 2:00. Damn, it seemed as though every time he was away from home overnight, he was ready to raid the refrigerator in the early-morning hours. A substitute for sex? he wondered. Or was he just seeking familiar comfort in unfamiliar surroundings? Well, hell, whatever it is, he could afford it. His weight had been dropping for weeks now. The doctor warned him to load up on the starchy foods for awhile, hoping it would stop the irrational drop in numbers, but he didn't much care. "180, 170, what's the difference?" was his retort to Jean, who merely shook her head and sent his pants to the tailor to take in the waist. She didn't even seem as worried as the doctor. Probably wasn't. These days, her serenity was completely unruffled, as though she only half-saw and half-heard him.

Meanwhile, though, he was hungry. And the chocolate shake he'd asked for hours earlier sat, almost untouched and probably warm by now, on the nightstand. No wonder. Marvin was the one guy in the Army who kept trying to get cottage cheese served to the enlisted men. Was it likely that a guy who watched his weight fanatically would consider high-calorie desserts a priority for his guests?

But Christ, I need something sweet. Maybe an egg cream—I haven't had one in years.

Hardly thinking, he punched the numbers for the main switchboard. "Any place still open around here where I could get an egg cream?"

The voice that responded was young and female, though throatier than most of the young women's he knew. And he detected a trace of hesitation before she spoke that puzzled him. "Our room service is open 24 hours, sir."

"I know about your room service," he said impatiently. "If your room service could make a decent chocolate soda, I wouldn't be talking to you now. Listen, I'm starving. There must be some drugstore or coffee shop nearby that still serves something sweet at this time of night. Any suggestions?"

He waited so long for a response he thought for a moment she'd hung up. "Hello?"

"Yes, sir, I'm here." And even in that throaty rasp he heard something familiar, something he was sure he'd heard before. "How about Miller's? It's about eight blocks away, but it's very clean, and the desserts are wonderful."

"How are they with chocolate?" he asked suspiciously.

Now the rippling laugh across the wire definitely sounded familiar. "If I could get off now, I'd meet you there."

"Okay. I'll take your word. You think they're still open?"

"Should be. The last time I was there—" She broke off. *I want to keep this job*, she reminded herself. *He's not going to take it away from me.* "I mean, I'm sure they still have all-night service." She gave him the address.

"Hope it's as good as you say. If it is, I'll drop a note to your boss."

"Thank you, sir. Good night." She disconnected quietly, but her heart didn't stop hammering for a long time.

***

Miller's was spotless, as she'd said, and quiet at 2:30 in the morning. With his first sip, he thanked God for that girl at the switchboard. He drank it down and asked for a second. It didn't go down as easily. Maybe he wasn't as thirsty as he thought. Maybe he was more tired. But when he thought about his unknown benefactor on the switchboard, he seemed to lose his appetite. He left half the chocolate soda and a generous three-dollar tip.

It was not quite midnight in L.A., and he knew he could still phone Jean, if he wanted. *And say what?* he thought. *'How's inventory going?' Do I care?* Oh, well, he supposed it was just as well. She would appreciate the concern, most likely.

Half-heartedly he placed the call, wondering dully what he'd say if she asked why he was calling. And put down the receiver with a thud when he realized why he actually was.

To avoid phoning the girl at the switchboard back.

Why should that thought even feel intrusive? He was simply returning a courtesy with a courtesy. Right? He thought of her voice making the suggestion, and suddenly could hear it clanging through his veins, fizzing in his blood. He sat down abruptly on the bed.

It's all Amanda's fault, he thought. On some subconscious level, he was always aware that every woman whose voice came to him first through a telephone wire was—could be—another Amanda. He shrugged it off. The silly little bitch. He had been more than patient with her—he'd bent over backwards to be understanding and thoughtful—and she had spoiled it all. *She'll get hers, one of these days*, he thought.

Meanwhile, he really should thank the woman at the switchboard. She'd offered a very palatable alternative to the dreadful room service. It was just good manners to let her know how much he'd enjoyed it.

Stop being so defensive, he told himself. *It's just a friendly call. And it's the middle of the night—she may* want *to talk to someone instead of just waiting for the board to light up.*

Thus fortified with a good excuse, he punched the phone.

***

She was almost asleep in her chair when the light flashed on the board. Surprising, too, since she'd been shocked so wide-awake at the thought that he was once again in New York. But she was more tired than she'd thought, and the jolt of adrenaline had finally worn off, leaving her languid in the plump chair. It felt good to be so relaxed.

She didn't hear the buzz the first time. Or the second. She was dozing with half-closed eyes when she realized the lines were alive again. "Yes?"

"It's about time. You asleep down there?"

She shook herself fully awake, but she didn't need to look at the switchboard to know the voice. "Can I help you, sir?"

"You did help me, Operator. That was one of the best chocolate sodas I ever had in my life. Both of them."

"Excuse me?"

"I had two. Miller's is a find. Goes right in my book next to Empire State Building. Thank you so much." He paused, then added swiftly, "This is the old buzzard in 422."

"I know."

He sounded pleased. "Do you? You're very quick."

"Not exactly. Our switchboard automatically gives the room number of every person calling in to us."

"Oh." This was more neutral. She couldn't tell what he was thinking.

"I'm glad you liked it," she said carefully, now vibrating-awake. "I had terrible visions of one of our guests starving to death before morning."

"Well, that's comforting. It's certainly more than I ever got from Marvin, on the battlefield or off. Do you people have a suggestion box anywhere about?"

A suggestion box? "No, sir. Why?"

"Because I'd strongly suggest you get a promotion for your quick thinking on the job. And I'd like to place the suggestion where I know Marvin would see it."

She blushed. Amazing that he could still do that to her. "Thank you. We aim to please."

"Come on, at least tell me your name. Marvin should know what a find he has."

"That's quite all right. I'll be happy to pass the message along."

"It's no trouble at all. Just tell me your name."

The insistence in his voice woke a panic in her. She had never imagined such a dilemma. *What were the odds?* she thought. *How could this possibly have happened?*

Swiftly she weighed alternatives. If she gave her real name, she'd be unemployed in the morning. If she gave a false name, and he really did follow through with Marvin, there'd be hell to pay. Marvin wouldn't know whom he was talking about and would likely blurt out her name in an attempt to clarify things. And that would lead to all of the above. Maybe even multiplied a little, because he'd think she was leading him on or making fun of him. Oh, God.

Maybe the best thing was just to play it light...

"Oh, that isn't necessary," she laughed, with as much poise as she could summon. "I'm just temping here tonight. I won't be around after the shift ends."

"Too bad. I thought I'd found myself a real ally." He paused. "Well, then," he said, thinking how inadequate he sounded, "thank you again."

"You're welcome—again."

"You know," he blurted out, wondering why it seemed safe to say it, "you remind me a little of—of someone I used to know."

"Oh?" Her voice, such a deep contralto, seemed more alert, and—unusually interested. "Someone you liked?"

He thought back for a second—Amanda ordering him a chocolate soda and a bagel for a breakfast. Amanda listening to him, so thrilled for his success. Amanda lying next to him, touching him so lightly... yet he felt as though no one had ever known him so well. He pushed the thoughts away. "Very much. For awhile."

"For awhile?"

"Well, things didn't work out the way I—would have liked."

"Oh." She didn't pursue it.

"I hope," he said impulsively, "that you'll be the one doing my wake-up call in the morning. I have an important meeting, and I don't want to miss it."

There was a pause. "No," she said finally, the throaty voice oddly appealing. "I'll be off by then. But I'll make sure they call you on time."

"I'm sure you will," he said slowly. "Good night."

She released the call with shaking fingers. It had sounded as though he actually had some... regrets. Like he actually somehow had missed her, which she had thought was impossible.

It reminded her of those calls they'd had at the beginning, just a year ago—and all the bright promise and joy she'd felt, which had suddenly and inexplicably vanished.

It felt almost, in that quiet little room, as though it were happening again at that moment, as though she were losing it all again.

She put her head down in her arms and cried.

***

Amanda called in sick the next day, for the first time since she'd moved to Parkside. She didn't think she could face going to work and wondering if he would call again in the middle of the night, just to talk. And there was too much hurt and confusion in her to concentrate on her job.

She spent the time in bed, and to her surprise and pleasure, her voice was almost back to normal the next morning. *Maybe,* she thought with a smile, *I just didn't want to sing at the Hot Grill.*

But she hadn't picked up her paycheck that day, and she needed it.

"Come by in the morning," Sandra, the bookkeeper, told her. "I'll have it ready for you."

"Thanks," Amanda said gratefully. "It's been one of those months."

"You don't have to tell me," Sandra laughed. "It's one of those months for me every month!"

It was cooler now; fall was definitely in the air. The hotel lobby was crowded with departing guests in heavy sweaters and coats and cleaning people keeping the rugs, lamps and mirrors sparkling.

Amanda stood in line, between a teenage male eyeing the girls at the desk and a harassed-looking businessman trying to balance and read the contents of a manila file.

Amanda smiled understandingly at the businessman and glanced around the lobby. The cleaning women were almost finished with the big oval mirror set in gilt; it was shining clean. A family of six was sitting in the conversation pit, waiting for the line to thin out. The little concession stand in the corner was doing a brisk business in newspapers, candy and tobacco.

Suddenly, she smelled it again—the feather-light woody scent of male cologne. It was close to her. Very close. She tried to sniff unobtrusively, but the two men closest to her weren't wearing scent.

Damn it, it was happening again!

The elevator doors had slid open, and Amanda glanced casually toward them. Suddenly, she went stock-still, and her arms and legs began to tingle.

Striding briskly out of the elevator, less than ten feet from her, was Beau.

He was alone, wearing a sports jacket and creased slacks, carrying a folded newspaper and a briefcase, not looking at the long line of people. He hadn't noticed her. He started across the shining floor toward the revolving doors.

She couldn't take her eyes off him.

Despite all that had passed between them, she felt such a pull toward him that it all but dragged her in his direction; she saw the soft silver hair and the pale skin and the snapping dark eyes, and she wanted to reach out and touch him. She wanted to say something, whatever would make things right between them, because here he was, so close to her—now was the time!

He had stepped aside for a young woman to pass, and gave her a nod and a smile.

He was less than two feet from Amanda, and he still didn't see her.

Amanda couldn't think of a thing to say. She wanted to reach out a hand to him.

But she couldn't bring herself to do it.

Too much had passed between them; too many terrible memories had intervened. For all the connection she still felt, there was too much rage, too much pain, too many silences on both sides, which had led to this separation.

Two women far ahead of her in line stepped back so Beau could pass through. "Thanks," she heard him say. He still hadn't noticed her.

She couldn't move.

She saw him slide through the revolving doors, saw the doorman speak briefly to him, then raise the whistle to his lips for a cab.

She stood frozen, wanting to run after him, to fix everything that had gone wrong. Caught between her longing and her fear of what he might say, or do. She'd thought she knew him so well, but she had no idea how he'd respond to her. It could be even worse than what she'd already lived through.

So in the end she just stood there, watching him walk away. And she knew then that she'd just been given—and lost—her last chance.

***

She didn't know how long she stood in the lobby, but after awhile, she found herself sitting in a high-backed chair near the mirror. She wasn't seeing anything around her; her mind was focused on the man who'd just walked away from her, yet again.

She knew now that everyone was right. It was over. For the first time, she realized that clearly, and knew that she somehow would cope.

He was gone from her life, and she had to move forward from this point. There could be no going back.

A small, quiet voice inside her told her she would laugh again, would feel joy again, would even someday love again. She knew it was all true.

But all of that would happen on the other side of this experience, and the woman it happened to was the one who had been touched by Beau Kellogg. Everything she became from this point forward would have his stamp indelibly on her being.

As long as she remembered him, he would never be entirely gone from her. But his part in her life was prologue; it was time now for the main event. He'd given her a new career and the confidence to go forward. Other men would want her in their lives for much longer, and the sooner she sought them, the better.

As his last service to her, he'd given her a glimpse of the road she was meant to travel.

Now, after waiting and watching and never feeling quite ready, it was finally her turn to step out on the stage.

CHAPTER 29

I t's the best thing we've ever done." Jules slapped a hand down on the piano keys, beaming. When the music evaporated, silence seemed to palpitate in the air. He waited for an acid comment from Beau, which seemed to be all he was hurling these days, or the occasional barbed witticism that elicited laughter despite its sting. When he realized nothing was forthcoming from the corner where Beau huddled over his pad, he busied himself re-marking a flat on his music sheet.

Beau gazed down blankly at the scribbles on his pad, hardly seeing the words he'd struggled with for two months. Jules was right—he knew it instinctively—yet the elation he usually felt after a productive work session was missing.

The score was finished, and it was terrific. Romantic, yeah, but also modern, even hip, God help them. The kind of music that Marie nodded to, first rhythmically, then approvingly, as she listened. *God forgive me,* Beau thought, *for having written songs that Marie will be whistling.*

It was as good as the best score he'd ever done; the pump was still yielding. He didn't have to concede to age yet. That thought finally evoked a smile.

"Once more on the last chorus," he suggested, rising and stretching. Jules nodded and dropped smoothly into the opening chords, and together, Beau's baritone and Jules' sweet tenor, they sang a song they'd written for a soprano.

"Pretty damn good," Beau approved.

"*Very* damn good," Jules concurred. "Perry'll have no problem finding backers for this."

Beau wasn't listening; he realized he was going to be late getting home again, and Jean would be less than thrilled. He began to stuff his pad and music sheets into his briefcase. "Let's run through everything one more time before the backers' audition. After what I went through getting Perry to set this up, I don't want to get caught with our pants down."

"We won't," Jules said confidently.

Beau grunted. "We better not." He patted his pockets, came up with his car keys. He almost ran through the hallway. "Good work today!" he called back as he let himself out.

Jules detoured to the hallway at the ringing of the phone. As he reached for the gold-handled French phone, he heard Beau's car engine catch.

Perry's voice at the other end was crisp but apologetic. No, sorry, nothing to do with you at all. Sudden financial crisis; can't contemplate going forward with a musical at this time. Seriously contemplating bankruptcy, in fact. Sure you'll find new backers, and so forth.

Jules set down the receiver slowly, disappointment licking at his entrails. They'd had enough problems finding old backers. And in that first minute of silence, he suddenly knew the show was dead. No matter that Beau had outdone himself, that they'd come up with a really terrific piece of theatre that was timeless and magical, that the songs were sure standards. It was dead.

He knew it was too late to call Beau back; he was already gunning the car at canyon-defying speeds. Jules shrugged and picked up the trendy antiqued telephone again. "Jean? Jules. No, he just left, and at the rate he's going, he'll be home in twenty minutes. Ask him to call me right away, will you? Thanks."

Jules heaved out the frustration searing his chest as he straightened the score sheets. Apart from the joy of producing a great score, he knew that working on the songs had somehow been therapeutic for his partner. He wished he knew what had started the tailspin he saw in Beau, because he wasn't the same man. The brittle, deep-rooted cynicism was gone. Instead, Jules felt an acute bitter anger and a throbbing sense of—was it loss?

He dusted a finger lightly, lovingly over the piano keys as he stacked the score sheets together for the score no one would ever hear now. A damn shame. He knew Beau would rail about it, and Jules didn't look forward to smoothing him down. Beau was always railing about posterity and his place in history; it seemed as though the pleasure of writing the stuff wasn't enough for him; it had to be *remembered*, too.

I'm getting too old and too tired for his fireworks, Jules thought. *Some things just aren't as important as he makes them out to be.* He surveyed the room contentedly. *God, I love working in here when I know Marie is in the next room.* He wondered what she'd planned for dinner. He switched off the lights, happily humming the song he knew would never be heard by a paying audience. Just writing them gave him joy. Who cared if anyone else heard them?

He'd leave the future to someone else.

***

The clutch felt less fluid in his hand. Beau noticed it again as he shifted. But the moment was filled as he sang the second chorus of *"Moving Mountains"*. Good tune, pretty lyric. It said just what he wanted to say. And this time, an audience would be paying to listen.

Unbidden, the thought of Amanda filled his senses again, suddenly, as though she was standing with that serene countenance on the hood of his car, listening to his words. He imagined for a moment the expression in her eyes as she heard it sung for the first time. He'd bet the house right now that she'd have opening-night tickets, if she had to work three jobs for the next year to pay for them.

Who cares? he answered himself, impatient at his own musing. *Since when is she the judge of a good piece of work?*

She'll be sorry, he assured himself, pushing the car harder. *When the show gets raves from the critics, when box-office lines form around the block, when people camp out for tickets—hah!*

The next bend was his favorite curve, but he never saw the thin film of oil spotting the yellow line. When the car reeled and twisted grotesquely, his first thought was that it had to be a mistake. He braked hurriedly, but the bend was much too close.

There wasn't even time for him to try to throw himself out. A younger man might have reacted faster, and his last thought as he realized it was the goddamned unfairness of it all. If it had to happen, why hadn't it happened when he was young and could have rolled with it?

And as the land dropped away in front of him—*Thank God the show was finished.*

At least he'd left behind something to remember him by.

EPILOGUE

<hr />

Autumn 1990

The chorus had just finished singing the new lyric when she smelled that strange, sweet cologne again.

The smell got stronger as she left her usual rehearsal seat near the front and headed down the aisle to Michael. It filled her nostrils, caressing her temples, which began to pound. *God, it's happening again, after all these years. Will I ever be free of this?* But it was her own fault, she admitted to herself ruefully. It was all her fault, for wallowing in the past, writing a libretto and lyrics for a show based on her own unhappy love affair with Beau Kellogg.

She'd done it, she told herself, only because the subject matter was so perfect for a musical, and no other reason. Tragic loves always were. *But I've learned*, she assured herself, stepping into the aisle. *I've grown up. I'm fine now. And it* was *seven years ago…*

… Except that the smell kept getting stronger, as she went up the aisle. She brushed back her short fine hair (she'd thought cutting it drastically would end her problems with its fineness; instead, it just fell in her eyes at every turn) and headed for the two people huddled in back, Michael, the show's composer, and Steph, co-author of the libretto. "Well?" she asked.

Michael shook his head. "I don't know… the ending still bothers me."

She shrugged. "That's how it ends."

"But it's… unfinished. They have a fight and he tells her off. She sees him on the street later and can't bring herself to go up to him. It just hangs there. There's no real resolution."

She shrugged again. "Let the audience fill in their own ending. We give them an up-tempo dramatic song at the end, and they'll go out happy."

Michael's eyes narrowed. "That's not like you. Since when have you become a cynic?"

"Since I began working on this show."

"It was your idea!"

"Maybe it wasn't a very good one."

"This is not what I need to hear," Michael muttered. "Not with a finished score, and two weeks into rehearsal. I think we have to rework it. Come up with some definitive ending, maybe a new song." He gave her a look that was meant to be tolerant. "And not that song you keep trying to push on me."

"*Being There*?" Stephanie asked. "It's a good song."

"I didn't write it. Come to think of it, neither did you."

"But I own it." Amanda's voice was even and calm, but the look she gave Michael was determined. "And you know it's perfect for the middle of Act I."

"Not the point. We can write something else. If I write a show score, I write the whole score."

It had been almost their only bone of contention since starting to work together. The problem was, it was becoming a bigger and bigger bone every day, with Amanda insisting on slipping it into the show and Michael resisting any addition that he didn't write.

Amanda gave him a tense little smile. Right now, she couldn't work up the strength to argue for the song, though she'd always intended, from the day she started to write the libretto, that the song Beau had written for her would be part of it. It was fitting, after all. And for that reason, she wouldn't explain to Michael why it was so important to her that it be part of the score. It's not that he wouldn't understand; it was that he would understand too well.

But now that smell was clouding all around her; she could feel it on her skin, in her nostrils... she couldn't help it. She knew she'd look odd, but habit was too strong. She took a deep breath, breathing in the oh-so-familiar scent. Closed her eyes for a moment, remembering...

"Hey, what's the matter?" Michael nudged her. She opened her eyes and deliberately smiled at him, to let him know her sudden flash of temper was gone.

"Nothing, Michael. Sorry if I sounded sharp. It's actually going pretty well. We might just have something here." She patted his arm lightly.

Michael was so good for her. Besides being the best young composer on Broadway, he was such a genuinely good guy: patient, loving and so proud of her. Unlike the other high-strung prima donnas she was used to working with, he was generous: he let the lyricist set the pace, but would just as willingly provide a melody first, if asked. He gave credit freely to librettist and lyricist and stayed in the background, letting his beautiful, soaring music speak for him.

She was lucky, no doubt about it. He was also a serious hunk, with those horn-rimmed glasses, curly black hair and broad shoulders, only three years her senior, and already racking up credits that made experienced Broadway insiders sit up and take notice. He'd done two major shows with top-flight librettists and lyricists, both well received, and earned both Tony and Grammy nominations.

He was marvelous as a boyfriend, too, funny and kind and sweet. They spent a lot of time together, though the tensions of mounting this show had understandably affected them both. They'd been lovers for two years, collaborators for the last nine months, and the last nine months had been the roughest. *When the show opens,* she told herself, *I can relax, give him more attention. He didn't understand why I was so demanding, writing it, and so difficult at every step. Once it's open we can take some time off, get back what we had. I'll make all the bad things go away.*

She just wished she could feel the... magic. Where was it? Why didn't her pulse pick up when she saw him? Why had her heart *never* skipped a beat in his presence, even when they were first getting to know each other?

Why did she still refuse to move in with him, as he'd asked her to, gently, again and again? What was she waiting for?

She didn't know.

Yes, she did. She wanted that heart-racing feeling she'd had... just once before. She wanted that sense that all the colors around her had brightened, that the air was sweeter, that life had suddenly lifted her beyond the everyday into something miraculous.

No, no, no... banish that thought forever. It was sick, didn't she know that? It was *sick.* That marvelous-to-be-alive feeling was prelude to the feelings of despair and anguish she'd finally relegated to the dark cellar of her heart, but only after months of pain. *I'm fine,* she told herself. *I'm fine. And what I have now is so much saner, so much healthier; everyone says so. It's so much* better *for me. I was a child before; that's why all that soaring joy seemed so right. But I've grown up, at long last. That wasn't real love. And I know what it leads to now. It leads to something I never want to feel again!*

Oh, God, those months of trying to get over it. Trying to forget, trying to focus on anything that would take her mind off the dull ache in her heart. The extra work, the double shifts, the scribbling of poetry that, slowly, with time and plenty of practice, turned into song lyrics.

The constant, never-ending reading, to keep her mind off the topic that brought such pain. If it was published in English, she had it on her night table. She read thousands of pages a week. It helped, a little, though now she didn't remember any of it.

She stuck the sheet music for *"Being There"* under all the other music in her piano bench, and took *Words for All Occasions* off her night table, wrapping it in an old sweater and burying it under two sets of sheets in her linen closet. She didn't want to look at it every day, though she couldn't quite bring herself to throw it away.

Finally, *finally* meeting Michael, after acres of blind dates, double dates, feeble attempts at romance that she always, finally, cut off when it was clearly useless. The cozy, familiar feeling of being with him, saying what she thought, doing as she pleased, knowing it pleased him, too. It was like falling into a warm bath that soothed her in its predictable, familiar heat. *I'm so lucky*, she thought, not for the first time. This *is what love is, real, healthy, sane love. Best friends, cozy companions, comfort and business combined. This is what everyone should be striving for, not artificial, ephemeral romance that can blow away with a change in the wind.*

That could break your heart.

That could damn near destroy you.

Michael seemed to sense her thoughts, and kissed her lightly on the cheek. She gave him a hug back, but her mind was on the smell. Her eyes, as always, darted around, looking for the source. As always, no one was there.

I'm losing it, she told herself. *Maybe it wasn't smart to revisit this part of my life. But it's a great story for a musical, and I was so sure I was over it, over him... Maybe no amount of time between the past and the present can erase these emotions.*

"Hey, Amanda, you with us?" Steph nudged her. "I said, is everybody squared away on the new lyric?"

Amanda looked up, startled. She had drifted off again, as she had so often recently, to the past. She shook her head, to clear out the cobwebs, and managed a lopsided smile. "Fine. They've got it down cold."

"Then what is it?" Michael ruffled her hair gently. "Another lyric problem?"

"No." She laughed, trying to sound lighthearted and casual. "I think I'm just—I don't know, hallucinating. It's weird. I smell something that isn't there... and it won't go away."

"What do you smell?" Steph asked curiously.

Amanda tossed her head, still trying to seem casual, though a pulse had begun to beat in her throat. "No, really, it's silly."

Michael shook his head. "If something's bothering you, tell me about it. Isn't that what we've always done?"

"But it's ridiculous," she protested. "And it's happened before, and it meant nothing then. Why should I bother you with it?"

He gave her a patient look. She knew from experience that meant he'd persist until he got a satisfactory answer. She couldn't avoid telling him.

Maybe if I just say it, *it'll go away,* she thought, *and I can take away its power to hurt me.* "Oh, it's just that I could swear I smell a—a man's cologne. I smelled it up on stage, but it's even stronger right here. Just like in our story." She attempted a laugh. "I told you it was silly."

"It's not like our story," Steph protested. "This one's real. I smell it."

Michael nodded. "Me too."

Amanda stared at them, feeling an icy cold in the pit of her stomach.

"You smell that?"

They sniffed again. Michael nodded.

"Absolutely," Steph confirmed. "Musk, I think."

"But there's nobody here except you two!"

"Well, there was that old guy—who was he? The man who was here a few minutes ago?"

She stared at Steph, as something began to jump in her stomach.

"Someone else was here?" she asked carefully. "Somebody... old? Who?"

Steph shook her head. "He didn't say anything. Just stood watching you and the singers for awhile, and left."

"No," Michael corrected her. "He stopped to talk to Greg at the stage door. I saw him on my way backstage."

She stared at them both. A man. An older man... wearing that cologne? She could actually feel her lips trembling. It was impossible. Yet somewhere in the deepest part of her, she *knew.* Without a word, she whirled and began to run down the aisle. In a second she had leapt to the stage, startling the singers, who were lounging or draped over folded chairs, talking quietly on their break, and disappeared through the curtains.

"What the hell—?" Michael said. "What's eating her?"

***

"Greg! Greg!" She clutched at the doorman's shirt before he even knew what was happening, his newspaper forgotten in his large fist. She looked wild, her hair flying around her face, her eyes enormous in her thin face.

"Hey, Miss Harary, everything in order?" He looked at her with concern, his faded blue eyes bewildered. "I got everything ready for you."

She struggled to speak calmly. "Greg, that older guy you were talking to awhile ago—"

He bristled. "Now, Miss Harary, that was on my own time! I got backstage all clean and the mail in the boxes and the refrigerator's stocked—you can look yourself—I was just talking to an old friend—"

"Greg, I know." She was trying very hard not to shriek. "But your old friend—who was he?" She searched desperately for an explanation and tried the truth. "I thought—I thought it was—someone I used to know."

"Oh." He relaxed into his comfortable sagging old armchair. "Well, that's not likely, not likely. Fact is, he was doing shows in this theater when you were in diapers, probably." He saw the look on her face and added hastily, "No offense."

"Greg, please—what's his name?"

"Well, fact is, he was—well, he *was* a damned good librettist himself, though you may not have heard of him. Had a show that ran at this very theater, *The Life and Times*. Terrible flop. His name's Beau Ke—"

That was all she needed. She clutched at him again. "Which way did he go, do you know, Greg? Please!"

Slowly, the puzzlement in his face dimmed. "He said he was gonna catch a cab at 45th. But he left awhile ago... "

"Thanks!" she gasped. She flew past him, out the door, though he called forlornly after her, "He must be long gone by now... "

She was running before she hit the sidewalk, running in flimsy heels she had worn to this rehearsal for luck, not speed. She winced as she felt her ankle turn, but after hopping around for a bit she sped on, her eyes darting in all directions at once. She headed toward 45th Street, the late-afternoon bustle fading around her, the sun sinking low in the sky. She jogged every other day, and she was in good shape, but her heart was thudding much harder than usual.

The taxi stand was just ahead. It was a good place to stop and look, or just catch her breath if she failed to find him.

She pushed past a woman with a twin stroller ("Excuse me!"), twisted past an old man balancing precariously on a cane ("Pardon—") and almost knocked into a messenger on a bicycle ("Sorry!"), before she reached the taxi stand.

She couldn't breathe. She had to stop.

As she pressed a hand to her aching side and scanned the oncoming taxis, she saw that at least she hadn't just missed him: no cabs were just pulling away from the curb. She had run as fast as she could to reach the stand, and now she whirled around completely, scanning the brisk foot traffic, but she saw no sign of him. *Oh, God, Beau...* if she'd missed him yet again, after all this time...

She had. He was gone. *Gone again*, she told herself. Still just out of her reach, as he'd always been, a feather-light spirit dancing on the wind.

She felt hot tears sting her eyes.

But maybe, in her haste, she'd flown right past him. Maybe...

Quickly, desperately, she turned back to the oncoming pedestrians, her eyes scanning the people she'd hurtled past in her rush. She saw no one behind her but the people she'd muttered apologies to a moment before, and they had all forgotten her. The woman with the twins was talking softly to them, pushing the stroller, and the messenger, oblivious and with headphones on, was flying past on his bicycle.

Behind both of them, glimpsed only in her peripheral vision, and walking slowly, was the old man with the cane, and a flush of shame came over her as she realized how close she'd come to knocking him over. It wasn't right, no matter how desperate she was, to endanger someone who seemed so fragile.

She stepped toward him to speak a few words of apology. And then as her eyes fell on him—

Before she actually saw him clearly—she stopped dead. Her eyes grew enormous, and her heart began to thud again painfully in her chest.

It was him.

She stared, unable to speak or move. The scent of the cologne was so pungent around her she could almost taste it, though he was still too far away to be the source.

Then he lifted his head. Idly his eyes went over her hair, focusing at last on her face. His abstracted look suddenly became animated, his liquid eyes darkening as he recognized her. He straightened and came toward her, his pace quickening with each step, his eyes never moving from her face.

She stood still. Her face was growing paler and paler, yet she couldn't tear her eyes away from him. He began to move faster, as though to forestall her darting away. Around them, late-afternoon traffic flowed; horns blared; buses rumbled to a halt; people yelled to one another.

They heard nothing of it.

He reached her. They looked at one another.

"Beau—" She whispered it, as though he might vanish if she spoke aloud. The smell of his cologne, so close to her, brushed her nostrils; it was overpowering to her dazed senses. *He's real; he's here. I'm not dreaming.*

He lifted his hand as though to touch her cheek, and let it drop. His eyes rushed over her, memorizing her face, her hair, her form. "You cut your hair."

Tremulously, she laughed. "Do you like it?" That rush of adrenaline she'd thought she might never experience again now threatened to drown her in waves of feeling, from her trembling knees to the roots of her hair. She felt as though not a day had passed since she'd last seen him. *Is it possible*, she wondered, *to erase seven years in a heartbeat?*

His eyes flicked over her again. "I—yes. It's different, but—it suits you."

"I'm not twenty-five anymore." Her eyes were beginning to sparkle as they once had; the smile on her wide mouth stretched across her cheekbones. "I can't just let my hair hang down like a teenager."

"Oh, stop it. You're still just a baby." He sounded so exactly like himself, even if the voice was a little rustier, a shade slower. Still impatient, still fussing at her, still... oh, God, still Beau. Her heart seemed to turn over as she looked at him.

She had to ask the question rushing through her mind. "Why did you leave the theater? Why didn't you wait to speak to me?"

"Look, I admit I was curious. But I wasn't there to speak to you, Mandy. I'm ancient." He looked at her, his mouth stern, and said implacably, "I don't belong in your life." She could see him almost physically drawing away from her, as he'd done so many times before.

And as always, he'd said something that hurt her. Once, it would have been a fist to her solar plexus. Once, she would have drawn back, too.

But she *had* grown up, it seems. Now she saw it for what it had always been: a warning to himself, a defense against his tumbling deeper into his feelings for her, an iron shield against the power and magnetism of her warmth, her attraction for him. *How could I not have seen this? How could I not have understood? How could I have been ...God... so young?*

Now, she just shook her head, feeling sure of her footing with him for the first time. "You're not ancient. You're Beau. Always the same." Her smile grew broader with the conviction in her voice. And she saw his stern look begin to melt into something softer.

They looked at each other, appraising, appreciating. He'd called himself old at sixty, but she could see now that he had become, in fact, much older. *Of course,* she reminded herself, *he's sixty-eight now. That's not late middle age anymore.*

She saw that his hair had thinned out, and there were new, deep lines at his eyes and mouth. Yet those eyes still had lights dancing in them, and his smile as he looked at her was as vibrant as before. The long slender fingers closed on his cane looked fragile, and his long lean frame was slightly bent, but she could sense the same restless energy inside him that had been there years ago. It still intoxicated her. The old, frail man was merely a shell. He seemed to read her thoughts. "I had a car accident some years ago. Broke my hip and my legs. I seem to feel a lot older since then." He tried to shrug. "It's not so bad. All things considered, I was pretty lucky."

"How long ago?"

"Mmm... seven years."

"After we—"

"Yes. Right afterward." He paused. "You didn't hear? It was in the trade papers."

She shook her head. "I never heard... anything."

They hadn't taken their eyes from each other. "What about you?" he said.

"Well—I have a show in rehearsal... but you know that."

He nodded. "The lyric sounded good. What's the show about?"

She looked up at him—she still had to look *up* at him—and suddenly laughed. "You don't know?"

"No. Should I?"

"It's about... us. Our... relationship. About a love that lasts—" She didn't want to say *forever*, so she choked off the rest of the sentence. The sudden softening in his eyes told her he knew what she had held back.

"Good subject," he said, with studied indifference, glancing away from her. "There's not enough romance on Broadway these days."

Is that all he'll say? she wondered. Does he care that I'm putting our lives up on stage, for singers to sing and dancers to dance, for audiences to watch? Does he even understand how much it means to me?

But she couldn't find a way to ask, so she settled for something more casual. "What are you doing in New York?"

"Doctors," he said wryly. "Specialists. Debating whether to operate on me again or let me go on as I am."

"Is that so bad?" Every nerve ending in her body was tingling as she looked at him. Yes, he looked older, but God, he still had the same knee-weakening effect on her that he'd always had. How was it possible for one person to affect another like this? And how could she ever have believed what she was told, that it was dysfunctional or illusory? How could she have believed it was anything *but* miraculous?

She wished that they could just talk forever, standing on the sidewalk with the traffic flowing past them, locked in their own little world. In fact, she would gladly settle for that; it was so much better than the half-life she realized she'd been living since he'd left.

He managed a smile. "It's tolerable. I don't like the cane, but I've gotten used to it. What really bothers me is that it makes me seem so much older. I don't know if I like the idea of being cut open again. I've been through that before."

She's still so beautiful. No, not beautiful. His mind, trained to accurate expression, automatically corrected him. Just—herself. Just as tender and sweet. The same, but a little different, a little older, the remembered slenderness of her body giving way now to some soft curves which seemed somehow even more appealing. Still holding her head the same way to look at his face, still cocking her chin at the same saucy angle. The tips of his fingers throbbed with the urgent need to touch her.

Tentatively, he reached out and brushed a lock of hair out of her eyes. An electric arc seemed to pass from his fingers to the soft, limp hair.

Amanda smiled at him, though she could feel herself trembling in every cell of her body, and tried to speak calmly. "I thought if I cut it, it would be less trouble. Seems I just exchanged one problem for another."

He smiled back at her, trying to seem as casual. "Isn't that what we all do?"

There didn't seem to be any answer to that, though the very air seemed to vibrate with the unspoken words between them. The silence lengthened, though neither of them made a move to walk away. Their eyes remained locked on each other.

"How is your wife?" She blurted it out, the thought that had loomed in her mind from the moment she saw him.

He looked at her for a moment before answering, as though he knew the impetus behind the question. "Thanks for asking," he said at length. "She died three years ago."

"Oh." She added, a moment later, "I'm sorry."

"She committed suicide." He didn't know why he added that.

Amanda looked at him, and a world of sudden understanding welled up in her heart, understanding not just his current situation but his past, and his obligations. When she spoke, her voice was gentler. "I'm really sorry. Is there something—I can do?"

"No. But it's kind of you to offer." He looked at her, feeling the blossoming warmth in his chest that she'd always evoked. *Why can't I tell her the truth?* he asked himself. *Why can't I just say, 'There's no one in my life; Jean wasn't even really a part of it when I knew you. I walked away not because I didn't love you, but because I felt so chained to her'? Because,* he answered himself, *she's still so young and she deserves a chance at real love, at a full life, at something much more than I can offer her. She doesn't need to be saddled with a sick old man and all my issues. Give her a chance at a future with no limits, not what little I can offer for the few pitiful years I have left.*

Still, he made no move to leave, just looked down at her.

As though propelled on its own, Amanda's hand reached over to gently touch the sleeve of his sports coat, while her eyes remained fixed on his, unwilling to break the contact. Her fingers fumbled and accidentally touched the skin on his wrist, instead.

They both felt the jolt of electric warmth that raced between them. He blinked; she shivered. Both had the same flash of thought: *It's still there, after all these years.* Then, quickly, they both began to talk at once.

"Are you going to—"

"When will you be—"

They stopped, looked at each other, laughed awkwardly. "You first," Beau said, with a hint of a bow and the slightly British intonation that she'd always loved.

But she couldn't think of what she wanted to say. She shook her head, indicating that he should speak.

He hesitated too, for a moment. "Quite a jump you've made, from singing and the hotel business to writing for Broadway. Jerry must have missed you plenty. Were you with him a long time after I—er—left the Lorelei?"

She stared at him, stunned. "What are you talking about? He fired me!"

It was his turn to stare. "Fired you? What for?"

She tilted her face to look up at him, pain twisting her features. "Because of you! Because you told him to fire me, and if he didn't you'd pull all the publicity from the hotel, and change the venue in your libretto, and—" Her voice trailed off. Beau was staring down at her, his face appalled.

"I never said any of that. I didn't, Mandy! I wouldn't have."

She was beginning to feel like Alice in Wonderland, the world tilting crazily around her. "But you called him that night, and you were screaming about me. He told me so, the next day. He said he'd never heard you so angry. And he told me you'd threatened to call the owner, too, if he didn't get rid of me, and... "

He was shaking his head furiously. "Never. I never did any of that."

She looked at him blankly.

"I swear, Mandy! I never asked him to fire you. I did call him and I *was* angry, but I wouldn't have done that. You have to believe me."

"But he told me... " Her voice trailed off.

"He told you what?" he said grimly.

She was startled by his transformation from frail to fiery. No, he hadn't changed. His eyes had gone as hard as steel. It mattered very much to him, apparently, that she believe him. And inside the paper-thin shell of the old man still lived the tempestuous spirit she'd always loved.

"I take it you didn't know that Jerry had skimmed money from the production funds the Fieldstons paid to the Lorelei?"

Her eyes widened. "Jerry?"

"Jerry," he confirmed. He looked at her and his tone softened. "He was the one I wanted to get away from. He obviously used you as the scapegoat. So you lost your job when he should have gone to jail." Even seven years later, he was obviously angry about it.

She spoke the first thought that came to her mind. "It was a long time ago. It doesn't matter anymore." She smiled again, that smile that lit up her face. "I would so much rather be doing what I'm doing now. Following in your footsteps."

He shook his head ruefully. "I suspect, Miss Harary, that you're going to surpass me in many ways."

She tilted her head toward him with a look full of disbelief, like the ones she'd given him so many times before, a look that had always made his heart tilt in his chest. *Careful*, he told himself. *Don't fall in love all over again.* Aloud, he said, "Am I keeping you from something? You must be busy with the show."

She gave him the same look again. "Trying to get rid of me?"

He bristled. "I'm just thinking of your commitments!"

Once, his tone would have set her teeth on edge. Now, she found herself feeling calmer, understanding what was beneath his words. *What do you know?* she thought. *I have grown up at last.* "Thanks, but I don't have any more at the moment." She didn't think of Michael; their two-year relationship might as well not have happened for all it suddenly meant to her.

The sun, sinking inexorably below the buildings, no longer warmed the air. A cool wind swept past them, and she glanced around. "There's a good coffee shop on the next block. Why don't we get a cup of coffee?"

He hesitated. "This won't change anything, Mandy. I'm so much older than you. Always will be."

She smiled slightly, trying to seem indifferent, though her heart was hammering almost through her chest. "It's just coffee, Beau."

"You must have somewhere else to go."

"Do you?"

He hesitated again. Finally, he said, "I guess—I'm free for a few minutes."

"Do you *want* to have coffee with me?"

It was his last chance to escape; she was giving it to him, giving him the chance to walk away, to turn his back on her and on everything they'd had. Inviting him to be blunt, to say something hurtful, to pull free. To run.

He looked into the soft gray eyes, which looked clear and straight into his. He had run once before, and he knew now, looking into those eyes, that she had suffered. If he said no, he knew she would suffer again, and it wasn't an ego-wish, but an unshakeable conviction.

And suddenly he didn't want to say yes just to assuage her pain, but also to ease his own silent suffering of so many years. He looked at the upturned face and elfin eyes, and suddenly understood how much he'd left behind years before. He felt a sharp, bitter stab of regret that lanced straight through his midsection.

The hell with this, he thought. *How long do I have, anyway? How much time have I already given up with her? Who in the world ever understood me better? Does the age difference really matter, after all these years? Does anything matter except being with her? Who am I hurting?*

She was still looking up at him, waiting for his answer. "Well," he said cautiously, "it is getting cold. Coffee's a good idea."

She gave a tiny smile, unwilling to show her elation. "Come this way." Without thinking, she reached for his arm to turn him in the right direction.

The electric jolt of their bodies, suddenly close together, sent both their pulses racing. He put out a hand to steady her, and unexpectedly found her in his arms, close to him in a way that hadn't happened in more than seven years.

He told himself he was just helping her straighten up when he put his arms around her. He didn't know which of them moved closer and initiated the spark until they found their lips pressed together.

In the middle of a crowded sidewalk on a street off Broadway, it was happening again.

They both pulled back suddenly, their faces flushed, a hint of laughter in Amanda's eyes, a suddenly sober look in Beau's.

"Just because circumstances are different now," he warned her, "it doesn't mean that... I mean, nothing's changed. Not really."

But as he looked at the soft flush in her cheeks and the sudden sparkle in her eyes, he thought: *Nothing's changed. It's never changed. I was a fool to believe it ever would—or that anything on earth could compensate for losing this.*

Amanda's eyes were luminous with joy, but she only answered quietly, "No. Nothing's changed."

She nodded toward the intersection, and when the light changed, they started across the street. After a moment, she slipped her hand into his. He didn't withdraw it; instead, his fingers locked onto hers, as automatically as he'd once tossed a tennis ball into the air before serving it over a net. The smiles they gave each other were full of rueful understanding; each knew, again, what the other was feeling, because each of them felt it.

Halfway across the street, she gave a sudden, ringing laugh. Beau looked down at her questioningly. "What?"

She shook her head, mirth flashing in her eyes. She had just realized what was wrong with the ending of the show. She knew now what had always been wrong with it, standing here on this busy street where her life had just begun again. Someday she might even tell him.

Some connections last forever. Some love doesn't die with absence or heartache or even, as she was realizing now, lies told by other people. It just remains quietly in hibernation until the moment of re-ignition that is nothing short of a miracle.

Why didn't it ever occur to me that my characters would meet again? she wondered. And answered herself silently, *Because we never did. And I thought we never would. And now that we have, I'll never let him go again. I'll never believe it if he tries to tell me he doesn't love me. He always did. He always will. We won't have years together... but however many months or days or hours, I'll hold onto him. Because we've always belonged together, and the hell with anything else.*

The smell of freshly brewed coffee came to both of them as he held open the door of the coffee shop. The warmth of the heated interior felt inviting to them both, a shelter for them now, together, after years alone in the cold.

"It's homey," he said, and smiled down at her.

No, darling. It's magic. But she didn't say it, just smiled back and stepped inside, toward the warm and waiting future.

A TIP OF THE HAT

Many people have supported this book over the long years it has grown from a handful of pages to a finished novel. Without them I doubt it would have happened, even now.

My deepest thanks and appreciation to:

Chris Halm, for the beautiful author photo, and for all his support over the years.

The crew who handled my production work, including Danny for her beautiful cover and Rosa for formatting and layout.

My mother, who instilled in me a lifelong love of the musical theatre—so much of this is due to her.

And most of all to Robbie Branscum, who loved and believed in this book from its infancy and never stopped urging me to finish it. Wherever you are, Robbie, I hope you're proud.

ABOUT THE AUTHOR

S usan Sloate is the author or co-author of more than 20 published books, including *Realizing You* (with Ron Doades), for which she created a new genre, the self-help *novel*, and the 2003 #6 Amazon bestseller, *Forward to Camelot* (with Kevin Finn), which took honors in 3 literary competitions and was optioned by a Hollywood company for film production. The revised version, *Forward to Camelot : 50th Anniversary Edition*, was published in October 2013.

The original edition of *Stealing Fire* was published in July 2013, and shot immediately to #2 on the Amazon bestseller list in its category. It was also a Hot New Release for its first 90 days, and was honored in the 2014 Reader's Favorite Literary Competition, in Women's Fiction. Prior to its original publication, *Stealing Fire* was a Quarter-Finalist in the 2012 Amazon Breakthrough Novel Award contest. It combines autobiographical experience with Susan's lifelong love of the musical theater. She is proud to be distantly related to Broadway legend Fred Ebb, the lyricist for *Cabaret, Chicago, All That Jazz* and *New York, New York*.

Susan has also written young-adult fiction and non-fiction, including the children's biography *Ray Charles: Find Another Way!*, which was honored in the 2007 Children's Moonbeam Book Awards. *Mysteries Unwrapped: The Secrets of Alcatraz* led to her 2009 appearance on the TV series *MysteryQuest* on The History Channel. She has been a sportswriter and screenwriter, managed two political campaigns, founded an author's festival in her hometown of Mount Pleasant, SC, and appeared in multiple volumes of *Who's Who in America, Who's Who in Entertainment* and *Who's Who Among American Women*.

Visit Susan online at www.susansloate.com.

AVAILABLE TITLES BY SUSAN SLOATE

Forward to Camelot (50ᵗʰ Anniversary Edition) (with Kevin Finn) Drake Valley Press, 2013

Realizing You (with Ron Doades) CreateSpace, 2013

Amelia Earhart: Challenging the Skies (*Great Lives* series), Fawcett, 2011

Abraham Lincoln: The Freedom President (*Great Lives* series), Fawcett, 2010

Pardon That Turkey! (All Aboard Reading), Grosset & Dunlap, 2010

Ray Charles: Young Musician (Childhood of Famous Americans series*)* Simon & Schuster, 2008

Mysteries Unwrapped: The Secrets of Alcatraz, Sterling Publishers, 2008

Ray Charles: Find Another Way! Bearport Press, 2006

www.ingramcontent.com/pod-product-compliance
Lightning Source LLC
Chambersburg PA
CBHW070834250626
47159CB00003B/779